alexandrabarlama

GEMS OF IXORA

OF STORM AND EMERALD

1

JESSICA HOFFA

Copyright ©2023 by Jessica Hoffa

All rights reserved.

No part of this publication may be reproduced, distributed, or transmitted in any form or by any means, including photocopying, recording, or other electronic or mechanical methods, without the prior written permission of the publisher, except as permitted by U.S. copyright law. For permission requests, contact [include publisher/author contact info].

The story, all names, characters, and incidents portrayed in this production are fictitious. No identification with actual persons (living or deceased), places, buildings, and products is intended or should be inferred.

Book Cover by *Moonpress* | *www.moonpress.co*

Illustrations by Jessica Hoffa via Canva

First edition 2023

ISBN E-Book: 979-8-9884142-0-9

ISBN Hardcover: 979-8-9884142-1-6

ISBN Paperback: 979-8-9884142-2-3

Welcome to Ixora!

Of Storm and Emerald

xoxo

Two souls are sometimes created together and in love before they're even born.

-F. Scott Fitzgerald

To the ones who like to get lost in another world when this one becomes too much. I see you, and I hope that you find home in Ixora.

Content Warning

The following lists all of the trigger/content warnings that you will come across throughout Of Storm and Emerald. You will encounter themes of vulgar language, explicit sexual scenes, edging, bondage, breath play, anal play, blood, poisoning, violence, murder, anxiety, depression, grief, and death of a parent. Your mental health is extremely important, so please take care as you dive into the world of Ixora.

Contents

Map of Ixora Left	XVI
Map of Ixora Right	XVII
Pronunciation guide	XVIII
Prologue	1
Chapter One	5
Chapter Two	12
Chapter Three	23
Chapter Four	39
Chapter Five	53
Chapter Six	56
Chapter Seven	63
Chapter Eight	70
Chapter Nine	79
Chapter Ten	92
Chapter Eleven	102

Chapter Twelve	114
Chapter Thirteen	117
Chapter Fourteen	134
Chapter Fifteen	144
Chapter Sixteen	157
Chapter Seventeen	177
Chapter Eighteen	181
Chapter Nineteen	191
Chapter Twenty	209
Chapter Twenty-One	218
Chapter Twenty-Two	226
Chapter Twenty-Three	238
Chapter Twenty-Four	248
Chapter Twenty-Five	253
Chapter Twenty-Six	260
Chapter Twenty-Seven	273
Chapter Twenty-Eight	284
Chapter Twenty-Nine	294
Chapter Thirty	301
Chapter Thirty-One	316

Chapter Thirty-Two	320
Chapter Thirty-Three	331
Chapter Thirty-Four	337
Chapter Thirty-Five	345
Chapter Thirty-Six	352
Chapter Thirty-Seven	359
Chapter Thirty-Eight	365
Chapter Thirty-Nine	372
Chapter Forty	378
Chapter Forty-One	384
Chapter Forty-Two	396
Chapter Forty-Three	409
Chapter Forty-Four	420
Chapter Forty-Five	424
Chapter Forty-Six	435
Chapter Forty-Seven	444
Epilogue	451
Bonus Chapter	453
Want more?	460
Acknowledgements	461

About the Author

COURT OF TOPA[Z]

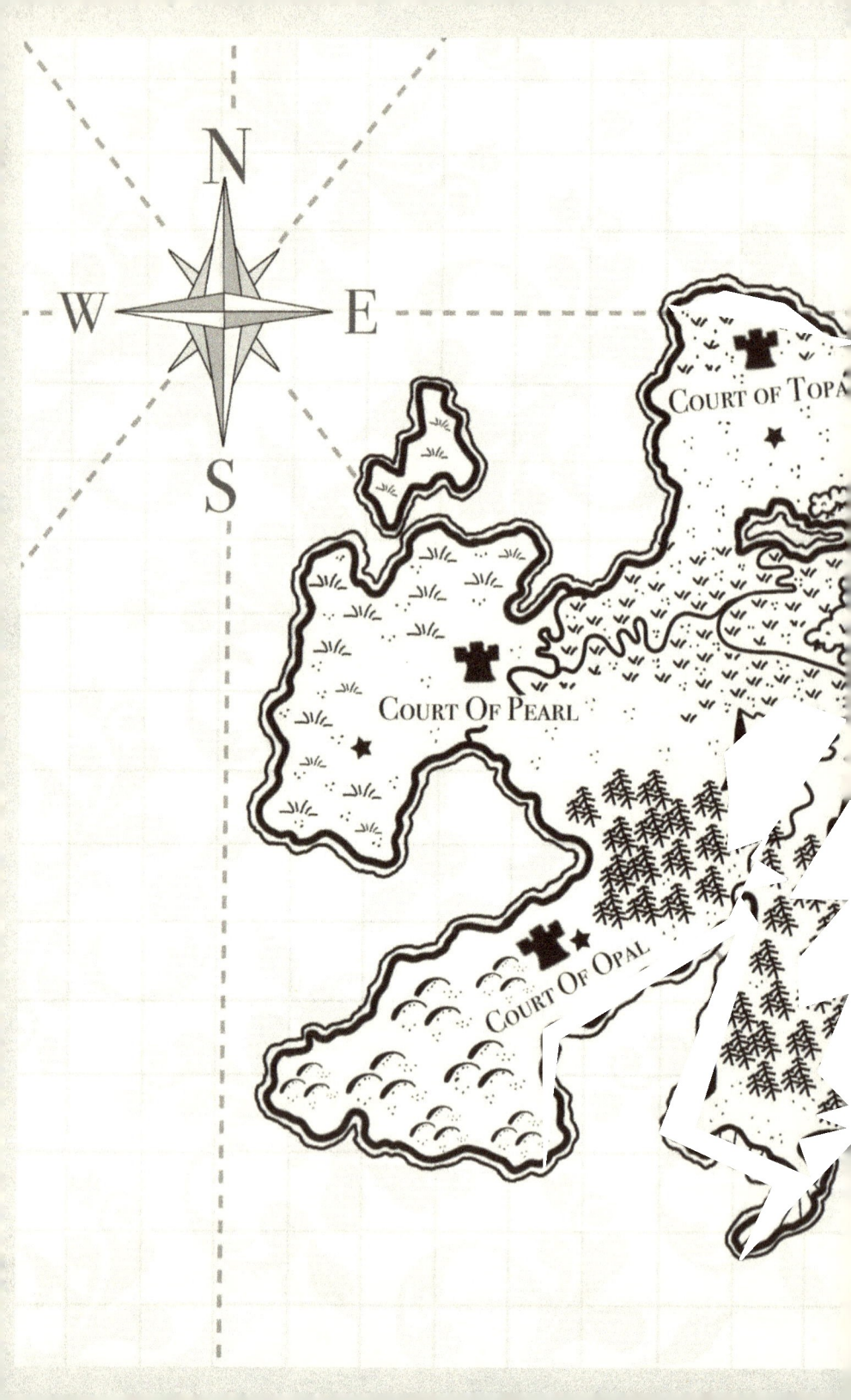

COURT OF PEARL

COURT OF OPAL

Ixora

Court Of Garnet

Onyx Mountains

Lyndaria

Kalmeera

Court Of Emerald

Cerulean Sea

Woods

The Court Of Sapphire Isles

Pronunciation guide

PEOPLE

AURAELIA: Ah-rae-lee-ah
DAEMON: Day-mon
XANDER: Zan-der
ADELINA: Ad-eh-leen-uh
AIDEN: Ay-den
PIPER: Pi-per
SYLVIE: Sil-vee
SER AERON: Sir Air-ron
ARAMIS: Air-a-miss
HARLAND: Har-land
OPHELIA: O-fee-lia
RIONA: Ree-o-na
DEMIR: De-meer
KYRA: Ki-rah
YVAINE: Ee-vain
AVYANNA: Ah-vee-ana
EVANDER: Ee-van-der

RANEESE GARRETH: Ra-nee-ce
CASSIUS: Cas-ee-us
SYRUS: Si-rus
SIMON: Si-mon
SARIAH: Suh-ri-uh
JODIE: Jo-dee
AESIRA: Ah-seer-ah
ARLO: Ar-low
ORNA: Or-nah
BLYANA: Bly-ana
KAEMON: Kay-mon
LAVENA: Luh-vee-na
DAVINA: Duh-vee-na
ERIX: Air-ix
ASTRAEA: Uh-strae-uh
KILLIAN: Kill-ee-n
ROAN: Roe-an
TORAN: Tor-an
ZARIA: Zuh-ri-uh

PLACES

IXORA: Ick-soar-a
LYNDARIA: Lyn-dar-ee-a
KALMEERA: Cal-meer-a
ARCELIA: Ar-cee-lee-ah
MALAENA: Muh lay-nuh
LYNARIA: Loo-nar-ia

DEITIES

GODDESS RAYNE: Ray-ne
GODDESS NARISSA: Nuh-riss-ah

Prologue

500 Years Ago...

As flames dwindled down to their embers, and the screams of the injured and dying drifted into the background, the ruling members of Ixora gathered round a makeshift table of scorched rosewood and ash.

The war that had plagued their lands for five years had finally come to an end.

The Court of Sapphire Isles had been the sole ruler over Ixora for centuries, but under King Erix's sovereignty, the realm had suffered.

Courts warred within themselves, and with others.

Plague and famine spread to every corner of the realm, taking countless lives, and still they were left to fend for themselves.

But when Lord Roan of Emerald–the largest of the mainland courts–had been murdered in cold blood and still there was no aid from the royals, his daughter, Lady Astraea, took matters into her own hands.

She spent the year following her father's death garnering support from the other courts to lead a coup against the king–and it worked.

Nobles from every court flocked to her aid calling for justice, and after five grueling years of battle against the crown, they finally won.

"You've ruled without contest for long enough, Erix," Lady Astraea proclaimed, using her power over the wind to amplify her voice above the gathered nobles.

A hush fell over the small crowd as all eyes turned in her direction, then she continued.

"For too long the people of Ixora have suffered under your rule. For too long my people— *our* people," she swept her arms wide gesturing to the other nobles, "Fought and died because you continue to turn a blind eye on the mainland citizens of this realm. But I say enough is enough."

A resounding wave of cheers echoed through the field as she finished speaking.

Erix, arms bound behind his back as he kneeled in the blood-stained dirt, sneered back at her. "You think *you* can do any better?"

"By myself? No. No one should have unchecked power—magic or otherwise."

"What are you suggesting, Astraea?" Lord Toran of Opal asked.

"I'm suggesting that we have a balance of power within Ixora, and that it be something everyone here agrees upon."

There was a jumble of murmurs throughout the group before Lady Iridessa of Opal stepped up next to her father, glancing at him for reassurance before she spoke. "I only speak for myself and my people, but we do not want to rule. We also do not want to continue the way that we have been."

A chorus of agreement followed her statement, and then Lady Zaria of Topaz stepped forward. "I propose a dual monarchy, with a system of checks and balances from the remaining courts."

"Dual monarchy?" Confusion laced Astraea's voice, and her brow furrowed.

"Yes. King Erix would step down, leaving his son to rule in his stead. And you, Lady Astraea, would take up the mantle of the second monarchy."

"Me?" Astraea asked. The matter-of-fact way that Zaria proclaimed her as a ruler–a *queen*–shocked her to her core, but the nods of agreement from the remaining nobility sealed her fate.

It wasn't until King Erix's voice cut through the noise like a hot knife that she was able to shake herself from her stupor.

"You think that I will simply abdicate?" A maniacal grin spread across his face as he laughed.

However, the sound was short lived, replaced by the unmistakable sound of a blade cutting through flesh.

Standing behind the body of the now slain king was his eldest son, Killian. She'd heard of the Prince's shadow magic and his ability to move from one place to another in the blink of an eye. Seeing it in person was a completely different matter.

"I think we've all heard enough of his ramblings, don't you?" he asked as he nonchalantly wiped his blade across his forearm. "Now, where were we? I do believe that in order for this to work, we will need a treaty of some kind. Do you agree?" His piercing green eyes locked in on Astraea as he posed the question, and it was as if a thread had been snapped between them.

She cleared her throat and nodded. "Yes, a treaty is definitely in order."

The nobles of Ixora sat around that burned tree for hours discussing the ins and outs of the new treaty. And in the end, the Treaty of Rosewood was formed.

The Treaty of Rosewood

With the end of the war between the courts of the realm of Ixora and the sovereignty of the Sapphire Isles, a new day has dawned. With the fall of King Erix, two monarchies shall rise. One of the Court of Sapphire Isles, and one of the Court of Emerald.

Each with their own duties and responsibilities to their people and the realm as a whole.

To keep the peace in the realm, no two persons destined to reign, shall share in the blessed tradition of matrimony if it should inter-

twine the two houses of rule. The Court of Emerald and the Court of Sapphire Isles agree to work with each other, and not against each other.

For the betterment of the whole of Ixora, there shall never be one in control. With a checks and balances system from the Lords and Ladies of courts surrounding our realm, may the goddesses shine their light down upon our people.

Every noble from the six courts of Ixora signed it.

First by Astraea and Killian, agreeing not only to become the new reigning monarchs over the realm, but to never allow their families to intertwine.

They were followed by nobles from Opal, Topaz, Pearl, and Garnet, with the hope that this treaty would stand the test of time and that peace would reign.

Chapter One

Present Day...

Auraelia

"You've got to be fucking kidding me." Whispered words, followed by an exasperated sigh, floated through the air as cold water seeped into the leather of her boot. Removing her foot from the puddle she'd landed in, Auraelia slipped down one of the old cobblestone streets just beyond the wall outside the Court of Emerald. Sticking to the shadows and trying desperately not to be noticed by the late-night crowd wandering the streets, she pulled her cloak tightly around her body and drew her hood further onto her brow. After a sharp turn down an alley, she was forced to an abrupt halt when she nearly collided with a stack of crates. Thankful for the fact that she was in trousers and boots, as opposed to her typical skirts and heels, Auraelia sidestepped the crates. Narrowly avoiding another puddle in the process, she made her way further into the night and away from the city.

Weaving through the streets she knew all too well, Auraelia stopped for a moment to take in the scene of homes around her. They varied in size, from single-family and multigenerational homes to multi-family dwellings, but the shape and design of each house was relatively the same throughout Lyndaria. They were all made of the same light gray stone in varying gradients due to age and weather, but the harsh lines and sharp corners were softened with beautiful landscaping.

Flowerbeds of snapdragons, rose bushes, and hydrangeas could be found throughout the city in varying shades and species. However, it was the beautiful climbing vines of purple wisteria that cemented the ethereal aesthetic found throughout this part of the realm.

The sound of trickling water down drainpipes, courtesy of the summer storm earlier in the day, gave a soft and soothing background to the dark and starry night.

Her world was as serene as it was beautiful—even in the dead of night—as fireflies danced through the flowers and vines like living stars that you could touch. She closed her eyes and took a deep, calming breath, before continuing on her way to the one place a woman in her position should not be going...a brothel.

"Two days. In just two fucking days, my life will be forever changed. My freedom, not that I had much anyway, will be gone." Auraelia sighed, then drained the last of her glass of whiskey before she slammed it down on the bar inside Madame Sylvie's *boarding house*.

From the street it looked exactly how a typical boarding house should look. Made of the same stone materials as the rest of the homes and buildings in Lyndaria, though slightly larger to accommodate the many boarders that were sponsored by Madame Sylvie. Beautiful gardens decorated the grounds, both in front of and behind the main house, as well as purple wisteria that draped along the sides, softening the look of the stone.

The inside was warm and inviting, with dark cherry wood floors covered in plush, multicolored rugs. Beautifully intricate chandeliers hung from the ceiling giving the space a comforting, yet regal, ambiance. But for the elite few, that was not what one would be seeking out when paying a visit to Madame Sylvie's.

Just to the left of the front entrance, in the main hallway of the house, was a door that blended in perfectly with the surrounding wood paneling. Where this door led was an entirely different world from what was presented upstairs. Beneath the façade of *Madame Sylvie's Boarding House for Girls*, was the real enterprise.

Madame Sylvie, or Vee to a select few, had transformed the lower level of her home into a luscious oasis fit for debauchery. Dim lighting set the mood while thick embroidered blood-red curtains draped the walls as both an aesthetic and to block sound from reaching the upper floors. The floors were softened by lush, woven rugs in the deepest wine-red shades, accented with gold damask patterns.

Black sheers that hung from the ceiling created individual lounge areas which allowed for the illusion of privacy as women of all body shapes and sizes wandered the space. They were all adorned in the same gossamer black gowns that draped down their bodies like pooling shadows. Though the ladies with patrons lounged in varying states of undress, the ones without walked around with so much grace that they seemed to float across the floor.

The dresses they wore were secured around their necks by thin gold chains that fell down their backs and ended in small teardrop shaped red stones. The two slits that cut through the fronts of their skirts ended at their hips–leaving little to the imagination.

In the back of the room was a small corner bar that stood out amongst all the lush and sensual spaces around it. Then again, that area wasn't meant to be inviting.

"It's there to supply liquid courage to those who need it. If you want to drown your sorrows, you should find somewhere else to do it." Madame Sylvie's words trickled back into Auraelia's mind as she sat at the small corner bar with her head shoved into her hands, and grinned.

Vee was a petite, curvy woman, with the most beautiful ivory skin that was sprinkled with freckles. Her bright auburn ringlets cascaded down to her waist, and her ice-blue eyes held an intensity that would freeze you where you stood, if looks could do such things. She stood approximately five-foot-two and was probably in her early forties–not that she would ever tell you her real age. Regardless of her stature, she was all fire and did not tolerate disrespect from anyone. She definitely did not tolerate people just hanging out at the bar; with the exception of Auraelia, but that was only because she refused to move.

"What are you whining about this time, girl?" Vee asked on an exhale as she rolled her eyes and continued drying various bar glasses that she had just washed.

Auraelia looked up from her hands and signaled for another whiskey, her shoulders slumping as she released a long breath. After Vee poured the amber liquid into the glass, Auraelia took a sip and let the taste settle on her tongue. Woodsy with a hint of smoke, and the tiniest whisper of honey that lingered in the back of her throat.

She swallowed and let out a deep sigh. "In two days, my life will be forever changed, and there's nothing that I can do about it." Instantly realizing what she had just admitted to a virtual stranger, her eyes widened. Taking a swig from her glass, she tried to act as normal as possible–and not like she'd possibly just revealed her biggest secret.

Auraelia readjusted her hood to shield more of her face and continued to nurse her drink. At the same moment she sent up a prayer, to any goddess that may have been listening, that she hadn't just revealed too much.

She'd been coming to Vee's for about a year now, in search of some semblance of freedom and normalcy. And the only thing that had ever been asked of her was to pay her bar tab before she left and to "*keep her trap shut.*" Vee never asked for her name, and even though Auraelia told her to call her Rae, she still called her "girl" and said that unless she was one of *her* girls, she didn't care what her name was.

After a few moments of strained silence, Auraelia lifted her eyes toward Vee to see her still drying glasses, only now, a tense look marred her face. Auraelia reached into the pocket of her cloak and pulled out her coin purse to pay, but before she could place them on the bar Vee gently grabbed her hand.

Auraelia's heart was beating faster than a hummingbird's wings when she looked up. She met those ice-blue eyes and saw nothing but understanding and for the briefest moment there was a little bit of pity too. Unable to take the intensity of Vee's gaze, Auraelia gave a small smile and then headed home toward her future.

As she wound her way back through the streets of Lyndaria, Auraelia looked up at the night sky and saw that the moon was almost at its peak. Quickening her pace, she stuck to the shadows as she turned down road after road until she finally saw the wall surrounding Emerald Castle.

Staying close to the stacked stone, she searched around for the notches that had helped her scale over the top and into the Queen's garden. Dropping to the garden floor in a crouch, she slowed her breathing and listened. When all she heard were crickets chirping sweetly in the background, she rose slowly and adjusted her cloak so she blended into the night.

The Queen's garden was typically hard to see in the dead of night, but with the full moon overhead, the entire garden was illuminated, and the smell of the flora cloaked the air with sweet perfume.

Peonies.

Rows and rows of bushes covered in a variety of delicate pink and white blossoms as far as the eye could see. This was the only place in all of Lyndaria where you could find these beautiful blooms, and for the next few days, they would be used to decorate the whole of Emerald Castle. After all, it was not often that two balls were hosted within the same week. It was an exciting and important time for the Court of Emerald.

As she stepped away from the wall, she took all of two steps down one of the worn paths before she heard a deep chuckle from her right. Hoping to find the source, she whipped around and simultaneously pulled a long dagger from the hidden sheath at her back.

The person who peeled away from the shadows, and now stood in front of her, was none other than her brother–Prince Xander of the Court of Emerald.

"By the goddess, Xander! Are you trying to send me to an early grave?" Auraelia whisper-yelled at her brother.

Xander smirked as he put his hands in the air in mock surrender. "No, sis, but are you still planning on taking my head off with that thing, or can we play nice?" Every word dripped with sarcasm.

Feigning indifference, Auraelia brandished her dagger around for a moment. Then with a sigh, a smirk, and an overly dramatic eyeroll, she finally put the weapon away.

Auraelia stepped back and took a good look at her brother. He stood tall, at around six-foot-four, with shoulder length sandy blond hair that was haphazardly secured in a high bun on top of his head. His beard was short and neat, and a shade darker than the rest. He also had impeccably straight, white teeth.

All of this would paint him as a generally handsome man, but it was his eyes that always had the women at court swooning. Beneath his long dark lashes were eyes that resembled a great storm. His irises were a bright silver that shone like the moon on a dark night, streaks of charcoal gray cut through the brightness like streams, then pooled at the edges to form the outer rim.

It was a genetic marker that most of the royal line in the Court of Emerald possessed, and there was no denying from whom that trait was obtained.

Queen Adelina, also known as their mother.

After a few moments, Auraelia began walking down the path that would lead her back to the castle. Not waiting to see if her brother followed, she asked, "So why are you out here this late anyway?"

Hearing his exasperated chuckle, she stopped and turned around to wait for his answer. Xander rolled his eyes as he walked toward her, eating up the distance between them until they were side by side.

"You know I could ask you the same thing, right? Does mother know you're still sneaking off in the middle of the night even with your cor–"

"SHHHHHHH!" Auraelia admonished, throwing her hand over Xander's mouth. "I really don't want to think about that until I absolutely have to. It's not exactly something that I'm looking forward to."

With a deep sigh, she began walking again as Xander kept pace beside her. They were both silent for a few moments before he asked, "Do you think that you're ready?"

Taking a moment to really consider the question, she looked up at the stars twinkling in the sky and gave the only answer she could with all honesty, "I don't really have a choice."

Chapter Two

Auraelia

"Pay attention, little bug, this is very important."

"Yes, Momma."

Queen Adelina walked around to sit on the bed behind Auraelia and began to brush her long hair. Her mother was beautiful beyond words.

She was dressed in a silver floor length silk shift that brought out the brightness in her soft gray eyes. Her chestnut brown hair was loosely braided down her back, and her sun kissed face was kind and without wrinkles, except around her eyes and mouth which were caused by years of laughter and smiles.

"You are six now, and it is time that you learn what is to come in your future." Her mother set the brush down on a side table, and pulled Auraelia into her lap, holding her lovingly to her chest.

"On your twenty-fifth year, a lot will change for you. All of Ixora will be here to celebrate you and this glorious milestone. But there is something you must learn first."

With wide eyes, Auraelia tried desperately to crane her neck around to face her mother, but the Queen just chuckled, pulled her closer, and tapped her nose. "Patience, little bug...within our great family, there is also great magic. And when your twenty-fifth year arrives, and the moon is at its peak, you will experience a change within yourself. Your magic will begin to manifest, and there's no way of knowing what it will be, or how great of a power you will possess, only that it will come. Everyone's journey into their power is different. Some feel a fullness in their chest or tingling in their fingers. Your vision may vastly improve or it could be something entirely different. It all depends on what our ancestors bless you with."

Auraelia jumped from her mother's lap and spun around with eyes the size of saucers. "Is that why you can move the water? Did my father have magic? Will Xander?"

Chuckling, Queen Adelina gently pulled Auraelia back into her lap and kissed her head, "Yes, little bug, that is why I am able to manipulate water. As for the man who contributed to your making, he had the ability to jump from place to place, but only if he'd been there before or seen a map of the location. It is unclear as to whether Xander will develop magic. Within my family, it's traditionally passed from mother to daughter, and is usually only held by the females. But since your father also possessed magic, it's possible that Xander will develop some sort of ability as well."

Sensing that Auraelia was about to ask a million questions, Queen Adelina continued. "However, regardless of whether or not your brother possesses magic, you will be crowned 'Heir Apparent' on your twenty-fifth year."

With a furrowed brow, Auraelia looked up and asked, "What does that mean, Momma?"

"It means, little bug, that one day when I'm gone, you will be queen. The crown will go to you, and you alone. It is how it has always been in our great family, and within the Court of Emerald. The only way that would change is if no daughters were born within the immediate royal line. Then it would go to the eldest prince, and if he later had a daughter, the crown would revert back to a matriarchal line, and the princess would be crowned queen."

After a few moments, she sighed and snuggled closer to her mother. "I don't want to be queen if that means I lose you, but if I have to be queen, then I hope that I'm as good as you are, Momma." Auraelia closed her eyes, her mouth stretching wide with a yawn, and started to drift off to sleep.

Shifting on the bed, Queen Adelina laid Auraelia down. Tucking her beneath her blankets, she kissed her goodnight, then headed toward the door. But before she left, she turned back to the sleeping form of her daughter, lit up by the moonlight that streamed through the large floor to ceiling windows, and with a smile on her face whispered, "You will be, little bug, of that, I am sure."

Queen Adelina closed the door, and Auraelia slept soundly with a small smile adorning her sweet face.

Jolting upright in bed, Auraelia looked around for the intrusive sound that snapped her from her dream. To her left, she saw her best friend—and lady in waiting—Piper, as she ripped back the curtains and placed them behind the metal stays on the wall.

"Morning, sunshine," Piper sing-songed from across the room with a huge grin on her face.

Groaning, Auraelia laid back down and pulled the covers over her head.

Piper had been her friend since they were in diapers, and since her family was part of the nobility within the Court of Emerald, she was immediately made Auraelia's lady in waiting. Although it may have started as a forced acquaintance, their relationship had quickly become a bond that only death could sever.

Piper was all-natural beauty and grace, with hair the color of the darkest night that hung just below her shoulders, and olive skin that was enviable. Her hazel eyes were framed by dark lashes and sparkled with mischief. Her lips seemed to be home to a permanent smirk that would lead anyone to believe she was up to no good...which she usually was, especially when it came to doing things with Auraelia. Though Piper was a fortnight younger than Auraelia, she was also an inch taller, which was something that she never let Auraelia forget.

The sound of Piper's steps filled the room before she threw herself on top of Auraelia and pulled the covers from her face. "Come on, Rae...I mean, *Your Highness*." enhancing her sarcasm with a mock bow, "It's time to get up. Today is a big day!"

With a disgruntled moan, Auraelia sat up and pushed the covers, and Piper, off her. "Two things, oh best friend of mine. One, please stop calling me 'your highness,' especially when we're in the privacy of my chambers; you know how much I loathe it. And two, I know what today is, but that doesn't mean that I need to rise with the sun as you continue to insist on doing."

Piper lifted one of her eyebrows, a look of bewilderment on her face. "Rae, it's nearly mid-morning. I had to bar the door to keep the lady's maids out of here so that you didn't bite their heads off for waking you." After a beat of silence, the two women launched into a fit of laughter.

Minutes passed before they finally calmed down enough for Piper to bribe her with hot coffee and breakfast. Slipping her arms into her dressing gown, Auraelia trudged into the sitting room.

The room itself was small and cozy. With a wall of floor to ceiling paned windows that held a set of glass doors in the middle, it was the brightest space in Auraelia's suite.

Beside the doors that opened out to a short balcony that overlooked a small portion of the queen's garden–sat a small iron dining table and two chairs with cushioned seats. There was a large fireplace with a cozy sitting area that had two armchairs with a small round table in between, and a matching settee. The floors were pine and covered in colorful, woven rugs.

On either side of the fireplace were two large bookcases, each holding countless volumes that ranged from romance novels to sword fighting techniques. As well as various knick-knacks that Auraelia had either collected or been gifted over the years.

A cool spring breeze drifted through the open balcony doors as she and Piper ate their breakfast of assorted fruits and pastries. They talked animatedly about everything that would be happening that day as Auraelia let the rich aroma of coffee wake her mind and calm her nervous energy.

A while later, a knock signaled that it was time to officially start the day, and Piper opened the door so that the lady's maids could enter and start their work. Finishing her coffee, Auraelia headed into her bathing chamber to wash away her adventures from the previous night, and to hopefully clear her mind enough to focus on the day ahead.

Auraelia loved her bathing chamber. It had a free-standing shower and a wash basin, but the main focus of the room was the large, gold soaking tub in the middle with a skylight above it. Being able to soak in a warm bath while looking up at the stars brought an unparalleled sense of calm to her soul.

When she entered, she was greeted by lavender and chamomile scented steam. Evidently, one of her lady's maids made it into the bathing chamber without her notice and had already drawn her a bath with her favorite oils.

Sinking into the hot water, she leaned against the curved side and closed her eyes, letting the heat seep into her bones and wash away her tension as she attempted to clear her mind.

Okay, today is my twenty-fifth year. It's the day that I should be coming into my magic...but I don't feel any different. Maybe the ancestors and the goddess didn't consider me worthy? What if I am the first future queen of the Court of Emerald to not have magic?!

Her pulse quickened as her thoughts spiraled.

Though unsure of what exactly she was searching for, Auraelia took a deep breath and reached within her mind and body for any inkling of magic. After what seemed like an eternity, and as every attempt came up empty, she climbed out of the tub and slipped her arms into her dressing gown. As she stepped into her chambers, her breath caught in her throat as Piper set a large ivory box on her bed.

It was time.

Excitement and anxiety warred for dominance as she walked across the room to sit at her vanity, wiping her slick palms on her robe as she took a seat. Piper stood behind her with a reassuring hand on her shoulder as she gave precise instructions to the lady's maids, before leaving to get ready herself.

They started with her hair, and Auraelia let herself get lost in the rhythmic ministrations of the strands being set into curls and waves, then watched in fascination as they wove delicate threads through braids before wrapping the ends to secure them.

When they moved on to makeup, she closed her eyes and let her mind wander.

She and Piper had dreamt of their twenty-fifth birthdays for as long as she could remember. They talked aimlessly about the dresses they would wear to Auraelia's birthday ball, the foods they would eat, and the many, *many*, boys that they would dance with.

They'd discussed what they thought were the best ways to flirt and practiced the subtle art of 'bedroom' eyes.

A chuckle escaped as a memory of Piper holding a comb across her lip as a faux mustache so that *"She could better get into character"* flitted to the forefront of her mind.

"We're finished, My Lady." The delicate chime of one of her lady's maids pulled her out of her reverie. She smiled and thanked each of them before standing from her vanity.

It was time for the dress.

Auraelia strolled across the room to where the box sat on her bed.

It was a work of art in and of itself. Ivory, with gold filigree inlaid on the lid, and if the royal blue satin ribbon that held it closed was any indication of what was inside, it was sure to be beautiful. She let the ribbon slide between her fingers as she gently pulled apart the knot at its center.

Inside, covered by a layer of royal blue silk organza, was one of the most beautiful gowns that she'd ever seen. Without taking it out of the box, she gingerly fingered the details of the bodice. She had no idea what the full dress looked like, but from what she could see, it was stunning.

Leaving the box where it sat, she headed to her dressing room where some of her lady's maids waited to help her finish getting ready. Untying the sash of her robe, she let it fall to the floor, and for the first time since this whole process started, Auraelia took the time to actually look at herself in the mirror while her ladies worked seamlessly around her.

Everything was in coordinated shades of deep royal blue. From her shoes to her panties–and everywhere in between. And despite how much she loathed corsets and garters, she had to admit that they did something for her confidence. Her lips tilted up into a sly smile as she watched her lady clip the garter belt to her stockings, and the way that the delicate silver embroidery caught in the lamp light.

She loved the way that her corset accentuated the narrowness of her waist and the fullness of her hips–as well as pushing her boobs up to her chin.

If you've got it, flaunt it, right?

The longer she looked at herself, the more the anxious butterflies in her stomach settled.

As the ladies finished cinching her into her corset, Piper walked in with the gown draped across her arms. Auraelia gingerly stepped into the pool of fabric, and as her ladies fastened the round satin buttons down the back, she looked in the mirror, a small gasp escaping her lips.

She looked beautiful.

Her long, honey-blonde hair cascaded in waves down her back, and while the fishtail braids added an edge to the structure of the waves, the iridescent thread that had been woven through them made her hair shimmer like moonlight on water.

Her cheeks looked sun kissed. The dark makeup around her eyes brought out the gray and blue hues of her irises, making them sparkle like the stars in the sky. Her lips were full, with a perfect dip in the middle of her top lip, and the deep berry-red of the lip paint made them look all the more inviting. They even left her nose piercings, which her mother would most certainly have a fit about, leaving the pinhead sized diamond stud in her nostril and the delicate hoop of opal through her septum. Although the septum piercing was customary for the royal women in Auraelia's family, her mother had not been pleased with the additional piercing through her nostril, regardless of how small it was.

But it was the dress that made her stand wide-eyed in the mirror.

With delicate touches, she ran her fingers over the bodice.

It was midnight blue with navy and pewter beading in intricate lines that looked like streaks of lightning. The design coalesced where the dress tapered in at her waist and shot upward over her breasts and then down the skirt in the opposite direction.

There was flesh-toned mesh across the upper part of her chest that continued down her arms, while branches of beading crawled up from her wrists in the same design as the bodice. The skirt–which was surprisingly light had a satin lining that felt cool against her legs and was topped with layers of organza in an array of blues and grays, which made her look like a walking storm cloud.

As Auraelia turned in the mirror, her mother strolled into her chambers, stopping a few feet in front of her.

The queen brought her hands to her mouth, and with glassy eyes, looked at her daughter with immense amounts of pride. "You look beautiful, little bug. Though, I suppose you're not so little anymore now, are you?"

With a smile on her lips, the queen walked to Auraelia, pulled her into a warm embrace and whispered, "How are you *feeling*?" in her ear, before leaning back just enough to look into her daughter's eyes.

Auraelia's heart sank as she looked back at her mother. Lowering her gaze, she hung her head and shook it slightly. Without missing a beat, Queen Adelina pressed a finger beneath Auraelia's chin and lifted it so that they were once again looking eye to eye. After a few moments, her mother grinned, "Give it time, my love. You'll see." And with those parting words, and a kiss on the cheek, the queen excused herself.

Curious about what her mother saw, Auraelia rushed to the mirror. When she didn't immediately notice a difference, she sighed and began to turn away from her reflection. But when she looked once more, she noticed a small change. Eyes that were usually a stormy blue-gray, briefly showed small flecks of green.

That's new.

As evening drew near, Auraelia's anxiety rose.

She had been so enamored watching the delicate movements of her ladies throughout the day, that she'd gotten a temporary reprieve from the turmoil of her thoughts. But now that they were finished, the reality of her not feeling any magic in her veins, and the fact that she was about to face all of Lyndaria–as well as nobles from throughout Ixora–came crashing back down.

Her shoulders slumped ever so slightly as worry and dread crept into her thoughts.

The only things keeping her from completely succumbing to her anxiety, were that Piper would be by her side through it all, that it was her birthday ball tonight...and that it was a masquerade.

As she walked back into her room, something on her bed shimmered beneath the lamplight. There, sitting on the lid of her dress box, was her mask. Navy swirls edged in pewter dipped and twined around each other. The colors had been perfectly matched to the beading in her dress, and the design reminded her of the way the waves crashed against each other in the midst of a storm. It was delicate and beautiful, and the perfect complement to her gown.

Once again lost in her thoughts, Auraelia hadn't noticed that Piper was now beside her.

"I'll help you with yours if you help with mine." Piper said as she nudged Auraelia with her elbow.

Nodding, she lifted the mask to her face while Piper secured the delicate silver ribbons behind her head. The mask fit the contours of her face perfectly, falling across her cheek bones to cut across the upper bridge of her nose.

"Thank you," Auraelia muttered under her breath as she turned toward her friend.

"Are you alright?" Piper asked, her words laced with concern.

Auraelia nodded and reached for Piper's mask. Piper was always gorgeous, but tonight she was resplendent. Her gown, which was made from satin in the color of the deepest teal, was draped and wrapped around her body before cascading out at her waist to form the skirt. Her hair had been braided and pinned into a simple updo with a few curls left out to frame her face.

"Damn, Piper. You just had to show me up on my own birthday, didn't you?" Auraelia joked, placing her hands on her hips for emphasis.

"You're the one who wanted to be all *mysterious* and not let anyone know who you were at your own party," Piper jested in return.

There was a moment of silence before they both broke into a fit of laughter, shattering the nervous tension that–once again–tried to take hold.

Motioning for Piper to turn, Auraelia grabbed the silver ribbons of the mask and tied them into a bow before weaving the tail ends through her braids. Once it was secured, Piper turned and grabbed onto Auraelia's hands.

"You ready?"

The previously calm butterflies in her stomach swarmed once more, and her pulse began to race. Auraelia took a deep breath and exhaled slowly. She refused to let her anxiety ruin this night.

Straightening her shoulders, she held her head high as she met the eyes of the friend who had been there for her through everything and smiled. "Let's do this."

Piper smiled in return and did a little dance. "That's my girl."

Hand in hand, the women made their way toward the doors of the suite. Auraelia's heart pounded harder with every step they took, only this time with eagerness and anticipation instead of nerves. Her body vibrated from the excitement of the possibilities that this night might bring.

With one final, steadying breath, Auraelia and Piper made their way through the double doors of her suite and toward the masquerade below.

Chapter Three

Auraelia

Entering the ballroom of Emerald Castle was like walking into a large aviary–that is if you replaced the colorful birds with people dressed in outlandish colors and feathers.

The walls and ceiling were made entirely of glass and the white granite columns that supported the structure had been decorated in gold painted vines. The floor–which perfectly matched the columns–was polished to the point of reflection, making the light from the gold chandeliers illuminate the tiles in a warm glow. The far-right wall was covered in tables full of fruit, cakes, and assorted pastries, as well as bowls of punch. Servers walked around with trays of sparkling wine, whiskey, and champagne. The orchestra was seated to the left and played loudly enough for the people dancing to hear the tune, but soft enough for couples and groups to have conversation.

It was perfect.

There were two stipulations that Auraelia gave her mother when it came to having a birthday ball. One, it had to be a masquerade. And two: she was allowed to simply be a guest at her own party. To mingle and enjoy the night as a woman and not as a princess to be crowned Heir Apparent the following day. Although begrudgingly, her mother understood and agreed.

As Aurelia and Piper walked into the ballroom, the only person who seemed to notice was the queen–giving them a subtle nod before continuing on with her conversation.

Grabbing a glass of sparkling wine from a passing tray, Auraelia started to scan the floor for potential dance partners.

"What about him?" Piper asked as she inclined her head toward a tall man across the way.

Auraelia squinted to try and get a better look as the man in question turned and smirked at them. Even with a mask obscuring half his face, she knew who it was within a second. With her lips turned down in faux disgust, she turned to her friend and snickered, "Being as that's my brother, he's not really my type."

Both women had to cover their mouths to try and suppress the giggles that threatened to escape as Xander approached them. With a raised, quizzical brow, he waited patiently for them to regain their composure. When they finally calmed themselves, he cleared his throat and directed his attention to Auraelia.

"I suppose since it's your birthday, I should ask you to dance. But I'm not sure how inconspicuous you would remain after that, dear sister." With a wink and a smirk, he turned his attention to Piper and bowed, "My Lady, would you care to dance?"

Piper and Auraelia shared a glance, then after a small shrug from Auraelia, Piper curtsied, placed her hand in Xander's, and they headed to the center of the room where other couples were dancing.

Left to her own devices, Auraelia began to observe the crowd around her. It was a different experience being on the outside of an event, rather than at its center. The ability to merely exist in a space, without the pressure of being perfect all the time, lifted a weight off her shoulders that was heavier than she realized.

Standing just outside of a group of women, she rolled her eyes and laughed to herself as they gossiped about the men in the room that they found attractive, which included her brother, and listened to their petty jealousies towards the women who were dancing or conversing with those same men—like Piper.

Her amusement grew when she witnessed the men doing much of the same. She had to suppress a laugh as she listened to them try to work up the nerve to ask any of the ladies to dance. Fixing their hair, straightening their lapels, all to just stand in a group and not make a single move.

A bunch of preening peacocks, the lot of them.

Standing by the wall of windows that faced out into the garden, Auraelia watched while couples twirled and dipped their way across the dance floor and realized for the first time that day that she was genuinely happy.

"Hello, my star."

She jumped. Lost in her own thoughts and the gentle sway of the music that coursed throughout the ballroom, she hadn't noticed the firm body pressed against her from behind, nor the warm breath at her ear as a large hand snaked its way around her waist, looking to pull her closer.

Shock turned to pure loathing and ran rampant through her at the sheer audacity that someone could be so forward, especially out in the open surrounded by people. Seething, Auraelia quickly pulled from the embrace, and–with an incredulous look on her face–spun around. "Excuse me, who do you thi—"

As soon as their eyes met, her seething turned into a simmer. Trapped in the depths of his gaze, she faltered, and her heartbeat quickened. Even with his mask on she could tell that he was gorgeous, and a feeling she couldn't quite place bloomed in the center of her chest, like a thread had been pulled taut between them.

Lifting one eyebrow, he smirked, and answered the question she hadn't been able to finish asking. "Who do I think I am? Oh, my star, that would negate the purpose of wearing a mask, now wouldn't it?"

My star? What the...why does he keep calling me that? Heat flooded her cheeks. "I'm sorry," though unsure of why *she* was apologizing, she continued anyway. "You must have me mistaken for someone else." She turned to leave, but before she could make it one step away, he caught her wrist and started tracing small circles on her pulse point with his thumb. His touch was like a brand on her skin, searing straight into her soul.

When she met his gaze, he smiled, and her knees went weak.

"Not a chance, my star. Now, would you care to dance? You're much too beautiful to be a wallflower."

Deciding to let this mysterious man guide her to the dance floor was the easiest decision she had made all night. His mere touch had her pulse racing, and she was drawn to him like a moth to a flame. And because he had no idea who she was, she could be absolutely, irrevocably, herself. It didn't matter that she was actually a princess. Tonight, she could be just a girl at a ball, but at that moment, she chose to be *his*.

He was taller than her—even with her heels, and as they took a turn around the dance floor, Auraelia took a good look at her mysterious partner. He wore a simple black mask that covered the top half of his face and coordinated beautifully with the rest of his ensemble.

Dressed from head to toe in black, it looked like the devil himself had whisked her onto the dance floor.

His vest had small, gold braided embellishments along the front edge, where matching buckles fastened across his waist. The lush velvet of his coat was soft beneath her fingertips and covered in an intricate brocade pattern while its edges were accented in the same braided gold as his vest.

His hair was as dark as his coat and there was a bluish hue to the strands under the lamplight. He wore it short on the sides and kept the top long and unkempt, like he constantly ran his fingers through it—something that Auraelia's fingers now itched to do—and he had a short well-trimmed beard that suited his square jaw line. His lips were full and pink, like he had been entangled in a night of kissing, and he smelled like sandalwood and the ocean breeze.

He smirked, and it was then that Auraelia realized she had been blatantly staring at his mouth. Quite positive that her entire face was the color of her berry lip paint, she quickly looked away to try and compose herself. Without missing a single step, he gently grabbed her chin and pulled her face back toward his. Eyes the color of moss agate, with swirling pools of gold that seemed to shine with a light all their own, looked back at her. Breathless and blushing, Auraelia opened her mouth to say something, anything, but no words came out.

"My name is Daemon," was all that he said as he returned his hand to hers and continued to lead her through the dance.

A million thoughts circled through her mind when he revealed his name. There was only one Daemon that she knew of that would have been invited to Lyndaria for her birthday *and* the impending coronation and that was Prince Daemon Alexander, Crown Prince of the Court of Sapphire Isles.

Thankfully, he still seemed to be clueless as to whom he was spinning around the dance floor, and she was determined to do whatever it took to keep it that way for as long as possible.

After a few more turns the dance came to an end and Daemon led Auraelia from the crowd. Grabbing two glasses of sparkling wine from a passing tray, he handed one to her before making his way toward the doors nestled in the wall of glass where this whole encounter started and headed into the garden.

Downing the contents of her glass, she followed him into the fresh night air. Curiosity, paired with not wanting the night to end, overruled any logical reasoning as to why she should have stayed in the ballroom.

This area of the garden grounds was separate from the Queen's garden. With its fountain centered hedge maze and its rose bushes, snapdragons, and wildflowers, it was an unkempt oasis nestled in the middle of a world of structure.

The Court of Emerald employed numerous grounds keepers to ensure that this garden continued to be kept in a state of disarray. They let nature do as it willed but made sure that the pathways stayed clear and kept unruly weeds and vines from places they should not be.

With the full moon illuminating the gravel pathways, Daemon and Auraelia walked in contented silence, their hands brushing in whispered touches that made her stomach flutter.

When they were far enough away from the party, he grabbed her hand and pulled her to a stop. "Will you tell me your name?"

Suddenly feeling more confident–whether it was from the wine, the full moon, or the way his eyes seemed to blaze when he looked at her–Auraelia's lips tilted up into a sly grin as she stepped toward him and parroted back his words from earlier. "That would negate the point of wearing a mask, now wouldn't it?"

She stepped away, but entwined her fingers with his as she led him further into the garden.

Daemon chuckled, seemingly content with letting her tug him along. "Where are you taking me?"

Turn after turn, she took them further into the garden, and as he pulled on her hand —probably thinking that she had gotten them extremely lost in the mazes—she stopped in front of an old, seemingly forgotten path.

Glancing at Daemon, she winked and tugged him forward, "Come on."

He shook his head, amusement radiating across his features, and let her lead him onward.

A canopy of leaves and crepe-like flowers hung overhead. Their foliage was so dense that only a few streams of moonlight were able to trickle through and light the way.

As she and Daemon wound their way down the path, they came to a large iron gate set into a stacked stone wall that was overgrown with wisteria and ivy.

Utterly confused, Daemon mumbled under his breath, "What is this place?"

"I believe it's a sanctuary," Auraelia responded, trying to keep her voice from sounding as breathless as she felt.

"A sanctuary?" he asked, sounding a bit confused as he quirked a brow in her direction.

But the only answer she gave was a mumbled, "Mm-hmm...Problem?"

She pulled her hand from his and sauntered over to the gate where she turned to lean against the cold iron bars. Auraelia gazed at him, taking in the sharp edges of his jaw, and the broad width of his shoulders. How his hands flexed at his side, like he wanted to reach out and touch her yet refused to make a move in her direction. When she met his eyes, they glowed with passion and desire, and a familiar heat filled her body.

"You got me all the way out here, my star, now what are you going to do with me?" The way that he said his nickname for her, deep and full of gravel like it took everything he had not to devour her whole, made her breath catch in her throat and had her heart pounding like rain during a summer storm.

"I'm not sure." Auraelia looked away, and let out a low chuckle as she continued, "It's not like I planned this." A moment passed before she met his intense gaze once more and asked the one question that she hoped would turn this already unforgettable night into the best birthday that she could have asked for.

"What would *you* do?"

That one question seemed to jolt him out of whatever trance he had been in. The smirk that she had come to know turned devilish as he slowly stalked toward her.

"Oh, my star, wouldn't you like to know."

Before she could nod her head more than once, Daemon was there, pressing her against the gate, his lips crashing into hers like a wave upon the shore. It was all tongue and teeth, while their hands blindly searched for any sliver of skin to sink into. Sliding her hands beneath his coat, she wrapped her arms around his back, trying desperately to pull him closer. All while he eagerly grabbed fists full of her skirt, inching it higher and higher up her legs.

But the moment his fingertips grazed where her garter belt held her stockings, he froze and pulled away. Resting his forehead against hers, their breaths mingling together in the shared space.

He let out a reluctant, "Fuck," on a breathy exhale, as he gently swept strands of stray hair away from her face and caressed her cheek with all the gentleness one would use to touch a flower.

Sighing, Daemon pulled away enough to look her in the eyes. "If you want this to stop at a kiss, I need you to tell me, and I need you to tell me right now. Because, by the goddess, no matter how much I want you to want this, if you don't, we will leave right now and return to the ball."

She searched his face for any sign of falsehood in the words he spoke. But as she stared into his eyes, the pools of gold in the sea of green seemed to be glowing brighter now than they had all night, and all she could muster was a whispered, "Yes."

Daemon maintained a soft, yet firm, grip on her chin, keeping her face tilted up and forcing her to maintain eye contact. "Yes, what? I need you to use your words. I need you to tell me what you want."

Even though she was no stranger to intimacy, having had both long-term partners as well as an occasional tryst, something about tonight felt different.

Maybe it was because he didn't know who she was, or perhaps it was because they were outside in a garden and could be caught at any moment, she didn't know.

What she did know was that for the first time in a long time, she didn't care. His gaze never faltered, burning its way into the depths of her soul. She stared straight back, drowning in his intensity.

"I'm saying yes, Daemon. Yes to you, yes to this. Here and now, whatever that may be."

With that, Daemon rested his brow against hers and let out a sigh of relief, and after a growled out, "Thank fuck," he crushed her between him and the iron gate, devouring her lips in a world-shattering kiss.

Pressed between the cold hard iron and the solid warmth that was Daemon Alexander, Auraelia was in pure bliss.

What started like a strike of lightning, turned into a long, steady roll of thunder. Their kisses slowed to nips and a languid tangle of tongues. Desperate hands turned into gentle and deliberate caresses trying to map out every dip and curve on each other's body.

Daemon pulled away and gently gathered her skirts as he lifted her leg so that it could rest on his hip. He took in every inch of her leg, letting his fingers weave feather light caresses up and up, only this time they didn't stop at the top of her stocking. A breeze through the garden, combined with adrenaline and the delicate touches from Daemon, sent a shiver down her spine causing her skin to prickle.

His hand slid higher, pooling her skirts at her waist and exposing the intricate silver embroidery on her garter belt. Daemon slipped a finger under the delicate strap, and as he inched his way higher, he let out a low groan that Auraelia felt straight in her core. "The skirts are a bit much, but this—" he snapped the ribbon against her thigh, "This I like."

A small whimper escaped, causing him to drag his eyes to hers. As he continued to run his hand further up her exposed leg, he leaned forward and planted hot, open mouth kisses on her shoulder, trailing them up her neck to her ear.

"Is there something that you want?"

Daemon's whispered words pebbled her skin, and her breath caught in her throat as his fingers skirted the junction of where her inner thigh met her pussy, causing her core to clench with need. Gently fingering the edge of her lace panties, Daemon kissed his way from her ear, following her jaw line back to her mouth. Through it all, he worked his hand around to fully cup her, and she couldn't help the moan that slipped from her throat.

Mindlessly, Auraelia rocked against his hand, desperate for the friction that she knew would get her off. But as soon as she found the rhythm she needed, the pressure he provided was gone. With a look of indignation, she opened her mouth to protest, but the fire in his eyes and the smirk on his lips shut her up.

"My star, I'm sure you're very competent at getting yourself off. But please, allow me the honor."

Before she could think of a retort, his lips were on hers once more as he moved his hand back to where she needed it most.

He stayed on top of her panties, using the lace to create extra friction as his fingers moved in relentless circles over her clit, edging her closer and closer to her climax but never tipping her over. He slid his fingers further down her center, and she knew he would find the fabric drenched with her arousal.

Daemon groaned as he ripped a hole down the center of her panties and pushed them to either side, giving him complete access to her sex.

Deepening the pressure on her clit with the heel of his palm, he tentatively pushed a finger inside her entrance causing her to gasp against his lips and her hips to rock forward, desperate to feel him deeper.

"All of this just for me?" he asked, as he worked his finger in and out of her, trailing kisses down her neck.

Auraelia reached between their bodies, aiming for the laces on his trousers when his other hand–that up until that moment had been holding her tightly against him–grabbed her wrist and pinned it above her head. "No, not yet. This may be the sanctuary of a goddess, but the only goddess that I want to worship tonight is you."

The quick nod of her head, followed by a breathy, "Okay," was all the confirmation he needed.

His relentless teasing never ceased as he alternated between slow circles on her clit and delving his fingers into her core. Daemon released the wrist that he held above her head, but the reprieve was short lived as he brought her other hand up and pinned them both against the gate.

Pure unadulterated passion burned in his eyes as he looked at her. "Hold on to the gate, my star. Let me make you shine."

As soon as she took hold of the gate, he was on his knees. Draping her leg over his shoulder, he dove under her skirts and put his mouth on her aching pussy. At the sudden onslaught of his tongue, Auraelia gasped and clung tighter to the bars.

Rotating between spearing her with his tongue, and gentle nips on her clit, Daemon seemed to take pleasure in bringing her to the edge over and over again, prolonging her release.

"Oh, for the love of—" Auraelia's breathing became more and more erratic, "Daemon, please. I'm begging you!" She could damn near feel him smirk against her.

"Oh, how I love the sound of you begging."

Adding his fingers, he ruthlessly thrusted in and out of her entrance. He curled them forward to tantalize that wonderful spot within her core, all while he sucked and flicked her clit.

Warmth filled her body as her orgasm barreled through her—much like the thunder that suddenly sounded overhead. Unable to contain herself, she let go of the gate and threaded her fingers onto his hair. And as she rocked against his mouth, another orgasm ripped through her.

Removing his fingers from her quivering pussy, Daemon drank in her release like he was a man parched and the only thing to satiate him was her.

As Auraelia worked her way down from the high caused by Daemon's tongue, thunder continued to roll through the sky. Daemon eased her leg down from his shoulder and stood, righting her skirts before he bothered with himself. His mouth glistened with proof of what had just transpired and eyes, still full of want, shone back at her. As well as something else...

Possession.

He wanted her, and from the smirk on his lips, he intended to have her. He took a step to close the minute distance that had been created between them, grabbed her waist, and once again had her pressed between him and the gate to the sanctuary. His kiss was soft as he tentatively traced the seam of her lips with his tongue, seeking entrance but waiting patiently for the invitation.

This was nothing like what they shared earlier. It was slow, a series of give and take, and tasting her own arousal on his lips was like her own personal aphrodisiac. As they kissed, Auraelia ran her hands up his chest to his neck then tangled her fingers into his hair, tugging slightly.

Groaning, Daemon pulled back, and when his eyes met hers, they widened slightly.

"Your eyes—" a mix of confusion and awe tinged his voice, "There are bright green streaks in them now that weren't there before." His eyes searched her face. Slowly, he reached up and gently fingered the edge of her mask, curiosity burning in his gaze. "May I?"

Auraelia stood there, wide eyed and frozen, her heart pounding in her chest. But just as he was about to lift her mask, thunder boomed above them as the sky opened.

"Shit!" They exclaimed in unison as the sky proceeded to dump water. Using the sudden rain as an excuse, she slipped out of Daemon's hold and took a few steps away.

"Where do you think you're going?" he asked, a bemused look on his face. The passion that blazed in his eyes banked momentarily before flaring to life again when she leaned over to remove her heels–a cocky grin on her face.

Standing in the pouring rain, most people would look like a drowned rat, but not Daemon. No, he stood there with his arms crossed and a smirk on his lips as the rain poured down causing his clothes to look like they had been painted onto his body. She wasn't even sure when he'd lost his coat, but now every muscled contour was clearly defined beneath his soaked shirt.

The sight made her mouth water and had her momentarily second guessing her decision.

Auraelia stood up straight, keeping the grin on her face, and started to back her way down the path that had led them to the sanctuary.

"I think this may be my cue to bow out gracefully," she shouted over the downpour.

Daemon uncrossed his arms and raised a brow. "Is that so? I thought we were just getting started." He took a step toward her, but she continued to steadily back away. "I wasn't quite finished worshiping you yet."

The devilish grin on Daemon's face–one that promised immense pleasure if the first two orgasms had been any indication–made her steps falter.

Keep it together, Rae. It's just a panty melting smile on a drop-dead gorgeous man.

Coming to her senses, she held out her hand. It may have brought him to an abrupt halt, but it didn't erase his smirk.

Keeping her eyes locked on his, Auraelia did the only thing that she could think of. She dropped into a deep curtsy, something that she only did for the queen. "*Prince* Daemon, thank you for the...eventful evening. I bid you goodnight."

At the sound of hearing his title, Daemon removed his mask.

"How is it that you know who I am?" Shock momentarily radiated across his face, but it quickly turned to amusement.

Auraelia produced a smirk of her own and winked. "I guess you'll have to figure it out."

Turning on her heel, she sprinted through the rain and back toward the ballroom. Leaving a drenched and confused prince standing alone in the garden.

Wanting to avoid leering eyes and questions about the state of her appearance, Auraelia skirted the castle wall away from the ballroom until she found one of the maid's entrances that led up a back staircase. Miraculously, she made it back to her room without being spotted and slipped into her suite.

As she leaned against the door, she took a deep breath and smiled. Reaching up to remove her mask, she walked across her sitting area, her soaked skirts leaving puddles in their wake. Just as she was about to walk into her bedroom, she heard the door to her suite open then slam closed.

"Where the hell have you been?! I swear to the goddess, Rae, are you trying to send me into an early grave?!"

A snicker escaped before she could stop it. Rolling her eyes, Auraelia called over her shoulder, "I'm sorry, Piper, I went for a walk and got...distracted." A grin spread across her face as she recalled exactly what that particular distraction had been.

As if she sensed the shift in her thoughts, Piper was across the room in the blink of an eye and spinning Auraelia around to face her. "Spill. I need to know everything. Starting with who that gorgeous man was that monopolized your time on the dance floor tonight."

"It wasn't just on the dance floor." With a wink, Auraelia turned and continued to her bathroom so that she could strip out of her clothes and take a bath to bring some warmth back to her body. Piper helped her out of her gown while the tub filled and peppered her with questions about where she had gone, why she was drenched, and who she had been with.

When Auraelia finished recounting the details, her friend stood with her mouth agape and stared back at her with shock and awe.

"Auraelia Rose, I didn't think you had it in you! I'm so proud," Piper said as she wiped an imaginary tear away from her eye.

"Oh, shut up." Auraelia gently pushed her friend's shoulder and rolled her eyes.

"Seriously though, Rae, I wasn't sure about the masks at first, but now I can see their appeal." Piper waggled her brows, then with a smug look on her face, turned toward the door and left Auraelia alone to soak.

Resting her head on the back of the tub, she looked up to the aperture in her ceiling and out at the sky above. The storm that had come on so suddenly seemed to have dissipated just as quickly. Sinking down into the warm water of her bath, she allowed her mind to wander.

"Your eyes...there are bright green streaks in them now that weren't there before."

Auraelia shot up in the tub as Daemon's words to her in the garden barreled their way to the forefront of her mind, colliding with the interaction she had with her mother while getting ready for the ball.

She stepped from the tub, sloshing water onto the floor in the process, and threw on her dressing gown as she hastily walked to her vanity. Peering into the glass, she saw it. Small streaks of green shot across her eyes like bolts of lightning. Closing her eyes, she once again felt for her magic.

Minutes seemed to pass with no noticeable changes, but as her frustration grew, the wind outside picked up and rattled the windows of her room. Then, just as she felt a warm heaviness in her chest, thunder sounded directly above the castle.

Chapter Four

Daemon

I can't believe she left me standing out here in the goddess damned rain. How the fuck did she know who I was? Who the hell is she?! Daemon stood frozen right where *she* had left him.

Shortly after she had abandoned him there, the rain let up and the clouds started to clear away. He headed back towards the castle, adjusting his cock–that was painfully hard, thanks to a certain little minx–to a more tolerable position in his trousers. He made his way through the maze of hedges, trying desperately to remember all the twists and turns that had led them to the sanctuary.

Halfway back, thunder rolled overhead and lightning struck in the distance. Decidedly not wanting to be caught in the middle of another freak storm, he quickened his pace. After a few wrong turns, he finally made it back to the entrance of the garden.

The party seemed to have dwindled down to a few drunken stragglers, but he still didn't want to draw attention to himself by walking into the ballroom sopping wet. Fortunately, while exploring the castle and its grounds before the ball, he'd discovered a few servant's entrances. Unfortunately, the door he'd chosen to make his discreet entrance also happened to be where supplies were delivered to the kitchen, and there was still staff meandering about.

At the sight of the crown prince in the kitchen–soaked to the core and dripping on the recently mopped floor–all work stopped, and the eyes of the kitchen staff went as wide as the saucers on which their delicious meals had been served. They all dipped into low bows, then an elderly woman at the back of the room, most likely the head chef, cleared her throat as she straightened. "Excuse me, Your Highness, is there something that we can make for you? Or help you with?"

Slightly embarrassed at his current state—and that he was most definitely putting these people out—Daemon plastered a grin on his face and shook his head. "No, I'm quite alright, thank you. Just got caught in the rain while taking a stroll through the lovely gardens and didn't want to disturb the party. Though it seems I may have gotten turned around. If you would be so kind as to point me in the proper direction of my rooms, I'll be out of your way."

Back in his suite, he roughly closed the door behind him and made his way across the space, once again adjusting his cock that still strained against the laces of his pants.

All the guests here for the coronation were settled into the east wing of the castle and separated by court affiliation. And although Daemon had an entire crew that traveled with him to Lyndaria, they remained on his ship in the harbor.

He'd only brought one person with him to the castle, so they ended up in a double suite. Both sides had a bedchamber and a washroom, the only shared space being the sitting area. For that, Daemon was relieved. He really didn't want to hear what went on after dark in the room that his companion occupied.

It was simple, but well decorated and furnished to keep guests comfortable during their stay. Woven rugs covered the dark wood floors, and a cozy sitting area with a small fireplace opened to the floor to ceiling windows which overlooked the mountains in the distance.

Storming into the bedchamber, he bypassed the large four-poster bed, stripping on his way to the shower. He needed to bring some warmth back to his body and see if he could do something about the heaviness that still weighed down his cock.

Stepping into the shower, he groaned from the delicious heat of the water as it cascaded over his body.

He'd heard that the castle, and most of the residents in the city, had updated plumbing that brought running cold and hot water directly into their homes. But he was never more grateful for it than he was at that moment. The bathing chamber was small but had all the necessary features and the last thing he wanted to do was drag some poor sucker from their bed to bring water to his room for a bath.

In Kalmeera, the capital city within the Court of Sapphire Isles, only the castle had new plumbing. Though they were steadily working on updating the rest of the city to hopefully make the lives of their citizens a little easier.

As the water rained down, he closed his eyes, propped one arm on the wall and rested his head against it. Gripping his cock in the other hand, he sucked in a sharp breath through his teeth. *Fucking shit, how am I still this hard?*

Tightening his grip, Daemon worked himself in a steady rhythm as he reminisced on his evening in the garden with *his star*.

The way her arousal tasted on his tongue, the feeling of her cunt gripping his fingers as he worked her to the edge over and over again until he finally tipped her over. The way her fingers tugged and tangled in his hair. How she smelled of lavender and chamomile, which would now forever be ingrained onto his soul. The way she looked at him like a wanton goddess for whom he would gladly get down on his knees for again so that he could worship at her feet.

He pictured her tight pussy riding his cock instead of his fist as he began working himself closer and closer to the release he so desperately needed. His imagination filling his head with the sounds of her pleasure-filled whimpers and moans. With one final stroke, he clenched his teeth as he painted the wall of the shower with his cum, the evidence of which was quickly washed away in the streams of water.

"Well, that was certainly intense. What cunt got you wound so tight?" A deep voice cut through the silence like a hot knife.

"Fuck you, asshole," Daemon replied without even turning around, "Give me a few minutes and I'll be right out."

"Take your time, you *obviously* have some things to work through."

"Oh, fuck off!"

Sighing, Daemon pushed off of the wall and washed quickly. After wrapping a towel around his waist, he stepped out into his bedchamber to find none other than his pain in the ass best friend, Aiden, lounging on his bed picking at his nails with a dagger.

Aiden was a good-looking man, standing just as tall as Daemon. His sun-bleached hair was perfectly coiffed at all times and his skin was golden from spending his days on ships. He kept his face clean shaven, claiming *'women prefer it this way, they don't want rug burn from my face.'* His eyes were the color of warm honey, framed by dark lashes and bushy brows.

Daemon crossed the room to his wardrobe where he pulled on loose black pants before he leaned against it and crossed his arms. "I've had a long night, Aiden. What's up?"

"I could ask you the same thing," Aiden replied with a waggle of his eyebrows and a smirk. "I've never seen you wound so tight."

"Fuck off."

"Look, *Your Highness,* don't be crabby with me because you didn't get your dick wet in some lame-ass Lyndarian pussy. There's still time. We'll be here for a few days."

Standing up straight, Daemon started to cross the room toward his *friend* and opened his mouth to respond. But before he could, Aiden continued.

"I came to see if you ended up back here. I saw you dancing with that girl—"

"Woman," Daemon interjected.

Aiden rolled his eyes, "*Woman,* and then you were gone. I didn't see you leave, so I'm just doing my civic duty and making sure that *Crown Prince Daemon Alexander, of the Court of Sapphire Isles* wasn't lying in a rose bush somewhere." His words dripped with sarcasm, and had he not been Daemon's best friend, it would have cost him dearly. But since he was, indeed, his best friend, he got a sucker-punch to the stomach instead, which caused him to double over and launch into a coughing fit.

"Asshole," Aiden wheezed between coughs.

"That *woman* is a fucking goddess—"

"So, you *did* get your dick wet," Aiden managed to get out in between labored breaths.

Daemon closed his eyes and pinched the bridge of his nose. "No, you asshole, I did not *'get my dick wet'* as you love to phrase it. I ate her pussy like it was my last fucking meal, and I'll be damned if it wasn't the sweetest I've ever had. But before we were able to get to anything else, it started fucking raining. Then she ran off, leaving me hard and soaked in the middle of the fucking garden."

Aiden–still holding his stomach from the blow Daemon dealt him–was now folded over in a fit of hysterics. But when he met Daemon's stoic expression, he quickly sobered. "Wait, you're not kidding, are you?"

"Unfortunately, no. And that's not all."

"What else could there possibly be?" Aiden asked incredulously.

"She knew who I was..."

"*What?* How in all of the realms did that happen? You had a fucking mask on."

Sighing, Daemon continued, "I told her my name was Daemon, but that was it. I assumed that would be a safe bet. I mean hell, there has to be more than one noble with my name, right? It's not like I have *'prince'* tattooed on my forehead."

"Wait, so she knew who you were, and she still bolted?"

Daemon glared at Aiden in response.

"Fuck. Did you at least get her name?"

"No, I didn't. I called her *my star*."

"*My star?* Damn, D, you've got it that bad after one taste of her pussy? Does it drip gold or something?"

He landed another blow to Aiden's stomach.

"Yeah, I probably deserved that one."

"You think?"

Immensely tired of this conversation, he kicked Aiden out of his suite and back into his own next door.

As he laid down on the bed, Daemon stared at the ceiling with an arm draped over his head and let his thoughts wander back to the unanswered questions that had been floating around since he was left standing alone in the garden. *Who is she? How did she know who I was? But more importantly, how am I supposed to see her again if I don't figure that out?* Groaning, Daemon rolled over onto his side and decided to try and sleep, he'd figure it out tomorrow...hopefully.

Tomorrow came too quickly, and it was bound to be a long day. At the sound of rattling metal trays, Daemon rolled out of bed and walked into the sitting area. He'd slept like shit and was pretty sure he looked like it too. Aiden, who sat in one of the chairs by the fireplace picking at the fruit on the breakfast tray, turned when he heard Daemon pad into the room.

"Damn man, you look like shit," Aiden stated after popping a grape into his mouth.

Well, that confirms that.

"Good morning to you too, Aiden. How are you today?" Daemon replied sardonically and quickly followed with, "Where's the coffee?"

Aiden picked up the carafe, holding it high in the air. "You want it in a cup, or...?"

"You want it in your lap, or...?" Daemon replied.

"Damn, D. I hope you find this chic—"

"For the last time, she's a woman. Not a *chick*, not a *girl*, a woman. Don't make me punch you again."

"Alright, shit. Come on, we gotta eat and get ready. Everyone is meeting outside the ballroom to walk to the sanctuary in an hour, so we need to hurry."

"The sanctuary? They're having the coronation here on the grounds?"

"Guess so. All I know is what I was told. Hurry up, so we can go."

Daemon sat in the chair next to Aiden and took a sip of his coffee, letting it warm his insides and erase some of the fog left in his mind from lack of sleep. Once they finished breakfast, they each went to their own chambers and got ready for the day.

Since it was a coronation and the attire was formal, Daemon chose to go with the colors of his court. His shirt was black linen with fasteners up to his neck, though he left a few undone at the top. His vest was cobalt blue with delicate silver embroidery–reminding him of a certain little minx's garter belt from the night before–and three silver buckles that fastened across his waist.

His coat, though similar to the one from the previous night, was a beautiful monochromatic brocade fabric in the richest shade of cobalt, and the cuffs were trimmed in the same silver thread as his vest. He paired everything with his nicest pair of black leather trousers and boots.

Aiden was already waiting for him when he walked into the sitting room. Their formal dress was similar, but where Daemon's ensemble was accented in silver, Aiden's was black.

"Ready to get this over with?" Boredom filled his friend's tone.

"No, but I don't really have a choice, do I?"

Neither of them particularly wanted to be in Lyndaria, let alone sit through a coronation, but Daemon's father was sick and couldn't travel so he had ordered him to take his place.

In Ixora, whenever there was a coronation for an heir apparent, or the crowning of a new monarch, a representative from every court had to be present so that there was no way to contest who was next in line.

So, there they were.

With a sigh, Daemon fastened his sword belt around his waist, and headed towards the door.

"Hey, forgetting something?" Aiden called from behind him.

He turned around just in time to catch the object that Aiden lobbed in his direction–his crown.

"Fuuuck." After throwing his head back in exasperation, Daemon righted himself and placed the crown on his head. It had been in his family for generations and worn by every Crown Prince of the Sapphire Isles.

From a distance, it simply looked like metal had been braided together, but up close, the details shone through. Each strand in the braid was different. One was made to look like the tentacle of an octopus, another was a simple hammered metal, and the last strand had waves carved into it and each crest of the wave was accented with crushed sapphires. It sat just below his hairline, allowing a few wayward silky strands to fall over it in the front.

Now that Daemon was looking *'properly princely'* as Aiden put it, they headed down to meet the rest of the guests and to head to the sanctuary.

Walking through the garden in the daylight was a stark contrast to the intimacy that it held in the dead of night. When they reached the sanctuary, Daemon's eyes grew to the size of a ship's helm as memories from the previous night flooded his mind. What he thought had been old and abandoned, was actually a beautifully maintained garden oasis.

Next to the gate was a gold plaque, one that he completely missed while he had his beautiful star pressed against him. The sanctuary was built for Rhayne, the goddess of love and war. Though he wasn't sure if the members of the Court of Emerald still worshipped her, there was something poetic about having the coronation in a sanctuary for a goddess of love and war. After all, even beloved monarchs had to take their people to war if it was warranted, and sometimes when it was not.

As they walked through the gate, Daemon looked around in awe. At first glance it looked like ruins from an old building, but upon closer examination, the intentionality behind the design of the space became apparent. The structure was made of the same light gray stone as the castle with giant columns towering like large oak trees throughout the space. There was no defined ceiling, instead it looked like a series of skylights without glass in varying shapes and sizes that let in natural light.

This would be beautiful at night to see the stars.

Following the group of guests further into the sanctuary, they walked through an archway that led to the ceremony area. The open ceiling continued, but the walls consisted of gothic-style arches in the stone that held no windows, allowing for a natural breeze through the space with a minimally obstructed view of the surrounding flora. There were natural wood benches lining the aisle down the middle that led to an upraised altar where a unique throne sat at the center.

A large wisteria tree grew behind the chair, and while its roots encircled and twined along the arms and legs, its branches draped waves of lilac-colored blossoms above it.

Lost in the serenity and ethereal feeling of the space, he hadn't realized that everyone else had taken their seats until Aiden cleared his throat and gestured to the empty space in the third row next to the aisle.

The ceremony commenced shortly after they took their seats as one by one people of importance filed into the ceremony space. The priestess performing the ceremony came first, shrouded in a white linen robe that trailed along the floor and a simple, silver circlet across her brow that was embellished with an emerald at its center.

Prince Xander was next, and had he belonged to almost any other house in Ixora, he would have been named next in line. But since the Court of Emerald was a matriarchal line, he instead headed the war council and served an advisor to the reigning queen.

Queen Adelina followed shortly after her son and looked resplendent in her deep emerald gown. The bodice was corseted and embroidered with a beautiful pattern in gold, wide straps draped off her shoulders with long, flowing gossamer sleeves while the full skirt was a simple satin in the same shade of emerald. Her hair was darker than Xander's, more of a chestnut brown in comparison to his sandy blond, and if it weren't for the few streaks of gray that framed her face, one might assume she was the princess. Which had him wondering, if their mother looked that beautiful at whatever age she was, what must the princess look like?

Fortunately, he didn't have to wait long.

Somewhere in the sanctuary were musicians, their music filtering through to the ceremony space as a woman with midnight black hair proceeded down the aisle. She wore the color of the court, but the fabric darkened from a pale green that reminded him of the foam on the sea, into a deep forest green that could have easily been mistaken for black. It twisted around her torso, then draped down to the floor in waves. Once she made it to the steps of the altar, she didn't go up, instead opting to stand next to Xander.

If that's not the princess, then who...

Before he could finish his thought, the melody changed to something soft and romantic as a soft breeze filtered through the space. Petals from the wisteria tree floated through the air and fell delicately like a mist of rain. Daemon kept his eyes forward as the princess from Emerald finally made her entrance. He didn't look in her direction until she reached the bench where he stood, but by the time he glanced her way, he could no longer see her face–but what he could see, he liked.

Her hair was lighter than her brother's, more of a honey-blonde and had been swept up into an array of different braids, twists, and curls which were secured at the nape of her neck. Her dress was emerald green and corseted like her mother's, though a shade or two lighter, and it accentuated the narrowness of her waist.

The bodice was flesh-toned mesh with strategically placed green and gold embroidery, and where her mother had a full skirt, the princess had chosen to have layers of fabric that brought a softness to the structure of the gown.

On her shoulders she wore what looked like golden armored plates connected by golden chains in varying lengths across her shoulder blades, while a long coordinating green gossamer cape trailed behind her. She also wore gold bands with chains that mimicked the ones draping across her back around each of her biceps.

When she arrived at the altar, she curtsied low to ground out of respect to her mother then ascended the steps. Standing in front of the throne, she turned, keeping her head bowed and her eyes downcast as the priestess began the ceremony.

Throughout the whole coronation, Daemon continued to try and get a better look at the princess. From the front, he could see that her dress pushed her breasts up to an inviting display while still being somewhat modest, and the chains that draped along her back also hung across her chest in delicate swoops.

She looked beautiful, even as she maintained a stoic expression through the entire ordeal, not once lifting her head to look out at the people gathered. When it was finally time for her to be introduced to the gathered witnesses, and the crown of the Heir Apparent was on her head, only then did she straighten and lift her eyes to the crowd.

Daemon froze. He would recognize those slate-colored eyes anywhere, even after just one night.

It can't be.

"Princess Auraelia Rose, you have been crowned Heir Apparent to the throne of the Court of Emerald. Do you accept this role, swear to uphold the integrity of your court, and defend your people until your last breath?" The priestess asked loud enough for all the guests present to hear.

Auraelia locked eyes with him and smirked, her gaze intense and mischievous.

"I swear it," she answered, her eyes never leaving his as she made her vow.

"Then with the blessing of the Goddess Rhayne, and the witnesses gathered here this day, I now pronounce you Crown Princess Auraelia Rose Morwen, rightful heir to the Court of Emerald and future queen of Lyndaria. May the Goddess shine her love and wisdom upon you, and may the ancestors guide you."

When the priestess finished her announcement, every guest stood and dipped into a bow or curtsy as a gentle breeze blew through the hall, once again sending flower petals to rain down in a flurry.

Once everyone straightened, applause and cheers erupted through the sanctuary as Auraelia descended from the altar and out of the space. Only then did she break eye contact with him, and even though he kept his gaze fixated on her, she kept hers trained forward–never once glancing his way.

As guests started filing out of the ceremony space, Daemon stared through the archway that the princess and her party had exited through.

"It's her." His words were barely more than a whisper.

"Who's her?" Aiden asked with a confused, and slightly concerned, look on his face.

"Princess Auraelia."

"D, you're gonna have to give me more than that, man. What's going on? What about the princess?"

Daemon turned toward his friend and something on his face must have made the pieces fall into place, because Aiden's eyes grew wide, and he ran both hands down his face.

"Fuck, D. Seriously? Shit. Of course, your ass would be the one to find the fucking princess during a mother fucking *masquerade ball*. You're an ass, you know that..."

Aiden continued rambling and spewing curses, but Daemon wasn't paying attention anymore. Just beyond his friend, he caught a glimpse of movement. He saw her, bathed in sunlight, as she spoke to the midnight-haired woman from her processional.

She glanced in his direction, and when their eyes met, he felt a strange pull toward her. Hers widened with surprise as he held her gaze. It was only slight, and only for a fraction of a second, before she broke the connection and turned her attention back to her companion.

When she grabbed the hand of the other woman and pulled her further into the garden, his lips pulled into a wide grin.

There was no way he was letting her get away from him so easily a second time. Thankfully, there was still a formal dinner followed by a celebratory ball.

You want to play cat and mouse, princess? Well, let the games begin.

Chapter Five

Auraelia

"Shit, shit, shit..." she kept muttering the word over and over again as she unceremoniously dragged Piper further into the garden and back toward the castle.

"Rae, for the love of all things good in life, would you please slow down!"

Coming to a stop, Auraelia looked at her friend, then behind her to make sure they hadn't been followed and took a few steadying breaths before she spoke. Her heart was racing, and she couldn't tell if it was from adrenaline or anxiety–possibly both.

"Did you see him?"

"Did I see who, where?" Piper asked with a quizzical look on her face.

"Prince Daemon."

"Prince Daemon...Oh, you mean the man who ate your pussy like it was his favorite flavor of cake, not twenty-four hours ago? *That* Prince Daemon?" Piper's eyes narrowed into slits as a devilish grin spread across her face.

Auraelia scoffed and rolled her eyes. "Be serious, Piper!" Her voice took a whiney edge as panic set in.

"Yes, Rae. I saw him. He was kind of hard to miss with you both throwing sex daggers at each other with your eyes."

"Wha—We were not."

"Oh, my dear, sweet friend, you most definitely were. Not that I blame you, he's gorgeous." Piper feigned a swoon and fanned herself for dramatic effect.

"You're ridiculous," Auraelia chuckled and gently shoved her friend, which sent them both into a fit of laughter. Regaining their composure, they walked through the garden back to the castle, arm in arm.

"I don't know what I'm going to do now that he knows that it was me from last night. We still have the banquet and ball to get through."

Piper pulled them to a stop and turned to her friend, grabbing Auraelia's hands in hers. "You are Crown Princess Auraelia. You are strong. You are resilient. You are beautiful. And you do not cower to anyone, not even a prince; regardless of how gorgeous he is," she added with a wink. "You will face this obstacle like you do everything else, with grace...and a stubborn head and sassy attitude, but that's why I love you."

A weight lifted from her shoulders with Piper's words, and she smiled as they began walking again. "Thank you, Piper. I don't know what I would do without you."

"You would be insufferably boring and utterly miserable, of course." And with that classic Piper response, laughter ensued once more.

As the castle came into view, Auraelia saw her mother waiting just outside the doors to the ballroom. Inside, half of the space had been turned into a banquet hall, while the other half remained open for the celebratory ball that was to commence once the meal was over. When they reached the doors, they curtsied to their queen before Piper went inside to find her seat at the table, leaving Auraelia with her mother.

"I'm so proud of you, little bug, and you look beautiful," Queen Adelina said as she looked at Auraelia with adoration and adjusted the delicate circlet that now sat on her brow. It was comprised of silver vines with delicate gold leaves that twisted and intertwined together. Resting right below her hair line on her forehead, it came to a point in the center where a large raw cut emerald was nestled into the tangle of silver vines.

"Are you ready?" Her mother's voice was light and full of hope.

Before she could answer, a stiff wind blew through the garden that sent a chill down her spine. Gently grabbing her chin, Queen Adelina forced her to meet her gaze, then smiled so large wrinkles formed at the corners of her eyes. "I see you've found your magic."

"What do you mean?" Auraelia asked as pure confusion and worry danced across her face.

"You truly don't know, do you?"

Auraelia shook her head and waited for an explanation, but one never came.

"You'll see it when you're ready to, my dear. But it's there and it is wonderful." With that, her mother lovingly stroked her cheek and walked inside the ballroom to take her place at the head of the table.

Auraelia took a deep breath to calm the nervous butterflies that had taken flight in her stomach. With her anxiety momentarily in check, she straightened her shoulders and walked through the ballroom doors.

Here goes nothing.

Chapter Six

Daemon

He felt her presence before he saw her.

It was like the room became charged with static as soon as she stepped into the space. She walked with the elegance of any lady, but with an air about her that demanded respect and loyalty. She was the embodiment of what a queen should be, and she wasn't even a queen yet.

When she got to her seat, she faltered, but only briefly, and he was pretty sure he was the only one who noticed the misstep. Her seat was at the table head opposite her mother, and once they both took their seats, the rest of the table followed suit. To Auraelia's right, was the midnight-haired beauty that he'd seen her talking to in the garden—her lady in waiting, Piper— and by a stroke of dumb luck, he'd been seated to her left.

Let the games begin, princess.

As everyone settled into their seats to start the meal, he had to force himself not to stare at the beautiful woman sitting next to him. He still couldn't believe that of all of the people he encountered at the ball the night before, the damn princess was the one who rode his face with free abandon in the middle of the garden.

When the first course was served, he took the chance to glance at Auraelia in hopes of catching her eye, but she was in a deep, hushed, conversation with her lady. Deciding to take full advantage of her distraction, he took it upon himself to get a better look at *his star*.

She was stunning.

Being this close, in a brightly lit room and without a mask disguising half her face, he was able to really take in her features. She had long lashes that brushed her eyebrows when she fully opened her eyes, and a straight nose that ended in a rounded, slightly upturned point. It was also pierced, which was uncommon in the Sapphire Isles, but it suited her face. Her lips were full with a dip right in the center, and when she laughed or smiled, her entire face lit up, making her eyes sparkle.

So completely consumed by the beauty sitting next to him, he hadn't noticed that people were staring at *him* until Aiden cleared his throat and Auraelia turned in his direction, catching his stare. When their eyes locked, all the memories he'd been trying to tamp down came flooding back to the forefront of his mind, and it was like she knew. Her lips tilted into a tiny smirk, her intense gaze full of the same passion and mischief from the night before.

"Is there a problem…Ser?" Her brow was furrowed in confusion, but there was a playful glint in her eye. A challenge to call her out on her white lie.

"Prince Daemon of the Court of Sapphire Isles, Your Highness," Lady Piper supplied, matching Auraelia's conspiratorial look.

"Oh yes, of course. My apologies, *Prince* Daemon," she replied, and inclined her head slightly in his direction in reverence to his title. After a few intense seconds of silence, she looked him in the eye and raised her brows. "Well, Prince Daemon. Is there a problem that I need to be made aware of?" The mischievous look in her eye never wavered, and the smallest of smirks graced her beautiful mouth.

He smiled and tilted his head slightly, feigning confusion, though he knew full well he had been caught staring.

Two can play this game.

"Not at all, Princess. Why do you ask?"

"Well, you've been staring at me like I have something on my face, or food stuck in my teeth."

After that comment, her lady could no longer contain the laughter that she had been trying desperately to suppress. She snorted, and the wine she had been drinking took an alternate route, coming out her nose instead of going down her throat.

The women looked at each other and after a beat of silence, erupted into a fit of hysterics. The commotion halted the other conversations at the table, as everyone turned their attention toward them. The queen cleared her throat, raising a reproachful brow at her daughter, which brought the laughing to an immediate halt, and a deep flush to spread across Auraelia's cheeks.

Daemon smiled to himself as images of Auraelia, flushed for an entirely different reason, flooded his mind.

As if his thoughts summoned her, she looked his way, and when their gazes met her flush deepened to a beautiful shade of crimson before she broke eye contact and turned her attention back to her friend.

Conversation slowly returned to the table as the second course was served and the rest of the meal went by in a blur of plates, glasses, and subtle glances. For the most part, Auraelia stuck to conversation with her lady, but she also politely engaged with the various court dignitaries that sat down the table from her.

She spoke with Lord Arlo and Lady Aesira from the Court of Opal about their warrior training techniques. Later, she complimented and thanked Lady Lavena for the beautiful fabrics she'd sent from the Court of Pearl–fabrics that were then turned into the gown from the night before and the one she wore now.

He watched the interactions in awe.

The air about her was one of superiority, but she never transferred that onto the people around her. She spoke to everyone as if they were old friends, and not as if they were below her station. Unlike the rest of the guests at the table, he could barely hold her attention for more than a few measly seconds.

When he turned his focus back to his friend, he chuckled to himself and shook his head. It was obvious that Aiden was immensely interested in Lady Piper, but like Auraelia, she barely paid him any mind. And from what he could see, she would probably chew him up and spit him out, and Aiden would say thank you.

Good luck, my friend.

As the meal came to an end, musicians began playing a relaxing tune on the opposite side of the room signifying that dinner was over and it was time for the ball to commence. Queen Adelina and Princess Auraelia both stood from their seats and were quickly followed by the rest of the guests at the table.

Silence rang through the room as the queen began to speak.

"I would like to thank you all for joining us on this wonderful day as we celebrate crowning my daughter as Heir Apparent to the Court of Emerald." The look that the queen beamed at her daughter was one full of pride. "And now that the meal has ended, please join us as we continue the celebration with Lyndaria's finest wines and whiskeys, and a night of dancing."

When she finished speaking, the musicians began playing a lively tune that was intended to pull people away from the table and onto the dance floor as servers filed into the room with trays of refreshments.

Guests began to meander away from the table and out into the area that had been designated as a ballroom for the evening. But as Daemon opened his mouth to offer to escort Auraelia across the room, Aiden caught his sleeve, pulling his attention.

"What is it, Aiden?" Daemon asked, clearly annoyed at the interruption.

Auraelia

The decorations from the night before were still present throughout the space, but her mother had added stems of peonies and roses to the vines on the columns as well as some bouquets around the room. It was beautiful, but she couldn't fully appreciate it when she felt the intense stare of Prince Daemon burning into her back.

Right after her mother finished her speech, his friend, Aiden, managed to grab his attention long enough for her to slip away from the table with Piper and make her way to the receiving line where mother was formally greeting the guests.

As they made their way across the room, she could feel the excited energy radiating off her friend.

"Would you settle down, please? You're making me anxious."

"Rae, you really did not do him justice when you described him. He's *hot*! And I don't know what you're so nervous about, he clearly likes you...well at least we know he likes *parts* of you." Piper wiggled her eyebrows to emphasize the innuendo in her statement.

Auraelia rolled her eyes and sighed, "Come on. Mother is waiting for us."

Standing in the receiving line, greeting every single guest that attended any function, had to be one of the most boring and tedious parts of being a royal, but she always did it with a smile. About halfway through the line, she could feel Daemon's heated gaze on her face from across the room–just as she had felt it on her back when she walked away from the table.

When she finally worked up the courage to meet his gaze, he gave her his signature smirk that made her knees tremble and started prowling in her direction.

Goddess, help me.

Before he even made it to the line, he was spotted by her mother. "Ah! Prince Daemon, I'm so glad that you were able to make it, and I'm so sorry to hear that your father is ill."

"You're too kind, Your Majesty." He dipped into a low bow and placed a chaste kiss on the queen's right ring finger where her emerald ring sat. The ring that signified her marriage to the kingdom, and that would one day be Auraelia's.

When he rose, his eyes immediately found hers, and a cool breeze drifted through the room as they held each other's gaze. She was drawn to him in a way that she couldn't quite explain, but her heart fluttered in her chest every time his eyes met hers.

"Princess Auraelia," Daemon said as he bowed, his voice low and smooth as silk.

"Prince Daemon," she replied as she dipped into a shallow curtsy, trying not to show how much he affected her.

When he turned his attention back to her mother, it was as if a tether between them had been snapped.

"Your Majesty, I know it's customary for the princess to receive all her guests. But I was wondering if I may have the honor of her first dance this evening."

Auraelia's eyes widened at his proposition, and it seemed to have taken the queen by surprise as well. But that minor shock quickly morphed into a mischievous smile that rivaled Piper's.

No. No, no, no.

"Oh, of course. That is, if she agrees..." Her mother may have said she had a choice in the matter, but the look in her pewter eyes said differently. She loved her mother, but there were times–like this one–where she could see the wheels turning in her head when she got an idea and wouldn't let it go.

When his gaze settled upon her once more, she was certain he could hear the rapid pace of her heart.

"Would you care to dance, Your Highness?" The golden pools in his eyes glowed in the lamplight, as he casually extended his hand, a subtle dare for her to reject his offer.

She took a deep breath to center herself and smiled as she placed her hand in his. "I would love to, Prince Daemon."

Grinning like a cat who caught a canary, he led her out to the dance floor.

Shit.

Chapter Seven

Daemon

*C*heckmate, Princess.

When they got to the center of the dance floor, they did the customary exchange of bows before he pulled her into his frame. After they made a full turn around the floor, other couples seamlessly joined in.

"You look beautiful, Princess."

"Thank you." A pink blush crept across her cheeks. "And you don't have to call me princess. My friends call me Rae."

"Are we friends?"

Her mouth lifted at the corners. "We could be. Probably should be since we'll both be rulers of our own courts one day and will have to work together."

He let her words sink in for a moment, then leaned down just a fraction so that his mouth was closer to her ear, "We can be friends, but I think I'll stick with *my star*, what do you think?"

When her skin pebbled beneath his touch and her blush deepened, he smiled. Reveling in the way she reacted to him. "Did you really think that I wouldn't figure out that it was your pussy that came all over my tongue last night? Or that I would let you slip away again?"

"I um, I—" she stammered, unable to get her words to form a coherent sentence.

"As I said last night before you so kindly left me standing rock-hard in the rain, I'm not done worshiping you, and I don't know that I ever will be."

He allowed Auraelia to lean back far enough to look into his eyes and see the passion that burned there, but also the clear intent of his words. Everything he said to her was true. "I've had a taste, and I want more." He tightened his hold on her waist, pulling her closer to his body, "Say yes."

"And if I say no?" There was a challenge in her voice, and her brows were raised in defiance. The mask of the meek woman who was in his arms a moment ago cracked, giving him a glimpse of the goddess he'd seen the night before.

There you are.

"Then you say no, and we finish this dance. And if you choose to dance with another partner, then I will bow out gracefully until I can take your hand once again. I want to get to know you, Auraelia. To know your mind. But I would be lying if I told you I didn't also want to hear you screaming my name in pleasure." He smirked as the words settled between them and left the decision up to her.

They continued the dance, and he held her as close as their bodies would allow. Auraelia searched his face, as though looking for any sign that he may be joking but knew she would find none. He assumed she would hesitate at his offer since she no longer had the anonymity her mask provided, but he meant what he had said. He wanted her mind just as much as he wanted her body. He'd gotten a taste of both, and it wasn't enough.

Out of nowhere, a cool breeze drifted through the closed room, causing the hair framing Auraelia's face to float around her. A question froze on his lips as he noticed the same green streaks of lighting shooting across her irises that he'd seen the night before.

Holy shit.

Before he could say anything, she got that beautifully mischievous look on her face, the same one she had before she abandoned him in the garden. Only, this time she followed it with one word. "*Yes.*"

Yes. The most beautiful word that he'd ever heard, and it was uttered by the most beautiful woman he had ever seen. Not wanting to waste another moment, he attempted to pull her from the dance floor.

When he felt her grip on his hand tighten, he stopped and watched the smirk on her lips grow into a teasing smile.

"What is it?" he asked, furrowing his brow in confusion.

"I can't exactly leave the ball that is being held in my honor after one dance, now can I?"

He narrowed his eyes, and his grip on her waist tightened. "What are you playing at, Princess?"

"I'm not playing at anything; I just can't leave yet. It would be rude, and mother would notice my absence this early in the night."

He studied Auraelia's face, trying to decipher the look in her eyes but before he could speak, she continued.

"You said you wanted my mind, as well as my body, correct?" she asked, and her eyes shone with passion as well as a challenge, one from which he would not shy away.

"I did."

"Well, here's your chance. Converse with me. Try to *woo* me. We already know that you are very talented at seducing me. You've had part of my body, and I have agreed to that again. But my mind and my heart are much harder to obtain."

All that he could do was stare into her eyes as he continued to guide them across the dance floor, trying not to falter as she spoke her truth.

"If you merely want me for my body, then by all means take me. I can give you that without giving you my mind or my heart. But do not speak sweet lies to me about wanting my heart and my mind if you don't mean it. If you want me, all of me, it won't come easily."

Auraelia straightened her spine and lifted her chin in defiance. "The choice is as much yours as it is mine, but I will not leave myself vulnerable to the heartbreak that you could undoubtedly cause, should I open my heart to you without forethought. If you want a dalliance, that's fine. We can play this game until you inevitably return to the Sapphire Isles. But if you truly want more... *Show* me."

Auraelia seemed to have timed her speech to end with the song and as it did, he gently pulled her from the dance floor and away from prying eyes and listening ears.

"Auraelia, I meant everything that I said. I want to learn every corner of your mind as well as every curve of your body. I am drawn to you in a way that I do not understand, and you intrigue me. Even from the short time we've been acquainted, I've seen different sides to you. I've seen the mischievous, wanton goddess in the dark of night. I've seen the political princess command the room. You are stubborn and challenging as well as beautiful and kind..." Daemon gently caressed her cheek, then grabbed her chin between his thumb and forefinger, making her hold his gaze, "I want *you*. For however long you will have me."

He watched as a beautiful pink flush crept across her cheeks.

Releasing his hold on her chin, he gestured towards the refreshments table that had been set out after dinner. "Would you like a drink, my star?" he asked while offering his arm for her to take.

Auraelia nodded and placed her hand in the crook of his elbow. As they walked across the room, she whispered, "Might I ask you a question?"

He snickered. "Of course, how else are we supposed to get to know one another?"

"Why did you call me *my star* last night, and why do you continue to do so now, even knowing who I am?"

When he glanced at her, he found her looking at him as well.

"I called you that last night because while you were observing the people around you, I was observing you. I noticed you as soon as you stepped foot in the room. The light from the chandeliers made your dress twinkle like thousands of stars in the night sky. You were, and continue to be, absolutely breathtaking."

Auraelia's blush deepened, and a small, demure smile broke across her face. "And now? Why continue calling me that, when you know my name?"

"A few reasons, really. The first being that I love seeing how it makes your eyes light with excitement," he said with a smirk on his face. "The second, being that your name means *golden one* so it kind of fits, don't you think? And finally, you remind me of home."

"I'm not sure I understand what you mean. How do I remind you of home? We've only just met?"

"Wine or whiskey?" he asked as they reached the refreshments table.

"What?" she asked, thrown by the change in questioning. "Oh. Whiskey, please."

He grabbed two glasses and handed one to Auraelia before guiding her to a bench set along the windows. They sat and he took a sip of his drink. The woodsy flavor was accented with a hint of blackberry that left a tingle in his throat and warmed him from the inside.

"Daemon?"

"Right, sorry. How much do you know about the Sapphire Isles?"

"Not much, if I'm being honest. Aside from the history between our courts, I know that you are seafaring people who control the majority of the imports and exports within Ixora, but not too much outside of that."

He let out a low laugh and smiled. "Yes, we are seafaring people, which is how you remind me of home."

When she drew her brows together in confusion, he quickly elaborated.

"When we're at sea, we use the stars to navigate. Sailors are drawn to the North Star because it is a constant fixation in the sky. Never faltering, always shining." He grabbed Auraelia's free hand from her lap and began rubbing tiny circles around her knuckles. He hadn't even realized he'd done it until her hand gently squeezed his, encouraging him to continue.

"I was drawn to you like a sailor to the North Star. I feel you when you enter the room, it's like the air becomes charged with static and I'm automatically aware of your presence. I don't know why; I wish that I did. But you, Auraelia, are my star. You have a gravitational pull that tugs at my soul." Releasing her hand, he nervously ran his fingers through his hair. "I know that it sounds crazy. Hell, it sounds crazy to me, but it is my truth."

Auraelia sat there in silence as the weight of his words settled between them. After what felt like an eternity, she smiled. "It does sound crazy, but what's life without a little insanity? Would you like to dance?"

He smiled.

It wasn't the courteous grin that he would freely give to those around him. Nor was it the smirk that he'd given her many times over, the one that always made her eyes widen and caused her breath to catch.

It was a real smile.

He grasped Auraelia's hand in his own once more and stood, pulling her with him. His eyes never left hers as he bowed and placed a kiss on her knuckles. "I can't think of anything I would rather do." Tucking her hand into the crook of his arm, he guided her back to the dance floor.

The room went quiet as all eyes turned in their direction, and groups of guests parted giving them a wide berth to make their way to the center of the dancefloor. Then he pulled her into his arms and let the world around him fall away.

Chapter Eight

Auraelia

She felt every pair of eyes on her the moment they walked across the room. Everyone watched and waited to see what the Princess of Lyndaria would do next with the Prince of the Sapphire Isles. But the ones that stood out the most were Piper, Xander, and her mother.

Piper had a smug *'you go girl!'* look on her face, which was nothing new. Xander was scowling, which was his typical overprotective, older brother reaction to any man who dared to come near her. Her mother, however, had a knowing smile on her face that said she saw more than Auraelia could fathom. There was a flash of worry, but overall, her eyes shone with approval over Auraelia's choice in partner–even if only for a dance.

But all of that fell away as soon as Daemon took her into his arms.

His hand was a hot brand on her back as he led her across the floor. Auraelia felt her heart swell and her chest warmed as a phantom breeze swirled around them, lifting her skirts as if they were suspended in water.

When Daemon's eyes widened, the pieces fell into place, and her jaw dropped with the realization.

Holy shit! Am I doing this?

Seeming to sense the turmoil in her mind, his gaze softened as he spoke in a low, soothing tone. "You didn't know, did you?"

She shook her head, "No. Mother wasn't sure how my magic would manifest. I think she'd been hinting that she saw something last night, and then again today after the coronation, but she wouldn't give me a straight answer." Auraelia rolled her eyes and took a moment to think back on everything that transpired over the past two days. "Last night...last night, you said something about my eyes, but by the time I got back to my chambers they looked normal, aside from a few traces of green."

Daemon's face turned contemplative as he glanced around them, and Auraelia did the same. They were the only ones affected by the swirls of air, leaving the rest of the room untouched. Finally, he smiled, "Well, my star, it seems like we have at least part of the answer to what your magic may be."

She cocked one of her brows, giving him a *'care to elaborate'* expression, which made him chuckle and raise a brow of his own. "The wind, Auraelia. Have you noticed that it is only affecting us?"

"Yes, but I don't know *how* I'm doing that. I've never summoned it on purpose, it just seems to *happen*."

"It's happened before?"

"I'm not certain. But just today, I believe it's happened a handful of times."

"The breeze through the ceremony that made the petals fall like a spring snow?"

She nodded.

"Do you think you could stop it?"

"I'm not sure." Panicked, she looked around the room, her anxiety squeezing the air from her lungs. The more anxious she felt, the stronger the wind blew, causing it to spread to other parts of the room.

What was a gentle cocoon of air around Daemon and Auraelia, soon became a strong breeze through the room that tousled the ladies' hair and blew through their skirts.

Daemon gently grabbed her chin and brought her focus back to him. "Auraelia, you need to breathe. Focus on my voice."

Nodding, she closed her eyes and took a deep breath to try and recenter herself.

"There you go, just keep breathing."

The wind in the room started to die down as Daemon gently stroked her cheek with his thumb.

"Open your eyes."

When she did, she saw the pools of gold in his moss-colored eyes shining like twin suns.

She saw desire and acceptance.

She didn't care that the way he held her face looked like a lover's caress.

Didn't care that her people and guests of the crown had just witnessed her use her magic without any control over it. That was something to worry about later.

All that she cared about was that somehow Daemon, a man she had known for no more than a full day, was able to ground her when her panic rose.

The world fell away again as Daemon gently cupped her cheek. Instinctively she leaned into it as he asked, "What do you feel when you're using your magic?"

Her head tilted to the side, and her eyebrows knitted together in confusion. "I'm not sure I understand."

"When I use my magic, I feel it throughout my body. My limbs feel weighted, like a heavy blanket is draped over me. It's all encompassing."

She thought for a moment, then it was like a veil had been lifted. "Right before the wind surrounded us, I felt a warmth fill my chest. It was heavy, but it was a comforting feeling. Like I was whole."

Daemon smiled, "Do you want to try it?"

"Try what?" Panic seeped into her words as her anxiety began to rise once more.

"Summon your magic, Auraelia. Show me what you can do. Show everyone in this room that you are in control."

She searched his expression, but when she looked into his eyes, she saw adoration. He truly believed that she could control her power this soon.

Daemon stroked her cheek as he spoke to her in a low voice, "Close your eyes. Take a deep breath and feel for your magic. Search for that warmth. Find it and hold onto it. Then visualize what you want to do with it."

She did as he said.

Closing her eyes, she took steadying breaths and let his touch ground her. She felt the warmth fill her chest, like the embers of a fire slowly being stoked back to life, and let it radiate out through the rest of her body. Then, focusing on what she wanted, she willed the air around her to do as she bid.

She was so focused on her magic, that she hadn't felt Daemon bend to whisper in her ear, "Open your eyes, my star."

When she did, she saw excitement in his gaze and that beautiful smirk. He flicked his head to the side, gesturing for her to look around. She turned her gaze from the man who was in the process of turning her world upside down, and what she saw took her breath away.

A gentle breeze drifted through the room.

It was calm enough to barely stir the loose hair around her face, but strong enough to knock petals loose from the flowers surrounding the room, and she watched in awe as they rained down on the guests.

It was beautiful.

Turning her gaze back to Daemon, she saw passion and desire burning in his eyes. And when his grin turned devilish, she was quite certain that her own eyes mirrored the sentiment.

The rest of the night went by in a haze of dancing, drinking, and conversation. Auraelia and Daemon rarely parted from each other, except when Xander cut in to demand a dance with his sister, so Piper danced with Daemon to keep him out of the clutches of the court ladies.

When the queen announced that she was retiring for the night, she shot a warning glance at Auraelia that only one of her children –and Piper– would notice. Her mother knew of her nighttime escapades and didn't care as long as she was smart about it. The look she gave was not one of deterrent, but one that said, *'Don't be stupid, and don't get caught.'*

Shortly after the queen left the ballroom, others followed suit and the room slowly emptied, leaving only a few stragglers–most of whom were drunk and draped over the benches.

"May I speak with you for a moment, Your Highness?" Piper asked. Her face was the perfect representation of a lady, but her eyes said something else entirely.

Auraelia excused herself from Daemon's side, where he was having a conversation with Aiden and Xander and walked out of earshot with Piper.

"What is it?" she asked in a tone that showed she wasn't buying anything that Piper said.

"What's the plan?"

"Excuse me?" Auraelia asked.

"What do you mean *'excuse me?'* it's not like you can just waltz him up to your room undetected," Piper retorted, and when she didn't answer, Piper's mouth dropped. "You can't be serious. Rae. *Please* tell me that you are going to take that man for a ride."

Auraelia laughed, and discreetly shrugged her shoulders. "We haven't really talked about the *how* yet. It's not really a conversation that you can have when you're surrounded by a hundred people."

Daemon walked up behind Auraelia and touched the small of her back, effectively cutting Piper off before she could come up with a snarky response. The small caress sent a wave of awareness through her and settled in her core.

"Would you like to take a walk through the gardens, Princess? I hear that they're lovely at night." Daemon's voice was laced with mischief.

She looked up with a passion in her eyes that mirrored his and smiled. "I would love to."

They inclined their heads to Piper, who desperately tried to hide a smirk.

But before he could drag her away, Piper pulled her in for a hug and whispered, "In that case, I guess I'll find something...or someone...to entertain myself with." When they pulled apart, Piper gestured toward Aiden with her eyes, then winked.

They parted ways, and Auraelia tucked her hand into the crook of Daemon's arm as he led her out into the garden.

The night was cool, and the air was still and quiet.

They walked down the familiar gravel path, and a sense of *deja vu* came over her. "Are you not tired of these gardens yet?" she teased.

"On the contrary, my star, these gardens are quickly becoming my favorite place to be." Daemon pulled her into his arms, and she tilted her face toward his.

The memories from the night before crashed into her mind. Echoes of fingers dancing along her skin, and heated kisses down her neck sent her magic into a tizzy. The soft breeze that coasted through the garden ruffled his hair, and when he smiled, her knees went weak.

I swear, this man is going to turn me into a puddle if he keeps looking at me like that.

Daemon rested his brow on hers and inhaled deeply, "Auraelia..." His voice was husky and low, like it took everything he had to hold himself back from whatever it was that he wanted to say.

"Daemon." She mirrored his tone, her voice a whisper in the wind.

"There's something that I've been dying to do all day today. And I–"

A growl rumbled deep in his throat, and she felt it in her core. His grip on her hips tightened as he stepped closer. Pulling her face away from his, she waited until he looked her in the eye.

"Then do it."

Those three words seemed to ignite something within him. His lips collided with hers, his tongue running along the seam of her mouth, begging for entrance.

She opened for him, and he wrapped an arm around her waist, pulling her flush to his front as he snaked his other hand up to the back of her neck.

She melted into the kiss, every one of her nerve endings standing on end as desire pooled between her legs.

Pulling away, he searched her eyes, "As much as I love this garden, I want you splayed on my bed with firelight dancing on your skin. Tonight, I want to worship you without the threat of rain interrupting me."

"How do you plan on accomplishing that? I can't exactly get to your rooms without being seen. Or you to mine."

The corners of his lips pulled upward into a Cheshire smile, and the golden pools of his eyes expanded, encroaching on the beautiful moss green of his irises. "Let me worry about that. Do you trust me?"

Auraelia narrowed her eyes, curious but also cautious, "I probably shouldn't since we barely know each other, but yes."

Was it reckless? Absolutely.

Did she care? Not a single bit.

Being with him stoked a fire in her soul like no one had ever done, and she wanted to let the flames consume her.

"Then close your eyes, and hold tight, Princess." Daemon pulled her as close to him as physically possible, then delicately pressed his lips to hers. It was soft and sweet but claimed her all the same.

She felt the air stir around her, not in the same way that it did when she manipulated it, this was more like a disturbance. Like the air around her thickened.

Though her eyes were closed, she could sense that the space around her had brightened. One minute, it was a dark and cool spring evening, the next it was warm, and she could see light peeking through her closed lids. Daemon broke the kiss, and she opened her eyes. They were no longer in the garden; they were inside a room in the castle.

His room.

As she looked around to get her bearings, a wave of dizziness overwhelmed her, and she swayed on her feet. Daemon's hold on her waist never faltered, supporting her weight as she waited for the dizzy spell to pass. Finally feeling that she wouldn't topple over, she hesitantly pushed herself away from him before meeting his gaze.

"What the hell was that? How did we get here?" She tried to sound calm, but even she could hear the wary tone in her words.

His signature smirk appeared once more, his eyes glowing with desire as he prowled toward her, eating up the space that she had placed between them.

"Magic," Daemon stated like it was the most obvious answer, his eyes twinkling in the light from the fire.

She crossed her arms, an incredulous look on her face. "You know what I mean, don't be obtuse."

Daemon chuckled, "Why don't I just show you."

Not waiting for her answer, he pulled the shadows from around the room. Gone were the fireplace and furnishings of the room and in their place were swirls of the deepest blues and darkest blacks, cocooning them in darkness. Her mouth hung open in awe as she took in her new surroundings, reaching out to brush her fingers against the shadows that swirled around her.

When she finally met his gaze again, her eyes were alight with wonder. "What is this? I've never seen anything like it."

Daemon smiled. "They're shadows. I have some of my own that I can use and manipulate at will. But I can also pull any shadow near me and bend it to my will. I also use them to get from one place to another, it's called *shadow walking*. Which, coincidentally, is how we got here."

As she processed the new information, she continued to stroke the shadows surrounding her, causing a shiver to visibly course through Daemon's body. Noticing the obvious reaction it had on him, she stopped and raised a questioning brow, then reached out to run her fingers along them again. As soon as her fingertips were a hairsbreadth away, Daemon winked and disappeared from view, only to reappear directly behind her. The sudden movements elicited a gasp from her lips.

Daemon wrapped his arms around her waist and pulled her flush against his chest. He leaned down, his breath a warm caress that sent shivers through her body as he whispered in her ear.

"When I am controlling the shadows, my star, they are an extension of me. When you caress them like that, you might as well be stroking every nerve ending in my body."

Chapter Nine

Daemon

He took his time as he trailed kisses down her neck, her head lolling to the side to give him better access. Her eyes fluttered closed as she melted into his touch, and a low moan sounded deep in her throat.

Pulling her waist flush against his own, he slid his hand up the bodice of her gown, and gently palmed her breast over the fabric. She arched into his touch as a cold wind blew through the room. Like a phantom touch, it caressed the shadows, causing them to shudder.

Daemon slid his hand higher, and lightly wrapped it around her throat. The new position tilted her head back onto his shoulder and gave him an unobstructed view down her body. From the swell of her breasts and the delicate gold chains that draped across them, to her narrow waist and the fullness of her hips.

The flush that he took pleasure in bringing to her face, now spread down her neck and colored her chest in a rosy-pink hue.

A groan rumbled deep within his chest as he nipped at her ear. "Oh, the things I want to do to you."

Auraelia's eyes fluttered open, and she tilted her head. Meeting her gaze, he saw the passion that swirled in their stormy depths.

"So do them," her voice was low and breathy, and he felt it straight to his cock.

She smirked, and with that slight tilt at the corner of her mouth, he threw all pretense out the window. Dropping the shadows that still shrouded them in velvety darkness, he spun her around and pulled her flush against him.

He molded her body to his and captured her mouth again.

Sliding his hand from the front of her throat to the nape of her neck, he threaded his fingers into the hair at the base of her skull, and gently tilted her face to a better angle.

Auraelia sank into his touch, matching every stroke of his tongue with her own, and every sweet moan that escaped from her was a straight shot to his groin.

"Auraelia, my star, you're wearing far too many layers," he muttered between kisses.

She chuckled and placed her hands on his chest, giving him a gentle shove as she slowly backed away. The memory of her leaving the night before crashed into his mind, and he grabbed her waist before she could take more than a step,

He nuzzled into her neck and nipped at the tender flesh there. "Where the fuck do you think you're going?"

She wriggled in his arms and laughed.

When he pulled back, his brow furrowed in confusion as Auraelia shook her head, and once again stepped out of his grasp.

"You said that I was wearing too many layers. I was *trying* to remedy that particular situation." She placed a finger in the center of his chest and pushed him backward until his knees hit the edge of his bed. "Sit."

Fuck. Yes, ma'am.

Though he typically liked to be the one in control in the bedroom, he was more than happy to oblige her. Sitting on the edge of the bed, he watched as she backed out of reach.

Her eyes burned with desire and mischief, just like they had in the garden the night before. But tonight, they were also glowing, the telltale signs of her magic shining through the slate-blue coloring of her irises in streaks of peridot.

He watched as she slowly trailed her hands up her body, caressing each of her curves as she made her way up to the chains that draped across her chest and back. As each one was unclasped, his heart picked up pace. When the final one was undone, she shrugged the plates from her shoulders and let the cape fall to the floor. Locking eyes with him, she slowly stepped forward.

"Care to lend me a hand?"

He widened the space between his knees to give her room to step into and his throat tightened as he drank in the sight of her. When she gave him her back, he ran his hands up her sides from her thighs to her waist before he slowly brought them to the middle where she was laced into the dress.

Daemon took his time working the laces, relishing her close proximity and the softness of her skin as his knuckles brushed along her back. When he finished, she clutched the front of her gown, and once again stepped just out of his reach.

This woman is going to be the death of me.

When she turned around to face him again, her eyes locked with his and she let her dress fall to the floor.

Eyes wide and mouth gaping, he took in the glorious woman before him.

She looked like a goddess. Her arms were toned and tan, her breasts were full with toffee-colored nipples, and her hourglass figure dipped perfectly into her waist accentuating her rounded hips. Her strength was evident, but she still had a softness to her curves and features.

Her long legs were encased in sheer stockings that ended at her thigh and held in place by a simple emerald-green ribbon that matched the heels she still wore.

And she was *bare*.

With no panties in sight, he had nothing blocking his view of the small patch of curls between her legs. His cock throbbed at the thought of being buried between them.

"Auraelia," he growled from where he was seated on the bed, "If you don't–"

"If I don't, what?" she asked, tilting her head slightly and placing a hand on her hip.

Her body language radiated defiance, but her eyes gave her away as need swirled in their depths.

Without moving from his spot on the bed, he summoned the shadows from around the room. She didn't even have a chance to react before he'd shadow-walked her across the room and unceremoniously dropped her onto the bed.

She landed on her back with a squeak and glowered in his direction.

Daemon stood and leaned over to place his hands on either side of where she lay. Caging her beneath him, he gave her a wicked grin. "As I was saying," he let his eyes rove over her body before he locked his gaze with hers, "If you don't get over here, I'm going to *bring* you to me."

He trailed a single finger down the side of her face to her neck, and then down her body, lingering in the valley between her breasts.

Her skin was soft and smooth, and the featherlight touches made the fine hairs on her body stand on end.

"*Daemon*," Auraelia half growled, half pleaded, as she drew out his name.

The desperation in her voice had him suppressing a groan. He wanted nothing more than to sink into her, but the need to take his time and savor this moment won out.

Leaning forward, he ran his nose up the side of her neck, stopping right below her ear to place a chaste kiss. "Patience, my star. We have all night."

When she moved to wrap her arms around his waist, he pulled away and stood, backing away from the bed just as she had.

Auraelia scoffed and leaned up on her elbows, throwing him a look that said if he didn't hurry up, she would take care of things on her own. As much as he would *love* to watch as she brought herself pleasure, that wasn't on the agenda tonight.

He pushed his coat off of his shoulders and laid it neatly on a nearby chair. His sword and belt were next, and his boots followed shortly thereafter. When he reached up to remove his crown, Auraelia stopped him.

"Leave it."

It was then that he realized she still wore her circlet and looked every bit like a queen while spread out on his bed.

"As you wish, Princess," he replied with a reverent nod.

He raked his eyes down her body as he unfastened the closures on his vest and shirt. Her back was arched, which pushed her breasts higher into the air, and the sight sent shock waves through his body. His cock, which was already straining against the laces of his trousers, grew harder the longer his gaze lingered.

The light from the fire across the room licked across her skin, setting her aglow in washes of gold and orange, making her look like the star that he claimed her to be. And even in the low light of the room, her arousal was evident–the curls at the apex of her thighs glistening.

Daemon pushed his shirt off his shoulders and let it fall to the floor. Auraelia's eyes widened as they raked down every inch of his exposed skin, and she sank her teeth into her plump bottom lip. The heat of her stare set him ablaze, and it took more restraint than he thought he had not to take her right then.

Prowling toward her, he unlaced his trousers as he went, letting them hang precariously low on his hips. Stopping in front of her, he nudged her knees open with his own, fully exposing her sex to him.

A warm breeze swept through the room, caressing his skin like a lover's touch, and tousling his hair.

Fuck, this is going to be fun.

Auraelia

She wasn't sure where to look when Daemon stalked toward her like a predator. He was divine. All sculpted muscles, with a spattering of hair across his chest and a trail from his navel that pointed like an arrow down that delicious *V* at his hips before it dipped into his trousers. While all of that was something that she'd expected, what she hadn't prepared for were the tattoos.

Across his chest were a myriad of nautical markings. On one side, there was a siren with octopus tentacles and strings of pearls woven into her hair, and a veil of netting that cut right below eyes that were left blank, as if she were all-seeing.

Opposite the woman, was a ship and compass overlaying the meridian lines that would be found on a map. There was an octopus on the corresponding shoulder that intertwined its arms around the compass and ship, giving the feel that it was being held there, and his arms were covered with an array of oceanic scenes that traveled down to his wrists.

Daemon nudged her legs wider with his knees, and every nerve ending in her body stood at attention. With her emotions running high, she unintentionally sent a breeze through the room, resulting in a roguish grin spreading across his face. *Goddess, help me.*

He slowly leaned over her, causing her to lay back against the bed. Resting his hands on either side of her head, he used his leg to add pressure against her pussy, sending a tremor through her body and eliciting a gasp from her lips.

After a minute that seemed to last forever, she couldn't take it anymore.

"*Daemon...*" she whined as she wriggled against his leather clad thigh, seeking out any form of friction that she could.

He lifted a hand from the bed and caressed her cheek, while dragging his thumb over her bottom lip. Gently pulling her mouth open, he pushed the end of his thumb through her parted lips, simultaneously using his thigh to add pressure right where she needed it. When he slipped his thumb further into her mouth, she closed her lips around it and sucked hard and was instantly rewarded with his sharp inhale.

Daemon slowly removed his thumb from her mouth and trailed his hand down her quivering body, his eyes boring into her own.

"I'm going to worship you. Map out every inch of your body. Every hill and valley. Every dip and every rise..." he whispered the words like one would whisper a prayer, and each word was met with a corresponding movement of his hands on her skin. He massaged each breast in equal measure. Pinched and pulled each of her nipples, the mixture of pleasure and pain sent waves of desire to pool between her legs. The featherlight touches from the tips of his fingers across her stomach and hips made her skin pebble.

She was already a quivering mess by the time Daemon reached his destination and slid his fingers through the slick curls at the apex of her thighs. Every promise of pleasure that fell from his lips was accented with a swirl on her clit or a tease of pressure at her entrance.

"I'm going to memorize what it takes to make you gasp." *Swirl.* "What makes you moan." *Pressure.* "What it takes to make you scream." *Swirl.* "I'm going to claim every inch of your body until we don't know where either of us ends, and the other begins." Driving his point home, Daemon thrust a finger inside of her, and she threw her head back and moaned.

He slowly worked his finger in and out and used the heel of his hand to add pressure and friction to her clit. Bending down, he took her nipple into his mouth before letting it go with a *pop,* and trailing kisses up to her ear.

"Then perhaps, my star, we will do it all over again." His mouth was on hers as soon as the last word passed his lips, collecting her moans with his kisses as his hand picked up speed.

Auraelia reached for his trousers that still hung low on his hips in an attempt to push them down, but from her angle, she was barely able to get them down a measly inch.

Pulling her mouth from his, she let out a disgruntled moan, "Daemon, take off your fucking pants."

Daemon, who was still knuckles deep in her pussy, gave her an innocent smile, "But, my star, I would have to stop *this* to do that." As if to prove his point, he shoved another finger inside of her.

Her breath hitched with every thrust, but she managed to nod, "Yes, but you can't *fuck* me with your pants covering your dick."

"I beg to differ." Daemon sped up the movements of his fingers and added the curling motion he used the night before that made her melt.

"*Daemon,*" she whined.

"Very well. As you wish."

He withdrew his fingers and stood. Sticking those same fingers in his mouth, he moaned around them, savoring her taste like he would a fine wine.

"I *will* have you coming on my tongue tonight, but not right now. Right now, I need to be inside you."

Auraelia propped herself back on her elbows and watched as Daemon pushed down his pants. The moment his cock was free from its confines, her eyes widened at the sight.

He had a small dusting of dark curls at the base, but he was anything but small. Standing erect, it nearly reached his navel. She watched as he stroked himself in front of her, his fingertips barely overlapping from the girth, as his eyes raked over her naked form.

Auraelia ran her tongue along her bottom lip before pulling it between her teeth and drawing her gaze away from his cock and up to his eyes. "Do you take a daily contraceptive?" she asked as her gaze burned into his.

"I do."

"Oh, thank the goddess."

She curled a finger in his direction, beckoning him forward. "Fuck me, Daemon. You promised to make me shine."

"Oh, my star, I'm going to make you *burn*." He leaned over and grabbed behind her knees, "Wrap your arms around my neck."

Auraelia did as he asked, and he lifted her from the edge of the bed. Rotating them around, Daemon took her spot with her straddling his lap. He slid his hands from behind her knees, and up the outside of her thighs before venturing back between her legs.

"I want you to ride me, Princess. And then I want to fuck you until you *see* stars."

"Someone's bossy," she said as she reached her hand between their bodies to wrap it around his cock. It certainly *looked* large enough, but in her hand, he was huge. Her fingers barely met around his shaft as she slid up and down his length, collecting precum from the tip to help her hand glide more smoothly.

Kneeling more firmly on the bed, she lifted up so that she could situate him at her entrance. He removed his fingers from her pussy, and she whimpered. But before sinking down his length, Auraelia rocked against him, coating him in her arousal.

"Damn it, woman." Daemon took a sharp breath through his teeth, his hands digging into her hips, guiding her movements while she slid her pussy along his cock.

She lazily ran her hand up his chest, tracing the lines of his tattoos. "You'll have to tell me what these mean."

His gaze snapped to hers, the golden pools in his eyes turning molten as desire burned in their depths. "You're really going to ask about my tattoos while you torment me?" A wicked grin spread across her face as she continued to slide against him. "Fuck that."

Before she could blink, he flipped them so that she was sprawled on the bed beneath him. With one hand braced by her breasts, his other reached between them, positioning the head of his cock at her entrance. Auraelia lifted her hips, in an attempt to close that miniscule gap between them.

"Oh, I see. You *wanted* this to happen."

A smile of faux innocence pulled across her face, and Daemon gave her a devilish grin in return. "You want me to fuck you, Princess?"

Pulling her bottom lip between her teeth, she nodded emphatically.

"So be it."

He didn't hesitate, pushing in halfway before he stopped to let her acclimate to his size. Auraelia's back bowed at the intrusion while her walls stretched to accommodate his girth and clenched around him.

With all their unfinished business from the night before, coupled with the anticipation building throughout the day, she was dripping. He withdrew slowly before plunging back in, fully seating himself inside her.

His movements were tortuously slow.

With each pull and thrust, his cock brushed that sweet spot on the inner wall of her entrance. When he increased his pace, Auraelia fisted her hands into the sheets as her climax built inside her. When he grabbed her legs and draped them over his shoulders, the new position brought about a new set of sensations. She didn't think he could get any deeper, but she was wrong. Leaning forward, he sandwiched her legs between them as he bent her in half.

"*Fuck!*" she exclaimed on a breathy exhale.

"I believe that's what I'm doing. But if you're unsatisfied, allow me to remedy the situation." Before she could protest, he withdrew swiftly, and flipped her onto her stomach. Grabbing her waist, he pulled her hips into the air, fully exposing her sex to him. He ran his hands over her ass before smacking one cheek, pulling a surprised gasp from Auraelia. He chuckled as he rubbed the reddening skin.

"Do you like a little pain with your pleasure, Princess?" He leaned down and licked long and slow up her center.

Auraelia moaned and pushed her hips back in encouragement, hoping that was answer enough. He ran his tongue through her slit once more before pulling away, only to drive his cock back inside her at a punishing pace.

"I believe I asked you a question." His statement was punctuated by another slap to her ass.

Auraelia moaned and pushed her hips back again, meeting him thrust for thrust. When another slap landed across her backside, warmth spread through her body and pooled at her center, and she yelped out, "Yes!"

He kept his hands firmly on her hips, holding her steady as he drove into her over and over again. But as soon as the word left her lips, the room darkened slightly as Daemon drew the shadows to him and used them to touch every inch of her.

The feeling of invisible hands as they roamed over her skin was an intoxicating contradiction to the unyielding grip on her hips and the punishing pace that he'd set.

His shadows swirled around her arms with featherlight touches before they moved on to her breasts, tweaking the sensitive buds of her nipples. Fully distracted by the sensations from his magic and her growing climax, Auraelia barely noticed the velvety ribbons wrapping around her wrists.

"Do you have any issues with being bound, Auraelia?" His tone was serious, but there was an undercurrent of mischievousness.

"No, wh–?" Before she could finish, her arms were pulled out from under her, and she fell face first into the bed.

Turning her face to the side, she sputtered to get the hair off her lips. "What the fuck, Daemon?!"

She tried pulling her wrists free, but the shadows only tightened and pulled her arms further out in front of her before looping through the bars of the iron headboard.

Slowing his pace, Daemon bent over her body and kissed his way up her spine. He swept the few loose hairs from her cheek, "You wanted me to fuck you, so that's what I'm doing. Say the word and I'll unbind you, but I don't think you want that."

He sat back and drove into her hard and slow while his hand skimmed around her hip to the junction at the center of her thighs, sending a flood of arousal to her core. The torturous circles on her clit and the hard thrusts of his hips, forced whimpers from her lips.

Auraelia felt her climax building like a crescendo, and as it edged closer, she turned her face into the mattress to try and stifle the sound of her moans.

But Daemon wasn't having any of that.

He slid his fingers into the hair at the nape of her neck and pulled just hard enough to lift her head from the mattress.

"Those sounds belong to me, Auraelia. I want to hear you." The gravelly tone of his voice combined with the possessive nature of his words were like a lightning bolt through her, pushing her closer to the edge of oblivion. With a few more swirls of her clit, stars swam through her vision and a loud moan escaped her lips as her climax barreled through her like thunder rolling across the sky.

Chapter Ten

Daemon

The feeling of her coming undone had him quickening his pace. The walls of her pussy clenched around him as she rode out her orgasm, coaxing him to follow her into oblivion.

Daemon never stopped circling her clit, trying to draw out her climax as he dove headfirst into his own. He pulled out of Auraelia, and a deep moan passed his lips as his cum painted her backside. Though he was spent, he made sure that the shadows that bound her fell away.

Collapsing beside her on the bed, he pulled her hands to him and gently massaged life back into her limbs. She watched him through half lidded eyes as he worked delicate circles over her wrists and hands. When he finished, he stroked her cheek, "I'd like to draw you a bath, if you'd let me."

Shock and confusion flashed in her eyes, but only briefly.

Has no one taken care of her after sex?

Daemon swept hair from her face, "Are you sore at all?"

Auraelia shifted a little and flexed her wrists, likely to test the tenderness there.

"Maybe a little, but it's not so bad."

Sensing her hesitation, Daemon grinned. "I need to clean up the mess I've made, and it will give us a chance to talk a bit. Plus, it will help with any soreness."

He placed a chaste kiss on her temple before he slipped from the bed and padded to the bathroom. As he walked across the room, he could feel her eyes on his ass. Calling on his shadows, he used them to smack hers and delighted in the yelp that echoed into the bathing chamber from the bedroom.

Once again thankful for hot, running water, he proceeded to draw Auraelia a bath. The tub was big enough for two people, but he had no plans of joining her unless she asked. While it filled, he rifled through the assortment of salts and oils meant for scenting the water and aided in healing and relaxation.

"What are you doing?" The sound of her voice nearly caused him to fall onto his ass from where he squatted next to the tub. "Sorry, I didn't mean to startle you," she said with a giggle.

"I was looking for an oil to add to your bath. But it seems I only have cedar, and possibly–" he sniffed one of the jars, "Vanilla?" There was a questioning lilt to his words.

He heard her cross the room, and when she stopped right in front of him, she ran her fingers through his hair–the simple touch bringing a level of intimacy as he kneeled before her. With every breath he took, his lungs filled with the scent of her. The soft notes of lavender that would forever be associated with Auraelia, and a heady combination of her sweet arousal and the salt on her skin.

Gripping his hair lightly, she pushed his head back so that he was gazing up at her. "Cedar and vanilla sounds lovely."

She ran her thumb over his bottom lip, then bent down and pressed her mouth to his. Daemon idly ran his hands from her calves up to her thighs, stopping at the tops of her stockings where he slowly untied the ribbons that held them in place. Breaking their kiss, he grinned up at her, "Let's get these off and get you cleaned up."

With deft fingers, he rolled her stockings down her legs, caressing the silkiness of her skin as his hands slid down. Having lost her shoes at some point–either during sex or after, he wasn't sure–he was able to slip the stocking over her foot. After placing a chaste kiss on the inside of her ankle, he repeated the process on the other leg.

Daemon stood and turned to pour the oils into the bathwater as it ran. Grabbing a cloth, he submerged it in the water before turning back to Auraelia. Gliding a finger across her cheek, he picked up the few strands of hair that had fallen out of her braids and twists and tucked them behind her ear.

"Turn."

Creases formed on her brow, as confusion painted her features. "Excuse me?"

He chuckled, then held up a finger and moved it in a rotating motion, gesturing for her to follow suit. "Turn around, Auraelia. I want to clean you off before you climb into the bath."

Realization dawned on her face, and she turned as her face flushed.

Daemon got to work. Taking the damp cloth, he slowly wiped away the evidence of their encounter. When her back was clean, he swiped the cloth over the round cheeks of her ass, then dipped it between her legs. A surprised gasp, which quickly turned into a moan, slipped from her lips. The sound sent a wave of heat straight to his cock.

Fuck, I could come just from the sounds she makes.

Keeping one hand between her legs, he snaked the other around her waist and pulled her to him. He nuzzled into her neck, then trailed kisses up the slender column. Her head fell to the side, giving him better access as the sound of her moans slipped through closed lips.

"Into the bath, Auraelia." He pulled away and heard her grumble as she stepped into the warm water. Daemon chuckled at her barely concealed outburst. *Insatiable creature.*

Auraelia sucked a sharp inhale through her teeth as she sank down into the heat of the water. When she was submerged up to her neck, her breasts barely breaking the surface, she let out a contented sigh and closed her eyes. Daemon watched as the tension in her muscles ebbed away with every second she soaked. Cracking an eye, Auraelia turned her head toward him with a smirk on her lips.

"Are you just going to stand there, or do you plan on joining me?"

He matched her smirk with one of his own, "Do you want me to? I thought you might like some personal space."

She sat up, and slid into the middle of the tub, making room for him behind her. "Would you just get in, already?" Her words were laced with annoyed amusement, and it brought a smile to his lips.

"As you wish, Princess," he replied with a mock bow.

Auraelia splashed him with water and rolled her eyes, "Ass."

He chuckled then climbed in behind her.

Once he was seated, he extended his legs out on either side of hers and pulled her to him so she could lean back on his chest.

"Is this ok?" he asked, unsure where to put his hands regardless of the fact that he had just had them all over her body mere moments ago.

Auraelia relaxed into him and rested her head on his shoulder, immediately releasing the tension he felt. He grabbed the sponge that sat on the ledge next to the bath and submerged it in the water. Daemon trailed it across her chest, squeezing out the water as he went and letting it trickle down her breasts and back into the tub. He repeated the process over again, while she absentmindedly traced circles on his raised knee.

After a few moments of companionable silence, Auraelia took the sponge from him and set it back on the ledge. Grabbing his hand, she started to trace the designs that were tattooed on his arm.

"Tell me about your tattoos." It wasn't quite a question, but there was a hint of hesitance behind it.

"What would you like to know?"

"Do they have any specific meanings? Why so many? How long did it take to do them?"

Sensing that the series of questions wasn't going to let up any time soon, Daemon chuckled. "Alright, alright. Yes, some have specific meanings, some don't. I have this many because I wanted them, and I will probably get more. As for how long it took? It took a while. I didn't get them all done at once, but my arms took the longest."

"Would you tell me about the woman on your chest?" Curiosity laced her words, and she looked up to meet his gaze.

Nodding, Daemon began to tell her the tale of the goddess who looks after his people.

"Narissa is the goddess of my court, just like the Goddess Rhayne is here in Lyndaria. She is the Goddess of the Sea and the Sky, and she protects the sailors that sail her waters with dignity and honesty. Those who don't meet the fate of her creatures that roam the deepest parts of the sea only surfacing to dole out her justice. On occasion, she has been seen perched on the rocks that jut out into the water, luring those with darkness in their hearts to their death with her siren song."

"Why are her eyes blank? How is she the goddess of the sky as well as the sea?"

Daemon shook his head and chuckled, "Patience, my star. I'm getting there."

Auraelia sighed as she rested her head back on his shoulder and began idly running her fingertips up and down his arm. When she didn't say anything, he continued.

"She's the goddess of sky as well as the sea; she can turn the sky to storms and, in turn, manipulates the sea. Anger Narissa, and the calm sea you knew could quickly turn into a raging surf that could capsize any vessel. She can also calm the sky and the seas in favor of her sailors."

"She sounds fierce and incredible," Auraelia mused.

Daemon leaned down and whispered in her ear, "As are you, my star, as are you."

Sliding a finger under her chin, he tilted her face up as he brought his down to press a kiss to her lips. Auraelia reached up and tangled her fingers into his hair, holding him in place and as she deepened the kiss.

He swept his tongue across the seam of her lips, and she immediately opened for him–their tongues battling for purchase in each other's mouths. Auraelia broke the kiss, and turned to face him, sloshing water over the side of the tub in the process. Straddling his hips, she fused her mouth back to his and he felt the heat of her core as it rested over his cock.

Fuck.

Wrapping his arms around her waist, he held her close to his body as her pussy slid over his length which had been hardening since she stalked into the bathroom. His hands splayed across her back and explored every inch of her body that he could reach while she rocked against him.

"Fuck, Princess," he growled against her mouth.

Breathless and flushed, she pressed her hands on either side of his face, "Yes, please."

Eyes that burned with desire stared down into his own.

"This was supposed to be a relaxing bath," he responded, raising a brow.

Auraelia rolled her eyes and rocked against him. "I relaxed. I relaxed right against your naked body and felt your cock harden against my ass."

She slid one of her hands down his chest until it slipped beneath the water. Taking him in her hand, she worked him from base to tip. Daemon threw his head back and inhaled through clenched teeth, then grabbed her chin and held her gaze to his. Her movements never faltered as she steadily worked her hand up and down the length of him.

"You want my cock?"

Auraelia nodded the best she could and sank her perfectly straight teeth into the flesh of her plump bottom lip–a seductive grin pulling at the corners of her mouth.

Goddess, I want to fuck that mouth.

Daemon grabbed her hips and lifted her slightly as he nestled the head of his cock at her entrance. "Then take it. I'm yours to do with as you please. Use me, Auraelia."

Excitement lit her eyes as she slowly sank down his rigid length. He kept his hands on her hips, his fingers itching to push her further down, but he let her set the pace. Her walls clenched around him as she slowly lowered herself until he was fully seated inside her.

Fucking Auraelia was something he was certain he would never tire of.

Her body was supple and strong. Her waist was trim, but the fullness of her curves gave him something to sink his fingers into. She was all woman, and the look in her eyes while she rode him said that she knew as much.

Daemon loved this position.

It gave up some of the control, but it still gave him the ability to take it back. It also put her perky tits directly in his face, which bounced along with every slide of her cunt. Wrapping his arms around her waist, he pulled her to him, and bent down to pull one of her nipples through his teeth. The sensation made her draw a sharp breath and grind harder against him. Sucking the pained nipple into his mouth, he lapped away the hurt with his tongue before turning his attention to the other breast–working the tip to a swollen peak.

Auraelia's pace never wavered. The walls of her pussy fluttering around him as her climax grew. Kissing and nipping his way up her chest, he gripped her hips in his hands and thrusted upward. Auraelia threw her head back and moaned as she dug her nails into his shoulders, anchoring herself to him. She matched him thrust for thrust as he speared her on his cock, and they both chased their release.

Reaching between their bodies, he circled her clit with his finger. "Fuck. Yes, Auraelia, give it to me. I want to feel you come undone."

As if on command, she lost it. The walls of her pussy clamped down around him as her orgasm ripped through her. Within a few thrusts Daemon felt his balls tighten and a tingle at the base of his spine. He grabbed her face, drawing her gaze down to his. The satisfied smile that graced her lips, made his cock throb. "Auraelia, unless you want me to fill this pussy, you need to get off of me."

Her sweet, satisfied smile morphed into one that would rival the devil.

Auraelia tightened her legs around his waist, fusing herself to him. Then, using his shoulders for leverage, she slammed her pussy down on his cock.

"*Auraelia,*" he growled in warning.

But her pace never slacked, and her wicked grin only widened.

"Alright then." Daemon met her smile with one of his own, and reached his hand between them again, circling her clit. "You want me to fill this pussy? Then fucking milk me dry, Princess."

With Auraelia still coming down from the previous orgasm, it didn't take much to send her tipping over the edge again. With one more thrust, he followed her into oblivion as her walls clenched around him and held his cock deep within her core.

Auraelia slumped against his chest as she came down from yet another climax.

He felt her smile against his chest, and then chuckled, "What are you grinning at?"

"That was probably the most relaxing bath I've ever taken," she replied, the sarcastic tone in her voice making them both laugh. Daemon pulled out with a groan and grabbed a cloth to cleanse between her legs. When she relaxed back into his hold, they fell into a sated silence.

The bathing chamber was quiet, the only sound coming from water dripping off of the lip of the tub and into the puddle that had formed on the floor. Daemon absentmindedly traced the line of Auraelia's spine as she laid on his chest, the now cool water causing her skin to pebble.

"We should probably get out, my star."

Auraelia groaned at his suggestion, and begrudgingly sat up. "You're probably right. My fingers have turned into prunes." Her nose scrunched up as she looked down at her fingers, and he couldn't help the chuckle that escaped.

Daemon rose first, wrapping a towel around his waist before wrapping Auraelia in another and lifting her from the water. A flush stained her cheeks and traveled down her chest as he set her gingerly on the floor. "Thank you."

He smiled and tucked a few damp strands of hair that were stuck to her face behind her ear.

"It was my pleasure." He pulled her flush against his chest, forcing her to crane her neck to look into his eyes. He gave her a Cheshire smile, "And it will continue to be my pleasure until you're begging me for mercy."

Then he leaned down, and pressed his mouth to hers in a bruising and all-consuming kiss.

Chapter Eleven

Auraelia

Staring up at the canopy that hung above the bed, Auraelia let her mind wander back to her night with Daemon.

After their bath, he'd carried her to the plush rug in front of the blazing fire in his chambers where he ravished her again and used his shadows to bind and blindfold her, heightening her senses. Then again on the bed, where he'd folded her body like a piece of parchment. Then on the chair, where she sucked him down until the salty streams of his release slid down her throat, and where he then bent her over the arm, driving into her until they both came in a slur of moans and curses. Against the wall, where the cold stone added a delicious contrast to the heat radiating off him while the rough texture of the wall dug into the soft skin of her back, the pain adding another level to her pleasure. Then pressed to the window in the common area after they'd drifted into the room in search of food and drink.

They'd spent the night bringing each other pleasure in every way possible.

When they were completely spent, Daemon shadow walked them to the bathing chamber again where they showered, taking turns washing each other and relishing the other's touch. When they finished, he wrapped her in his dressing gown and carried her to his bed.

They laid there in a comfortable silence, their limbs tangled together as she traced patterns on his chest until the sun began to rise over the mountains.

"The sun's rising, my star," he whispered before pressing a kiss to the crown of her head, "And as much as I want to keep you wrapped in my arms and in my bed, it probably isn't the smartest idea."

Auraelia chuckled, "You're probably right. Plus, if Piper doesn't beat them to my chambers, my lady's maids would be inclined to call in the queen's guard if I'm not present."

After a beat of silence, she pushed onto her elbow. "The question is, how am I to get back to my chambers undetected? I sure as hell can't traipse around the castle in your robe, let alone my gown from last night."

"Let me worry about that." He grinned and his eyes twinkled with mischief as he pressed his lips to hers before sliding off the bed and to his feet.

She watched as he strode around the room, his ass flexing with every step, as he gathered her belongings. They were mostly in a neat pile where she left them, but her circlet had been removed at some point and she wasn't sure where it ended up.

Once they were both dressed, Daemon pulled her to him. Her back firmly pressed against his chest as his arms encircled her waist. Her eyes fluttered closed as he peppered kisses along the column of her neck.

"Keep your eyes closed and think of your chambers. Of your bed. Hold that image in your mind's eye and don't let it go."

Auraelia squirmed in his embrace, "It's really hard to concentrate on that when your cock is pressed against my ass."

He chuckled, but his voice was low and gravelly, "You keep squirming like that, and I won't let you leave this room. Queen's guard be damned."

Auraelia smirked and pushed her hips back into his. "Is that a threat or a promise?"

Daemon gripped her hips and spun her around, pulling her flush against his chest. Lightly gripping her chin, he tilted her head up so that their gazes were locked. "Don't tempt me, Princess. I'll pull you into my shadows and never let you go." Then he devoured her mouth with his before turning her back around. "Now, be a good girl, and do as you're told."

Though his tone was joking, it still sent a flood of desire between her legs.

She did as he commanded and focused on her chambers.

She pictured her cobalt and silver embroidered coverlet draped across her bed, and the starry midnight blue canopy that hung above it. She felt the air stir around her as darkness consumed the light outside her lids. She felt him press a kiss to her temple then whisper, "See you soon, my star."

The next thing she knew, the world was temporarily stripped away, and when she opened her eyes, she was in her chambers.

Alone.

Auraelia shuffled to her bed, still dressed in Daemon's dressing gown, and climbed in. Pulling the soft fabric tighter around her body, she inhaled his scent as she stared at the beaded stars above her, a smile on her lips.

"You dirty, dirty, bitch," Piper shrieked as she bounded into Auraelia's room, breaking her pleasant reverie. Jumping onto the bed,

Piper grabbed a pillow to make herself comfortable, "You better spill all the filthy details."

Auraelia smiled at her friend, then subconsciously pulled the lapels of Daemon's dressing robe higher.

"Wait a goddess damned minute. Is that *his*?!"

Auraelia turned the color of her mother's peonies and nodded before burying her face into her own pillow.

Piper shrieked and began hitting her with the pillow she'd snagged earlier. "Oh, no, ma'am. You're going to tell me every sordid detail of that encounter last night–"

"Encounters," she interrupted, a smirk on her lips.

"Oh, my goddess. Rub it in, why don't you." Piper rolled her eyes and emphasized her mock disdain with another hit of her pillow. "Either way, I need to know. Preferably before your nosey lady's maids come in here and start asking questions about where you got a *man's* dressing robe."

At that, Auraelia jumped up from her bed, a slew of curses leaving her mouth as she stripped out Daemon's robe and tried to find hers to replace it, all while Piper went into a fit of hysterics on her bed.

"Rae, calm down. I sent them to get your breakfast before I came in here. Give me some credit."

Auraelia stopped and took a deep breath before looking back at her friend. "I will tell you everything. Just help me get dressed."

Excitement flooded Piper's face, as she swiftly climbed from the bed and rushed to Auraelia's side. "Don't forget, we have training with Ser Aeron this morning. Oh, and then your mother wants you to sit in on the council meeting with all the nobles this afternoon."

Ser Aeron, the commander of the queen's army, was the only father figure in Auraelia's life. He was a large man, standing taller than Xander and as wide and strong as an oak tree. His beautiful ebony skin was a high contrast to his hair, which looked like someone spilled pepper into a canister of sugar. It was twisted into locs that hung to his waist and were secured at the nape of his neck. Being the commander of the queen's army, he was responsible for overseeing the training of all the soldiers, but he took it upon himself to personally train Auraelia and Xander. When Piper would distract her from the sidelines–which lead to numerous nicks and bruises–he *insisted* that Piper join in on the lessons stating, *"Every man and woman needs to learn to defend themselves at the very least, and since Piper is your Lady in Waiting she needs to be able to guard your back, in more than just the politics of nobility."*

He was correct, of course.

Piper was well versed in the politics of court and made sure that Auraelia didn't falter, but there was an added layer of comfort knowing that she could hold her own in combat should the need ever arise.

"Do I have time to change in between?" Auraelia asked.

Piper's brief hesitation was answer enough.

Auraelia pulled out clothes for the day and started to dress, all while she relayed every dirty detail to Piper, whose eyes sparkled like the stars with delight.

"Holy shit, Rae! I'm all hot and bothered just hearing about it," Piper exclaimed, fanning herself as she slid down the pillows while Auraelia finished recounting her night with Daemon.

Auraelia giggled at her friend's theatrics and shook her head. "You're ridiculous."

Sitting up, Piper forced a serious expression onto her face. "How big are we talking here? I need specifics." She held up her hands and slowly started pulling them apart. "Just tell me when to stop, okay?"

"Piper!" Auraelia's eyes widened in shock and she hit her friend over the head with her pillow. "I am not giving you *that* detail!"

Piper pouted and stood, then muttered under her breath, "You're no fun."

Resigned to the fact she wasn't getting any more details, Piper skipped away to let in the lady's maids who had arrived with their breakfast. The smell of fresh croissants and coffee wafted through the suite and made her mouth water. As she finished lacing her boots, there was a knock at the suite door.

"Come in," Piper shouted from the sitting room.

Auraelia could hear the door to her suite open. The sound was quickly followed by the grating sound of a chair being pushed back as someone stood in a haste, and a mumbled, "*Your Majesty,*" which meant that Piper had her mouth full when the queen walked into the suite. Chuckling to herself, she headed into the sitting area.

"Good morning, Mother." Auraelia strolled across the space and placed a quick kiss on her mother's cheek. "What brings you here this morning?"

"Can't a mother come see her daughter?" Queen Adelina asked, hand held to her heart as if she had been fatally wounded by the question.

Auraelia rolled her eyes at her mother's dramatics, "Of course you can, Mother. I was merely wondering if there was an actual *reason* for your visit this morning."

"Yes, well. In that case, I have a gift for you. I was going to present it to you yesterday, but you seemed–" she took a moment, searching for the word she wanted to use, "*distracted.*" Her mother finally finished, giving her a look that said, *"I may be older, but I'm not blind."*

Across the room Piper coughed as she choked back a laugh, effectively breaking the awkward silence between the queen and her daughter.

Queen Adelina turned and motioned to her lady who had been standing by the door to come forward. As she walked toward them, Auraelia noticed that she held a long, slender emerald-green box with gold leaf filigree along the edges in her hands.

She handed it to the queen, who reverently fingered the gold leaf.

"This is a tradition that has been a part of our family for generations. Presented to the Heir Apparent by the reigning monarch." When she looked up from the box, her eyes were lined in silver. But it wasn't sadness in her eyes, it was pride and love.

Handing the box to Auraelia, the queen grinned. "I hope you like it. I've been holding on to this since you were born." A small, nervous chuckle filled the quiet room.

Auraelia lifted the lid, and inside–set on a cushion of velvet the color of fresh cream–was the most beautiful dagger she'd ever laid eyes on. The blade was long and slender, and made of a solid piece of emerald. The hilt was made of gold vines that twisted and wrapped around the base of the blade, flowing up to a singular round cut emerald that was set in the pommel and seemed to glow in the low light of the morning.

"It's beautiful," Auraelia said, more to herself than to anyone else in the room, as she traced the delicate veins running through the stone.

"Would you all excuse us a moment, please," Queen Adelina said it as more of a statement rather than a question. "You too, Piper–" she added when she noticed her hovering by the table of food. "I'm sure she will explain everything to you later, but this is a conversation that needs to happen between a queen and her heir, first."

Auraelia furrowed her brow in confusion. "What's going on, Mother?"

When the door to her suite was finally closed, leaving the two women alone at last, her mother summoned a wall of water to blockade the door. Auraelia's eyes widened, and the queen chuckled as she shrugged her shoulders, "A bunch of gossips, the lot of them."

When Auraelia's expression didn't change, she added, "It's a sound block, to keep them from eavesdropping, little bug. Here, come sit."

Her mother walked over to the dining set that Auraelia kept by the balcony doors and sat–eyeing the spread of food that was set out on the table.

Joining her, Auraelia sat and offered her mother a cup of coffee before pouring one for herself–she had a feeling she would need it for this conversation. Taking a large sip, she squared her shoulders and readied herself for whatever information was about to be bestowed upon her.

"My love, you look as if your world is about to come tumbling down onto your head," the queen joked as she popped a berry into her mouth.

"Well, being as I have no idea what this conversation is about–never mind that whatever it is, is so private that you felt the need to throw up a wall of water in my room–so I am a *tad* nervous about its outcome."

"Auraelia, do you know why we are the Court of *Emerald*?"

"Aside from a large portion of this estate being made of, and being built upon a large deposit of emeralds...I don't think you've ever told me a specific reason, no."

Queen Adelina took a deep breath, "What gift was bestowed upon you by the Goddess Rayne and our ancestors?"

The sudden switch of direction gave her whiplash. "What? What does that have to do with–"

"Just answer the question. Please. I promise I will answer every question, but this is where we must start."

With an exasperated sigh, she answered her mother's question. "It seems I have the ability to summon wind."

Queen Adelina raised a questioning brow. "Is that all?"

Her mother's question was a blow that she hadn't expected, and her face fell. She quickly schooled her features, donning a mask of indifference, but she wasn't fast enough to escape the eyes of her mother.

"Oh, my love, I'm not suggesting that it's a minor ability. I merely think that there is more to your magic than you know. But only time will tell at this point. You're sure about the ability to control and manipulate the air around you?"

Auraelia nodded.

"Can you show me?"

Nodding again, she did what Daemon had shown her the night before when they had been curled together as they came down from their bliss.

She could almost hear him whispering in her ear as she went through the motions.

"Close your eyes..." She closed her eyes.

"Feel how the air moves around you." Opening her senses, she felt the air around her. How it flowed from the windows and coursed throughout the room. How it felt like feathers on her cheeks and fingers in her hair.

"And then command it to do something else." Auraelia thought back to the sanctuary when she had managed to pull the wisteria blossoms from their stems and suspend them in the air like they were falling in slow motion. She hadn't realized then that she had been the one to do it, but after her night with Daemon, she realized she had been manipulating the air around her constantly over the past two days.

She focused on the air flowing through the garden below–through her mother's beloved peonies. Envisioned it plucking the delicate petals from their bulbs and floating them through the open window.

When she heard her mother's sharp intake of breath, she opened her eyes.

Petals of pale pink and ivory swirled around them, cocooning them in a bubble of soft air and the delicate fragrance of peonies.

When she met the gaze of her mother, she saw awe and pride sparkling in the smoky pools of her eyes.

"So, the display in the ballroom yesterday. That was you?"

When she nodded, her mother's smile stretched across the entirety of her face.

"Auraelia, that's amazing."

Auraelia smiled, then floated a few of the petals down to land strategically in her mother's hair, before sending the rest of them back outside to rain down on the garden.

"I want you to try something."

Auraelia narrowed her eyes and looked at her mother with suspicion. The spark of pride in her mother's gaze had grown into glowing embers of excitement.

"Okay?"

"I want you to hold your dagger and use your magic."

"What? Why?"

The embers in Queen Adelina's eyes were a raging fire now. "Trust me."

Auraelia looked at her mother like she had gone slightly mad, but despite her hesitance, she lifted the dagger from the velvet cushion.

It was the perfect weight.

The heaviness of the gold hilt was perfectly balanced to the width and length of the emerald blade. Even with the twisting vines around the hilt, it was surprisingly comfortable to hold.

"We formed the Court of Emerald because our ancestors realized we were able to channel our abilities through the gems. We can use emeralds to heighten and focus our abilities."

Auraelia's eyes widened to the size of saucers, her gaze shifting between her mother and the dagger.

The hilt warmed in her grip while the emerald in the pommel and the blade seemed to glow delicately, as if the moment she gripped the dagger it woke in the presence of her magic.

Magic that she could now feel running rampant through her veins.

The tips of her fingers tingled, like they were full of static or a crackle of lightning. The air around her was heavy, yet light at the same time—like being wrapped in a lover's embrace.

She felt safe.

She felt...*powerful.*

The air in the room was still, but it stirred around Auraelia, lifting her hair so that it floated around her.

"Oh, my darling. There is so much more to your magic than you know, and I can't wait to see you pull back all its layers." The look her mother gave her was one of promise, and something else that she couldn't quite place.

Auraelia placed the dagger back in its case, watching as the light faded from the stones.

Queen Adelina stood from the table and with a swish of her hand, removed her watery barricade from the door. If Auraelia hadn't witnessed it herself, she would have never known that it had been there.

Crossing the room to the door, the queen halted and turned back to her daughter, a small smile on her lips. "You better finish getting ready for the day, or you'll be late for your lesson with Ser Aeron, and you know how much he *loves* when you're late." She winked at her daughter, then opened the door and left.

Auraelia sank into her chair and tried to process everything that she'd learned about her family's legacy and its attachment to the land that they lived on, but also her magic. She heard mutters of reverence as her mother made her way down the hall, before her door finally closed.

"What the hell was that about?" Piper asked as she crossed the room to where Auraelia was still slouched in her chair.

She sighed, then pushed herself upright. "I'll explain later. But for the time being, would you get my lady's maids, please. I need them to work their magic on my hair and lace this damn corset before we're late for our lesson with Ser Aeron. And I don't know about you, but I sure as hell don't want to muck stalls today."

Piper's eyes widened at the reminder of the last punishment they'd received for being late to a lesson and rushed to the door to let the ladies into the suite.

It didn't happen often, but regardless of status, Ser Aeron believed that everyone had lessons to learn. Unfortunately, most of those lessons were spent mucking out stalls for the horses after hours of training, when their limbs were sore, and their muscles were liquid.

Auraelia made her way over to her vanity so that her ladies could work on her hair. Sitting down at the mirror, she let her mind drift back to everything her mother told her. The static feeling in her hands and fingertips was new, she wasn't quite sure what it meant, but she was excited and determined to figure it out.

Maybe her mother was right. Maybe there was more to her magic. Only time would tell.

Chapter Twelve

Daemon

In the moments after he shadow walked Auraelia to her chambers, he seemed to be rooted in place. Looking around his room, memories of their night together shone in every corner of the space. Her lavender scent still clung to the air around him, despite the numerous showers and baths that they had taken throughout the night.

Taking a deep breath, he walked toward his bed, deciding to try to sleep a few hours before he had to start his day. He still hadn't decided when he wanted to head back to Kalmeera. The original plan was to leave today, but that was...*before.*

Before the smell of lavender enveloped his senses.

Before waves of honey spread across his pillows, and soft curves filled his hands.

Before eyes that reminded him of the sky before a storm drew him in.

Before he watched those same eyes shift to a combination of blues and greens like the ocean he loved so much. Eyes that held lightning within them and shot across them at the discovery of the magic that coursed through their depths.

Before he met *her.*

Before Auraelia.

Fuck.

A loud crack resonated around the room as Aiden came barging into their common area, unceremoniously slamming the door behind him in his haste.

"Hey, D!" he shouted through the space. "You up?"

Letting loose an exasperated sigh, Daemon closed his eyes as he pinched the bridge of his nose. "If I wasn't already, I would be now, asshole."

"Oh good, so when are we..." Aiden trailed off as he stepped into Daemon's chambers. "Hey, uh, D. I appreciate the offer, but you know I prefer the ladies."

"What the fuck are you talking about?" Daemon lashed back at his friend, spinning around to face where he stood at the door. Seeing the look on Aiden's face–eyes wide and lips curled in as he tried to suppress the laugh that was bubbling to the surface–Daemon quirked a brow, then looked down–he was still fully nude.

"Oh, fuck off." A mumbled stream of curses slipped as he rummaged through his wardrobe looking for a pair of trousers since Auraelia still had his robe.

Pulling on a pair of soft, black leather pants, he turned to see Aiden leaning against the door frame picking dirt from his nails.

"Is there a reason you're bursting into my room as soon as the sun crests the horizon?" Daemon asked as he moved past Aiden. Stopping in the middle of the room, he looked around before turning to glare at his friend, "You didn't even bring coffee with you?"

Rolling his eyes, Aiden pushed off of the door frame, "My apologies, Your Highness." His words dripped sarcasm as he bowed dramatically, then walked to the door and spoke to someone in the hall.

"Now that your precious coffee will be here shortly, when are we leaving?"

Daemon avoided eye contact with his friend and rubbed the hair at the nape of his neck.

"We *are* leaving today, aren't we?"

When he still didn't answer, Aiden threw his arms in the air.

"Come on, are you serious? Surely, you're not that hung up on this g–"

Daemon turned and narrowed his eyes at Aiden in warning.

" *–woman* already."

Daemon threw himself down into one of the wingback chairs in front of their fireplace just as a knock at the door announced the arrival of breakfast and coffee.

When they were alone once more, he sat up and rested his arms on his knees. "I don't know I really don't. There's just *something* about her that I'm drawn to. I couldn't explain it if I tried." He bowed his head and ran his fingers through his hair as he pushed out all the air from his lungs.

"Shit. All jokes aside, I wish that I could tell you what to do, but I can't. We have to go back to Kalmeera." Aiden walked over and placed a hand on Daemon's shoulder, "Sooner rather than later."

That final statement held more meaning than it should have. Daemon's father was ill, and as far as he knew, no one knew what was causing it or how to cure it. He knew that he needed to get home. His family depended on him.

So did his people.

Daemon rubbed his hands down his face, took a deep breath, and let it go. "Come on, let's eat. We'll leave tomorrow, I just have some things I need to take care of first."

Aiden glanced at Daemon and shook his head. He didn't say anything, but Daemon knew his friend well enough to know that Aiden knew–and didn't approve of–the *things* he needed to take care of.

Chapter Thirteen

Auraelia

"Is it just me, or is Ser Aeron being a royal prick today?" Piper whispered between pants as they, once again, had to run a lap around the training field because their stances weren't perfect.

"Pick up the pace, ladies, or I'll have you running laps until you collapse," Ser Aeron bellowed across the field.

The area they practiced on was near the stables outside the east wing of the castle. It had a range for archery, and a dirt pitch for combat and sword training. It also happened to be the only place that Queen Adelina hadn't decided to put a garden, making it the only available space near the castle.

They had been out in the heat for hours now, but it didn't matter. Ser Aeron seemed determined to run them ragged today. When they finished their final lap, they nearly collapsed, but somehow managed to stay on their feet. "Alright, ladies, grab some water. We're starting close combat in five."

Both women groaned with appreciation and stumbled their way toward the decanters of water that sat on the table near the weapons rack.

"Your Highness, might I have a quick word?"

Auraelia's body stiffened slightly before she turned. "Yes, Ser Aeron?" Even though he was like a father figure to her, he was still the Army Commander, and could be extremely intimidating. But seeing the small smile on his face, she relaxed.

It took but one step for Ser Aeron to catch up to where she stood, and then gestured for them to continue walking toward the table.

"How's the magic coming along?"

She sighed. "It's *coming*. Mother seems to think that there is more to what is currently presenting itself, but I'm not so sure."

Ser Aeron placed his hand on her shoulder, pulling her to stop. When she looked up, eyes a beautiful shade of amber looked back at her.

She'd always loved his eyes; they were so unique and a beautiful contrast to his deep ebony skin. Even when he was vexed, his eyes always held warmth in their depths. That warmth washed over her now and calmed her racing mind.

"It's only been two days, Auraelia. There's still time to figure it out. Give yourself some grace, it's still new to you."

She smiled up at the man who had been in her life for as long as she could remember. "I know, you're right. It's just hard to remember that sometimes when so much is expected from me. I don't want to let my mother, or our people, down."

"You'll be brilliant. At the very *least*, you'll do everything that you can for your people."

"That's the *least* that I would do?" Auraelia chuckled.

"You and I both know that everything that you *can* do will never be enough for you. You will always find a way to do more. But only at the detriment to yourself, never to your people."

When she smiled, Ser Aeron's brows pulled together. "That's not always a good thing, Auraelia."

"Yeah, yeah. I know. I'll work on it."

Ser Aeron chuckled and shook his head. "No, you won't. Go on now, get some water. It's time for you to kick Piper's ass." He winked, and then she walked off to do just that.

Grabbing the decanter from Piper, she drained the last of it, then wiped her mouth with the back of her hand. "You ready to get your ass handed to you?"

Piper scoffed and offered a mock bow. "You wish, *Your Highness*."

"Game on, bitch."

The two women shook hands. Even though they were bone tired, this was their favorite part of training. There were only a few rules, mainly for safety, but also because Auraelia was the Crown Princess, and she couldn't very well walk around with a black eye or broken nose.

"To your marks, ladies," Ser Aeron bellowed from where he was perched against the stone wall of the castle.

Auraelia and Piper took their places on the training pitch as Ser Aeron called out the rules. Even though they did this multiple times a week, and had been for years now, he still called them out as a reminder.

"Alright, ladies. There will be a slight shift to the rules today."

They turned toward him with looks of uncertainty on their faces–looks that quickly morphed into concern when they saw the Cheshire smile on his face.

Daemon

Daemon and Aiden took a walk down to the stables after breakfast. Since they'd decided to leave the following day, they needed to make sure that everything was arranged with the stable master for their departure.

As they rounded the stairs that led to the stables, the sound of shouting stopped Daemon in his tracks. It sounded like they were explaining rules. *Interesting.*

"Rule one: Stay away from the face. Below the neck only. Rule two: Fist and feet only until round two. Rule three: this is where things are going to be different this time ladies…"

Ladies? What the hell.

Daemon quickened his pace, stopping when a training field came into view. Standing in the middle of the dirt pitch was a tall brunette with hair the color of midnight, and a honey blonde that he would recognize anywhere.

Auraelia.

"What's going on?" Aiden asked when he caught up.

Daemon tilted his head in the direction of the field.

"What the fuck is going on over there?"

"I would presume training, Aiden. It *is* a training pitch."

"Is that…?"

"Looks like it."

"Shit. Wait, are you just going to stand here and watch?" Aiden asked incredulously.

Daemon's smirk was the only answer, as he directed his attention back to the training field and the two women upon it.

"When round two starts, you may both use the weapons you possess. Also, Your Highness, since you now possess magic, you may now use it."

"What?!" The woman with black hair screeched, throwing her arms in the air.

"Ser Aeron, I don't think that's such a great idea," Auraelia chimed in.

"Whether you think it's a good idea or not, it's *my* training pitch, and what I say goes. Got it?"

The women nodded, and grumbled a short, "*Got it,*" in response.

"Your Highness, you need to learn to wield your magic in combat, and we both know she is one of the last people that you would ever intentionally hurt. So, you can and *will* use your abilities. But keep in mind, she gets hers in a fortnight."

Both women grinned at that, and it was then that Daemon realized who was opposing Auraelia on the pitch.

"Fuck, is that Piper?" It seemed as if he and Aiden had come to that realization at the same moment.

"Would you shut up?" Daemon hissed through his teeth.

Aiden threw his hands up in surrender, as they both turned their attention back to the two noble women who were about to come to blows.

"Rule number four: First one knocked out of the dirt, loses."

When both women nodded in agreement to the rules, the man in charge of the exercise called for fighting stances, then raised and dropped his arm, signaling them to begin.

As the women circled each other, gauging when and where to make their first strike, Daemon took the opportunity to take in this side of Auraelia. The few times that they interacted, she was either in a ballgown or naked and writhing beneath him. So, this was a new side. One that he relished the sight of.

Her hair was pulled away from her face into a series of braids. There was a large loose one down the middle and two smaller and tighter ones down each side of her head, then they were all joined together in a braid that fell down to her waist. Her outfit was simple but accentuated all of his favorite places.

Her black corset was more casual than he had previously seen her in—or out of as the case may be—and the way it cinched her torso made her breasts swell over the top. The crisp white of her tunic was a stunning contrast to her sun kissed skin, and her black leather breeches formed to the luscious curves of her hips and accentuated the fullness of her backside. Her boots stopped above her knee and had a small heel with laces that ran the entirety of the shoe.

How in the hell does she fight in heels?

She even had a dagger sheathed to her thigh. Every inch of her was intoxicating, but seeing her block blow after blow, all while countering with strikes of her own, sent all of the blood in his body south.

"Round two, ladies...fighting stance...begin," the man bellowed.

With round two starting, Daemon descended the rest of the stairs. But instead of heading to the stables, he walked toward the training field.

"You've *got* to be kidding me..." Aiden huffed behind him from the bottom step.

"You go on ahead. I'll catch up."

Daemon monitored his pace. Even though he was eager to see the look on her face when he showed up, he didn't want to distract her to the point where she lost.

Coming up to the pitch, he went to stand next to the man in charge. A man, who from a distance looked large, but the closer he got to him the more he realized how much of an underestimate that was. Though he seemed to only be an inch or so taller, his size was intimidating. His arms were the size of tree trunks, and he did not look pleased to see Daemon standing there.

Daemon extended his hand, "Prince Daemon of the Sapphire Isles."

The man's eyes narrowed slightly at the mention of his title, throwing Daemon for a loop. He withdrew his hand, running it through his hair before he crossed his arms across his chest and leaned against the wall.

"And you are?" Daemon prodded as he watched the women continue to spar. Neither woman had drawn their weapon yet, and it seemed as if his reluctant companion was growing frustrated.

"Ser Aeron, Commander of the Queen's Army," he finally responded in a curt tone.

"Ladies, if you don't follow the rules, you'll be mucking stables. I don't think her majesty would appreciate the smell of equine shit filling the council chambers this afternoon. Auraelia, that goes for magic too."

Both women looked over to Ser Aeron to nod in confirmation, but the moment Auraelia saw him standing there, the flush on her face from exertion, deepened. Daemon smirked, and her eyes widened as she hastily turned away to refocus on the task at hand.

"If you distract my students, I'll put you in the ring with me. I don't care if you're a prince, I'll beat your ass."

Daemon cleared his throat, "Understood."

With the commander's threat hanging overhead, both women drew their daggers. Piper's was a simple blade of steel with a loop on the hilt that she slipped her finger through and began to swing it between different grip styles.

Auraelia's on the other hand, was like nothing he'd seen before. The gold hilt caught the sun's rays, but the stone in the pommel seemed to glow from within as soon as it was in her hand. The blade itself was long and slender, and when he saw its unnatural gleam, realization struck like a bolt of lightning.

She held an emerald dagger.

Daemon watched them dance around each other on the pitch. Their footwork was impeccable, both dodging and parrying one another with ease.

Piper had been the first to draw blood, slicing Auraelia on her forearm after spinning out of her strike. But Auraelia retaliated shortly after when she dropped into a crouch to avoid an attack, slicing Piper across the meat of her outer thigh as she went. Then, using the momentum from her drop, she swung her leg around, swiping Piper's legs out from under her–causing her to fall flat on her back.

As they both got to their feet, Daemon noticed that Auraelia had put her dagger away. It seemed Ser Aeron noticed as well as his whole body stiffened and he started to pull away from the wall. Daemon watched as he opened his mouth to shout–presumably to tell Auraelia to draw her weapon–but before Ser Aeron had the chance to say anything, Daemon felt a shift in the air around them, and a cocky grin spread across his face.

There's my star.

A look of bewilderment crossed Ser Aeron's face as he took in the shift in Daemon's demeanor. When they turned their attention back to the women, Auraelia had encased herself in a sphere of wind. Her hair floated around her as she manipulated the air to block every blow that Piper attempted.

Daemon could see the frustration growing on Piper's face. She was getting tired, and obviously didn't like the fact that she didn't have a way to retaliate.

Next to him, Ser Aeron shouted, "You have one minute to finish this, or you're mucking stables."

What is it with this man and mucking stables?

Daemon watched Auraelia, eager to see what she would try to do. They had worked on her magic in between rounds of sex the night before, but she was still new to her abilities, and he could see it taking a toll on her strength already.

The next thing he knew, she broke apart her sphere and pushed the air at Piper. She was, quite literally, trying to blow her competition away.

"Thirty seconds, ladies!" Ser Aeron barked.

Daemon could see the sweat running down Auraelia's face from exertion. Saw her jaw tighten from clenching her teeth. *Come on, princess, you can do it.*

As if she could hear his thoughts, Auraelia threw her arms forward, attempting to channel her magic through her hands. Pulling the air from the sphere, she used what remained of her strength to push it onto Piper. The force wasn't strong enough to hurt her, but it was enough to knock Piper out of the circle and land her square on her ass.

Daemon knew that she was powerful but seeing her concentrate her magic through her hands was something that took most people months–and sometimes years–to master. He was in awe, especially since she was still figuring out how to suppress it when it came to her emotions.

"Winner, her Royal Highness, Princess Auraelia," Ser Aeron exclaimed, a proud smile plastered across his face.

"Oh, come on!" Piper complained from where she sat.

Daemon saw Auraelia stagger on her feet and shadow walked to her before she could stumble.

"Oh shit, neat party trick there, *princey*," Piper remarked, clearly impressed but not surprised.

Daemon ignored the comment for a moment and focused on Auraelia. She had clearly over-exerted herself. Her eyes were closed, and her face was bleached of all color, but her breathing was steady. Running his fingers across her brow, he brushed away some of the hair that had escaped from their braids.

Her eyes fluttered open, and slowly began to focus on him. "Daemon?"

Her voice was barely audible, but the sound made his heart swell all the same.

"Hello, Princess," he whispered, "do you think you can sit on your own?"

When she nodded, he helped her sit up, keeping his hand on her lower back. If anyone had asked him why, he would have said it was to steady her, but in reality, it was more than that. There was a strange compulsion to be near her, to make sure that she was safe.

Ser Aeron came over with a full decanter of water, and Auraelia took it gratefully. While she drank, the commander kneeled beside her and held his hand over the gash that Piper inflicted during their training.

Auraelia's face screwed up in pain, but it quickly faded as a small golden glow emanated from his hand and spread over her arm. When he withdrew, a pink line of new skin was revealed where moments ago split flesh had been. Daemon openly stared at Ser Aeron as he stood and walked to Piper, presumably to do the same for the injury inflicted by Auraelia.

As the color returned to Auraelia's face, he turned to Piper. "*Princey*? Really?"

Auraelia choked on her water and turned wide eyed to her friend.

Piper merely shrugged, and now that her leg was fully healed, she pushed up from the ground.

Turning his attention back to Auraelia, Daemon gently rubbed her back, "Are you okay to stand?"

She nodded and gave him her hand—only wavering a step before she found her balance.

"You should eat something. You just exerted a lot of energy with that amount of magic."

Ser Aeron's hulking frame shadowed over Daemon, watching him closely with narrowed eyes. Daemon looked up to match his stare. "If you would be so kind as to grab someone and ask them to bring the princess something to eat, I would be eternally grateful."

He tried to keep his voice even, but he didn't like being scrutinized and watched over like a child.

Auraelia placed her hand on the commander's arm and nodded. "It's alright. I'll be right here."

When she smiled at the bristling man, the wrinkles in his brow smoothed and his shoulders dropped away from his ears, the tension visibly leaving his body. Ser Aeron grabbed her hand in a brief squeeze then turned to complete his task, leaving Piper, Auraelia, and Daemon to stand in a circle of awkward silence.

"Well, this is fun, but I'm going to go check and see if Ser Aeron needs any help." Piper gave Auraelia an indecipherable look as she excused herself.

He watched in fascination as the two women seemed to have a silent conversation, something only people who knew everything about each other could do. When Auraelia sighed, clearly giving up whatever silent argument they were having, Piper smirked.

"Your Highness...es." After a quick nod in their direction, and a wink in Auraelia's, Piper turned and skipped away.

When she disappeared from view, Daemon guided Auraelia over to a bench nestled under a line of trees at the edge of the training field.

"She seems like fun."

Her eyes were downcast, but she smiled. "Understatement of a lifetime."

"How long have you been friends?"

"I can't remember a time when we weren't."

When they reached the bench, Auraelia sat down and leaned back on her hands. Tilting her face to the sky, she let the sun that filtered through the leaves dance over her. She smiled, and it was full and unhindered, and Daemon's heart skipped. He knew she was beautiful, but here in her element, completely at ease and enjoying the sunshine, she was radiant.

Auraelia inhaled through her nose, then continued her train of thought. "She's been my lady in waiting since we were babes, and I guess being around someone every day for your entire life, you start to connect. When we were no more than ten, she and I snuck away from the governess and into the kitchens." Shaking her head, a small chuckle escaped at the clearly happy memory. "We stole a plate of sweets and hid in the garden. Obviously, it was a terrible idea and we got extremely sick, but we bonded over puking in the rose bushes. Neither of us ever told a soul...until now." A blush crept onto her cheeks. "She's been my sister and partner in crime ever since. My life would be immensely dull without her." After a few minutes, she turned to him, "What about you and Aiden?"

Daemon smirked, "Our families have been friends for generations. So, like you and Piper, we grew up doing everything together, and a lot of things that we shouldn't have been doing, too," he said, ending in a laugh. "He's a pain in my ass, but he keeps me grounded."

They drifted into companionable silence, the only sound around them coming from the breeze as it drifted through the leaves.

After a short while, Ser Aeron reentered the training field holding a small basket in his massive hands. The image of a large, burly man holding a tiny basket–one that presumably belonged to a small child–was certainly a sight to behold, and Daemon could barely contain the amusement in his voice when he reached them. "Ser Aeron."

Quickly narrowing his eyes at Daemon in warning, he then turned his attention to Auraelia with a smooth bow. "Your Highness, the kitchen put together an assortment of your favorites. I've also informed Her Majesty of the incident and that you may be a few minutes late to the council meeting this afternoon." Completely ignoring Daemon, he handed Auraelia the basket full of goodies.

When she smiled, his icy exterior seemed to thaw a fraction. "Thank you, Ser Aeron. Truly."

As if on cue, Auraelia's stomach made its presence known, triggering a flush that colored her cheeks.

"I'll leave you to it then." Ser Aeron bowed, and gave Daemon one more withering stare before he left.

"Oh, my goddess," Auraelia said under her breath, as she stuck her head in her hands.

Daemon shook his head and laughed "Okay, Princess, let's get some food in that stomach of yours, shall we?"

Picking up the basket from where it sat between them, he pulled back the cloth that had been draped over the top, revealing various foods that all smelled divine.

"What is all of this?" he asked in awe.

Auraelia chuckled. "Well let's see here. We have chocolate croissants, cheese, strawberries, and oh my goddess, they even put in a bottle of blueberry wine."

Daemon watched in wonder as Auraelia's eyes danced with joy.

Picking up one of the chocolate pastries, she took a bite. Her face melted into one of pure bliss. "You really must try this."

Before he could protest, she shoved a piece into his mouth.

A moan rumbled deep in his throat, as the deliciousness of the pastry melted on his tongue. The shell was crisp, flakey, and salty from the butter. But the center was warm and full of melted, decadent chocolate, and he snatched the remaining piece from Auraelia.

"Hey!" she half shouted with a laugh.

"Sorry, this is mine now." Daemon shoved the rest into his mouth.

Auraelia chuckled, then pulled two glasses from the basket and poured them both some blueberry wine.

Taking a sip, he let the sweet notes and bubbles dance across his palette. "May I ask you a question?"

Auraelia popped a strawberry into her mouth and nodded.

"What is the story behind the commander?"

Auraelia straightened, seemingly trying to steel herself for this conversation, and looked out over the training field that was in front of them.

Daemon reached to place his hand on top of hers, but thinking better of it, pulled back at the last minute. "You...you don't have to tell me if you don't want to."

She took a deep breath, blowing it out in a stream of air. "Ser Aeron is the only father figure I have, or have ever had, in my life.

The man who contributed to my genetic makeup has never been in the picture. He was around when Xander was born, and obviously around to make me, but he left shortly after as far as I know. Mother doesn't talk about him. Xander and I have never needed him. And since lineage is determined through the matriarchal line, it really didn't matter if he was present or not. But my mother–oh, my mother is a force to be reckoned with."

A small laugh escaped. "She insisted that I be treated as any male would be. I was to learn everything Xander did. And when it came to physical training, there wasn't a doubt in her mind that I, too, would be out on the training pitch. There were many, *many*, officers and soldiers that had been assigned to train me in combat, but they all treated me as if I were a delicate flower."

Auraelia stood, the memory clearly one that still rubbed a nerve. She turned to face him but didn't make eye contact. Instead staring down at her fingers as she picked at the skin around her nails.

"When mother had enough, she wrote to the Lord and Lady of the Court of Opal and asked for them to send someone to come instruct me; they sent Ser Aeron."

At the mention of the Court of Opal, bits and pieces started falling into place. His size, the style of his hair, and the unusual color of his eyes. Opal was known for producing the greatest warriors in Ixora, both men and women.

Everyone in the Court of Opal was trained in defensive and offensive basics at the very least, and if a citizen chose to join the training academy there, they had to go through extensive trials to make sure that they would survive. The fact that they sent one of their warriors here spoke volumes of Queen Adelina's reach and influence.

"How long has he been here?"

"Since I was around six. He started with training the queen's guard, then took over Xander's private lessons. When I turned ten,

I started my own lessons, and after a year or so, he started training Xander and I together."

"What about Piper? It seems unusual for a lady in waiting to participate in combat training."

Auraelia looked up, embers burning in her gaze as she crossed her arms over her chest, "No more *unusual* than a princess learning combat training."

"That's not—"

"No, it is. I understand it's not a common thing throughout Ixora for women to know how to protect themselves. But my mother refused to leave me defenseless. Magic can only get you so far."

"I'm sorry, Auraelia, I truly didn't mean to cause offense."

Auraelia uncrossed her arms and walked back over to the bench to sit down. "Piper joined my training sessions shortly after I started them, actually. Ser Aeron grew tired of her distracting me on the sidelines, so he made her join in. He also said that as the future of Lyndaria, I needed to have someone that I could trust to guard my back not only in the politics of court life, but also in imminent danger."

"He's a smart man. A tad prickly in the people department, but he seems like a good one, too."

"He really is. He's never coddled me, but he's also never been cruel. He's extremely respected by all the soldiers and guards. He treats everyone with respect and expects it in return. I'm extremely grateful for everything that he's done for my family, and my people."

Silence settled over them before he turned to Auraelia, confusion marring his features. "If he's a member of the Court of Opal, how is he Commander of the Queen's Guard?"

"Ah, that. Well, the short answer is that my mother asked if he wanted to stay, and he said yes." A small smile graced her face. "The long answer is more complicated. When my mother saw the wonderful job that he was doing with Xander, Piper, and myself, and saw the difference in her own guard, she asked him if he would want to stay. He agreed, but it also meant clearing it with the Lord and Lady of Opal."

"But your mother is a queen."

"She is, but she doesn't stay queen by taking things from the courts. Ultimately, it was Ser Aeron's choice to stay or go. She would never keep him here if he wanted to leave. But she still wanted to extend the courtesy of asking the Court of Opal if they had any objections or needed any compensation for the loss of one of their greatest warriors. Diplomacy goes a long way, Prince Daemon. You should know that." The last bit was said with a mocking lilt and a knowing smile.

"Touché, Princess."

They ate the rest of their picnic alternating between contented silence and light conversation.

Daemon told her more about his family and Kalmeera while Auraelia countered with her own stories of her favorite places in Lyndaria.

When they finished their meal, Auraelia repacked the basket.

"Are you feeling better?"

"I am, thank you."

What was once a comfortable silence was now heading into an awkward one. Neither of them sure of where to go from here.

"I–" they said in unison.

Auraelia smirked, "Go ahead."

Daemon ran his fingers through his hair, his nerves standing on end. "I'm leaving tomorrow."

"Ah, I kind of figured as much. You do have a kingdom to return to, after all."

She wasn't mad, and if anyone understood his duty to his family and people it was her. But still, it stung a little to hear her be so accepting of it.

When she stood, he felt his heart sink.

"I really should head back. I don't want to be too late for the council meeting."

"Can I see you later?" The question was rushed, anxious almost.

She shrugged one shoulder and smiled, "Sure, come find me after."

He was about to say something in response, but just as he opened his mouth, Piper came barreling around the corner and across the training field to where they were.

"Aurae–Your Highness, we really need to get you to that meeting," Piper said as she approached, eyes flitting back and forth between them.

When a look of clear disappointment briefly crossed her features, Daemon smirked.

"Yes, yes. I'm coming." Auraelia took a few steps before she looked back over her shoulder, heat blazing in her eyes, "See you later?"

"I'll come find you."

After a quick nod, she started walking. She made it a few feet before she stopped once again, "Oh, and Daemon?" she hollered before she turned around to face him fully, a smile once again lighting up her face. "Thank you." Before he could respond, she turned again, quickening her pace to catch up to her friend.

Leaving him to watch, as the two women linked arms, and walked back to the castle.

Chapter Fourteen

Auraelia

Still feeling a little drained from her use of magic, Auraelia took her friend's proffered arm as they walked toward the stairs that led back into the east wing of the castle.

"Soooo?" Piper bumped their shoulders together as she drew out the word.

"So, what?" She kept her face blank as she mimicked her friend.

Piper let out an exasperated sigh, "You're no fun."

"Nothing happened, Piper. We sat, ate, and talked."

Piper gave her a sidelong glance, her face a picture of every depraved thought that was clearly running through her mind.

"Oh my goddess, do you think of nothing else? We ate *food*, Piper. Food."

Piper scoffed, "See? No fun."

Auraelia rolled her eyes, but there was a small smirk on her lips. "You're incorrigible."

"Yes, but you love me, regardless."

Both women laughed and were still laughing when they saw a figure heading their direction from the stables.

"Who's that?" Auraelia wondered aloud.

Piper squinted, but then immediately looked away as a small flush crept onto her cheeks.

When the person in question came into better view, Auraelia noticed the sun-bleached hair, without a single strand out of place despite the breeze, and recognized them immediately.

Aiden.

The closer he got to them the deeper Piper's flush became.

"I see," Auraelia said, feigning hurt feelings.

Piper snapped out of whatever trance she had been in, her face now the color of crimson roses. "You see what?"

"You've been hounding me about *my* current relations to avoid sharing information about *yours*."

"I have no idea what you're talking about," Piper scoffed, as she feigned indifference.

"Mm-hmm." She gave Piper a sly look before turning to face the man heading their way. "Good afternoon, My Lord." She gave a small nod in his direction.

"Your Highness. My Lady," he responded, bowing at the waist–his eyes lingering on Piper a fraction longer than would be considered decent. When he realized that Auraelia noticed, he straightened quickly and cleared his throat. "Have you seen Prince Daemon?"

"Yes, we just left him sitting under the trees on the opposite end of the training field."

"Thank you. If you'll excuse me."

When Auraelia nodded, signaling that he was indeed free to go, he bowed quickly and then hurried in the direction that they had just come from.

Both Piper and Auraelia turned, watching him scurry across the field.

When he was far enough away, she turned to Piper with a Cheshire smile. Piper, on the other hand, looked like a cat who had been caught with a bird in its mouth. "Spill."

"I-I'm not sure what you're talking about," Piper stumbled over the words.

"Mm-hmm. You're lucky that I need to get to this council meeting. But don't think that you're getting out of this conversation, *Lady Piper*."

Piper let out an exasperated sigh. "Fine. But let's hurry, before your mother has both of our heads."

They both cringed. Auraelia loved her mother dearly, but the one thing that the queen of Lyndaria didn't take well to was tardiness. And although Auraelia had been permitted to be late *this* time, she didn't want to push her luck.

As they headed toward their destination once again, Auraelia looked back out to the trees where Daemon and Aiden should have been.

But they were gone.

She scanned the area once more, coming up empty, then continued up the stairs after Piper.

The meeting was held in the northern wing of the castle, in the queen's council chambers.

The entire wing was dedicated to the reigning monarch. From personal chambers for the queen–and king, if there was one–to sitting areas, private entrances to the queen's garden, and of course the council chambers.

Auraelia had been in there numerous times, but it was one room that she would never tire of, and this time was no different.

It was shaped like an octagon, with half of its walls housing gothic windows that looked out to the garden of peonies, while the other half were covered in bookshelves that held the history of not only Lyndaria and the Court of Emerald, but of Ixora as a whole.

The windows were framed in ivory drapes that brought a lightness to the room, but overhead, the ceiling had been painted to look like the sky at dawn. Swirls of pinks, lavender, and deep sky blues, and clouds in hues of orange to mimic the way that the sun bounced off their surfaces.

In the center of the ceiling hung a chandelier made of aqua and clear shards of glass that when illuminated, cast tiny pinpricks of light onto the mural above, giving way to the illusion of stars not yet ready to surrender to the light of day.

There was a large round oak table in the center of the room with a detailed map of Ixora carved into its surface, surrounded by carved low back chairs with plush cushions. But at the far end of the table, sat three high back chairs, with one rising taller than the other two. The one in the center was reserved for the queen, and the two flanking either side were reserved for Auraelia and her brother.

As she stepped fully into the council chambers, the meeting paused, and the members of the council stood to bow. She nodded to the group and headed to her seat, taking notice that there seemed to be more people present than usual.

To Xander's left sat Ser Aeron, who was not only the Commander of the Queen's Army, but also one of her advisors. Next to him was Lady Ophelia, the queen's lifelong friend and lady in waiting, who also happened to be the court's Mistress of Coin. Her family had been head of the court's finances for generations, and since she had no siblings to take up the mantle, she took on the role in addition to her duties to the queen.

Moving around the table, there was the Master of Hunt and Harvest, Lord Harland; the High Priestess of Rhayne, Priestess

Ríona; and Mister Amaris, who was the emissary for the Court of Emerald. The only person who seemed to be missing was Master Demir, who was the Master at Arms and weapons specialist for the whole of Lyndaria.

As she rounded the table, Auraelia noticed her mother in deep conversation with someone sitting in the chair next to her empty one.

Someone with perfectly messy hair, the color of a raven's wing.

Auraelia froze. *What in the name of the goddess is* he *doing here?*

As if he could hear her thoughts, Daemon turned his head in her direction. He didn't even need to say anything, his eyes did it for him. Eyes that bore into her hers, glowing as brightly as the embers of a new fire. She could almost hear '*Hello, my star*' being whispered to her as if he were standing behind her, his mouth pressed into the shell of her ear. Said mouth was now curved into a grin. *Shit.*

The memory of their first meeting came barreling to the forefront of her mind. Her heart sped up, her breath hitched, and goose flesh rose on her arms. It wasn't until Piper discreetly nudged her from behind that she realized she had stopped walking.

Finally making it to her chair, she sat down, exhaling a breath that had been stuck in her throat since she and Daemon locked eyes. Piper, who took a seat on a settee by the window, was newly flushed, and when Auraelia met her gaze, she flicked hers away to the far side of the room by the doors. Discreetly, Auraelia looked to where Piper had gestured.

Aiden. Well shit, looks like we're both going to be uncomfortable today.

"Now that we're all here," Queen Adelina said, giving Auraelia and Piper a quick, narrowed glance before continuing, "let us begin."

So much for not being in trouble for being late.

"Lord Harland, the floor is yours."

Auraelia sat through presentation after presentation from the lords and ladies of the council. She tried to pay attention when Lord Harland talked about how well the crops were doing and how they were expecting a bountiful harvest in a few weeks. She even successfully fought the yawn that threatened when he talked about how the Court of Topaz was also having an excellent growing year and that Lyndaria should be getting a shipment of fall crops from them in a few months' time.

The Court of Topaz and the Court of Emerald had a long-standing agreement to exchange seasonal crops throughout the year, and it was a mutually beneficial relationship that had lasted decades. Topaz maintained an environment and temperature that was conducive to growing autumnal crops such as corn, potatoes, gourds, and apples. Whereas Emerald, with its mild and rainy spring climate, was more suited to growing crops like beans, peppers, leafy vegetables, and berries.

Auraelia tried to ignore the way Daemon's hair fell in gentle waves over his forehead while Lord Harland discussed how the population of deer, wild boar, and other local game were thriving, which meant a successful hunting season later in the year, and how the current pheasant season was a huge success.

The memory of Daemon's fingers trailing up her thigh barely even crossed her mind while Lady Ophelia made sure that the crop exchange balanced out evenly between cost and profit. She surely didn't fantasize about his whispered words from the night before as talk turned to the upcoming solstice celebrations.

When Ser Aeron updated the queen on how training the new recruits was going, she very deliberately ignored the burning looks that Daemon would cast her way when no one was looking.

She really did try to keep her focus on the important things around her, but her mind continuously wandered to the man on her right.

It wasn't until Mister Aramis started to speak that her focus was fully wrenched from Daemon.

"I'm sorry Mister Aramis, would you please repeat that?" Auraelia asked, wanting to make sure that she had indeed heard correctly.

"Of course, Your Highness. I've received word from my associates in the Court of Garnet. There have been some...stirrings within their court that could become of concern, should they escalate."

"What kind of stirrings, Aramis?" Xander asked, his voice was laced with concern and his brows were knitted together in confusion.

The Court of Garnet was located on the other side of the Onyx Mountains and had always kept to themselves. It was the one court that was always glossed over in her lessons, though she never understood why. When she asked anyone about it, the response was always the same. Either *'they keep to themselves and don't bother with us, so we don't bother with them'* or an incoherent mumble followed by *'please excuse me, Princess.'*

So, the fact that the Court of Emerald had contacts *in* Garnet, and that they were warning the crown of possible discourse, was troubling to say the least.

Before Mister Aramis answered Xander's question, he shot a questioning look at the queen.

Auraelia furrowed her brow as she turned to her mother. "Mother, what's going on?"

Queen Adelina kept her eyes trained on Aramis, her face impassive as she answered Auraelia, "Nothing to concern yourself with, my dear." There was a brief nod from Aramis before he sat back down, his eyes downcast.

Auraelia turned to her mother, poised to question her further, but with one look, she shut her mouth. Fury and concern swirled in the stormy depths of her mother's eyes, and her lips were pressed into a thin line. She wasn't sure what was going on, or why she and Xander were deliberately being kept out of the conversation, but the tight set of her mother's jaw said that now wasn't the time to prod.

When she looked at Xander, he looked as puzzled as she felt. She needed to get to the bottom of whatever it was, but it wasn't going to happen right now.

Lost in her own thoughts, Auraelia hadn't realized that Queen Adelina had started addressing Daemon.

"Yes, Your Majesty. Lord Aiden spoke with your stable master this morning and squared away all of our needs. We are to take our leave tomorrow morning after breakfast, if that's alright with you, of course," Daemon replied to whatever question the queen had asked.

"Yes of course, of course. And I'll have our kitchen staff make sure to pack some things for you to take on your journey, as well."

"We would appreciate that very much, Your Majesty, thank you. The princess introduced me to chocolate croissants this afternoon, and I must say, I would be remiss if I didn't bring some back to Kalmeera with me for our chefs to recreate."

"Did she now?" the queen asked, pinning Auraelia with a curious look that made her want to shrink down into the cushion of her chair.

"Ser Aeron brought them to me after my ordeal this afternoon at training. I did the courteous thing and shared. That was all," she said in a whisper that only her mother would hear. It was received with pursed lips, and a *'hmm'* then the subject was dropped.

"Back to business. Prince Daemon, I didn't ask you to sit through this council meeting without reason. I have a letter that I need delivered to your mother and father. It entails information on our current trade agreement with the Sapphire Isles as well as a few new propositions that I would like them to look over at their leisure. If you would do me a kindness and deliver it to them, I would greatly appreciate it."

"Of course, Your Majesty. Lord Aiden is the emissary for my court, so it would be no trouble at all. Your letter will be delivered without fail."

"Well, then that settles it." Queen Adelina rose from her chair, signaling the end of the council meeting and for the others to rise as well. Seeing as this room was part of the queen's suite, the council members bowed or curtsied before making their exit.

Auraelia hung back, but nodded to Piper letting her know it was alright for her to leave, and followed her mother over to one of the benches that overlooked the garden.

When everyone had filtered out of the room, Auraelia turned from the garden and looked at her mother. "Mother, what's going on? What aren't you telling Xander and me about the Court of Garnet?"

Queen Adelina didn't look away from the garden, she didn't sit up straighter, she simply exhaled a breath. "It's nothing to concern yourself with right now, little bug. I will tell you both when the time is right, but now is not that time."

Queen Adelina finally turned from the window and gave Auraelia a small smile as she squeezed her hand. And though the smile didn't reach her eyes, Auraelia decided to let it go.

For now.

Auraelia sat with her mother for a while, watching the sun make its way down to the horizon, changing the sky from a pale blue to one painted in pinks and oranges. When Lady Ophelia came back into the room a while later with dinner for the queen, Auraelia excused herself. Kissing her mother on the cheek, she left the council chambers in search of her own dinner.

And Daemon.

Chapter Fifteen

Daemon

Daemon hid in his shadows outside the council chambers and waited patiently for Auraelia to emerge. He'd been surprised when Aiden explained that a messenger had been sent requesting their presence at the council meeting this afternoon. He, of course, agreed to attend. He loved the idea of surprising Auraelia and seeing how off kilter his presence would make her.

He made a point to arrive before her, and since her brother was already seated at the table, it was easy to discern which seat was designated for her. So, to make it even more interesting, he chose the empty seat next to hers.

Daemon's mere presence was a large topic of conversation prior to the start of the meeting, and he'd received a few interesting glances from the members of the council. However, the look from Ser Aeron was one of pure distrust. His eyes narrowed as soon as Daemon stepped foot into the chamber, and when they locked eyes for a moment, it was as if the words *"I'm watching you"* had been forced into his mind.

The commander had seen them together away from everyone else at court. He'd seen the way that Daemon looked at Auraelia.

He knew the exact moment she walked into the room. His body had become acutely attuned to hers since the night they met and his magic writhed beneath his skin when she was near. He heard her mumbled acknowledgements to the other members of the council as she made her way across the chambers, but he felt it the moment her eyes landed on him.

When Queen Adelina glanced behind him to acknowledge her, Daemon took that as his cue to turn her way. Her breath caught the moment their eyes locked together, and it was as if the world slowed. A beautiful flush colored her cheeks radiated down her chest, and his cock stiffened at the memory of seeing how far down the color went. She was frozen in time with him, and it wasn't until Piper nudged her back into motion that the spell was broken.

A sense of satisfaction washed over him at knowing that he had the same effect on her as she did on him.

Throughout the entire meeting, she was bound and determined to ignore his presence. She avoided his gaze while he stole glances when no one was looking, but he felt her eyes every time she would turn his way, no matter how brief. The icing on the cake was when he mentioned the chocolate croissant they'd shared, and she looked like she just wanted to sink into her chair and disappear.

Daemon knew he was in trouble. Knew that he shouldn't have started something that he was quite sure would ruin one or both of them. But they were both consenting adults, and goddess be damned, he wanted her, and she clearly wanted him too.

When she finally emerged from her mother's suite, he pushed his shadows out until they encircled her. Reaching through them, he grabbed her wrist and pulled her to him as she let out a surprised yelp. When she was flush against his chest, looking up at him with a bewildered expression on her face, he smiled.

"Hello again, my star," he whispered, then crashed his lips to hers.

He felt the moment she let go and let herself get lost in his embrace, sinking into his hold as she snaked her hands up his chest to twine her fingers into his hair. He growled, the sound emanating from deep within his throat.

Suddenly, she was pulling back.

"Daemon." His name was a breathy exhale on her lips. "Someone could see us."

When she moved to look around and step away, Daemon tightened his arm around her waist and used his free hand to tilt her face back to his.

"My star, all that anyone would see is a shadow in the corner. If they looked close enough, they might see a shimmer of magic, but they would never get close enough to do that. I've got you. I promise."

Auraelia's eyes reflected so many emotions back into his that it was hard for him to discern them all. But the one that stood out the most in that moment was longing.

His original plan had been to whisk them away to one of their rooms. He had even strongly considered the garden, where they could repeat their first night together–only this time he wouldn't let her run from him–and then they could spend the rest of the night wrapped in each other in the comfort of a bed. But now? Now, he wanted to show her another facet of his magic.

He turned her around, pulling her back to his chest, before leaning down to whisper into her ear, "Close your eyes, Auraelia."

She stiffened slightly before relaxing back into his embrace. When he could feel the last bit of tension ease away, he took a deep breath, letting his magic bleed out of him and into the shadows. What had once been ribbons of darkness twining around them, similar to a pot of ink being poured into a basin of water, was now so much more.

"Open your eyes."

Auraelia's breath caught. "Daemon, this is–" She shook her head, seemingly unable to find the words to process what she was seeing.

All around them was a sky that one would only see during the darkest part of the night. Clouds of purple, orange, and white spiraled around one another creating kaleidoscopes of colors. Specks of white that resembled stars twinkled all around them, like an artist flicked paint from the bristles of his brush, creating constellations and groupings you wouldn't see under normal circumstances.

It was the sky that Daemon only saw when he was out on the water. It was this sky that he was most at home under, and it was this sky that Auraelia reminded him of.

Daemon pulled her closer and peppered kisses up her neck, stopping right behind her ear. "This was once my favorite sight in the whole of Ixora. The stars were so bright, and I would get lost in their swirls for hours."

"Why is it now past tense?" she asked, tilting her head to the side, giving him better access.

Daemon chuckled and turned her back around so that he could look her in the eyes. He cupped her face in his hands, and gently stroked her cheek, "Because you, *my star*, in the short amount of time I have known you, have somehow managed to outshine them all."

Her eyes softened at his words, but she didn't say anything.

"I've told you once, and I'll gladly tell you again. I'm drawn to you and have been since I saw you walk into that ballroom two days ago. I don't know why, I couldn't explain it if I tried, but I think you feel it too. Or at least I hope you do."

Daemon removed his hands from her face and leaned down until their noses brushed.

"Daemon–" She paused and reached one of her hands up to stroke the side of his face. He leaned into her touch, waiting for whatever truth she would tell. If there was one thing that he was absolutely certain of with Auraelia, it was that she wouldn't skirt around the truth. She had been candid from the moment they met.

She dropped her gaze and sighed, and in that moment, Daemon felt his heart sink, but he waited for her to continue. When she finally looked up to meet his gaze once more, her eyes were soft, and she had a smile on her face. Her smile could light the way in the darkest of nights, and when it was directed at him, it was as if the sun was shining for him and him alone.

"You're not alone. I feel it too and though I don't understand it, I don't want to fight it. I don't know what that means going forward, especially with you leaving tomorrow and every other complication that is sure to arise. But I do know that I want to see what happens."

Daemon was too stunned to speak, so instead he did the only thing that he could think of, he pressed his lips to hers.

He had expected her to end things there. Say that it was just a fling, that it didn't mean anything. But she hadn't.

Auraelia pulled away and rested her brow to his. "This is crazy, you know that right?"

"I do. But I also don't care."

"We probably should care. We need to figure out how this is going to work," she said as he started trailing kisses across her jaw, and then down her neck.

Daemon sighed and rested his head on her shoulder before standing upright. "I know, and I do *actually* care. We will figure it out, I promise." Daemon let his smile turn devilish, "But first, Princess, I want you. *Now.*"

Auraelia's eyes widened, a moment of fear passing through before being consumed by her desire. "Right here?"

"Yes, Auraelia. Right here, among the stars."

"We're in a hallway, Daemon." She raised one of her eyebrows, as sass bled into every word.

"Are we?"

Her eyes narrowed slightly, as disbelief swarmed her features.

Daemon stalked forward, forcing her to take a few steps back and collide into a wall of solidified shadows that he'd conjured moments ago.

When she looked around to see what she was now pressed against, Daemon pulled her face back to his.

"Don't worry, my star. No one but me will hear your pleasure." He ran one finger down the side of her face in a feather light caress, then furthered his descent as he continued speaking. "No one but me will hear how your breath hitches before your orgasm rips through you." His finger was now down her neck and trailing across the swell of her breasts. "No one but me will see how your eyes roll back when I bite right here." He pressed his thumbs against her nipples behind the fabric of her corset, causing her to inhale sharply, then he continued his descent.

"Daemon," she moaned, want evident in her voice.

"Needy little thing, aren't you?" he asked, as his finger hooked into the top of her pants right above the laces. "Where was I? Ah, yes." He started undoing the ties. "No one but me will hear you scream my name as I bury my cock to the hilt into your pussy."

Ever so slowly, he slid his hand behind the laces, and was met with nothing but her bare skin and a soft patch of curls.

Fuck.

Slipping his hand down further, he cupped her, and the feeling of her slick core had him clenching his teeth to keep from ripping her clothes off right then. He loved watching her squirm under his touch. Loved watching her need and desire build.

Auraelia whimpered as she attempted to rock against his hand, seeking any kind of relief from the growing need pulsing in her core.

He began to slide his fingers back and forth through her slit, her desire coating his digits with every swipe. Every time he would graze her clit, her entire body would shake with anticipation.

"You're mine, Auraelia. I know that we have a lot to figure out but say you're mine."

Her face was flushed as her orgasm built, but her eyes were locked onto his.

"I'm as much yours, as you are mine."

"I'm yours, for as long as you'll have me. I'm yours."

She smiled. "Amazing. Now that we got that out of the way, would you please, for the love of the goddess, fuck me?"

"Only because you asked so nicely." Daemon smirked, then simultaneously drove two fingers into her core and crushed his lips to hers, devouring the gasp that tried to escape.

Auraelia's fingers tangled into the front of his shirt, both pulling him closer and using him to hold her up as he worked his fingers in and out of her while using the heel of his hand to add friction to her clit.

He slid his other hand around to her back, deftly undoing the laces of her corset, loosening them enough that he could pull her breasts over the top. Moving from her lips, he trailed hot, open mouth kisses down her neck, sinking his teeth into the junction where her neck met her shoulder, then easing the hurt with gentle kisses and flicks of his tongue. The sound of her moans, her whimpers, and heavy breathing shot straight to his already hard cock. Dipping his head lower, he pulled one of her nipples into his mouth. Auraelia, finally abandoning the strong hold on his shirt, ran her fingers through his hair at the root, holding him in place at her breast.

After lavishing both sides, leaving bite marks and purple bruises from pulling the tender flesh into his mouth, Daemon withdrew his hand from her pants and dropped to his knees in front of her, placing a tender kiss to the laces blocking her mound. "Princess, as sexy as these boots and pants are, they really are making this much more difficult than I would like."

Auraelia looked down at him and snickered. "And do you have a solution to this problem?"

Running his hands up her thighs, he stopped at her waistband and grabbed her hips. The soft give of her skin beneath his hands had him suppressing a groan.

How did I convince this woman to be mine?

A small smirk pulled at his lips as he spun her around and pressed her front to the wall that she had just been leaning against.

He worked her pants down until they stopped at the top of her boots, giving her only a few inches of movement. "Put your hands on the wall by your head, Auraelia. Keep them there until I give you permission to move. Understand?"

Auraelia whimpered, her head bobbing slightly in answer to his question, but he needed more. Standing, he positioned himself behind her and slapped her right ass cheek–light enough that it wouldn't leave a mark, but hard enough that it would sting. She jolted at the sudden pain, and her sharp inhale was music to his ears.

"I need to hear you, Princess. Tell me you understand," he said as he rubbed and soothed her stinging flesh.

"I–I understand."

He could hear the need in her voice when she answered him.

One side of his lips tilted up, from both her playing along with his games and also from the sight of her glistening pussy. "Good girl."

He slid two fingers through her arousal, and his sharp intake of breath sounded like a hiss. "Fuck, you're so wet."

Auraelia pushed her hips back into his touch, earning her a slap on her other cheek. Repeating the care he took on the opposite side, he gently rubbed the area. "Is there something you want, my star?"

"Yes." Her voice was a breathy whisper.

Daemon leaned over until his mouth was right behind her ear. "What do you want, Auraelia? Tell me what you want."

"I want you to fuck me."

"How? Be specific."

She shifted slightly underneath his weight, and he slid a hand around to her front to swirl his finger on her clit.

A groan rumbled through her, and she rested her head on the wall. When she didn't answer his question, he stopped. "Answer me, Auraelia, and I'll give you whatever it is you want."

Blowing out a breath, Auraelia turned her head to the side as much as she could and stared at him through the corner of her eye. "I want you to eat my pussy like it's your favorite meal until I come all over your face. Then I want you to fuck me. I want to feel your cock stretch and fill me."

Shock rocked through him at her words and ricocheted down to his aching cock. When he opened his mouth to respond, she smirked and continued.

"Then I want you to take me to dinner, because I'm starving and if we're going to repeat last night, I need sustenance."

Daemon laughed. "Oh, my star, last night is going to look like nothing when I'm done with you."

Lifting her head, Auraelia craned her neck around so that she could see him fully. Desire, passion, and a challenge filled her gaze. "Prove it."

Daemon matched her wicked smile with one of his own. "Challenge accepted, Princess." Then he dropped to his knees and did exactly as she asked.

He started slow. Flattening his tongue and taking long slow laps up her pussy, then using his hands to spread her as wide as he could, giving him better access to her core. With her boots stopping above her knee, her pants could only go down so far, so he had to work with what little maneuvering space he had.

Alternating between long licks and flicking the delicate bundle of nerves at the apex of her thighs, he could feel her being wound tighter and tighter.

Every gasp and moan that met his ears was a straight shot to his cock. He loved how responsive she was to his touch. How *natural* being together felt. Whether they were dancing in a ballroom, laughing beneath the trees, or finding pleasure in each other's bodies. Being with her just felt *right*.

Her breathing became erratic when he curled his fingers forward, massaging the sweet spot just inside her entrance. Her legs started to tremble, and her arms were beginning to sag from the way she desperately tried to keep them on the wall in front of her.

When he felt her walls start to clench, he ran his tongue along her slit once more before drawing her swollen clit into his mouth, sucking hard.

She combusted, her head thrown back in ecstasy.

Withdrawing his finger, he lapped up her release like it was the finest wine the world had to offer. He could have died right then, with her taste on his tongue and his name on her lips and he would have died a happy man.

Once her breathing slowed, he stood and wrapped an arm around her waist. Leaning forward to kiss her shoulder, he pressed the evidence of his arousal into the soft flesh of her ass.

Auraelia moaned and pushed her hips back into his.

"You doing ok, Princess?" he asked, sweeping loose strands of hair away from Auraelia's face.

She hummed in response before nodding and mumbling, "Yes."

"Good. Because I'm nowhere near done with you." Punctuating his statement with a firm press of his hips before straightening and reaching down to unlace his trousers–pushing them down far enough to release his length.

Daemon slid his hand through the arousal that still dripped from Auraelia's pussy. She hissed through her teeth at the feel of his fingers trailing over the sensitive flesh, and he circled her clit until she relaxed under his touch. Sliding his cock through her slit, he spread her arousal along his length before aligning the head of his cock at her entrance.

Ever so slowly, he worked his way into her. Her body stretched to accommodate his size while her walls clenched around him from being stimulated so soon after orgasm.

When he was fully seated inside her, Daemon ran his hand up her back and pulled her braid from where it was draped over her shoulder. He wrapped the plaited tresses around his hand and pulled gently, tilting her head back and causing her back to arch.

"Keep your hands on that wall, Auraelia."

Her murmured, "Ok," was all he needed to start moving.

He withdrew slowly before slamming back into her slick entrance. Auraelia stumbled forward a step, before she braced herself for whatever he had in store.

"That's it, Princess," he praised as he thrusted into her again and again.

Keeping one hand wrapped with her braid, he slid the other one from her hip around to the front and up to her breasts. Palming a heavy globe in his hand, he pinched its small bud into a peak.

Every moan and explicit word that fell from Auraelia's mouth fed his need for her.

Abandoning the hold Daemon had on her hair, he moved to wrap his hand around her throat. Tight enough to restrict blood flow, but not enough to cut it off. "Let go of the wall, Auraelia. I want you to play with your clit. I want to feel you come all over my cock."

Auraelia didn't hesitate. She dropped her hands from the wall, one going to her clit while the other reached back to pull Daemon's head forward so that she could devour his mouth.

He went willingly, capturing her lips with his, consuming every part of her that she would give him.

As she feverishly strummed her clit, Daemon drove into her in the same manner.

When he could feel his climax build to the tipping point, his grip on Auraelia's throat tightened, further restricting her blood supply. Her movements faltered a moment, but then she picked up her pace and crashed over the edge into oblivion, pulling him with her.

Daemon erupted with a roar, as her pussy clenched around him, milking his cock dry. A strangled scream slipped past her lips as he held a firm grip on her throat.

Lightning crackled across the sky, startling them both, and Daemon eased his hold on her neck. "What was that?" he asked between pants as he smoothed hair back from her face, and slowly withdrew, righting himself and pulling his trousers back up into place.

"You didn't do that?" Auraelia asked, her voice trembled, but he was unsure if it was from their coupling or from the lightning.

"No, my star. I can only manipulate the shadows and project images from my mind. I can't *create* lightning." He stooped down to pull up her pants while she tucked her breasts back behind the confines of her corset. When she had righted her clothing, Daemon gingerly turned her around to face him.

Pressing a finger below her chin, he tilted her head up so that he could look into her eyes. Eyes that were usually the color of blue calcite, were now the color of emeralds with bright streaks of peridot lightning streaming through her irises.

"I think there is more to your magic than you know, my star." When Auraelia wrinkled her nose, Daemon bent to press a chaste kiss to its tip. "I, for one, can't wait to see what all you're capable of."

Auraelia took a moment to absorb his words. "You think I caused the lightning?" she asked, disbelief evident in her voice.

Daemon shrugged, "Could be, but only time will tell."

Nervous energy radiated off of her in waves.

"Auraelia, try not to worry about it. Your magic will manifest in full when it's supposed to."

He could see that the uncertainty pertaining to her abilities was causing her to deflate and didn't want their last night together to be spent analyzing the details of the unknown. Magic was fickle and would only progress with practice.

"I believe I still have one more request to fulfill," he said to lighten the mood

Auraelia looked at him in confusion before the implication dawned on her.

"Food?" she asked hopefully, her eyes alight with delight.

Alright, food makes my woman happy. Note taken.

"Yes, my star." Daemon pulled her flush against his chest. "Food. As much as you want."

When she smiled, his heart leapt in his chest. "Just one question. Your room or mine?"

The smile on her face said everything that he needed to know. Pulling her as close as he could, he wrapped one arm around her waist and used the other to cup her cheek, lifting her face to his. "Close your eyes and think of where you want to go, then take me with you." Then he lowered his mouth to hers.

The stars around them winked out, turning back into swirls of ink and smoke as Daemon manipulated the shadows, transporting them to wherever Auraelia had chosen.

Chapter Sixteen

Auraelia

"*Just one question. Your room or mine?*" Goddess, save me, this man is going to be my ruin.

Auraelia knew exactly where she was taking him as soon as the question left his lips.

When the swirls of shadow finally rippled away, they were standing in the common area of her suite. Thankfully, Piper was nowhere to be seen, and she sent a quick prayer to the Goddess Rhayne to keep it that way. The last thing she wanted–or needed–was her best friend barging in.

She watched as Daemon took in the space around them, his arms still tightly wound around her waist. A cool evening breeze filtered through the open doors on the balcony, causing her skin to pebble and a shiver to run through her body.

"Are you cold?" Daemon asked as he pulled her further into his embrace.

Heat radiated off him as she wrapped her arms more firmly around his torso and smiled up at him. "No, just a chill."

He placed a chaste kiss on her lips before releasing his hold and making his way around the room.

Stopping at the bookcases, he traced the spines on various volumes that sat on their shelves. "I didn't know that you liked to read." His tone was wistful, and the sound made her stomach flutter.

"You never asked." She let her amusement shine through her tone and produced a smug grin when he turned around to face her.

Daemon continued his perusal of her suite, running his hands along the back of the settee and chairs. But when he picked up the romance novel that sat on the small table in her sitting area, heat flooded her cheeks.

Please don't open it. She silently begged from across the room, and when he merely flipped through the pages and set it back down, she sighed in relief.

A gentle smile pulled at his lips as he made his way back to where she stood, and every step he took toward her was a pull on her soul. When he finally reached her, he reverently stroked her cheek, and she leaned into the touch.

"Auraelia, I'm assuming your bed chambers are around here somewhere, correct?" Eyes full of hunger burned into her own.

"They are." She spoke the words in a low, breathy, tone.

His pupils expanded until there was only a sliver of green and gold left; the sight sent a wave of heat straight to her core. When Daemon leaned down to capture her lips, she reached up and placed a finger on his. Confusion flashed across his features, but it vanished just as quickly as it appeared. "You promised me food, *Prince Daemon.*" She enunciated every letter and syllable in his name.

Relief washed over his face, and he shook his head slightly, "How remiss of me, *Princess Auraelia*. Please allow me to rectify the situation." Then with a smirk and a wink, he was gone.

In Daemon's absence, Auraelia walked out onto her balcony and began to undo the braids that pulled at her scalp. It was one of her favorite places. She could look out over her mother's garden, and on a bright, clear night like tonight, she could see beyond the wall where a field of wild lavender grew in abundance.

Closing her eyes, she envisioned the air around her and the way that it blew through the field. She thought of the way that the tall green stems, with their delicate purple blooms, would bend and bow beneath a breath of wind. Saw the way they would dance to soundless music and pulled that breeze to her. The scent of lavender washed over her, its calming essence soothing the rough seas of her soul.

"The scent of lavender will forever be embedded onto my soul."

The sound of Daemon's voice startled her out of the calm she'd achieved. She spun around, a hand clutched to her chest as she took deep breaths to try and slow her accelerated heart rate.

"What the fuck, Daemon! How long have you been standing there?"

He chuckled, "Not long, but long enough to see you pull a breeze from clear across the castle grounds and past the wall." When he quirked a brow, it wasn't accompanied by his usual cocky smile. He actually seemed impressed.

"Are you going to just stand there staring at me, or are you going to come eat? Because personally, I'm ready for dessert." One corner of his mouth kicked up into a smirk that promised more than just a plate of chocolate and berries.

Auraelia didn't miss his thinly veiled innuendo. Passion still burned in his gaze as it slowly raked over her body. Even if she had somehow managed to miss it, the evidence was clear behind the laces of his trousers. The sight of his ample cock straining against the front of his pants made her mouth water, and she squeezed her legs together in an attempt to alleviate the pressure that was building there.

Daemon, of course, didn't miss the movement.

His eyes dilated further, the muscles in his jaw straining as he clenched his teeth, and the veins on his hand stood out as he balled it into a fist. *"Auraelia."* Her name was a promise and a warning.

She stared for a moment, lost in his burning gaze as she debated how much she really *needed* food. When the smell of whatever he had brought back with him hit her nose, her stomach growled.

The loud, and utterly embarrassing, noise broke the tension that had been building between them. Daemon's eyes reverted back to something close to *normal* as he let out a laugh full of mirth. "Come eat, my star. I have plans for you later."

Auraelia made her way toward the table just inside of the balcony doors, her eyes never once straying from his. On the table sat a few covered dishes. He'd even found candles and set those out as well. She'd never been with anyone who had taken the time for the little things. Who had taken the initiative to make the simple act of sharing a meal more intimate. But here was a man who she'd barely known for longer than two days, who seemed to think of nothing other than making her smile. The thought made her heart swell.

Choosing the chair furthest from the window, she slid between Daemon and the table. The space was wide enough that she could fit between the two without issue, but she made sure to lightly brush against his growing erection. When she made it to her chair, she glanced over her shoulder with a look of feigned innocence. "Excuse me."

A groan sounded deep within his throat, *"Auraelia."*

Daemon was riding on the edge of control, and she thoroughly enjoyed nudging him to see how much it would take to tip him over.

Taking the seat across from her, he lifted the silver cloches that covered the food. Steam rolled off the dishes, and the smell of roasted chicken with rosemary potatoes and green beans filled the air. It smelled divine, and Auraelia's mouth watered for an entirely different reason now.

Her eyes fluttered closed as she took a bite, moaning as the flavor exploded on her tongue. She may have grown up on these dishes, but the chefs in the kitchens really knew how to prepare food. It also helped that the ingredients were always fresh.

When she opened her eyes, Daemon was leaning back in his chair with his fingers laced together in his lap as he watched her, his eyes full of joy and a small smile on his lips.

Suddenly self-conscious, she swallowed. "What? Are you not eating?"

Daemon sat up and picked up his fork and knife, "I am, but I love how much you like food."

"I don't like food, I *love* food. If you couldn't tell," Auraelia gestured to herself, "I'm not the tiniest person."

Daemon's eyes glowed in the candlelight, "Trust me, my star, I've noticed." His heated gaze raked down her frame before coming back up, and she felt a flush creep across her cheeks.

Growing up, Auraelia had always been thin. As she got older, her girlish figure shifted into one of a woman. Her hips widened and rounded. Her stomach was no longer taught and flat, despite the amount of rigorous training she did. She had stretch marks on her thighs and her breasts. She had to learn to accept and *love* the body she was in, and she did. If she hadn't, the hungry look on Daemon's face as his eyes roamed over her body would have nipped those thoughts in the bud. He looked like he wanted to devour her and sink his teeth into the ample curve of her ass.

The longer she held his gaze, the more intense it became.

Clearing her throat, Auraelia finally looked down, spearing a few beans on her fork as she shifted in her chair, trying to abate the throbbing between her legs

Daemon chuckled as he brought a piece of chicken to his mouth, "Is there something I can help you with, Princess?" he asked before pulling the meat off his fork.

When she looked up, his gaze burned hotter than the sun.

"N–" a piece of food lodged in her throat as she tried to speak, "No, I'm fine. Thank you."

Daemon didn't say a thing.

He didn't need to. The knowing smile on his face said more than enough.

The rest of the meal passed in tense silence, while heated gazes were exchanged across the table. And Auraelia made a point to *casually* run the toe of her boot along Daemon's leg whenever she would shift in her seat.

Finally, Daemon lifted the remaining cloche to reveal a tray of chocolate, berries, and a bowl of sweet, fluffy cream. "Would you like to stay here, or would you like to take these...elsewhere?"

His question sent a shiver of anticipation through her, making the fine hair on her arms stand on end and the corners of her lips tilt up into a Cheshire smile.

Auraelia stood from her chair, and walked over to where Daemon was still seated. She didn't say anything, merely extended her hand for him to take.

When he placed his hand in hers, a tiny spark of energy passed between them. Jolting away from the contact, she clutched her hand to her chest–her eyes widening at the sensation. She looked to Daemon for an explanation, but his face mirrored hers.

"Did you–do you know what that was?" she asked.

"No, I'm not sure what that was, actually. But I'm sure that it's nothing." He grabbed her hand, pulling it from where it was still clutched to her chest, and rubbed his thumb over her knuckles in soothing circles.

The contact made her stomach flutter.

Gently, he pulled her to his chest, and wrapped an arm around her waist.

Using his free hand, he tilted her face up to his, "Did you still want dessert, my star? We can stay here if you like."

Daemon's eyes were swirling pools of moss green and liquid gold. Concern banked the fire that had been burning brightly, but the embers were still present, and she was determined to stoke them back to life.

Auraelia pulled her bottom lip between her teeth before replacing it with a smile and nodded.

He hesitated a moment, and then dropped the hold he had on her waist.

Backing away slightly, she once again grabbed his hand in hers. The lack of energy sparking between them was both a relief, and a conundrum. She wasn't sure what it was, and until she figured it out, Auraelia knew it would bother her.

Tucking those thoughts away, adding them to her growing list of problems for another day, she focused on the man standing before her, before walking them back towards her bedchamber.

Her eyes stayed locked on his as they crossed the room.

As they reached her door, Auraelia set a gust of air to push it open, her use of magic bringing a smile to Daemon's face. Once inside her chambers, she sent another breeze to close the door behind them, tousling his hair in the process.

With the door closed, her room was cast into darkness–her fireplace was cold, and her drapes were drawn.

"Stay here." She pulled her hand from his and slowly backed away, thankful she could navigate her room with her eyes closed.

Padding across the floor to the sconce by her bed, she turned the dial on the bottom and set about illuminating the space in a warm glow.

When she turned back around, she found Daemon's searing gaze was once again locked onto her, heating her from the inside out.

She felt it lick over every inch of her being. The way it caressed every curve before traveling back to her face where their gazes interlocked. The heat in his eyes burned into her soul and her arousal pooled between her legs.

Pulling herself from her lust filled stupor, Auraelia strode over to where Daemon stood in the center of the room. The once golden pools that graced the fathomless green of his eyes, turned to crystalized amber in the lamplight.

When she was close enough, he pulled her to him. The scent of sandalwood and the ocean breeze enveloped her senses as he wrapped an arm around her waist, while his other hand wrapped around the back of her neck and pulled her to his lips.

The kiss wasn't rushed.

He didn't devour her like he had earlier when they were surrounded by shadows and stars.

It was slow and tender, but it burned with a passion that was all consuming.

He took his time.

Coaxing her to open for him with a flick of his tongue.

She let him in. Let him consume her, body and soul.

Wrapping her arms around his waist, she let her hands rove over his back and the ridges of muscles there.

Let the world fall away in that kiss.

His hands never wandered as he continued to hold her tightly to him, like he could meld them into one.

Like magnets that only an outside force could pull apart.

Minutes or hours passed, she wasn't quite sure, by the time he pulled away. Leaving her breathless.

"I want you. But I want to take my time with you tonight."

For a moment, she let herself drown in the swirls of green and pools of amber that peered back at her before she nodded, "I'd like that."

Daemon placed a quick kiss to her lips before pulling her toward the bed, sitting on the edge as he guided her into the space between his parted knees.

He ran his hand down the outside of her thigh until he hit her knee, lifting until she placed her foot on the edge of the bed between his legs. The toe of her boot acting as an arrow pointing directly to the hard ridge of his cock.

Leisurely, Daemon slid his hands up both sides of her booted calf until he reached the tops of the laces just above her knee and began to unlace them. Pulling her foot free, he set it back on the ground before repeating the process on the other leg. His hands never leaving her body for more than a fraction of a second.

When both feet were free, he gently turned her around so that her back was to him.

Achingly slow, Daemon slid his hands from her hips up her sides and around to the laces that held her corset together. Every pull of the laces was like a direct line to her throbbing clit. When he finished, and the corset started to slide from her front, he stood and ran his hands up her sides to her shoulders where he gently pushed the straps down her arms, his fingers scorching a path along her skin. She felt the heat of his breath as his nose trailed up the column of her neck, leaving pebbled skin in his wake. She couldn't help it when her head tilted to the side and fell back onto his shoulder, coaxing him to continue the blissful torture, and a moan fell from her lips when he placed a feather light kiss behind her ear.

"I'm going to get you right to the edge and begging for my cock without even touching that sweet pussy."

His words were barely a whisper, but they made the blood running through Auraelia's veins feel like liquid fire. Her knees felt weak, and she sagged against his chest, closing her eyes. The arm around her waist was like a brand on her skin. Without her corset, she could feel the heat radiating off him through the thin linen shirt she wore, and it sent another wave of arousal to her core.

"If I slid my hand into your pants right now, would you be drenched for me, Princess?" She could feel the smirk of his lips as he purred sinful words into her ear. He slid his hand down her stomach to the top of her legs, skirting the edge of her pussy.

Oh my, sweet goddess.

Auraelia whimpered at the lack of contact, making him chuckle behind her.

"I'll take that as a yes."

"Oh, fuck off."

Her retort only earned her another chuckle as he pulled his hand back up her body. His fingers slipped beneath the hem of her shirt, and skimmed the skin of her stomach, her muscles jumping under the touch.

While his hands continued their slow exploration of her body, his little finger dipped under the waistband of her pants. Traveling deeper with each pass but never going far enough. His thumbs skimmed the underside of her breasts while he narrowly avoided the sensitive buds of her nipples, and the fabric from her shirt added delicious friction to every slide of his hand across her torso. Some touches were like a feather being dragged along her skin; others were like brands that would mark her flesh for life. But every touch and caress pushed her closer and closer to the edge of ecstasy.

Auraelia was putty in his hands, and she was quite sure he knew it.

But two could play this game.

She pushed her hips back into his growing erection. Grinding into it, eliciting a groan that sounded deep within his throat.

"*Auraelia.*" Her name was a warning on his lips, but the firm grip he now had on her hips was a promise.

Slipping both of his hands under the hem of her shirt, he coasted his hands upwards, dragging her shirt with him.

The rough calluses on his hands from years of hard labor on a ship and handling a sword scraped against the soft skin of her side as they slid higher. When he could go no further, he leaned down, his voice a low growl, "Lift your arms."

She did as he commanded, and he continued to slide the garment up and over her head. Tossing it to the side, he slowly trailed his fingers back down her arms, ghosting the sides of her breast and spreading goosebumps in his wake.

Auraelia let her arms fall back. Grasping the back of Daemon's head, she dug her fingers into his hair and pulled his face down to where her neck and shoulder met.

He went willingly. Trailing languid kisses across her shoulder and up her neck, while his hands slid down her torso to the laces on her trousers where he deftly loosened and undid the ties that held them in place.

Strengthening his hold, he rotated them around until she was facing the bed.

Pulling her hands from his hair, but keeping a grip on her wrists, he placed another kiss on her neck before turning her around so that she faced him. Placing her hands around his neck, he lifted her below her knees before crawling onto the bed and placing her on the plush spread, her hair fanning around her head like a goddess' halo.

Daemon nuzzled into her neck, leaving a searing kiss before trailing lower and kissing his way down her chest, but never straying from the valley between her breasts. Every touch was equally wonderful and agonizing as he slowly made his way down her torso.

Placing a final kiss below her navel, he hooked his fingers into the top of her pants and–in one swift movement–pulled them down to her knees, then off completely, leaving her completely bared to him.

"Fuck, Auraelia." His gaze was molten as he took in her naked body.

The next thing she knew, she felt phantom touches everywhere.

Strokes trailing down her neck. A whisper of something over her nipples, tightening the buds into painful peaks. Light caresses sliding up the inside of her thighs urging them apart, exposing her glistening core.

Daemon watched as she writhed under the ministrations of his shadows. Watched as they pushed her closer to the edge and then he pulled them back when she was close to tipping over, only to start the process over again when she started to come down.

It was torture.

Pure, blissful torture.

She didn't know how much longer she could handle Daemon's edging, and it only got worse when he began to remove his own clothing.

He began by slowly undoing the laces at his neck, and Auraelia watched as every delicious inch of golden skin and every intricate line of his tattoos was exposed.

She committed every line, both ink and muscle, to memory before letting her gaze travel to the vee of his hips where a trail of hair led down into his trousers. Down to where the hard ridge of his erection strained against the buttons that held his pants together. Her fingers itched to free the massive length behind them, to lick him from base to tip. She'd never been overly fond of taking a man into her mouth, but feeling the hold she had over him, the way he came apart at the seams for her, was a turn-on that she'd never expected.

When he released the final button, her breath hitched as his length sprang free from its confines–a bead of precum glistening on the tip. Her mouth watered at the sight, she just wanted to touch him.

Unfortunately, Daemon had other plans.

While she'd been watching him, swirling tendrils the color of smoke had encircled her wrists, keeping her from touching anything–herself included.

Even with the velvety shadows binding her wrists, he still had plenty more that continued to caress every other inch of her body.

He wasn't even touching her, and she was going to combust.

Standing gloriously naked at the end of the bed, Daemon began stroking his cock from base to tip as his eyes burned into hers. When he placed one knee on the bed, it was as if the world had stilled around them. Starting at her ankles, he gradually swept his fingers up her legs, and she nearly came from the contact alone.

She was closing in on the precipice of it being too much. The ache from the buildup was becoming too great. She needed release and she needed it now.

Sliding his hands further up her legs, he skimmed the inside of her thighs, closing in on the place she longed for his touch before retreating down the opposite side.

Auraelia pinched her eyes closed as a desperate whimper escaped.

"*Daemon, please.*" She could hear the whine in her voice, but she didn't care. She needed him. Needed to feel the weight of his body pressing onto hers as he sank into her.

When he reached the backs of her knees, his movement stopped. Curious, she cracked her eyes open to peer at him.

His eyes were glowing embers of need...and possession.

"I do love it when you beg." His lips lifted into a smile of pure wickedness, and before she could blink, he'd yanked her to the end of the bed and dropped to his knees. Then his mouth was on her.

Long, languid strokes of his tongue up her slit had her seeing stars, but when he sank two fingers into her pussy, she saw whole constellations.

"Fuck, Princess. You taste like the sweetest wine."

Auraelia fisted the sheets under her hands and threw her head back in ecstasy.

An incoherent stream of words along with his name fell from her lips, mixed together with moans of pleasure.

Daemon took his time working her back to the edge, alternating between sucking her clit and flicking it with his tongue. While his fingers pumped in and out of her core, curling to stroke that delicious spot that made her legs quake.

When the walls of her pussy began to pulse around his fingers, he stopped and looked at her over the dusting of curls at the apex of her thighs. His face glistening with evidence of her arousal, "Be a good girl and come all over my face, and I'll give you my cock."

When his head went back down, it was with renewed vigor.

His fingers pumped faster as his tongue assaulted the bundle of nerves between her legs.

Auraelia felt it building, the heaviness in her stomach. The tightening of her muscles. Her breathing sped up as her legs started to shake, and when he sucked her clit into his mouth, the world exploded around them. Her release ripped through her, the way thunder rolled across the sky and was followed by a bolt of lightning. Slow to build, then catastrophic and beautiful.

She clamped her legs around his head, her hips jerking as she rocked against his mouth and rode out her orgasm.

Daemon didn't slow. His fingers were still coiled inside her, steadily stroking the walls of her sex, all while his tongue issued a punishing pace on her clit.

Before she could even begin to come down, he slid a hand up her body to her breasts. Taking the painfully stiff peak of one nipple between his thumb and forefinger, he pinched and twisted.

The painful sensation mixed with the heady euphoria of her first orgasm sent Auraelia flying back into the stars.

Daemon withdrew his fingers, sucking the evidence of her release from the digits before returning to her drenched pussy. She could feel it slipping out of her entrance and down her ass, but he dragged his tongue up her slit, catching every drop.

"I could lick this pussy all day and never tire of your taste."

When he released the shadows that had been holding her wrists, she threaded her fingers into his hair and pulled his head up until he was looking at her.

A look of indignation crossed his face. "I'm not finished with my dessert, Auraelia. Do I need to restrain you once more?" Silky ribbons of shadow wrapped along her arms to emphasize his threat.

"No, but I do believe you promised me your cock if I came all over your face." Her eyes were heavy with the post-orgasmic bliss that had ripped through her, but they burned into his all the same. Knowing the effect it had on him, she bit her bottom lip. When his eyes dilated, a wave of exhilaration ran through her.

Checkmate.

Ever so slowly, Daemon withdrew from his spot between her legs, wiping the remaining evidence of her cum from his face and then sucking it off of his fingers.

Heat flooded her core once more.

Daemon's gaze was one of a predator stalking its prey.

Slow.

Meticulous.

Calculating.

Something primal took root when he looked at her like that, the need to claim him and be claimed by him. It was foreign, but something about it felt right. There was no denying the pull between them, and the fact that he was leaving the following day only intensified the draw.

Auraelia's eyes traveled down his body, landing on the impressive shaft between his legs. The head had a purple hue from lack of release, precum dripped from the tip, and the veins seemed to be pulsing with every heartbeat. She licked her lips as her gaze traveled the expanse of Daemon's muscled torso.

Drawing her eyes back to his face, she was met with a wicked smile.

"See something you want, my star?" Daemon's voice was husky with need, and his eyes seared into hers as he stroked himself.

His movements made it hard for her to keep her eyes on his face. They kept traveling back to where his hand worked his cock, and her pussy throbbed with every slide of his hand.

"Ye–" she cleared her throat, "Yes," she answered, licking her lips once again.

Daemon sucked air through his teeth, "Auraelia, if you don't keep that tongue in your mouth, I'm going to give you something to do with it."

She felt the heat of the flush as it crept across her cheeks.

Daemon tilted his head to the side, a cocky smirk on his face, "Is that what you want, Princess?"

When she only nodded, he tsked in disapproval.

"I need your words, Auraelia. Maybe if you behave, I'll let you suck my cock later. But right now, I want your pussy wrapped around me and you screaming my name."

Auraelia's eyes widened at his words.

Fuck, that was hot. Wait...Why was that hot?

Under normal circumstances, she would have snapped back at comments like that. She didn't like being talked down to or degraded. But for some reason, when Daemon did it, her pussy throbbed, and desire pooled between her legs.

Auraelia nodded once more. "Okay."

Then licked her lips.

She knew the moment her tongue swept across her bottom lip that she was about to be in a world of trouble.

A growl rumbled deep in his throat before he prowled up her body.

Reverently, his hands glided over the soft flesh of her legs, stomach, and breasts. The calluses on his palms creating an exquisite juxtaposition to the tender kisses that he left trailing in their wake. Slowly, he made his way up the center line of her torso, stopping at her sternum before venturing off to lavish her breasts.

His hot mouth encased one of her nipples, sucking it into his mouth and gently scraping it with his teeth while his hand palmed the other, pinching the stiff peak between his fingers.

Auraelia groaned and arched her back, shoving her chest further into his hold.

Making sure to pay equal attention to both breasts, he switched sides before trailing further up her body. Daemon removed his hand from her breast, gliding it up to encircle her throat in a light hold while he nipped and sucked various areas on her shoulder—marking her with deep purple bruises.

With his hand still wrapped around her throat, he sat up—his erection hanging heavily between them. Gently, he stroked the racing pulse point in her neck. "Is this okay?"

His grip was light enough that she could still breathe and speak. "Yes."

Daemon tightened his grip, cutting off some of her blood flow, "How about this? You can nod or shake your head if speaking is difficult."

His eyes were nearly black, burning with unadulterated desire, and Auraelia was pretty sure that her gaze was a mirror of his own. When she nodded her head, Daemon smiled. "Good girl."

Those two words set her ablaze, and her clit pulsed with every beat of her heart.

Daemon released his grip, allowing her to breathe more freely.

"If that ever gets to be too much, I want you to tap my thigh twice. Do you understand?" Retightening his grip on her throat, more thoroughly cutting off her oxygen, he waited until she tapped his thigh twice before releasing her once more, earning her another, *"Good girl,"* that made her flush.

Feeling bold, Auraelia slid her hand up his thigh to the point where his cock jutted out from his body.

Wrapping her fingers around his shaft, she began to work her hand over his considerable length. Daemon hissed through his teeth and squeezed his eyes closed as her hand slid up and down his shaft, using his pre-cum to lubricate her movements.

When he opened his eyes, fiery passion stared back at her as his gaze locked onto hers.

Daemon leaned over until he was so close that their breath mingled. She moved her hand faster, and a growl sounded deep in his throat. "Guide me home, my star." His grip on her throat tightened as she aligned the head of his cock at her entrance. Daemon took a deep breath, then pushed his way inside.

Auraelia felt the delicious burn of her body stretching to accommodate his girth, and when he started pumping into her, it was pure bliss. He filled her so completely; she had a feeling that no one would ever compare.

His grip on her throat was firm, but it loosened when he pressed his lips to hers.

It wasn't anything like the kiss they shared earlier. This kiss was a battleground.

It was all teeth and tongues.

Lips being sucked and nipped.

He devoured her mouth, while he pulverized her pussy with his cock.

Daemon sat back on his heels and propped one of her ankles on his shoulder before shadow walking a pillow from the head of the bed into his awaiting hands and shoving it under her hips. The new angle was full of new sensations. She felt him deeper than before and the ridge at the head of his cock rubbed against the front wall of her entrance with every stroke, guiding her back to the edge.

Auraelia was in sensory overload.

It was as if he had hands everywhere. With one hand on her hip and his other holding her ankle on his shoulder, his shadows played over her body. Some ghosted over her in feather light touches, while others were more deliberate in their functions. Phantom hands made of sparkling shadows, like the stars from sky had been caught in their depths, tantalized her most sensitive parts. There were ribbons of smoke rubbing her clit, while another massaged her breasts and tweaked her nipples.

Shadows soft as satin wrapped around her throat, allowing Daemon control the pressure without using his hands. He didn't bind her wrists this time, making sure she was able to tap his thigh if things got too intense. She felt him everywhere, and it was too much and not enough at the same time.

The familiar heavy warmth of her growing release settled into her bones.

There was a tingle in her extremities, which could have been from her impending orgasm or lack of oxygen–possibly both. But a split second before she tapped his thigh, her orgasm ripped through her.

As her eyes rolled to the back of her head, she could have sworn she saw the goddess' in Arcelia. But Daemon's stream of curses, followed by her name being said like a prayer as he followed her into oblivion, brought her back to the present.

Daemon released the hold his shadows had on her as the walls of her pussy clenched and pulsed around his cock, milking every drop of his release.

When they were both spent, he withdrew and laid down next to her. Pulling her into his side, he nuzzled into her neck and placed a kiss behind her ear.

"You're so beautiful, my star."

Auraelia smiled to herself and sank into his embrace. "What now?"

"Now? Now, we rest. Because I am nowhere near done with you yet." His words were a promise–one that Auraelia fully intended to make sure that he kept.

"Plus, we still have dessert to eat," he added.

The next thing she knew, the tray of berries, chocolate, and sweetened cream from the table in her sitting area was swathed in shadows and sitting next to her head.

Auraelia chuckled, "Show off."

She felt his chest shake as he laughed. "Rest, my star," then after placing a chaste kiss below her ear he whispered, "you're going to need it."

Chapter Seventeen

Daemon

He laid awake, staring at the deep blue canopy, feeling at home under the constellations of stars that were beaded there. Auraelia had fallen asleep in his arms, their legs tangled together, and her arm draped over his chest.

It seems we both like to sleep under the stars.

She hadn't been out long, but he could tell that she'd already entered a deep slumber; her breath coming in deep and steady.

As the early morning sun began to peek around the edges of her dark curtains, signaling the end of their night together and the beginning of an unknown time apart, Daemon idly ran his fingers up and down her arm, his cock growing hard with the memories of last night.

The chocolate and whipped sweet cream from their dessert hadn't been used on the fruit that accompanied them on the tray. Instead, he'd dripped and painted Auraelia's naked body in the decadence, turning her into his own personal dessert. The salt of her skin mixed with the sweetness of the cream and the rich notes of the chocolate were a heady combination.

Not to be outdone, she returned the favor.

Coating his length in sweetened cream, she then took him deep into her mouth and sucked him clean. He'd fucked her mouth after that–just as he told her he would. Shoving his cock deep into her throat.

She took him so beautifully.

Swallowing around his cock when he hit the back of her throat.

Tears running down her face, staining her cheeks, as she struggled for air.

But every time he gave her words of praise her eyes shone with pride, and lust.

They'd violated every surface of her chambers, just like they had in his. Auraelia rode his cock in the shower after they washed off what remained of the chocolate and cream. He'd then splayed her out on the cold tiles of the bathing chamber, and devoured her pussy like it was his last meal.

When they eventually made it back into her bed chamber, he'd bent her over the foot of her bed, taking her from behind–then again against the wall.

Between her mouth and her pussy, he was certain he'd died and joined his goddess in Arcelia.

Hours had passed, and when they were officially spent, their bodies weak and exhausted from pleasure, Daemon had shadow walked them into her bathing chambers and drew them a bath.

Auraelia's golden tub was beautifully crafted, and large enough for four people to fit in comfortably, but what pulled his attention was the skylight directly above it. Perfectly framing the moon and constellations that hung in the night sky. As their light trickled into the space, it cast Auraelia in an ethereal glow. She looked like a star that had fallen to shine just for him.

The water had chilled by the time they emerged. Auraelia's eyes were heavy as he dried her body and wrapped her in a thick towel, and she was completely at ease in his arms as he took them back to the bed–where she'd fallen asleep as soon as he pulled her into his embrace.

She's a fucking goddess, and I have to leave her here.

Daemon released a deep sigh, disturbing the hair on top of her head. As the morning light grew brighter, the birds began to sing their songs, and it was only a matter of time before Piper or one of Auraelia's lady's maids came into her room to rouse her for the day. He needed to leave. Goddess knows, he needed to leave. But he had a hard time walking away from the slumbering beauty next to him. He didn't want to just vanish without saying goodbye, but he also wanted her to get the sleep she needed.

Detangling himself from Auraelia's limbs, he resigned himself to the fact that if he didn't go, it would cause more trouble than either of them needed to deal with. Carefully lifting her arm, he slid out from the bed, holding his breath and praying to every goddess that she didn't wake.

When she curled in on herself, he let out a breath of relief. Gently sweeping hair out of her face, he bent down to press a light kiss to her temple; then took one last moment to drink in the beauty that was Auraelia, Crown Princess of the Court of Emerald.

In the three days that he had the pleasure of knowing her, he realized three things with utmost certainty.

She was beautiful.

She was fierce.

And she was *extremely* out of his reach.

She was the heir to her throne, just as he was the heir to the Sapphire Isles. The political ramifications that could come with them having a relationship would either be amazing or catastrophic. But that didn't stop him from wanting her or doing whatever he could do to try and keep her. Where they went from here was up to her, he just hoped that they were on the same page.

Every fiber of his being rebelled against this. Against leaving her. But he needed to get back to his people, to his ill father.

Daemon pulled on his shadows, using them to gather his belongings from around the space. Then, with one last look at Auraelia, ribbons of obsidian coalesced around him until they swallowed his form and walked him out of her room.

Possibly out of her life.

Chapter Eighteen

Auraelia

Auraelia woke to sun streaming in around the edges of her curtains, a contented smile on her face. Rolling over, she stretched her hand out, feeling for the warm body that had been pressed against her all night–only to be met with an empty space and cold sheets.

He was gone.

Left and didn't even have the decency to wake her and say goodbye.

Auraelia scoffed and shook her head. *Of course, he's gone. Stupid. Stupid girl.*

She took a deep breath and pushed all of her anger through a ragged exhale.

He's just a man. So what if the sex was spectacular? It's not important. He's *not important. He's just another cock. You knew he was leaving. Get it together.*

Even as she repeated the words in her head, her heart knew they were false.

Eyes still closed, she sat up, and steeled herself for the day and the inevitable bombardment of questions from Piper.

Pushing her anger and hurt away into the darkest recesses of her heart and mind, she inhaled and held it until her lungs screamed for air.

Then slowly released her breath and opened her eyes.

"Well, that was fun to watch." Piper sat on the edge of Auraelia's bed, leaning against the bedpost with her legs crossed at the ankle, twirling a rose between her fingers.

"What the fuck, Piper! Are you trying to kill me?" Auraelia's hand flew to her chest, her heart racing beneath her palm.

Piper chuckled and continued to twirl the rose. "This was sitting on the pillow next to your head when I came in this morning. There's also a note." Her eyes flicked toward the pillows to Auraelia's left before she tossed her the rose.

Auraelia's heart skipped.

Stupid.

Picking up the rose, she turned to where Piper had indicated.

There, sitting on the dark blue fabric, was a folded piece of cream parchment, sealed with a midnight blue wax seal. *Daemon.*

Deciding to ignore the letter for the time being, Auraelia turned back to where her friend was still perched on her bed.

"You're not going to read it?" Piper asked as she lifted a brow, curiosity lacing her features.

Auraelia shrugged, feigning nonchalance. "Not right now, no."

Piper's smile turned devilish. "Is it from who I think it's from?"

"Hmm?" Auraelia lifted the rose to her nose, inhaling its sweet fragrance.

"Oh, ok. I see." Piper jumped off the bed and rushed around the side in an attempt to grab the note.

Throwing herself at her pillow, Auraelia barely managed to grasp the note before Piper got her fingers on it. Clutching it to her chest, she narrowed her eyes at her friend, while Piper stared back–a knowing smile on her face.

"I'll leave you to it then, and I'll let the ladies know that they can set up breakfast in the sitting room. Oh, and Rae, put some clothes on, yeah?" Piper winked, and then left the room, pulling the door closed behind her.

Auraelia looked down to where she clutched the letter to her chest.

Nude.

She was completely and utterly naked, and her sheet had fallen down to her waist in the mad dash to grab her letter from Daemon.

Pulling the loose sheet from her bed, she wrapped it around herself before crossing the room to pull back the curtains. She stood there a moment, basking in the early morning glow that streamed through her windows. Then, taking a deep breath, she broke the seal on her letter and steeled her heart and mind for whatever it contained. As she unfolded the parchment, something clattered to the floor. Laying by her feet attached to a delicate silver chain, was a magnificent sapphire that glittered in the light. Stooping to pick it up, she palmed the stone and began to read the letter.

My Star,

I'm sorry that I left without saying goodbye. I've regretted that decision since I made it. You looked so peaceful, and if I hadn't left when I did, I don't think that I would have been able to leave at all.

I meant what I said, Auraelia. I want to see where this can go.

I want you.

I want to get to know you.

And I know that there may be repercussions with us both being who we are and the responsibilities that we hold, but I'm willing to try if you are.

I'm leaving this in your hands. Like everything else we've done, you decide where this does or doesn't go. If you want to end it here, we will. But I hope you choose this.

Enclosed is a raw sapphire that I've imbued with my magic. If you choose this journey with me, you can use it to send letters directly to me, instead of relying on others to make it to and from Kalmeera. Simply grasp the stone in one hand and the letter in the other, think of me, and the magic will take it from there.

I hope I hear from you soon.

If you choose not to pursue this, I understand. And if that is the case, I feel I must tell you once more. You are beautiful. You are fierce. And I am a better man for having met you.

Until we meet again, my star.

-D

Auraelia read the letter again, her heart hammering in her chest as she committed every word to memory. But despite her eagerness to be with him, to see where this could go, she needed to think. There was so much that needed to be processed and figured out, but none of that was going to happen right at this moment–or without coffee.

Taking a deep breath to calm her racing thoughts, Auraelia shifted her attention to the pendant nestled in her palm. The stone was a deep cobalt with veins of white coursing throughout, and upon closer inspection, it looked as if there was something *living* within it. Swirling ribbons of sparkling onyx moved deep within the heart of the stone.

Daemon's shadows.

Auraelia looped the chain around her neck. It was long enough that the sapphire pendant hung between her breasts, and it seemed to pulse and warm against her skin.

She refolded the parchment and tucked it beneath her pillow, placing the sheet back onto her bed, Auraelia hurried into her bathing chamber to wash up.

"Piper!" she shouted as she crossed her room.

Within seconds Piper was poking her head into the room. "You bellowed?"

"What's on the schedule for today?"

"I believe it's just training with Ser Aeron, why?"

She met Piper's curious gaze with one of mischief.

"Oh, I know that look. Where are we heading?"

"It's a beautiful day for a swim, don't you think?"

Piper's smile was brighter than any star in the night sky as she turned and headed out of the bathing chamber.

Auraelia called after her, "Oh, and Piper? Please don't destroy my chambers. The letter is under the pillow. Put it back after you're finished snooping, okay?"

Piper's laugh echoed back into the bathing chamber. "Understood!"

Once she was dressed and had finished her coffee, she sat down in one of the chairs framing the fireplace in her sitting area. Piper had returned to her own chambers to finish readying for the day, leaving Auraelia alone with her thoughts.

Taking out the necessary items from the table next to her, she wrote a response to Daemon's letter. When she finished, she folded the parchment and grabbed a sprig of lavender from the dried bundle she kept with her stationary. Placing it on the opening of the letter, she dripped sage green wax over the stem, and stamped it closed with her sigil.

Pulling the sapphire from between her breasts, she concentrated on the instructions that Daemon gave in his letter. Stone in one hand and letter in the other, Auraelia closed her eyes and thought of him.

Of his perfectly tousled raven hair.

Of eyes the color of spring grass with pools of liquid gold.

And a smirk so sinful that even the memory made her flush.

The stone pulsed in her hand, and then she felt it. The silky caress of his magic as it slid over her skin, then it–and the letter–were gone.

It fucking worked.

Auraelia opened her eyes and stared down at her now empty hand in disbelief.

Tucking the stone back into her blouse, she stood and headed for the door.

After an intense night with Daemon, followed by yet another equally intense training session with Ser Aeron, Auraelia was spent. Her muscles were liquid, and she was looking forward to soaking in the cool waters of the lake. She and Piper had stumbled across it on one of their excursions outside of the castle walls and it quickly became one of their best kept secrets.

Despite their exhaustion from training, they were giddy with excitement and headed straight for the stables when training was finished.

Piper had already spoken with the stable master that morning, so their mounts were already saddled and ready to go. Auraelia sidled up to her horse, a huge grin on her face and an apple in each hand.

"Hello, Jasira." The mare whinnied, shaking out her mane and stomping her hooves in excitement.

Jasira wasn't her first horse, but she was her favorite. She was beautiful, with a chestnut coat, and stockings the color of fresh snow on all four legs that matched the color of her mane and tail. The mare had been a gift from her mother on her twentieth birthday, and Auraelia had spent every day with her. Learning her quirks, understanding her movements, and growing their bond. They were a perfect match. Both reserved, but wild when they were allowed to roam free. They also both had a temper, which had almost gotten Auraelia thrown more times than she could count. But one look into the large brown eyes of that horse, and she knew that they would be companions for life.

Auraelia idly stroked Jasira's velvety nose, while she fed her the apples in her hand. Piper had already climbed into the saddle of her own mare, a painted beauty of chestnut and white named Miara.

"Rae." Piper kept her voice low, but it was enough to spur her into motion. It wasn't often that they didn't have a full schedule, and if they wanted to keep it that way they needed to leave. *Now.*

Auraelia quickly mounted her horse, and once she was fully seated, she nudged Jasira into a walk and led the mare out of the stables with Piper following close behind.

When they were far enough away from the castle, they urged the horses into a gallop and shot through the trees that lined the training field. The same trees that she had spent the previous afternoon under with Daemon.

As they skirted the last of the large oak trees that lined the wall surrounding the castle, Auraelia looked for the vines that concealed a secret door. It was an escape door built into the wall in case the castle was under attack. Far enough away that it wasn't obvious, but close enough to be useful. It was also long forgotten, which made it perfect for sneaking out of the grounds without guards.

Finally locating the door, they swung down from their saddles. Auraelia swept the vines aside to open the latch and push the door open, while Piper gathered the reigns of both mares.

Auraelia held the ivy out of the way while Piper led both of their horses through the opening, before slipping through herself. Once they were all on the opposite side of the wall, the women remounted their horses and set off towards their lake.

Just beyond the field of lavender, was a grove of crape myrtle trees. The blooms varied in color, from a variety of pinks to soft whites and delicate purples that would break away from their stems at the slightest breeze. The blossoms would float in the air like paper confetti, before they drifted to the ground and coated the paths between the trees in a carpet of color.

It was like riding into another world.

At the end of the sea of crape myrtles, was a large willow tree whose branches and leaves draped down and pooled on the ground below. The contrast between the dark vines of the willow and the colors of the crape myrtles was like toeing the line between a dream and a nightmare. But through those thick vines and leaves was a piece of heaven.

Auraelia and Piper had named it Nefeli Lake, which loosely translated into *Cloud Lake*, and it was the perfect embodiment of its name. The water was so clear that there was a perfect mirror of the sky above, giving the illusion of swimming amongst the clouds.

Surrounding the lake was a dense forest of trees that grew so close together that a person would have a tough time weaving between the trunks and their large roots. Leaving the only entrance into the mystical place through the draping willow vines.

Once the women reached the willow, Auraelia called upon her magic. Letting it fill her body with warmth and radiate down into her fingertips. Casting it out until she felt the breeze flow from her hand and in the direction of the tendrils of leaves flowing from the branches above. Gently moving them to the side like a curtain, she nudged Jasira through the opening, making sure that Piper made it through as well before releasing the hold she had on the vines.

When the lake came into view, they dismounted and let the horses roam free so that they could nibble on the spring grass that grew along the shore.

Stopping where the grass merged with the golden sand that surrounded the lake, the women sat down and let the tall grass tickle their arms in the breeze. They sat in contented silence, both basking the sun's rays and soaking in the melodic sounds of the woods around them.

Birds sang from the branches in the trees.

Frogs croaked on rocks nearby.

Water as it trickled over rocks and flowed into the lake from a stream.

It was perfection.

After a while, Auraelia removed her boots, and buried her toes in the warm sand. She was leaning back on her hands, her face tilted to the sun letting its rays warm her skin, when Piper unceremoniously tossed her blouse onto her face.

Auraelia scoffed and yanked the cloth from her face. "Bitch!"

Piper laughed and jogged the short distance from where they had perched on the beach, diving head-first into the crystal blue water.

Auraelia tossed the shirt to the side before standing and stripping out of her own clothing, and dove into the lake after Piper.

Fully submerged in the water, she let the coolness wash over her and seep into her aching muscles. Between physical training, her *vigorous* activities with Daemon over the last few days, and learning to use and control her magic, her muscles were knotted and sore.

Breaking the surface of the water, Auraelia pushed her hair out of her face.

"This is pure *bliss*," Piper whispered from where she floated on her back an arm's length away.

Auraelia leaned back, found her center, and floated along beside her, humming in response. As they floated there in silence, a sense of calm washed over her and she let her mind wander to thoughts of Daemon and the letter that she had sent him.

And smiled.

Chapter Nineteen

Daemon

Daemon stood on the bow of his ship, the Nevermore, when he felt the telltale signs of his magic coiling around his arm before funneling into the pocket on his vest and dissipating. His heart stopped for a fraction of a second.

Hello, my star.

He chuckled to himself, then took a deep breath and inhaled the warm salty air of the sea. Reaching into his pocket, he palmed the small piece of parchment that was nestled in the satin lining. Despite the fact that he was anxious to read what she'd written, he opted to wait until he was in the privacy of his cabin before opening the letter. There was too much to do before they arrived in Kalmeera, and life on the sea could go from calm to potentially disastrous in mere seconds. Thankfully, the trip home was only a day's journey on the Nevermore, and it seemed like the Goddess Narissa was with them. The seas were calm, and the wind was in their favor, filling the sails as she coasted across the Cerulean Sea.

The Nevermore was a beautiful vessel, the fastest in the royal fleet, and she was Daemon's baby.

His father, King Evander, was going to gift him one of the royal vessels when he came of age, as was tradition within the royal family of the Sapphire Isles, but he'd opted for commissioning his own.

He'd overseen everything.

From the initial design and the sourcing of the lumber to her actual construction and maiden voyage. She was small and sleek in comparison to the rest of the royal fleet, with a black stain covering the entirety of the ship and charcoal sails that blended into a stormy sky. Her hull was crafted and carved into the Goddess Narissa's creature of the deep, its tentacles twining as they stretched down the length of the vessel.

She was night incarnate.

A raven sailing on the sea.

And a physical representation of his shadows.

Daemon looked up to where the sails billowed in the wind, their darkness a steep contrast against the bright blue sky above, and smiled. It reminded him of how Auraelia's eyes would shift from a slate gray to one tinged with blue. She was beautiful, but it was when she used her magic that she really took his breath away.

He loved seeing the color of her irises shift to a beautiful shade of green ringed in dark teal, while streaks of peridot shot across like lightning.

When she was completely one with herself and her magic.

Raw and natural.

And he had the sneaking suspicion that she hadn't even tapped into the full weight of her abilities yet.

Reaching back into his pocket, Daemon grasped the letter firmly in his hand as he hollered a few commands to the sailors on the deck before he turned and headed below to his cabin.

The cabins below deck were simple. A bed, a desk, an armoire, and a toilet; all of which were bolted to the floor to keep them from sliding about. Even as a crown prince, he kept the unnecessary frills from the ship. The sea was his comfort. He didn't need down pillows and the finest bedding. He needed the sea, the stars to guide him, and his crew behind him.

With the thought of the stars, *his* star flooded his mind.

Daemon sat on his bed, Auraelia's letter firmly grasped in his hand as he ran his thumb over the sea-green wax seal that kept it closed. He had been doing that for what seemed like hours now. Wanting to know its contents, but afraid to read them all the same.

Breathing in through his nose, Daemon steeled his spine and slid his finger beneath the seal. Unfolding the letter, he closed his eyes and let out the breath he had been holding, then opened them to finally face whatever it was that Auraelia had written.

Dearest Daemon,

I must say, the sapphire is a neat party trick...and hopefully a useful one. It's also beautiful, thank you.

I'm not going to lie and say that I wasn't disappointed when I woke, and you were gone. Thanks for the rose by the way, Piper loved it. But I also understand why you did. Goddess only knows what would have happened if we had been caught together in the early light of the morning. You were right when you said that there could be repercussions from us being together, and I don't know if either of our kingdoms would approve of us exploring whatever this is between us.

What we want, and what is right are conflicting at best. Detrimental at worst.

There is so much that could go wrong, and not just with us. Our kingdoms are in a delicate balance, and the last thing that I want is to put that in jeopardy.

But I also want to be selfish and see what could grow between us.

So, I guess what I'm saying is, yes. Yes to you, and yes to this. But you must understand that my kingdom, and my people, will always come first.

If we are in agreement, then I look forward to this new adventure.

Until next time.

-A

Daemon read and re-read her letter until he had her words memorized.

She wants this.

A real smile graced his face for the first time since leaving Lyndaria.

Refolding the letter, he pulled the sprig of lavender that had been trapped beneath the seal and brought it to his face. Closing his eyes, he inhaled the scent, letting images of Auraelia flood his mind. His cock stiffened behind the laces of his trousers.

With his mind full of thoughts of her, he'd intended to alleviate some of the building pressure of his erection when a quick knock on the door pulled him from his reverie.

You've got to be fucking joking.

Groaning, he reached down to adjust himself, and pocketed the letter before standing to answer the door.

Standing on the other side was none other than Aiden. He leaned against the wall, his hair unusually disheveled, and a cocky smirk on his face as he took in Daemon's appearance.

"Damn, D. You still hung up on the princess?"

"Are you still hung up on her lady in waiting?" Daemon asked, matching Aiden's snide grin.

When his grin faded into a scowl, Daemon rolled his eyes. "Is there something that I can do for you, *Lord* Aiden?"

Matching Aiden's posture, Daemon crossed his arms over his chest and quirked a brow in his friend's direction.

"Nope," he responded, popping the *p* for emphasis. "But we're almost to port. So, you might want to get your ass out of that stuffy box of a room and up on deck." Aiden pushed off the wall and stalked away and up the stairs that led to the main deck of the vessel.

At the mention of home, Daemon's mood immediately lifted. He had planned on replying to Auraelia, but that would have to wait.

Kalmeera had one of the most stunning ports in all of the Sapphire Isles, and the place where ships docked was not a typical port. Instead, boats were met by narrow tunnels of waterways that had been formed into the cliff face surrounding the city. Inside the tunnels, were arches made of black sea rock that the ocean had polished into a shine. Each archway had been inlaid with mother of pearl and depicted beautiful mosaic scenes of the ocean and the world beneath its waves. Traveling under those arches and into the heart of Kalmeera was like sailing into the world of their goddess.

The tunnels themselves were dark as night, but bioluminescence beneath the water's surface transformed the paths into glowing rivers of light. That light was then picked up by the rocks that formed the tunnels, and the mother of pearl in the arches, turning the ceiling and walls into a sparkling night sky.

Every ship that came to the island docked there. Crews would then disembark their own ships with goods, and board the smaller flat boats that would carry them into the city.

Every ship that ported in Kalmeera had to follow these requirements.

Every ship, except the Nevermore.

With her small and sleek design, Daemon's crew was able to navigate her through the narrow passages, bringing her right into the city. Kalmeera was full of bridges and thorough ways that linked different areas of the city, making it easier for citizens to travel throughout the island.

The Nevermore was well known by the citizens, and when her storm cloud sails would crest the line of buildings at the far edge of the city just outside of the tunnels, bells would ring out to welcome their prince home.

Daemon followed Aiden to the upper deck where the captain of the ship was at the helm. The Nevermore may have been his ship, and he may have spent most of his life on the sea, but Daemon knew his strengths–and he knew when to let someone more knowledgeable take over. The captain was Raneese Garreth, the first–and currently the only–female captain in the royal fleet.

Raneese was a beautiful woman, with strong features and a stronger attitude. Her hair was the color of warm coffee that coiled into tight ringlets and bounced around her face. Her bronzed skin glowed beneath the warm rays of the sun, and she had chocolate-colored eyes that sparkled when she laughed and ignited when she was angry. She even had a dimple in her right cheek that would show itself on the rare occasions when she would laugh.

"Captain," Daemon said as he reached the top of the steps.

Raneese stood at the helm, confidently navigating the ship through the tunnels that lead into the city. "Highness."

Daemon met Raneese when she tried to sneak aboard his ship while he was ported along the region of the Court of Opal. She was originally from the Court of Pearl, but something from her past had sent her running. When she landed in Opal, Lady Aesira took her in and gave her asylum.

Raneese spent five years under Lady Aesira's tutelage, learning how to defend herself and seeking counsel for ways to work through her past. But when her past seemed to catch up to her in Opal, Raneese decided to run once again–right onto Daemon's ship.

He found her stowed away below deck, hiding behind barrels of fruit in the kitchen, a few days after they had left the port. When he asked her who she was and why she was on his ship, she tried to fight him right then and there. But when that didn't work, and he'd assured her that he would do her no harm, she explained she was on the run but would say no more. The look on her face was haunting, and there was pain in her eyes, so Daemon didn't pry any further. Instead, he extended her the same asylum that she had been offered in the Court of Opal.

Throughout the rest of the journey back to Kalmeera, Daemon discovered her skill when it came to sailing. As it turned out, she grew up working on boats in Pearl, and was an asset when they encountered a storm. She'd managed to steer the ship safely through the tempest, saving both his crew and the vessel in the process. When they made it back to Kalmeera, he made her a permanent member of his crew and named her captain. Not only giving her citizenship in Kalmeera and the safety that it provided, but also a family who accepted her for who she was without prying to things she didn't want to talk about.

Since then, she had become one of his closest friends and confidants.

As they made their way through the tunnels, Daemon looked over the side of the Nevermore and into the illuminated water below. Smiling as the sound of bells filled the air, welcoming him home.

The city was beautiful.

Full of cottage style homes with beams that crisscrossed the stucco forming the outer walls. There were windows of multi-colored sea glass that cast kaleidoscopes of color when the sunlight shone through at the right angle. Tall stone bridges throughout the city linked different areas together with ease, giving its citizen's full access to the city that they lived in. And dozens of small, flat skiffs carried boat crews and their goods to the market in the heart of the city, contributing to the health and wealth of Kalmeera's, and Ixora's, economy.

He smiled and waved as people came out in droves to welcome him and his crew home. He took in the men, women, and children that walked the streets going about their daily routines and envied the simplicity that their lives held.

"It's good to be home," Aiden said as he walked up to stand beside his friend.

"That it is. The question is, what are we coming home *to*?"

Daemon hadn't heard from his father or mother since he left for Lyndaria and had adopted the *'no news is good news'* mentality while he was away.

A week before King Evander was to leave for Lyndaria, he had mysteriously fallen ill. None of the doctors in the Sapphire Isles could determine what was causing his illness, or how to cure it. They'd tried everything under the sun, all to no avail. King Evander was bedridden and pale, and unable to keep much of anything down.

With his father wasting away day by day, and with no cure in sight, Daemon was reluctant to leave his side. By the time he was to leave for Lyndaria in his father's stead, King Evander was no better, but also no worse. Leading the doctors to believe that they had at the very least staved off the illness, but it still left him too weak to travel. So, against his better judgment, Daemon left and headed to see the princess in Lyndaria crowned.

And despite his earlier reservations regarding the trip, he had never been happier to carry out his *'princely duties'* as he had been when he was tangled in the sheets with his star.

The closer that the Nevermore got to the castle of Kalmeera, the more anxious he became. The castle was the jewel of the island. Built on the edge of the Seraphine Mountains, it overlooked the ocean beyond. Tall white towers, with ivy draped stairs spiraled along their outer walls shot into the sky. Each tower was topped with a dome of sapphire blue glass that made the space inside look as if it were under water. The front of the castle opened up into a grove of fruit trees, from guava and fig, to avocado and banana.

A long stone bridge connected the grounds to its people, giving them unfettered access to the wealth of produce that was available. There were rows of plumeria trees, whose buds varied from the purest white to vibrant pinks that faded into yellow, giving even the prettiest sunset pause.

Throughout the island, bird-of-paradise and hibiscus grew in abundance, while towering palms provided shade. Birds as bright as the colorful flora flitted from tree to tree, their songs filling the air.

There was color and life everywhere.

By the time the ship finally docked, and he was once again on Kalmeeran soil, Daemon smiled. After four long days away, he was finally home, and it was time to see what had happened in his absence.

When Daemon entered the castle, he was greeted by the glittering smile of Queen Avyanna.

"Oh, my son, welcome home." The queen wrapped him in a warm embrace, before releasing him and cupping his cheek in her hand.

"Hello, Mother," he replied, leaning into her touch. "And where is my lovely sister today?" His tone dripped with mirth.

"Oh, she's around somewhere, you can catch up later." She waved off his question, clearly more interested in the ones that were tickling the tip of her tongue.

Queen Avyanna stood there looking resplendent in her gown as she gazed lovingly at her son. The clothes in the Court of Sapphire were very different from most of Ixora–the hot and breezy climate of the islands calling for thinner fabrics and fewer layers.

The queen wore a gown of pale blue silk with a chiffon overlay that shifted into darker shades as it fell down the length of the solid underskirt. While geometric panels constructed the bodice, giving structure to the otherwise airy garment. The back was cut low, framing the floral tattoo that stretched down the length of her spine, and white strings of pearls draped across the opening.

Her straight, raven hair had been coiled into a knot at the nape of her neck, and atop her head sat a spired tiara of pearls and sapphires. Her eyes matched the color of the gems in her crown and were framed by arched brows and dark lashes, and her olive skin was golden from frequent time spent in the sun. When her full lips tilted up, showing her bright smile, Daemon smiled one of his own. He hadn't realized how much he missed his mother until he was once again in her presence.

"How was your trip? And your voyages there and back? How was the coronation? Did Queen Adelina treat you well?" The queen's bombardment of questions made him chuckle.

"Mother." Daemon tilted his head, a look of amusement on his face as he rolled his eyes.

"What? Can't a mother ask after her son?"

"Of course, but we have plenty of time to catch up." He chuckled once more and shook his head. Moments passed before he cleared his throat, his tone taking on a more serious tone. "How's father?"

Queen Avyanna sighed, "Your father is much the same when it comes to his illness, but his body is tired. I fear that without a cure, or at the bare minimum knowledge of what it is that ails him, he will soon leave this world and join Narissa in Arcelia."

There was a moment of tense silence between them as Daemon let the information soak in. He was about to speak when she looped her arm through his, a smile stretching across her face as she gazed up at him. "Come, we'll go see him together."

Daemon looked at his mother and saw beneath her smile.

Saw the sadness and fear in her eyes despite the mask she tried to keep in place to pacify everyone around her.

It made his heart ache.

Laying his hand over his mother's, he gave her a gentle, reassuring squeeze. "Lead the way."

A glimmer of light entered his mother's cornflower blue eyes before she turned and led the way to his father.

They made their way through the castle to the master suite. Taking a deep breath, he reached for the tarnished gold handle of the door, but before he could turn the knob, his mother squeezed his bicep, snagging his attention. She gave him a warm, reassuring smile, then nodded. Daemon steeled his spine, then turned the knob, and stepped into the room.

Just as his mother had said, his father was in the same condition that he had been in when Daemon left. But he looked...small, and King Evander was anything but a small man. He stood six-foot-five and was as strong as a hurricane. His father's once golden skin was now pale and ashen. His chestnut hair was muted, and there seemed to be more gray than not. The strong man that taught him almost everything he knew, laid frail in a bed propped up by pillows. Yet his moss-colored eyes still held the fire that had always burned in their depths.

Daemon spent hours sitting with his father, telling him all about his trip to the mainland of Ixora. He told him of the coronation, and the balls, the food, and focused entirely too long on the deliciousness of the chocolate croissants that Auraelia had introduced him to. He spoke of the kindness he'd received, and of the council meeting that he had been invited to attend. He told him everything.

Everything except about his time with Lyndaria's princess.

"You seem to have had a pleasant time." His father's voice was strained, like he hadn't used it in days.

Daemon nodded and pulled the letter from Queen Adelina out of his pocket. "I almost forgot. Queen Adelina asked that I give this to you. Something about trade agreements and some other information?"

He watched as his father opened the letter and read it carefully. Watched as his father's brows furrowed, then passed the letter to his wife. When Queen Avyanna finished, she sighed and gave her husband a questioning look. King Evander shook his head in response to whatever unspoken question had been asked, the queen sighed once more, then stood.

Daemon rose too, his eyes flitting between his parents. "What's in the letter, Father?"

King Evander was barely able to shake his head. "Nothing that needs to be discussed right now, my son. Now, if you'll excuse me, I'm tired and think I will rest for a while."

Queen Avyanna came around the other side of the bed and fluffed the pillows behind the king's head. Sweeping hair off of his brow, the queen stooped down to place a kiss on her husband's temple before turning toward her son. "Come on, Daemon. I'm sure you're exhausted." Grabbing his arm, she led him toward the door.

When they were on the other side, she pulled the door closed softly behind them. Her shoulders dropped as she let out a breath he hadn't realized she'd been holding. She then straightened her spine and turned to her son with a sly smile on her lips. "So," she began, "Tell me about Princess Auraelia."

He must have had shock written on his face because his mother chuckled and shook her head. Placing a warm hand on his cheek, she smiled. "Your eyes were glowing when you spoke of her, and I know it wasn't because she introduced you to chocolate croissants, Daemon." Her eyebrows were raised, and a knowing smirk was on her lips. "Walk with me. You can tell me all about her while we walk and then while we eat. I'm sure you're hungry."

Daemon released a resigned sigh as he extended his arm for his mother.

He escorted her through the castle to the dining hall, and as they sat down to eat, he told her about Auraelia.

About her beauty and her sass.

Her stubborn head and her pure heart.

And he told her about the way that his soul pulled to hers.

When he finished, his mother's eyes were rimmed in silver and full of love and pride. From across the table, she grasped both of his hands in hers, and gave them a tight squeeze. "Invite her to the summer solstice celebration."

Daemon was wide-eyed and speechless. The summer solstice celebration was a huge event in the Court of Sapphire Isles. It had been decades since they had invited anyone outside of the islands to the festivities, let alone a princess from another kingdom.

"Wh–what?" He stumbled over his words, unsure if he had heard his mother clearly.

"Invite her to the summer solstice," she spoke slowly, enunciating every word to make sure it sunk in the second time.

"You want me to invite Princess Auraelia...to our solstice celebration? Why? What was in that letter, Mother?"

The queen sighed. "Why? Because I want my son to be happy. Is that such a terrible thing for a mother to want? As for the letter, Queen Adelina mentioned that you and her daughter seemed...cozy, during your visit. She's just being cautious and sharing information. You know that the treaty between our kingdoms states that the heirs can't marry. So, if you're serious about pursuing whatever it is between you, and if she is of the same mind, you need to discuss that not-so-little detail. Okay?" Her eyes bored into his own, conveying the importance of everything that she had just told him.

Daemon nodded and squeezed his mother's hands. "I understand, mother. I'll keep that in mind. In the meantime, I think I'll head up to bed, if that's alright?"

She smiled and released her son. "Of course. Rest well."

Daemon circled the table to where his mother sat and leaned down to press a kiss to her cheek. When he pulled away, she grabbed his chin. "Promise me that you'll consider inviting her to the celebration. I would love to meet the woman who has stolen my son's heart in a matter of days." With a wink, she released his chin, allowing him to stand to his full height once more.

He shook his head but smiled. "I'll think about it. Goodnight, Mother."

"Goodnight, my son."

As the Crown Prince, Daemon had one of the largest suites in the castle; not that he spent much time in it. There was a study, or sitting area, that had two sets of large paned glass doors that opened onto the attached balcony and looked out over the castle grounds and out to the city beyond.

His study was simple, with pale gray walls that gave it an airy feel.

He had a desk, and a simple sitting area with worn leather furniture surrounding a low table–that still held the maps and books of Lyndaria that he had been perusing before he left. There was an entire wall of bookcases that held everything from his private collection of novels, to information and history on Kalmeera, The Sapphire Isles as a whole, and all of Ixora.

Opposite the windows, was his bedchamber, which was the complete opposite of his study. Swathed in dark shades of charcoal and the deepest teals.

His bed was stained the same color as his ship, while the bedding and rugs brought a pop of rich color to the space. A bronze chandelier hung from the ceiling, and there were coordinating sconces that hung on the wall over twin side tables that matched the bed frame.

Black stone made up the majority of his bathing chamber, all except for the large tub that sat in the center of the floor. It was large enough to fit four people and made of marble that contrasted the rest of the room. Black veins coursed through the white stone of the tub, reminding Daemon of the tendrils of his magic.

Daemon stepped into his suite and pulled the door closed behind him. Leaning against it, he ran his hands through his hair before dragging them down his face. Letting out a groan, he strolled across the room to the bar that was nestled between the floor-to-ceiling windows. He poured himself a finger of whiskey, and he drained the glass—not even letting the flavor settle on his tongue before pouring another.

Taking the crystal glass and decanter with him across the room, he sat behind his desk and let his body sink into the worn leather. Pinching the bridge of his nose, Daemon finished his drink before pulling Auraelia's letter from his pocket.

Unfolding it, he laid it out on the desk and reread the words that were still ingrained in his mind.

She wants this.

Grabbing a piece of parchment, he picked up the black feather quill that sat on his desk and began to pen his response to *his star*.

Daemon sat at his desk for what seemed like hours, writing and rewriting his response to Auraelia. He couldn't seem to turn the words swirling around in his mind into a coherent thought on paper.

Between the words he wanted to say, and the ones that his mother had planted in his head, he was a mess. He was unsure if he wanted to invite her to the solstice celebration as his mother had suggested. Their relationship was new and balanced precariously on the edge on a blade. One false move could send them teetering over the edge. That aside, his mother's reminder of the treaty was enough to send his mind spiraling all on its own.

He knew of the long-standing treaty of course, but it had been written centuries ago so he had just assumed it wasn't a prevalent issue. But his mother bringing it to light showed just how real, and how current, that treaty was.

"No two persons destined to reign, shall share in the blessed tradition of matrimony if it should intertwine the two houses of rule. The Court of Emerald and the Court of the Sapphire Isles agree to work with each other, and not against each other. For the betterment of the whole of Ixora, there shall never be one in control. With a system of checks and balances from the Lords and Ladies of courts surrounding our realm, may the goddesses shine their light down upon their people."

Thinking of how much that treaty complicated the already challenging situation between him and Auraelia, made his head throb. As the crown prince, he knew his duty to his position and his people; as did Auraelia. But as a man of flesh and bone and blood, he knew what was in his soul, and his soul called to hers.

Daemon took a deep, cleansing breath and pressed his quill to the parchment. When he was satisfied with the letter, he folded the parchment and sealed it with midnight colored wax and pressed his signet ring into the warm liquid. Then with a wave of his hand, it was gone.

He let a small smile form on his lips.

Sliding his chair back from his desk, he stood, and headed into his bedchamber for a much-needed shower and sleep.

Chapter Twenty

Auraelia

Auraelia woke to the sound of curtains being drawn away from the windows. The sound, coupled with the bright light of the early morning, had her reaching for a blanket to cover her head, only to find there was none. She sat up abruptly, the book she had been reading the night before toppling to the floor. Reaching for the fallen novel, she lost her balance and rolled from the couch in her sitting room onto the floor, landing with a surprised yelp. Groaning, she rested her head on the cool wooden floor.

"Well, that was certainly graceful," Piper quipped from across the room.

"Shut up," she responded without changing position.

"Do you need help, Rae?"

Auraelia sighed, then pushed up into a kneeling position and blew her hair out of her face.

"No, I'm fine. I must have fallen asleep while reading."

"That much is obvious. Couldn't sleep or was the book too good?"

"Nope." She popped the *p* for emphasis before pushing up from the ground. "Couldn't sleep."

When she picked up her book from the floor, a folded piece of parchment fell out from between its pages and fluttered to the ground. Auraelia stood, frozen in time. The midnight blue seal staring back at her from the floor. Even from this distance, she could clearly make out the scripted '*D.A.*' that was stamped into the wax.

He wrote back.

Memories of the previous day, of the hours she spent wondering if he would write back, filtered back into her mind.

After they had gone swimming in Nefeli Lake, the rest of the day had gone by in a blur. They'd stopped at the lavender field on the way back and spent hours cutting sprig after sprig of blossoms to bring back with them so that fragrant flowers could be turned into whatever was needed. But the green in the stems reminded her of Daemon's eyes.

When they returned to the castle, they dropped the flowers off in the kitchens and ended up staying to help the chef prepare for dinner. It wasn't often that Auraelia got to spend time in the castle kitchens, but she treasured the time all the same.

It started after she and Piper had stolen sweets when they were ten. Their punishment had been to help the ladies in the kitchen remake what they had taken. Ever since then, both Piper and Auraelia would sneak away to the kitchen to help whenever they could. But as she chopped chocolate for tomorrow's pastries, her mind drifted back to sharing those same pastries with him.

When there was nothing else for them to do in the kitchen, both women retired to their suites to bathe and get ready for dinner. They ate in the dining hall and played drinking games with Xander afterwards, then they all retired to their rooms for the evening.

She'd been bone tired when she got back to her chambers, but her mind was everywhere. And no matter how hard she tried, it always drifted back to Daemon and the million questions surrounding their new-found relationship.

What were they to each other?

How would this even work?

Did her letter actually make it to him, or was it some magical fluke?

But the question that had been circling around and around all day, was whether or not he would even respond to her.

With questions swirling, and after hours of tossing and turning, Auraelia decided to read. She slipped from her bed, wrapped herself in her dressing robe, and padded into the sitting room.

She'd stoked the fire back to life and grabbed her favorite romance novel from the shelves. One that she had read so many times that the cover was worn to the point of being unrecognizable. Then, curling up on the plush settee, she let herself get lost in the world of a book.

Shaking herself from her wayward thoughts, Auraelia stooped to pick up the letter. Letting her thumb run over the rise and fall of every curve to the initials that were embedded into the wax.

Clutching the letter in her hand, she tucked it into the pocket of her dressing gown and crossed the room to where Piper was setting up breakfast.

Later. I'll read it later.

Across the room, Piper was removing the cloches from their trays. The smell of freshly brewed coffee and hot pastries wafted through the air, making her stomach grumble.

Piper chuckled, "Would you come eat, please."

Pulling up the chair opposite her friend, she sat at the table and piled her plate with croissants and berries while Piper filled both of their cups with coffee.

"So, what fell out of the book that had you staring so intently at the floor?" Piper asked before popping a berry into her mouth.

Does she miss nothing?

"What are you talking about?" Auraelia's feigned confusion did nothing to dissuade her friend.

"Are you seriously going to look me in the face and tell me that I *didn't* see something fall to the floor? And then subsequently watch you stare *at* said floor for goddess only knows how long before you picked up whatever it was?" Piper chided, her eyes laced with annoyance.

Auraelia sighed. "It was a letter."

"A letter?"

"Yes, a letter."

"Damn, Rae. You're really making me work for it this morning."

"It was from Daemon, okay? I haven't opened it yet. I'm not even sure when I got it."

"Wait...What do you mean you got a letter from Daemon? *How* did you get a letter from Daemon?"

Shit.

Auraelia pressed her fingers into her temples, massaging the area in hopes of staving off the growing tension headache that was forming. She sighed, then began to tell her friend of the sapphire Daemon had given her and imbued with his magic. Giving them an open line of communication without the breach of privacy that came with traditionally sending letters to or from a royal.

When she finished explaining everything, she pulled the sapphire from behind her shift. Showing Piper how the shadows of Daemon's magic danced within the stone.

Piper sat still as a statue. Then, ever so slowly, she dragged her eyes from the stone in Auraelia's hand up to her face.

"You kept *that* from me? Of all things to keep from me, you keep a magic necklace that a drop-dead gorgeous *prince* gave you?!" Piper all but yelled at her friend, her hands firmly grasping the arms of her chair, turning her knuckles white.

"Piper, come on. It hasn't even been a day, and I didn't even know if it worked until I saw his letter this morning." When she was met with silence, Auraelia leaned back and crossed her arms. "So, are you ready to tell me what happened with Aiden, or are you still deflecting?"

Piper choked on her sip of coffee. "Excuse me?"

"Oh, you heard me. You've been hounding me for details about my time with Daemon. Now it's your turn. So spill."

Piper sat in silence, chewing on her lip as she fiddled with the napkin that was draped across her lap.

Eventually she sighed, resigned to the fact that Auraelia wasn't going to relent.

"The night of the masquerade, do you remember when Xander asked me to dance?"

Auraelia nodded, not wanting to say anything in case it spooked Piper into stopping her story.

"Well, after our dance, he escorted me from the floor back to where we left you, but you were no longer there. He offered to stay with me, but I told him that I could find you on my own, so he bowed and left me to my own devices. I admit, I didn't *immediately* look for you." Piper stopped a moment, a shameful look crossing her features, but it was gone faster than it appeared. "I knew you wanted to experience the ball from the perspective of a *normal* guest, so instead I walked toward the refreshments table."

A small flush crept across Piper's cheeks, staining them crimson, as a smile tilted up the corners of her mouth with whatever memory she was reliving.

"Piper?" Auraelia's voice was low, but it still pulled Piper out of her daydream with a jolt.

"Yes, sorry." Piper's flush deepened with her embarrassment. "While walking to grab a drink, I bumped into a very tall, very solid man. Our eyes locked for a moment, and I drowned in the two pools of honey that stared back at me. And, Rae, when he smiled–" Piper sank down into her chair, tilting her head back as her eyes rolled back in their sockets, fanning herself.

Auraelia laughed. "Piper, you're worse than I am."

"Maybe. But the moment only lasted a few seconds and then he disappeared into the crowd."

"Wait...what?"

"Hush, I wasn't finished." Piper waved off her friend, and Auraelia threw her hands up in mock surrender.

"As I was *saying*, he disappeared into the crowd, so I turned and went to fetch the drink I was after, then I started meandering around the room in search of you. But that's when I saw you with *him*. Mister tall, dark, and *smoking hot* was spinning you like a top around the dance floor, and I don't think I'd ever seen you so...so...intrigued? Happy? Maybe both? But either way, I decided to watch from the sidelines.

"Eventually, you left the dance floor, and I watched as Daemon pulled you toward the garden doors. I had taken one step in your direction, when a hand encircled my wrist, and spun me away from you and into the very firm chest of the man I had collided with earlier in the night."

"I'm assuming that was Aiden?"

"Can't a girl tell her own story?"

"Sorry, sorry. Please continue." Auraelia chuckled to herself.

Piper had an affinity for dragging out her tales, making sure that everyone knew every detail. So, it wasn't a surprise that she was weaving this tale into a wall sized tapestry.

"Thank you, now where was I?"

"You collided with mister *'eyes like pools of honey.'*"

Piper glared but continued. "You took the fun out of it, but yes, it was Aiden, and he used the stupidest line of them all, but I couldn't help it. I was stuck in his sticky gaze and drunk on his smile." She sighed and picked up her coffee cup. Inhaling the rich scent.

"What line did he use?"

Piper rolled her eyes as she took a sip of her coffee, then placed her cup back on the table. "He said, and I quote, *'We really need to stop bumping into each other like this.'* I mean really, he couldn't come up with anything more suave? Say, I don't know, *'Hello, My*

Star' is a good one." Piper winked and then they fell into a fit of laughter.

When they settled, both women sighed and sank into a few moments of contented silence.

"So, what happened next?"

"You're really not going to let this go, are you?"

Auraelia lifted her brows and cocked her head to the side. "Would you?"

Taking a deep breath, and then pushing it out through tight lips, Piper conceded and continued her tale.

As it turned out, Aiden had pulled her onto the dance floor and swept her off her feet. Then Piper whisked him off to the castle library where they made good use out of the couches, and no use of the books. But when they had returned to a mostly empty ballroom, they parted ways–her to find Auraelia, and presumably Aiden to find Daemon.

The day of the coronation, Piper remained aloof throughout the dinner. Focusing most of her attention on Auraelia, then continuing the trend long after the meal concluded. Seemingly not used to being ignored by someone he wanted, Aiden had followed her around like a lost puppy begging for scraps. When Auraelia became preoccupied with Daemon, only then did Piper give Aiden her attention.

It seemed that Aiden had a thing for being told what to do, and according to Piper, was quite good at following directions. When Piper had concluded her tale, both women sank into a comfortable silence. Consuming their breakfast with peaceful smiles on their faces.

Thankful that the tension between them had been lifted, Auraelia reached across the table and grasped her friend's hand. "Thank you for telling me. But I must ask, how are you now that he's gone? Are you okay?"

Piper shrugged one shoulder. "I'm fine I suppose. The sex was good, but it wasn't world altering."

A pregnant pause followed her statement, and Piper suddenly became very interested in her plate, pushing around the few remaining berries that lay there.

"What is it, Piper?"

Piper covered her face with her hands and groaned. "Okay, the sex was better than good, it was great. Still not world altering, but do you know how fun it is to boss a man around in the bedroom?!"

Auraelia laughed, full and loud, at her friend's outburst. "No, I can't say that I can attest to that particular scenario. All my dalliances prior to Daemon–with both men and women–were merely two people seeking their pleasure. Though in my experience, women are more *giving* than men. Even in relationships, it was never anything world shattering. No *one* person was in control, and when it was over, we went our separate ways. But, with Daemon, it's...more."

"More?"

Auraelia sighed, and a small smile played on her lips as she shook her head. "Yes, more. I don't even know that I really understand what I mean by that, but it is. There is this electricity between us. It's hard to explain."

Quite literally if those shocks the other night were anything to go by.

Piper raised one eyebrow in confusion. "Try."

Rolling her eyes, she continued. "In the bedroom, he's almost animalistic. He's very dominant and likes to be in control. But at the same time, he would give up some of the control to me. It was very give and take. Each of us seeking out the other's pleasure instead of focusing solely on our own."

Piper locked eyes with her friend, mouth agape. "Since when did you like that?!"

"Since Daemon, I guess." She shrugged, then continued.

"But Piper, outside of the bedroom?" she sighed. "It's like I'm standing outside in the midst of a hurricane. The wind and rain lashing at me from every direction. Then he looks at me, and it's like the storm pauses and I'm grounded. The wind freezes in place, rain and debris are suspended in the air around me. The whole world just...stops."

Auraelia stared off into the distance as a flush crept across her cheeks. Her fingers trailed across her mouth, the memory of his kiss still lingering on her bruised lips.

"Oh, Rae. You've got it bad."

"What?"

Piper snickered. "Nothing. Come on, we need to get ready for the day, and you still have a letter to read."

As they were finishing their breakfasts, Auraelia received word from her mother that she was to see her before heading to training with Ser Aeron.

Before going their separate ways, Piper called the lady's maids into the suite while Auraelia made her way to her chambers to get ready for the day.

Her letter from Daemon left, unread, in her pocket.

Chapter Twenty-One

Auraelia

The moment she stepped through the door of her mother's suite, she was pelted with a stream of water. And it had been nonstop ever since.

Despite the fact that she still had training with Ser Aeron later, her mother kept pushing her. Trying to get her to dive into the well of her magic and find the bottom. To find what all lurked in the depths of that well. They had been at this for hours, with no end in sight.

Hours of her being soaked to the bone when she hadn't shielded her mother's advances. Hours of her mother telling her to *'feel for her magic'* and *'just let it come to you, don't think so hard.'* Only for her to then tell her to *'focus'* and *'concentrate'* two moments later.

"Auraelia, you need to focus. Concentrate on your breathing. Feel your magic fill your body, and then expel it."

Her mother's annoyingly unhelpful mantra for the day rang through the garden courtyard outside the queen's suite.

Goddess, help me.

"I'm trying, Mother. I haven't been doing this for *years* like someone else in this garden." She knew as soon as the snide words left her lips that she was in trouble.

Queen Adelina tilted her head to the side, her eyes wide and a hard set to her jaw, as she cast a wave of frigid water at her daughter. Auraelia shrieked at the sudden onslaught but managed to put a shield of air between herself and the wave.

When her mother recalled her magic, Auraelia hesitantly dropped her shield. As mist created by the clash of magics fell through the air.

"Better! Much, much better. Come, let's eat."

Wet, and out of breath, she followed her mother to the doors of her suite. The smell of roast and potatoes wafted through the air and out to the courtyard, making her mouth water and her stomach grumble.

When they reached the doors, Queen Adelina stopped in her tracks and turned to her daughter. "I would appreciate it if you wouldn't track water into my rooms, my love." The small tilt to her mother's lips giving away the challenge behind her words.

"You've got to be kidding me. *You* caused the soaked clothes," Auraelia, exhausted and hungry, lashed out at her mother.

Completely unfazed by the minor tantrum, the queen shrugged. "I did, yes. But last time I checked, you have the ability to remedy that situation."

Auraelia stood frozen under her mother's gaze, at a complete loss of words.

"Now," she continued, "When you're dry, you may enter and eat." Then she turned on her heel and headed into her suite to the table of food that had been set up. "Oh, and dear? I would hurry. It's almost time for your lesson with Ser Aeron, and you know how much he loathes you being tardy."

You have got to be kidding me.

Auraelia expelled an exasperated sigh, throwing her head back in the process.

Okay. Dry clothes. It shouldn't be that hard, right?

Shaking out her hands as she rolled her neck from side to side, Auraelia closed her eyes and tried to concentrate. But it wasn't her mother's voice coaxing her to concentrate. It was the deep, gravelly timber of Daemon that whispered in her mind.

"Close your eyes, my star. Breathe. Think about what you want, and then will it to happen."

A small smile tugged at the corners of her mouth. Images of her and Daemon intertwined in her sheets as he helped her play with her newfound abilities between rounds of sex crept into her mind.

She let his phantom voice ground her as she dove into her magic. Letting it warm her center before spreading out to her extremities. Let the tingles in the tips of her fingers build until it felt like she was holding static in her hands.

Holding onto that feeling, she opened her eyes as she willed the air around her to wrap her in a cocoon of warmth. Drying her clothes and hair in the process.

Her eyes locked onto her mothers, as a smug smile pulled at the queen's lips.

Auraelia pulled her magic back into her center, calming the surge of air that she had summoned and stepped into the suite.

By the time she made it back to her room, the sun was setting beyond the castle wall, casting the sky in hues of pinks and oranges. Her sore muscles screamed at her from over-exertion, as she hauled her weary body through her suite and toward her bathing chamber.

When she reached the door to her room, the sound of water running and the smell of lavender and chamomile permeated the air. She took a deep breath, letting the relaxing scents fill her lungs. Hauling her body through her room, she came to the doorway of her bathing chamber.

There, squatting next to the tub as it filled, was Piper.

"Have I ever told you that you're my favorite person? Because you most definitely are at this moment," Auraelia said with a sigh.

Piper chuckled and stood. "I believe that you've mentioned it on occasion, yes." She winked at Auraelia as she wiped her hands off on a towel. "I figured that you would want and *need*, if that stench is anything to go by, a nice hot soak." Piper scrunched her nose to exaggerate the statement. "But maybe you should shower first, because Rae, you reek."

Auraelia looked down at herself and pulled the edge of her shirt up to her nose, recoiling at the stench that burned her nose. "Oh, sweet goddess." Her lips tilted down in disgust. "You weren't kidding."

Piper released a full belly laugh at her friend's expense. "Come on, I'll even help you out of your corset. But after that, I'm shoving you in that shower if you don't do it yourself."

Auraelia laughed and walked across her bathing chambers to where Piper stood, turning so that her friend could unlace her corset.

After her lesson with her mother, she had to sprint across the castle and the grounds to make it to her lesson with Ser Aeron. Unfortunately for her, she was still late which meant that she had to clean the horse stalls afterward.

Between magic training with the queen, combat training with Ser Aeron, and sparring with Piper, Auraelia was exhausted. Tack on mucking stalls to the tail end of it all, and she was spent. Her muscles were sore, and she just wanted to collapse into her nice, warm bed.

Piper stripped Auraelia of her corset and prompted her to lift her arms so that she could help her out of her tunic. "Do you think you can handle the rest, or do you still need me?"

"No, I've got it. Thanks, Piper."

"No problem. I'll go down to the kitchen and let them know that you're ready for dinner."

"Thanks, really. I appreciate you." A small, tired, smile bloomed on her face.

"I know, I know. Now stop being sappy and go get un-stinky. I'm begging you." Piper turned and walked out of the chambers. Her chuckle echoing back into the bathroom.

"Love you, Piper!" Auraelia hollered after her.

"Yea, yea. Love you too. Now go shower!"

Auraelia stripped the rest of the way down. The cold tiles were bliss on her sore feet as she walked over to the shower stall that was tucked into the corner. Not bothering to wait for the water to warm, she stepped into the frigid streams and washed quickly.

By the time she was finished, her large tub was full and waiting for her.

She sank into the deliciously warm water. Letting her head rest on the edge, she closed her eyes. Her mind wandering back to the last time she had been in this tub, and with whom, as the heat melted her cold, pebbled flesh and soothed her screaming muscles.

When the water began to chill, she stepped from the bath and dried off. Twisting her hair into a towel, she put on her dressing robe and padded into her bedchamber. Piper still hadn't returned from the kitchen with dinner, so Auraelia laid down on her bed and pulled the letter from her pocket.

Prying the wax seal off, she took a breath, and unfolded the letter.

My sweet Auraelia,

The sapphire is indeed a 'neat party trick,' and I'm glad that you've put it to use.

Though I hope that you forgive me for the disappearing act that I had to pull, I'm so glad that Piper liked your rose.

You're right about our circumstances, and normally I wouldn't pursue something that may hurt not just myself or the other party, but my kingdom as well. Like you, my kingdom and my people come first. But I would be lying if I said that a part of me wouldn't give it all up if it meant that I got to explore this with you.

Those thoughts scare me if I'm being quite honest. But it's something that pulls at the back of my mind on the daily. I already miss the smell of lavender on your skin and the way your eyes ignite with challenge. I miss that smart mouth of yours, and the fierceness of your soul.

I hope that I get to experience it again soon.

I hope that I get to experience you again soon.

Write back soon, my star.

Yours,

-D

She clutched the letter to her chest, a smile tugging at the corners of her lips.

Since Piper still hadn't returned, Auraelia rolled onto her side and reread her letter until exhaustion claimed her and she drifted off to sleep.

She woke hours later to a dark room and the sound of crickets outside of her window. As she pushed up into a sitting position, the rattle of metal against porcelain pulled her attention. There, laying on the bed next to her, was a tray of goodies…and a sleeping Piper.

She grinned at the sleeping form of her friend–sprawled out against the pillows, hair stuck to her face, and small snores escaping from her throat.

As Auraelia carefully reached over to grab the small plate of fruits and cheeses from the tray, she noticed a familiar piece of parchment resting near Piper's hand.

That little sneak!

Auraelia rolled her eyes and snatched up Daemon's letter before she slipped from her bed and padded out into the sitting area, leaving Piper to sleep.

The curtains in her sitting area were still pulled back, allowing the bright light of the moon to shine through the tall panes of windows. Crossing the space with delicate steps, she set her plate down on the table and opened the glass door that led out to her balcony, inhaling the night air, and letting the breeze drift through the space.

Grabbing her plate, Auraelia headed over to the settee that faced the windows so that she could sit and look out at the night sky.

When she finished her food, she fetched her stationary from the table and settled in to write Daemon back.

Dearest Daemon,

I wish that I could say that this would be easy, but that would be a lie. I haven't even told my mother yet, and goddess only knows how that is going to go. If it's anything like the way Piper reacted to me keeping the sapphire a secret, it most likely won't go over well.

By the way, were you aware of the tryst between Piper and Aiden? From what she said, she could have stepped on his face, and he would have said thank you. So, it looks like our relationship might not be the only one navigating rocky waters. Fortunately for them, they don't have a treaty keeping them apart should things progress.

That stupid treaty. I understand its purpose, I really do. But it certainly does complicate things, doesn't it?

Sorry, that got heavy. How are your parents? Your sister? Tell me more about you and your life there. I've never been to Kalmeera, but I've heard that it's beautiful.

And before you think differently, I miss you too. It's strange. We barely know each other, but also know each other very intimately. I keep expecting to see you lurking around a corner with that stupid smirk on your face.

It's too bad that you can't shadow walk across the sea and back to me.

Until next time,

-A

Auraelia folded the parchment, once again sealing it with a sprig of dried lavender and her sigil pressed into the wax before sending it off to Daemon.

Chapter Twenty-Two

Daemon

Daemon laid in bed, arm draped over his face, as images of slate-blue eyes and golden waves filtered through his memories.

Weeks had passed since his time in Lyndaria.

Weeks since he'd felt her velvety-soft skin under his fingertips.

Since he'd kissed her supple lips and felt her writhing beneath him.

Too long since he'd seen her eyes ignite with that internal fire, as her melodic voice challenged him at every turn.

Their letters back and forth had been a comfort. A bandage to the ever-growing ache in his chest at being away from the one person that his soul clung to.

Once the initial awkwardness of long-distance communication ebbed, their letters had become an almost daily occurrence. Sometimes writing more than once a day, depending on their schedules.

They talked about everything under the sun. From their families to their likes and dislikes.

Where he preferred darker shades of blue and grays, she preferred bright colors. Her favorite was a vibrant shade of teal that matched the waters of the Cerulean Sea, and Daemon remembered thinking how much she would love his court with its multitudinous shades of blue.

Favorite food? Bread dipped in a concoction of egg, milk, sugar, vanilla and cinnamon. Which was then cooked and dusted in finely milled sugar. He'd never had it, but it sounded delicious, and was determined to get the castle chefs to attempt it.

She'd told him more about her brother. How even though they were close, their duties often pulled them in opposite directions, so they rarely got to spend time together outside of royal duties and occasional dinners.

He'd told her about his sister–Yvaine–and all the trouble she managed to get into.

She kept him up to date on her and Piper's shenanigans. Told him about their trips to Nefeli Lake, and about her horse–Jasira. About her magic lessons with her mother, and her training with Ser Aeron.

He did his best to match her colorful imagery with some of his own when he described Kalmeera. Knowing she had never been there; he wanted to try and give her a mental image.

He told her about his conversation with his mother, where he had relayed his time in Lyndaria. And how she could tell that there was more than just chocolate croissants between them.

Letter after letter, they opened up more and more. Learning about each other.

It was beautiful, and wonderful.

But it wasn't enough.

He wanted *her*.

Wanted her wrapped in his arms and pinned beneath his body. Wanted to be with her to share meals with. To spar with her, physically and verbally. He wanted to witness her magic flourishing, not just read about it. He wanted to witness her coming into her own.

But despite all of that, he still hadn't decided whether or not he was going to invite her to spend solstice with him in Kalmeera.

Early morning light filtered through the crack beneath his bedchamber door, signaling that it was time to rise and start the day. He was exhausted. He'd been up late, scouring over the treaty between his kingdom and hers, looking for loopholes and concessions.

Just in case, he'd told himself, just in case this *thing* between them turned into more than just letters.

And he'd found one.

One.

One of them would have to abdicate their claim to their throne. One of them would have to give up the thing that their whole life was built around.

And that one thing, was something that he knew she would never do.

Daemon sat on the edge of his bed. Elbows resting on his knees, head in his hands, and let out a deep sigh.

He looked up, glaring at the miniature figure of the Goddess Narissa that sat on the table next to his bed. "You just had to tie my soul to someone I couldn't readily have, didn't you? Couldn't have made it easier on both of us? Picked someone *accessible*?"

He shook his head. *I'm talking to a fucking statue.*

Just as he rose to head toward his bathroom, there was a knock on the door to his suite. Lounge pants slung low on his hips, he stalked out of his room and toward the offending noise.

As he reached for the knob, the person on the opposite side whined. "Come on, D! Open up!"

Daemon sighed and shook his head. *Yvaine.*

"I have coffee," she trilled from the other side of the door.

"You better have food too," he quipped back, opening the door for his sister. Blocking her path until he saw that she did, indeed, come bearing food as well.

"Can I come in now? And good goddess, baby brother, put a shirt on. I don't want to stare at your abs over breakfast."

Yvaine was two years his senior and had the Sapphire Isles followed the same line of succession as Emerald did, she would have been crowned heir instead of Daemon. But the moment air entered his lungs outside of the womb, that future had been stripped from her grasp—as were all the responsibilities that came with it.

Of which she took full advantage.

When she wasn't preoccupied by her duties, she traveled all over Ixora, simply for the pleasure of traveling. Whereas Daemon traveled for the betterment of his kingdom, and to keep contracts and treaties between courts current.

She slept in and stayed up late, hanging out with friends instead of schmoozing stuffy lords who only wanted to push their own agendas.

For as long as he could remember, he'd accepted his role with pride and grace. Fully taking on all of the responsibilities that came with being not only a prince, but with being the one who would one day take the throne.

He made a point to spend as much time with his people as possible. From getting his hands dirty with work out in the cities when they needed a helping hand, to being the mediator for issues—both large and small. He'd dedicated hours upon hours learning everything he could about the histories of every court within Ixora. Especially since the Isles had trade agreements with the majority of them. He never once doubted his role.

Never once begrudged his sister for passing that role onto him—not that she actually had a say in the matter.

He had been happy with the way his future had been laid out. Never once questioned it.

That was until *her*.

Now his mind was full of questions that made both his head and his heart ache. Thoughts that made him second guess his future within the monarchy of the Sapphire Isles. But those were thoughts that he was determined to keep to himself.

At least for the time being.

At least until he knew better where they stood with one another, and if this could indeed be something real. Tangible.

Permanent.

Daemon let his sister into his space, watching as she placed the tray of food and coffee on the table in the sitting area of his study. Then, as requested, he padded to his room to pull on a shirt.

The scent of lavender enveloped his senses as soon as he stepped into his chambers. There, sitting on his pillow, was a new letter.

Closing the door softly behind him, Daemon shadow-walked across his room and snatched it up. Carefully pulling the lavender from the wax, he inhaled its soft scent before breaking the seal.

Dearest Daemon,

Is it rude to say that I just ate my weight in chocolate croissants? It is, isn't it? Well, I guess you'll have to ignore that statement. Or come back to Lyndaria and get some yourself.

Honestly, it probably has something to do with the fact that my body is mad that there isn't a baby currently nestled in my womb. So, crisis averted there.

Also, you're super sweet, and I really like you...but right now I really think all men suck.

Aside from my micro-pity party over here, tomorrow is Piper's birthday. And despite being uncomfortable, I'm determined to make it the best birthday possible.

I think she's more nervous about her magic manifesting than I was, and I was a wreck. So, to combat the nerves, we're having a read-in.

We'll be spending all day in comfortable clothes, reading various dirty romance novels, and eating ridiculous amounts of food.

Basically, what I'm trying to say is that you probably won't hear from me tomorrow.

But don't worry, you're still the only man I'll be thinking of while I'm alone in my room with my hand between my thighs.

Yours,

-A

The laugh that had been bubbling up from the rest of her letter died at the last line.

Fuck.

Daemon skimmed through the letter once more, before sticking it in the drawer of his side table with the others.

Adjusting his now semi-hard cock to a more comfortable position, he threw on the first shirt he found in his wardrobe and headed back out into his study.

Yvaine was lounging across one of the couches, coffee cup in her hand. "What took you so long?" she asked without looking in his direction.

Daemon scoffed. "Is it really any of your business? This is *my* room after all."

She sat up as he approached the couch and gave him a questioning glance over its back. "Well now. What's got your knickers in a twist?"

He sighed as he sat on the couch opposite his sister and poured himself a cup of coffee. Inhaling its rich scent before taking a cautious sip. "I just have a lot on my mind, okay?"

Yvaine nodded knowingly, a slight purse to her lips as her head bobbed. "Auraelia?"

At the mention of her name, he choked on his coffee. "Excuse me?"

She laughed. "Oh, come on, baby brother. You didn't seriously think that mother *and* Aiden would be able to keep that secret, did you? My baby brother has a crush that has gotten his head and heart all tied up in knots. Mother is worried. Aiden thinks it's hilarious. Of course, they're going to be blabber mouths."

He scoffed, "Aiden thinks it's hilarious, does he? I think that's called deflecting."

Her eyes grew wide with curiosity and mischief. "You're not holding out on me are you, D? You know I *love* a good bit of gossip. Especially if it will give me something to tease my other *little brother* about."

Daemon smirked. *Fair is fair.*

"Next time you see him, ask him how Piper is doing."

"Oh my goddess!" Yvaine screeched. Bouncing in her seat before readjusting to sit on her feet. "You *both* found someone to pine over in Lyndaria? Shit, maybe I should have gone too."

Picking up her coffee from where she had set it on the table, she took a sip.

"What happened to Sariah? I thought she was '*the one*?'"

"Sariah is great, but she's ready to settle down. And that's just not me. I'm not there yet."

Daemon nodded in understanding; he knew that feeling all too well. For the last few years both his parents and the council had been strongly hinting at him finding a wife and future queen. They had pushed countless ladies into his lap to get to know and potentially court. None of them held his attention. Most of them just wanted the prestige that came with being seen with the future king of the Sapphire Isles, not the man himself.

He didn't just want someone to hold the title of wife and queen, he wanted someone to share his life with. Someone who would share the burden of ruling. He needed someone to help carry the responsibility when it grew too heavy upon his own shoulders, needed someone who understood it.

He wanted a friend and a partner.

Unfortunately, the person he *wanted* was someone he wouldn't be able to have in that capacity, and it made his stomach turn.

Setting down his coffee, Daemon stood from the couch causing a look of confusion to cross his sister's face.

"Everything okay?"

"Yeah, I just–" he sighed. Casting his gaze downwards and running a hand through his hair. "I need to think."

Yvaine seemed to understand and stood from where she was perched. "Have you given any more thought to inviting her to solstice?"

Daemon kept his eyes trained on his feet. "Some, and as much as I want to see her, I just don't know if it would be a good idea. I haven't made up my mind yet."

She nodded and placed a hand on his shoulder. Giving it a gentle squeeze, which pulled his gaze to hers. "I know this probably won't help, and I'm sure mother has hounded you enough already. But I think you should. Maybe seeing her again would help clarify some things in your head as well as your heart."

Daemon nodded. "You're right. But it could also complicate things far worse than they already are."

Yvaine scoffed, then punched him in the arm.

"Ouch. What the fuck was that for?"

"If you're going to keep being morose about the whole situation, call it off instead of dragging her along. Don't be an ass. I don't know the woman, but I *do* know that she doesn't deserve to be led on. Figure it out or let her go."

She paused, then pulled him into a tight embrace. When she released him, her eyes were soft, but also stern. "I mean it, Daemon. No one deserves to be led on. If you can't figure out a way to have her, let her go."

He nodded his assent, and she turned to head toward the door, hollering, "I love you, little brother!" before she pulled the door closed behind her.

After Yvaine left his chambers that morning, he decided to shower to clear his head. But it did the opposite.

Instead, the last line of Auraelia's letter played on a loop, causing his cock to harden. Images of her spread out on his bed with her hand between her thighs as he watched played on repeat. Flashes of her pressed up against the cold marble in his shower as he sank into her pussy coursed through his mind.

Fuck.

Cock in hand, he stroked himself to the images flooding his brain until his release coated the black stone.

He'd dressed quickly after that. Heading out for a day of unrelenting princely duties.

There were council meetings to discuss the trade agreements between the Isles and the other courts. And with his father still ill, it was his job to step in and sit beside his mother to conduct them.

The Sapphire Isles provided exotic fruits to the majority of the realm. As well as fresh seafood, obsidian, and colored glass. Topaz provided grains, gourds, and a variety of fruits that weren't conducive to be grown in the Isles or other parts of Ixora. For the Court of Pearl, it was high quality fabrics and pearls–of which his mother was quite fond. Emerald provided leafy greens, beans and berries, as well as game from their various hunting seasons. The Court of Opal traded in game as well, but also allowed courts to send their commanders to learn how to effectively train their soldiers.

The only court that the Sapphire Isles didn't have a trade agreement with was the Court of Garnet. Tucked away on the other side of the Onyx Mountains, Garnet kept to itself. As far as he knew, they didn't trade with any of the other courts either.

When the talk of trade agreements ended, the next line of business was discussing the solstice celebration. His mother's eyes never left his face, boring holes into the side of his head that asked the unanswered question, *"Did you invite her yet?"*

Daemon tried not to zone out as the talk of guest list and food options drug on and on. Tried to ignore–and not look annoyed at–every not-so-subtle hint at him spending time with eligible ladies of the court.

After hours of discussion, he finally called the meeting to a close and excused himself before he could get pulled into yet another trivial discussion about canapes.

Slipping from the council chambers, he aimed for the garden at the far end of the castle grounds. He needed to be out under the open sky. Needed to feel the wind on his face.

Needed out of that stuffy room with its pushy politicians and his mother's unflinching gaze.

Outside, the sky was painted in an array of vibrant pinks and fiery oranges as the sun set on the horizon. The moon, already high in the sky, was waiting for its moment to shine.

Two steps down, a voice called to him from behind.

"What is it, Aiden?" he asked without even bothering to turn in his direction.

"Want to work off some of that foul energy that's pulsing off of you in waves?"

Daemon half turned to where his friend stood on the top step, a cocky grin on his face. "Are you *offering* to get your ass kicked, Lord Aiden?"

Aiden's laugh boomed across the open courtyard. "In your dreams, *Your Highness*."

By the time Daemon made it back into his rooms that night, the stars were out, glittering like fragmented glass that had been scattered across the inky black sky. Bone tired and weary, he grabbed a glass of whiskey before heading into his bedchamber.

It had been a while since he'd sparred with Aiden, and neither of them pulled punches. His now swollen and throbbing jaw was proof of that–as was Aiden's newly formed black eye.

After a quick shower, Daemon pulled Auraelia's letter out from his side table. Too tired to walk back into his study, he conjured parchment and a quill from his desk. Smiling as he penned his response.

Deciding to give her a taste of her own medicine.

Chapter Twenty-Three

Auraelia

"Rae. *Rae!*" Piper screeched as she shook her awake.

"What?" she responded, her voice scratchy from sleep.

Piper shoved her once more. "Get up. Lover boy wrote you back and it fell on my face."

Rolling over, she snatched the parchment from her friend's hand and sat up.

"Can he not write at normal hours of the day? These late-night correspondences are a bit much...unless they're *that* kind of late-night letter." Piper's eyes grew wide, and her lips pulled into a feline smile as she prowled over to where Auraelia was sitting.

Jumping out of bed, Auraelia hurried to her bathing chamber and closed the door. Pressing her back up against the wood to keep Piper from trying to open it. "Come on, Rae. Sharing is caring. Let me read it," Piper begged from the other side of the door.

Laughing at the ridiculousness that was her best friend, she shook her head and started to pry the wax from the parchment. "*Maybe* after I read it, I *might* let you read it."

Piper sighed audibly. "*Fine*. But at least tell me if it's dirty. It's not fair to live a scene from a dirty romance book, and *not* share it with your friend. It's just rude."

"Would you go find food or something, and leave me in peace please?" Her voice was light and full of mirth.

When Auraelia heard Piper's steps recede from the door, she finally unfolded the letter, taking in the scratchy texture of each letter as it formed words.

Oh, My Star,

Your mention of chocolate croissants may have been a tease, but it wasn't rude.

What was rude was your intentional tease at the end of your letter. Was your intent to make my cock hard for you? Did you want to fill my mind with images of you spread out on my bed, pleasuring yourself while I watched?

Because if that was the case, then you were successful. But that's not all that I saw while I stroked myself in the shower.

Images of my head between those luscious thighs, devouring your pussy was one of my favorites. But imagining the way my cock would disappear into your tight pussy as I pressed you against the wall in my shower, the water running in rivulets down your body is a hard one to beat.

If your intention was to remind me that your mind isn't the only thing I'm missing, consider me informed.

Only you could make my cock weep from across the sea. But remember, two can play this game, Princess.

Oh, and tell Piper happy birthday for me.

Your move.

-D

Fucking hell.

Auraelia's entire body felt flushed from his words, and she felt as if she had melted into the floor.

Daemon had always had a way with words in the bedroom but seeing them written out on parchment for her to read over and over again was something else entirely.

His deep gravelly voice filled her mind as she read it again. Like he was behind her, whispering filth into her ear, sending heat throughout her body only to pool between her legs.

Leaning her head back onto the door, she took a deep breath, and blew it out between pursed lips.

Fuck.

Pushing off the door, she walked over to the wash basin to splash water on her heated face. While patting her face dry, she heard someone hurrying across her room, followed by incessant knocking on the door of her bathroom.

What the hell?

"Rae? Are you okay in there?" Piper's voice sounded panicked.

Confused as to why Piper would think she wasn't ok, and concerned about the panic in her voice, she stepped away from the wash basin and stepped into water that had pooled on the floor and slipped.

"Fucking hell," she groaned.

"Rae?! That's it, I'm coming in."

Piper pushed the door open to find Auraelia lying flat on the floor, staring up at the ceiling. "Are you ok?"

"Yeah, I'm fine. Just slipped and fell on my ass. Give me a minute."

After a moment, she rolled onto her side and pushed up into a sitting position. Leaning against the tub, she looked to her friend who still stood in the doorway, wringing her hands–a nervous habit of hers.

"What's up, Piper? What's wrong, why were you so panicked?"

Silver lined her eyes when she finally looked up at Auraelia. "I–I think my magic manifested."

Excitement coursed through her body at her friend's confession. "That's amazing, Piper! What is it?"

"I um–I *saw* you fall. So, I came running to the bathroom to make sure that you were okay. But in doing so, I think that I may have caused you to slip. Rae, I'm so sorry."

"Piper, you didn't cause me to fall. I got water on the floor when I washed my face and didn't pay attention to what I was doing." Auraelia looked to her friend, willing her to understand that it wasn't her fault. But then something clicked. "Wait. You said you *saw* me fall? Like–like a dream or a vision?"

Piper nodded her head.

"Piper! That's amazing!"

"Amazing? What exactly is amazing about seeing your best friend bust her ass?"

Auraelia looked at her friend with her signature *'you've got to be kidding me right?'* expression. "Other than the obvious reason of that being hilarious. You can clearly see that I am *fine*. But, Piper, your magic is clairvoyance. That's incredibly rare and, well, pretty fucking cool!

"You know that's not a common gift in our court, and it's been decades since a known clairvoyant existed. And the fact that you, my best friend since diapers, are now the holder of it? I'm so fucking excited for you!"

"Well, when you put it like that, I guess it is pretty awesome." A smile pulled across her face, and there was a light shining in her eyes.

Auraelia nodded in confirmation, then patted the floor in invitation for Piper to join her on the floor.

Piper slid down next to her and rested her head on Auraelia's shoulder. The two women sat in silence, their breathing the only sound in the room.

"Do you think you can get up?" Piper asked.

Groaning, Auraelia pushed up from the floor and winced. "Great, not only am I menstruating, but now I have a bruised ass."

Piper fell over in a fit of laughter.

"Oh, shut up. Come on, I'm hungry. Let's see if Chef has any snacks hidden away in the kitchen for old times' sake."

Pushing up from the floor, Piper took a moment to stand fully up-right. "Fucking cramps. Also, I went to find food after you locked yourself away in here. By the way, what was in the letter?"

A flush covered her cheeks, and radiated down her neck, coloring her a shade of strawberry red.

"Oh, so it *was* one of those kinds of letters, after all."

Auraelia smiled. "He also said to tell you happy birthday."

"Well, that's the least he could do since his letter dropped onto my face."

Both women laughed, and linked arms as they exited the bathroom in search of snacks.

The knock at the door, and the flurry of people flitting into the sitting area of her suite signaled that it was already midday, and time for lunch. The gloom and rain that persisted outside the windows made time look as if it were standing still.

True to her word, Auraelia had canceled all training sessions for the day so that she and Piper could just relax and enjoy her birthday. She even convinced her mother to let her take the day off from magic training. And with the weather outside, they wouldn't have gotten much training done as it was. As it turned out, staying in ended up being a smart idea anyway while Piper got used to her newfound abilities.

Throughout the night, Piper had a multitude of visions. All of them were small and inconsequential, but they still took her by surprise. Anytime she was walking, she would either freeze in place or run into a piece of furniture. Which was funny the first few times, but then Auraelia made her stay put on the couch or walked with her whenever she needed to go to the bathroom or get across the room.

There was a point when Piper grabbed her arm during one of her visions, and it was like being pulled underwater. Glimpses of them laughing so hard that they fell off the couch rolled through her mind like a memory. The reason for the hysterics was unknown, but completely probable with their history.

The projection of Piper's visions was a new facet of her magic, and it sent them both into a stunned state of shock—it wasn't common for new abilities to progress that quickly.

They sat there in silence, staring out the windows, and when they finally *did* look at each other, hysterics ensued and the series of events from her vision came to fruition.

Over the course of the day, they'd had the time gap between vision and reality figured out.

Five minutes.

They had approximately five minutes to figure out whatever Piper's vision meant before it happened in real time. So far, they hadn't been able to keep anything from happening. And any time that they *did* try, it happened anyway—just not necessarily the way that it was originally intended, though it wasn't for a lack of trying.

Piper's visions ranged to a variety of things. From simple things like a berry rolling under the couch, to lightning striking a tree in the garden.

As the lady's maids set up their lunches on the table by the windows, Piper made sure to stay as far away from them as possible. There had been a few times where she'd bumped into Auraelia and triggered a vision. And since she was still working on controlling the frequency and severity of her visions, Piper had told Auraelia she didn't want to take any chances.

"You can just leave them on the table, ladies. We've got it from here, thank you."

"Of course, My Lady. We also brought in some more hot water bottles for your cramps if you need them." The tall blonde lady's maid, Kyra, replied with a small curtsy. "Are the old ones in your chambers, My Lady?"

Auraelia nodded, a sweet smile pasted onto her face.

"And will you be needing any other supplies? New linens?"

"More pads would be much appreciated, Kyra, thank you. I believe the bed linens are still fine though."

"Of course, and I'll check on the linens and take care of them if need be."

Auraelia nodded her assent.

Kyra strolled through the sitting area, muttering instructions to the other ladies with her before they dispersed to complete their tasks. Once they finished, they bid Piper and Auraelia farewell and exited the way that they came.

"Are we sure she's not a spy for your mother?" Piper asked as she plopped down in one of the chairs by the table of food.

Auraelia chuckled, "I'm quite sure. It wouldn't do her much good since I tell mother practically everything as it is, so why would she need a spy?"

"I don't know, maybe she's trying to make sure that I'm still a good influence on you or something."

Laughter erupted from both women, but it was Auraelia who spoke first. "Piper, my dear, sweet friend. My mother thinking you're a good influence on me is about as likely as Xander being crowned *Queen*."

Laughter continued on throughout lunch. Between bites of turkey and cheese finger sandwiches–their favorites– and berry and cheese plates, they reminisced over their adventures throughout their friendship.

From sneaking out to go to pubs in the city and swimming in their secret lake, to late night conversations over broken hearts and sometimes broken minds.

They wholeheartedly believed that they were soulmates.

Not in the lover's sense of the phrase, but in the sense that two souls were meant to travel this world together. To be there for each other no matter what.

They believed that your soul could pull to different people in a multitude of different ways. That some people even had more than one soulmate, just maybe not in the same capacity or purpose.

Though she'd never experienced that particular sensation until she met Daemon.

Daemon.

Sensing the trailing of thoughts, Piper kicked her under the table.

"Ouch, what the hell was that for?"

The look on Piper's face was incredulous. "You're really going to sit there and tell me you *weren't* just drooling over mister tall-dark-and currently unavailable?"

"I–I um–"

"No, ma'am. It's *my* birthday. No broody, tattooed, male fantasies allowed. I don't care how delicious they are...unless they are found in those novels we're supposed to be reading."

"Fine, fine."

The rest of the day went by in a blissful blur. It had been a while since they didn't have to run all over the castle to be one place or another. Whether it was training, council meetings, or grievance mediating, they rarely got to just *be.*

They spent the rest of the day alternating between reading their novels and trying to trigger Piper's visions– and avoiding the outcomes. They ate copious amounts of mini cakes and pastries that they would undoubtedly regret later. Drank wine until they thought they were going to be sick and read a handful of novels.

Kyra had come back at some point to bring fresh menstrual supplies and to change the bedding. As well as keeping them in full supply of hot water bottles for their cramps.

It was a much-needed day of rest and fun, for both of them.

One that Auraelia wouldn't have traded for the world.

As the day turned to night, the sky began to clear. Giving way to the stars, and the bright white light of the moon.

Piper had fallen asleep on the settee, her open book dangling by her fingers over the floor. Slipping from her chair, Auraelia pulled a blanket over her friend's sleeping form, then carefully removed the book from her fingers–slipping a sprig of lavender between the pages to mark her spot before setting it down on the table.

Between romance novels, and a heavy wine buzz, Daemon's letter had been coursing through her head all evening. And with Piper finally asleep, she needed to do something about it. Carefully, Auraelia grabbed her stationary from the drawer in her table and stumbled into her room.

Closing the door softly behind her, she smirked. Time to herself, and a buzz from liquid courage, was exactly what she needed to write Daemon back.

Two can play this game indeed.

Chapter Twenty-Four

Daemon

The scent of dried lavender permeated the air, seeping into his slowly waking consciousness. Daemon rolled onto his side, facing the middle of his bed, mindlessly stretching out his arm as he searched for the warm body that wasn't there.

Searched for the soft and supple curves that his mind and heart associated with that smell.

When he was met with nothing but cold, empty space, he begrudgingly cracked his eyes, and a saddened sigh slipped through barely parted lips.

Ever so slowly, he let his eyes fully open, taking in the early morning light that filtered into his chambers from underneath the door. When they finally focused, he noticed the folded parchment that rested on the pillow next to his.

A lavender sprig pressed under sea green wax stared back at him.

He sat up and rubbed the sleep from his eyes, then grabbed the small, folded letter.

It lacked her usual tidy perfection. The lavender that was always set just so was off kilter, and barely secured by the seal. The wax that always made a perfect circle was large and misshapen. Like it had been poured on haphazardly before she pressed her signet into the warm liquid.

He chuckled to himself. *What in the hell?*

This was a side of Auraelia that he hadn't seen yet. She was always so put together, so sharp witted and concise. This...this was new. Different.

Endearing.

This was the chaos in her beauty.

Unfolding the letter, he soon realized the *why* behind the chaos.

My dearest Daemon,

Oh, my sweet. You know, it's really unwise, and quite mean, to make a girl all hot and bothered during her best friend's birthday. Especially when you're not here to remedy the situation or reap the benefits of it.

Instead, I'm here all by my lonesome. Hot, frustrated, and slightly buzzed from unhealthy amounts of wine. In this large bed of mine, with nothing but your words to keep me company.

No strong hands to coast down my body and cup my breasts. No mouth to kiss and lick and suck my pussy until I'm writhing beneath the touch. No phantom shadows to lend their velvety touch as they bind my wrists and caress my body.

No, instead you choose to play a game that you my dear, sweet Daemon, have no chance at winning. Because while you slept, I had my fingers deep within my soaked pussy. Felt the way that my walls clenched around them as I came to thoughts of your cock sinking deep within me. To you fucking me into oblivion before you followed me over the edge. I came to the sound of your moans and my name on your lips as it echoed through my memories.

Then I showered and did it all over again.

If you still want to play this game, then I look forward to your response. But until then...Your move, Prince Daemon.

-A

Fuck!

Daemon's cock throbbed.

Her words painted a perfect picture in his mind that would stay with him for years to come. Auraelia splayed out on her bed, a golden halo of waves surrounding her head as her soft, sculpted, body glistened under the glow of the lamp light. A beautiful pink flush to her tanned skin. The sound of her moans and his name on her lips as she rode her fingers to release.

Daemon sent shadows skittering across the space, flipping the locks on the doors.

He slipped his hand beneath the thin satin sheet on his bed and gripped his cock. Swollen with need and begging for release, he read her letter over and over. Letting the images play on a loop in his mind while he worked toward his climax.

Temporarily sated, he slipped from his bed and padded into his bathroom to shower. There he was bombarded with vivid imagery of Auraelia riding his cock in the tub the night of her coronation.

Fucking goddess.

Daemon groaned in frustration as he switched the shower to cold. Hoping he could freeze out the beautiful torment that was his memories. He dressed quickly and headed into his study.

She was good at this game of theirs, but he was determined to be better.

Sitting at his desk, he secured parchment and quill, penned his response and sent it off.

As much as he loved the back and forth teasing and flirting, he wasn't sure how much he could take before he *had* to see her.

Had to have her, taste her. Just be near her.

They were teetering precariously close to the edge of a delicately balanced blade. It was only a matter of time before it tipped over.

Daemon stood from his desk and headed out for the day.

There was a solstice to plan, and his mother to disappoint. Because no matter how much he wanted to see her, he knew he couldn't invite her to solstice. If his mother, or sister, got their hands on her, there was no way that he was going to be able to let her go.

He would have to go to her. He didn't know when, or how, but it needed to be soon. His world grew more and more gray with every day they spent apart.

And he couldn't help but wonder if she felt the same.

Chapter Twenty-Five

Auraelia

One and a half months of letters.

One and a half months of not feeling his touch or hearing his voice. With only his written words to dull the ache in her soul.

And over the last few weeks, those letters had become fewer and farther between. Their game of teasing and flirting turned into short and unfeeling correspondence.

They lacked the emotion and laughter that she had become accustomed to.

They lacked depth and feeling.

They seemed to lack *him* altogether, almost as if they had been written by someone else.

And then they just stopped.

She knew he was busy. Summer solstice in Kalmeera was said to rival the Fall solstice celebration that Emerald threw in conjunction with Topaz. And with King Evander still ill, she knew that he had a lot on his plate.

So, she let it go, and let him be. She was not the type of woman to wait around for a man.

So, she didn't.

She set about her days, doing everything she could do to occupy her time. She sparred with Piper, and even Xander when he wasn't too busy.

Her mother tested her limits with magic and pushed her boundaries. Ser Aeron helped her feel and focus on growing her connection to the magic around her. He had her focusing on archery as of late, wanting her to practice using the air around her to bend the path of the arrow.

She went to council meetings, where her mother continued to skirt around any information regarding the Court of Garnet, shutting down any and all questions that Auraelia and Xander would ask. It was always the same. Always, *'nothing for you to concern yourself with,'* or *'we will discuss it later.'* And despite their constant protestations, she stood firm.

Auraelia spent most of her free time in the kitchens helping the staff prepare for summer solstice. Despite their celebration being smaller than the one in Kalmeera, they still celebrated the longest day of the year. The castle kitchens worked tirelessly to get sweets and pastries made in time for the parties that would be held throughout the city. Then, days before the celebration, Auraelia, Piper, Xander and a few other nobles would ride into the city to help their people set up and pass out goodies.

"Your Highness, you really don't need to do that," the head chef said as she watched Auraelia chop vegetables.

Auraelia smiled and looked up from her task. "I know, Liza. But I like doing it. It keeps my hands busy and my mind still. Plus, this is where I hear the best gossip." She winked at the plump woman who shook her head and returned to stirring the many pots on the stove.

She'd hoped that she'd be able to pick up something about Garnet during her time in the kitchen, but it seemed that either no one knew anything, or they got extremely tight lipped when they saw their princess.

Auraelia bounced and flitted from one task to another, filling her days to the brim.

But when the nights came, and she was alone, she missed the man she had come to know. And couldn't help but wonder if he'd tired of their games... If he was tired of the distance.

"Auraelia...*Auraelia*."

"Rae," Piper whispered as she dug her elbow into Auraelia's ribs. "Your mother has said your name at least twice now."

Shit.

Lost in a daydream, she hadn't heard her mother calling her name. Or had any idea as to what was being discussed in the council meeting.

"Sorry, Mother. I don't know where my head is at today. What were we talking about?"

"We were discussing the letter that I received from Queen Avyanna, of the Sapphire Isles."

Shock blew into Auraelia like a hurricane force wind. "I'm sorry—what?"

Her mother chuckled. *Actually* chuckled.

"I received a letter from Queen Avyanna, requesting the presence of our court at their Summer solstice celebration."

"But, why? We haven't been, in what, nearly five hundred years? Why now?" Her heart pounded so loudly in her chest that she was certain her mother could hear it.

"Evidently, Prince Daemon and Lord Aiden spoke highly of their time here, so she is returning the invitation."

Surprise that was laced with confusion, was evident on the face of everyone at the table.

"Your Majesty," Lord Harland cut in, "Surely you can't attend with our own preparations in full swing."

"Of course not, Lord Harland. I wouldn't dream of it."

A collective sigh of relief rang through the space from the lords and ladies at the table.

"But," all eyes snapped back to the queen, "that doesn't mean that Princess Auraelia shouldn't go. Being as she is the future of our court, and a future reigning monarch of Ixora, I believe it could be beneficial for her to attend."

Dumbfounded.

That was the only explanation for how she was feeling. Completely and utterly dumbfounded.

"Of course, she wouldn't be going alone. Lady Piper would need to go with her and attend to her duties as her Lady in Waiting. And of course, Prince Xander would attend as well, as a chaperone and personal guard."

"Mother–"

"Auraelia–" Her mother cut her off with a curt tone. "I don't want any argument. You're going, and that's final. Plus, I think it would be *good for you*."

The inflection that her mother added to the end of her statement said more than the words themselves.

She knew something. Auraelia wasn't sure what it was, but she knew *something*.

Auraelia nodded her assent, as did Piper and Xander.

"Great, now that that is settled. You will all leave within two days' time. Queen Avyanna is sending Lord Aiden to escort you to the Sapphire Isles and has informed me that gowns and appropriate attire will be provided for the night of the celebration since their fashions differ from ours."

With that, the council meeting was adjourned, and Queen Adelina dismissed everyone–including Auraelia.

As they left the council chambers, Auraelia and Piper were still too stunned to speak.

They were going to Kalmeera.

She was going to see Daemon.

In person.

The prospect was exciting and caused thousands of butterflies to take flight in her stomach. But the next thought that crossed her mind was one that sent them plummeting.

What if he didn't want her there?

The following two days were like walking through a thick fog, and before they knew it, they were walking the gangplank to the most beautiful ship that she'd ever seen.

It was small and sleek, and the color of shadows with small silver accents in the details.

"Welcome aboard, Your Highness. My Lord. My Lady." The voice was light and airy, like a cool breeze through wildflowers, and belonged to a stunning woman. She looked to be around five-foot-ten, with stunning bronze skin and an abundance of coffee-colored curls that coiled and bounced around her face with every step. There was a stern look on her face, but her eyes gave her away. She was happy...but there was also a sparkle of mischief.

"My name is Captain Raneese Garreth, and this beauty is the Nevermore. Prince Daemon's private vessel."

Auraelia stopped in her tracks at the mention of Daemon. "Is–is the prince on board?"

"No, ma'am. This was a private voyage sanctioned by the queen."

"Basically, we stole his boat." A deep tenor coursed through the air.

Aiden.

Auraelia chanced a quick glance at Piper. To anyone else she would appear indifferent and aloof. But to Auraelia? She saw the tight clench in her jaw, the way she subtly pulled at her knuckles, and heat in her eyes that would make flames second guess their nature.

Clearing her throat, Auraelia directed her attention back to Aiden. "Lord Aiden." Her tone curt and unfeeling.

He smirked. "Your Highness," he said with a flourished bow.

Arrogant asshole.

"If you'd follow me, I'll show you where your cabin is for the remainder of the trip. The journey only takes a day, so we should be there shortly after nightfall, as long as the wind is in our favor." He paused a moment before throwing Auraelia a knowing look over his shoulder. "But you could help us out with that, couldn't you, Princess?"

Anger boiled in her veins, but before she could say anything, Xander cut in.

"She may not be *your* princess, Lord Aiden. But I will remind you that she is still *a* princess, and you will give her the respect she is owed."

Aiden's smirk dropped immediately, and he paled under Xander's intense stare.

She smiled up at her brother. Xander was a typical older brother. Constantly picking on and pushing his baby sister, but he always had her back. Just as she always had his. And she was immensely grateful that he was here with her on this trip.

As they continued down the hall to their cabins, a barely suppressed giggle escaped from Piper.

When Auraelia gave her a questioning look, Piper grabbed her arm. A vision of Aiden tripping on nothing but air and falling onto his face flooded her mind.

As much as she loved that Piper could share her abilities and felt safer around other people as time went on and her magic stabilized, Auraelia didn't think she would ever get used to the feeling. It felt like being held underwater, as milky clouds parted to show whatever image her friend needed to share.

When she released her arm, her vision cleared, and it was her turn to smirk.

Winking at Piper, she sent the tiniest gust of wind to trip up Aiden's cadence–bringing Piper's vision to fruition.

When he looked back at the two women, like twin minds, they both tilted their heads to the side and smiled.

Chapter Twenty-Six

Auraelia

Kalmeera was beautiful, even under the cover of darkness, and she now understood why Daemon told her that he could get lost in the swirls of the stars for hours. Out on the sea, the colors were bright and vibrant, and the sky looked clear enough that if you extended your arm far enough, you could reach them.

When they reached the port outside the city, she was stunned into silence. Tunnels so dark and narrow that you could barely see the different entrances were formed into the cliff face. The only thing breaking up their looming darkness was the water that crashed against the stone, and the hull of the ship. Glowing streaks of cyan-colored light shot through the inky depths. Lighting the way with every wave and movement of the creatures beneath the water's surface.

Auraelia watched in fascination as they made their way through the tunnels, and into the heart of Kalmeera.

When they reached the castle, it was near midnight and most of the staff had already retired for the evening. The few that remained, escorted Auraelia and her party to their rooms in the east wing.

They each had their own chambers, complete with personal bathing chambers, but Piper and Auraelia shared a common space between them. With the late hour, they hadn't had the chance to explore their new surroundings, but the light of the moon through the windows illuminated the space enough to see.

The common area was beautifully simple, with light natural wood floors, ivory furniture, and aquamarine-colored accents throughout the space. There was a small writing desk to one side of the room, and a fully stocked bar cart nestled between two tall bookshelves on the other.

But Auraelia's breath caught as she stepped into her room. Deep, rich, turquoise hues touched practically every surface.

Crossing the room, she ran her hand along the bed. The frame was brushed gold, and the teal bedding was light to counteract the heat of the isles but heavy enough for when nights were cool. Pulling back the coverlet, she ran her hand along the sheets, the satin cool and silky beneath her fingers.

There were chairs with gold frames and teal velvet cushions, and golden sconces hung on the wall over two matching side tables.

It was luscious.

Luxurious.

And all Auraelia wanted to do was sink down into the covers of her bed, and sleep.

Slipping out of her travel dress, she pulled her robe from her trunk and wearily padded into the attached bathing chamber to freshen up.

She vaguely remembered Daemon mentioning that the castle had updated plumbing. So, she crossed her fingers and prayed to the goddesses that her memory wasn't playing tricks on her. When she was greeted by a large clawfoot tub with a spout and handles, she sighed in relief.

As the tub filled, the sound of her door opening pulled her attention.

"Rae?"

"I'm in here, Piper, just trying to run a bath before I collapse into bed."

Piper shuffled into the room; towel wrapped around her head.

"I see I wasn't the only one with that idea," she chuckled.

"I smelled like sweat and salt water, it was gross."

A tired laugh escaped. "Touché. Are you ok? We haven't really had a chance to talk about you seeing Aiden again after almost two months of no contact."

Piper sighed and perched herself on the counter next to the wash basin. "I'm fine. He's an asshole who comes crawling as soon as he doesn't get what he wants, and I get to have my fun when I want to."

"Piper–"

"Look, Rae. I'm not looking for anything serious. I'm not. I don't know why I let myself get wrapped up in a good lay, but I did. If it turns into something more, that's fine. But don't you think for one second that I would ever leave you and Lyndaria for a fine piece of ass." She winked, trying to bring humor into the conversation. But there was still lingering sadness and hurt behind her eyes.

Deciding not to pressure her oldest and dearest friend and crack open a wound that she was trying to mend, Auraelia laughed. "As if I would let you leave anyway. You're stuck with me."

"Forever and always?"

"Always and forever, Piper. Always and forever."

Piper hopped down from the counter and bounded across the space, pulling Auraelia into a firm embrace. "Thank you, Rae. I don't know what I would do without you."

She pulled back and clasped Piper's cheeks between her hands. "You would be terribly bored."

They both chuckled, and then she placed a quick kiss on her friend's cheek before releasing her hold.

Once Piper left, Auraelia slipped into the warm water of her bath–letting the heat seep into her tired muscles. After a short soak, and a quicker wash, she stepped from the bath. Drying her body with one of the fluffy teal towels, before wrapping another around her hair.

She padded into her room, quickly changing into her nightgown, and then she let herself sink into the bed, the cool satin gliding across her clean skin like a lover's touch.

Towel still wrapped around her hair she drifted off to sleep. Her final thought of the night was of Daemon, and whether he knew that she was under the same roof that he was.

It was midday by the time she rolled out of bed. The afternoon sun streamed through the windows of her room, warming the space.

Slipping from the bed, she pulled on her dressing gown and padded over to the windows. Throwing them open to reveal a balcony that overlooked the sea.

Oh my goddess. This is beautiful.

She stood in the doorway, looking out at the crystal blue water and white foam that formed on the peaks of the swells that built as they came barreling towards the shore.

"Piper!" she bellowed across the room.

Throwing the door to her room open, Piper leaned against the frame slightly out of breath. "What is it? Is everything ok?"

"Yes, of course. Did you see this view?!"

Piper stood upright and crossed her arms over her chest. A look of indignation marred her features. "You *did not* just holler across the suite, sending me into a state of panic, I might add, all because you opened your damn window."

Auraelia shrugged, a sheepish smile on her lips. "Sorry?"

Piper huffed in mock agitation. "To answer your question, yes, I have seen the view. It's absolutely breathtaking. The ocean and mountains in one direction, and bright colors everywhere else. It's like another world here."

Auraelia nodded in agreement.

When a knock came on the door to the suite, the women exchanged a look of confusion.

"Maybe it's lunch?" Piper supplied.

Shrugging her shoulders, Auraelia followed Piper out into the sitting area. Taking a seat on the settee while Piper crossed the room to open the doors.

"Good afternoon." The words chimed through the room and seemed to belong to more than one person. The sweet melody from the tones were warm and inviting, pulling her from her spot on the couch.

Standing, she looked toward the door, where two gorgeous women stood. They were both tall with raven hair, their resemblance uncanny, and they were both dressed in stunning gowns. The younger of the two wore a dress the color of muddled berries that faded into a rich burgundy. It wrapped around her neck and had diamond shaped cut outs in the bodice—one between her breasts and the one on each side of her waist. And there was a slit up one side of the skirt that almost reached her hip.

The other woman wore something of a similar design, but it was slightly more modest with smaller, silver mesh lined, cutouts. It was the color of a saltwater pearl and was embellished with them as well. They were absolutely stunning.

"Won't you please come in?" Piper offered as she stepped out of the way.

"Thank you," the older of the two women said as they stepped into the space.

They looked familiar, like she'd met them before but couldn't place them.

As she took in their features, the pieces began to fall into place.

Bright green and blue eyes shone behind long, thick lashes.

Dark raven colored hair, that took on a blue hue when under the lamp light.

And a smirk.

One that she knew like the back of her hand.

Fuck.

Desperately trying to keep her cool, she sank into a deep curtsy. "Your Majesty."

Auraelia watched as Piper's eyes flitted back and forth between her and the strangers in the room and saw the moment everything clicked into place for her friend. An *'oh shit'* expression briefly crossing her features before she, too, dropped into a curtsy.

The two women chuckled, and the older of the two clasped her hands together–Daemon's tell-tale smirk still on her lips.

"Well, let's get these introductions out of the way, shall we? I'm Queen Avyanna, but you seem to have pieced that together already. This is Daemon's sister, Princess Yvaine."

"It's a pleasure to meet you both and thank you so much for inviting us to your celebration. I've heard it's spectacular." Nervous flutters traveled throughout Auraelia's body, and she had to focus on her breathing to keep her anxiety in check.

"I'm Princess Auraelia, and this is Piper, my Lady in Waiting. My brother, Prince Xander, came with us as well, but I'm not sure where he is at the moment."

"It's a pleasure to meet you both. Now, we've come bearing lunch and gifts." Queen Avyanna gestured toward the doors where a line of people began entering the suite with trays and trays of delicious smelling food, who were then followed by two ladies carrying garment boxes.

Auraelia and Piper stood in awe as the flurry of people maneuvered around each other like a flock of birds flying in unison.

When the room cleared out, an awkward silence ensued.

Finally remembering her manners, Auraelia gestured to the sitting area in their suite, "Please, sit."

Queen Avyanna smiled and inclined her head in acceptance of the offer. Then she and Yvaine took the matching armchairs, while Piper and Auraelia sat on the settee.

"I'm sure that you find this...odd."

"Just a little." Piper mumbled under her breath.

"Piper!" Auraelia admonished, then turned toward the Kalmeeran queen and princess, "I am *so* sorry." An embarrassed flush crept over her cheeks.

Queen Avyanna laughed. "It's quite alright, my dear. Why don't we clear some things up for you, hmm?"

Auraelia nodded.

The queen gestured toward the food that was laid out before them. Piles of fruits, smoked meats, and cheeses–and it all smelled delicious.

While they all helped themselves to the spread, the queen spun her tale.

"First things first, Daemon does *not* know that you're here. Let's just call you a surprise and an incentive–"

"I'm sorry, an incentive for what?" she cut in.

"For the last month and half, I have watched my son sulk around this castle. Doing everything he's supposed to be doing and enjoying nothing outside of that. The night he returned home, he sat down with me for dinner. And after some prodding, he finally told me about *you*. Obviously, I was curious, so here you are.

"As to being an incentive, my dear, you deserve more than just letters–yes, I know about those, he's not as sneaky as he thinks he is. You deserve to be wooed, and you both deserve to be happy. I'm hoping that him seeing you here will push him into figuring out what he wants. And I do apologize for making you an unknowing pawn in all of this. But a mother does what she must for her children."

Auraelia took a moment to take all that in. Letting it ricochet through her mind as she searched for what that meant for *her*.

Piper, however, didn't miss a beat and wasn't afraid to speak her mind to anyone–including a queen. "And what of what Auraelia wants?"

"Piper," Auraelia grasped her hand, "It's fine."

"No, Rae, it's not. I know we would have come regardless because your mother said so, but what about *you*? This is your life too."

Auraelia's eyes softened as they met the stubborn gaze of her best friend.

"She's right, you know," Yvaine chimed in before popping a piece of yellow fruit into her mouth.

"*Yvaine–*" Queen Avyanna started, before she was cut off by her daughter.

"No, mother, she's right. She does get a say in this. They're on an even playing field. Both of them are heirs to their respective kingdoms, and *that* is a huge factor in all of this. Almost as much as where their hearts lead them."

Auraelia took in Daemon's sister. Her long and lean frame draped over the chair like she hadn't a care in the world. Her raven hair fell to just below her chin in a stylish, blunt cut, and she had the same moss green eyes as her brother. But instead of gold, there were streaks of blue. The perfect combination between Daemon and his mother's eyes, and it made her wonder if King Evander was where their green eye trait was obtained.

She had the same olive complexion as her brother, and when Yvaine caught her gaze, her lips had the slightest uptick into the smirk she loved so much.

"As much as I love my friend for standing up for me, and for Princess Yvaine–"

"Just Yvaine, please. I don't do titles in informal settings."

Auraelia smiled, she completely agreed with the sentiment. "Yvaine, for agreeing with her. I'm not completely opposed to this idea. I too, would like to know where his head is at."

Queen Avyanna smiled a Cheshire smile, as mischief and acceptance twinkled in her cornflower blue eyes. "I had a feeling I would like you."

A comforting silence fell over the group as they finished their lunch.

Auraelia and Piper tried all kinds of new fruits. The yellow one that Yvaine had eaten earlier was pineapple and was sweet and acidic. Then there was pink dragon fruit, which was sweet and reminded her of a pear. There were also bananas, papayas, and mangos. Even apples from the orchards in Topaz. All of which were delicious and paired beautifully with the assortment of cheeses.

When the ladies had finished their lunches, the queen's gaze lit with excitement.

"It's time."

Both Queen Avyanna and Yvaine stood from their seats.

"Time for...what exactly?" Piper asked, her forehead wrinkling with confusion and worry before her face relaxed, and her eyes went vacant.

Auraelia watched as whatever vision Piper was having played out in her mind, and when she finally came to, her eyes were lined in silver as she looked at Auraelia.

Yvaine lifted a solitary eyebrow in question. "What just happened?"

Queen Avyanna smiled, "You are quite gifted, my dear." Her voice was laced with awe.

Shock radiated out from Piper in waves.

"Would someone mind clueing me in, please?" Yvaine asked, as she put her hands on her hips.

Piper cleared her throat. "I um–I'm clairvoyant. I only came into my magic a few weeks ago so they're still sporadic. But I can also project them. So far just to Rae–Auraelia. But it's something."

Yvaine's eyes widened. "Gifted, indeed. It's been years since there was a known clairvoyant in Ixora. And projection too? Marvelous."

Piper nodded and turned towards Auraelia. "I don't want to show you, because I don't want to ruin the surprise, but Rae. The dress they brought for you? You're going to be more beautiful than I have ever seen you. Daemon's not going to know what hit him."

A flush colored her cheeks as she turned her attention back to Queen Avyanna and Yvaine. "Well, let's get to it then I guess. We have a party to get to and a prince to shock."

Piper and Auraelia stood, exchanging conspiring smiles with the women from Daemon's family, before leading the way into Auraelia's chambers.

Piper wasn't kidding when she said that she would look beautiful in the gown that Queen Avyanna had designed for her. It was stunning. The fabric was light and airy, and floated on any whisper of a breeze. A swarm of butterflies took flight in her stomach as she thought of Daemon's reaction to seeing her there. To seeing her in *this*. The fashion in Kalmeera was very different from Lyndaria, and she was embracing every aspect of it.

When they were finished getting ready, Queen Avyanna and Yvaine escorted them down to the ground floor of the castle where Xander stood waiting. His eyes widened when he saw them, and a small smile graced his usually stoic face.

"You look beautiful, sis," he said when they reached the bottom of the staircase.

Piper cleared her throat and looked away nonchalantly.

A chuckle bubbled up from Xander's throat, and he shook his head. "You look good too, Piper."

Piper brought her hand up to her chest in mock shock. "Why, Xander. Thank you ever so much." She waggled her eyebrows and threw him a wink–a broad smile lighting up her face.

Auraelia rolled her eyes at their interaction. "You're both incorrigible, I swear."

When both Piper and Xander shrugged their shoulders in response, she shook her head and took Xander's proffered hand to help her down the final few steps.

With their party complete, they were then led to the far side of the castle, where a grand set of stone steps led out into a garden oasis. Even with it being the longest day of the year, the sun had started its downward progression in the sky, casting hues of orange on the garden.

Auraelia peered out through the columns that lined where the castle ended, and the garden began.

The party was in full swing.

Brightly colored flora surrounded the space, filling the air with a mixture of floral scents. There was a pond nestled in the middle of the garden that was surrounded by lit paper lanterns and there were tiny candles floating atop the water amongst the lily pads and lotus flowers.

She took in the space with wonder in her eyes. It was so beautiful, and so different from the celebrations that were held in Lyndaria.

Queen Avyanna stepped up next to her. "Beautiful, isn't it?"

She nodded. "I don't think I've ever seen anything quite like it."

A small smile graced the queen's lips before she grasped Auraelia's wrist and pulled her from the column. "Take a few minutes if you wish. But when you're ready, simply step out to the top of the stairs and we will have you and your party, announced. Okay?"

She nodded her assent, then turned back toward the column while the queen and princess made their own entrances into the celebration.

Piper came to stand next to her, and they peered out at the crowd covering the lawn.

"Did you find him yet?" Piper asked as she scanned through the sea of faces.

"What? Oh, no. I haven't seen him. I haven't really been looking."

"Auraelia Rose, you're a *much* worse liar than you think, so I don't know why you even bother. Now, let's find that mot–"

Piper's words trailed off as her eyes widened and her mouth set into a firm line.

Auraelia knew that look. Knew that *no one* wanted to be on the receiving end of that look. She turned her head in the direction that Piper was looking, "What is it–"

The words died on her lips.

You've got to be fucking kidding me!

There, standing across the garden, was Daemon, talking and laughing with a beautiful woman as she ran her fingers through his hair.

Fire raged through her veins, and her breath came out in barely controlled huffs.

She'd given him grace for his lack of correspondence when she thought it was due to his duties. She'd even given him grace when she thought he was no longer interested. But it was another thing entirely to lead someone on while seeking company from someone else.

And that was where she drew the line.

Auraelia pulled away from the column and straightened her spine.

Taking a deep breath, she walked out to the top of the steps just as Queen Avyanna instructed, with Piper and Xander trailing behind her.

With her emotions bouncing all over the place, her hold on her magic slipped a fraction. An angry breeze pushed through the garden, causing the flames on the candles to flicker.

Daemon turned toward the steps, just as the footman at the end of the stairs started his announcement.

"Introducing, Crown Princess Auraelia Rose of the Court of Emerald. Escorted by Prince Xander of the Court of Emerald, and Lady Piper."

She felt his gaze on her throughout their introduction. She saw him move toward her out of the corner of her eye. But she refused to give him one minute of her attention.

If he wanted to *mingle* with other people, then she would do the same.

She wasn't a doll to be kept on a shelf, only to be played with when the mood struck. She was Princess Auraelia Rose, heir to the Court of Emerald.

And it seemed he needed to be reminded of that fact.

'My Star' indeed. Checkmate, asshole.

Chapter Twenty-Seven

Daemon

Daemon was deep in conversation with Sariah when he noticed Aiden walking purposefully across the garden, an anxious gleam in his eye.

"Where's the fire, Aiden? Also, where the hell have you been, I haven't seen you in two days."

Aiden took up a spot next to Daemon and took a large sip of his drink. "I uh–your mother sent me on a last-minute errand for solstice." At the conclusion of his sentence, his eyes widened to the size of a full moon, a thin sheen of sweat coating his brow.

Was he nervous?

He was poised to ask him just that, when a strong breeze coasted through the garden.

He would know that magic tinted breeze anywhere. It carried with it the subtle scent of lavender, something that wasn't grown anywhere near Kalmeera.

Only in Lyndaria.

Daemon immediately turned on his heel toward the grand staircase at the front of the garden, where a vision in blue stood at the top.

Holy shit.

Aiden patted his friend on the shoulder and mumbled an apology before slipping away into the crowd.

Sariah sidled up beside him and leaned in. "Who is that?"

Daemon choked on the words as he tried to force them out. "It's umm–it's–" But before he could get them out, the footman at the bottom of the stairs announced the newcomers to the crowd.

The words became background noise as he forced his way to the front of the garden. A million thoughts running rampant through his mind. The *what*, the *how*, and the *why* of it all disappeared as soon as he was merely a breath away from her.

She was dressed in a traditional Kalmeeran gown. The top was midnight blue and faded into lighter and brighter shades toward the bottom. She looked like the night sky fading into the bright blue of the day.

The fabric wrapped around her chest before crossing at her neck and forming straps along her upper back. There was a cut out between her breasts, where the sapphire pendant he'd given her swayed gently in the gap, and two cut outs at her waist that wrapped around to leave her lower back exposed.

Two slits went up either side of her skirt, exposing her long, lean legs to her upper thigh. And wrapped around one of her thighs was a thin strip of midnight blue lace to mimic the look of a garter, only it held a series of chains and pearls that draped a few inches down her leg instead of a stocking.

There weren't enough words in his vocabulary to accurately describe how beautiful she looked.

When he stepped up to extend his hand toward her, Xander–who had escorted her down the steps–shot him a look that could have killed him where he stood. And Auraelia didn't even spare him a glance as she crossed his path.

What the hell was that about?

He watched as Xander escorted her through the crowd to where his mother was standing with some of the noblemen from their court...and their very eligible, very single, sons.

Fuck!

His anger began to build, sending his shadows to pool at his fingertips.

As he watched her walk away, realization dawned.

Her hair had been left down. Only a singular wide braid hung down the middle and there were a few smaller braids throughout the remainder of her honey blonde waves. All of which had strings of saltwater pearls woven into them, and there were three individual strands strung across the crown of her head. It was a very common hair style amongst women in his court. However, the only women who wore pearls in their hair were members of the royal family. *His* family.

Goddess, damn it, mother.

If he hadn't figured it out by then, then the way Auraelia and her party were just embraced by his mother and sister would have been a clear indication.

He knew in an instant that this was all his mother's doing.

This was the last-minute errand that Aiden had been sent on.

He didn't invite her, so *she* did.

Shit.

Daemon made his way over to the group surrounding Auraelia and his mother. When his sister saw him coming, she winked and then scurried away.

I'll deal with her later, I guess.

But just as he reached the outer edge of the group, Auraelia placed her hand in another man's and Daemon had to watch as he led her out onto the dance floor.

With the *main attraction* gone, the rest of the group dispersed. But there were rumblings between other men about when they would get to spin the dazzling young princess around the floor.

Never, if I have anything to say about it.

By the time he made it to his mother, she had a cocky smirk on her face.

"Gloating doesn't become you, Mother."

"No more than sulking becomes you, son. I gave you the opportunity and you squandered it, so I took matters into my own hands. What I did *not* see coming, however, was you somehow managing to spur the women before you even clapped eyes on her. Whatever did you do, my love?"

"If I had an answer to that question, I would gladly give it to you." He sighed. "Did you really have to pawn her off on Syrus, of all people?"

"Syrus is an excellent dancer, and since she didn't seem too interested in dancing with *you* at the moment, he was the next best option."

Daemon scoffed. "Syrus is a snake, as is his father, Lord Cassius. Thankfully, my star can hold her own." A smug grin crept onto his face.

Queen Avyanna laughed loudly, before quickly placing a hand over her mouth. "Oh, my dear, sweet boy. Are you sure that she's still *your* star? Seems she's burning awfully bright for someone else at the moment."

Daemon glanced towards Auraelia on the dance floor, and to anyone else it would look as if she was having the time of her life. But he saw traces of annoyance in the lines around her smile, and the laugh she produced was forced. He knew what genuine joy and amusement from her sounded and looked like, and that was not it.

It seemed as if he wasn't the only one who noticed, because just as he took a step in her direction, Xander cut in, and he watched as her shoulders relaxed in the arms of her brother.

"Why don't you ask Sariah to dance? She looks like she could use some fun." His mother asked from behind him.

Daemon sighed but nodded his assent and headed off to find his friend.

Sariah was Yvaine's ex-girlfriend, but she was still a dear friend of his. They'd all grown up together, so she was like another sister to him. She was beautiful. Her ivory skin had freckles scattered like constellations. Her eyes were unique, one a vivid blue and the other like crushed amber. But it was her fiery red hair that stood out like a beacon in the sea of souls at the party.

She stood alone by the table of refreshments, nursing a glass of sparkling wine.

"Care to dance?"

"Oh, thank the goddess, yes."

Daemon took her hand in his and led her out to the floor. As the previous song came to an end, Auraelia was facing right at him.

Daemon watched as her eyes traveled from him to Sariah and back.

He noticed the subtle shift in the color of her eyes. Eyes that pulled more blue than usual, courtesy of the blue in her dress, were now a deep green and streaked with bright peridot lightning.

As he and Sariah approached, she inclined her head slightly in greeting. "Prince Daemon."

The words were formal and drenched in ice water. There was no warmth in them, but an immense amount of anger.

He turned to watch her exit the dance floor, and it took everything in him not to go after her–he still had to be a welcoming host. As much as he wanted to, he couldn't just fall at her feet and beg forgiveness for whatever had directed her ire in his direction.

Taking a deep breath, he turned back toward the floor, pulling Sariah with him.

"Well, she certainly was chilly. Want me to warm her up a bit?" Sariah joked, trying to lighten the mood. And since her abilities were related to fire, it normally would have worked.

"She's mad at me for something."

"Wait, you *know* the princess? Like, well enough for her to be mad at you? What did you get up to in Lyndaria, Daemon?"

"So, *so* much."

Sariah's eyes widened slightly when she realized what he meant and nodded her head.

The rest of their dance was silent, both lost in their own worlds. And when it ended, he sought out the one other person who would know what was going on–Piper.

She was standing with Auraelia and Xander, a group of men surrounding them all vying for a chance to dance with the two new beauties at the party. Even Xander had his fair share of ladies itching for his attention.

But as soon as Daemon entered the circle, the twittering ladies turned their attention toward him. Auraelia's scoff was barely detectable, but he heard it all the same. But before he could get a word in, she was off to the dance floor with some other lord's son.

"Ladies, I'm so sorry, but I'm previously engaged. If you would, please excuse me." Daemon added a warm smile that usually made the ladies blush, and then pulled himself from their grasp.

As they turned their attention back to Xander, he sidled up to Piper.

"Lady Piper."

"You."

"I'm sorry, did I do something?"

Piper released a chuckled scoff and angled herself away from him but kept her eyes on Auraelia on the dance floor.

Ok, that's it.

Daemon stood in her line of sight, causing her to lift her gaze to his. "If you would do me the honor of a dance, Lady Piper." His tone was slightly clipped.

A sickly-sweet smile crept onto her face, and it made his stomach sour. "I would rather stick my hand in an open flame. Thanks, though."

Daemon smirked, "That could be arranged, you know. I have a friend who I'm sure would be more than willing to accommodate."

Piper narrowed her eyes at him, and then at his still extended hand.

"Piper, you are a guest in *my* court. I danced with you when I was a guest at *yours*, it would be...*diplomatic* of you to return the gesture."

She rolled her eyes but placed her hand in his. "You do know that dancing with me isn't going to win you any favors, right?"

"I just want to know what's going on." Daemon turned his softened, pleading, gaze toward her as they made their way to the dance floor.

"You really have no clue, do you?"

When he shook his head, she sighed. "You're an idiot."

Daemon listened intently as Piper explained what was going on. "You stopped writing."

"I-"

"Whatever excuse you have, I'm not the one who needs to hear it. *She* is. You stopped writing and that fractured something inside her. She hid it well, but I could see straight through the facade."

Daemon continued to lead them around the floor, but his heart cracked as every detail was laid at his feet.

"When we got the letter from your mother inviting us here, I saw a tiny spark come back into her eyes. Then we arrived and found out that *you* didn't want her here. And to top it all off, she saw you flirting with someone right before we walked out."

"What? I wasn't—"

Piper cut him off once more, "Again, whatever excuses, or reasoning you have, I'm not the one who needs to hear them."

Daemon was silent. He didn't know what to say, or if there was anything that he could say.

"You see how bad this looks from her perspective don't you? You convinced her to give this—give *you*—a chance and then she comes here and sees you talking to another women. Sees women throwing themselves at you at every turn."

"I wasn't flirting with anyone," he said through clenched teeth.

Piper's eyes widened as his tone. "That's not what we saw."

"How–how do I fix this, Piper?"

"Oh, Daemon, that's not something that I can help you with."

Piper's icy exterior seemed to have thawed during their conversation. But her walls went straight back up as soon as she locked eyes with Auraelia. And with the song coming to an end, he graciously let her leave their dance.

He turned, looking for Auraelia on the dance floor, and found her about to enter into yet another dance with a man who was not him.

Fuck that.

Daemon walked calmly, yet quickly, across the floor before coming to an abrupt stop at her side.

His sudden appearance startled her.

The smile she gave him was manufactured and her eyes were still icy and hard. "Prince *Daemon*. If you will excuse me, I was about to dance with–sorry, what was your name again?" She gave her pathetic excuse of a dance partner a kind smile.

"Uh–Simon, My Lady."

"Right, Simon. So, if you would please excuse–"

"Princess, I'm sure that Simon is a splendid dancer, but I am offering my hand in his stead," Daemon said as he shot a look at Simon that said, *'bow out.'*

And he did, bowing to both Daemon and Auraelia, before he excused himself.

Auraelia's head moved back and forth on a swivel between Simon's retreating form, and Daemon's smug smile.

"You've got to be joking right now."

"On the contrary, Princess. You'll find I'm quite serious. Shall we?"

"The hell we shall."

"Auraelia, it's one dance. You're a guest at my court, it would be expected that we shared at least one."

She looked away from him for a moment and took a few deep breaths and she flexed her fingers. The amount of control she'd gained over her magic in the few weeks since he'd seen her was amazing.

"Fine. *One* dance."

Daemon bowed. "As you wish, Princess."

As he led her out onto the dance floor, the other couples seemed to vacate the space–leaving only them on the floor.

"Did you plan this?" she asked, her annoyance clear as crystal.

"I didn't. But it's the first time, in a *very* long time, that we've had visiting royals, and the fact that we are on this dance floor *together* is a big deal. So please, try not to look like you want to blow me off a cliff."

"What a wonderful idea."

Daemon's eyes widened at her response. *Fuck, in her current mood she probably could.*

With her disingenuous smile firmly in place, Daemon began to sweep her around the dance floor.

The feel of her once again in his arms made his heart swell. Her scent enveloped his senses, and with them pressed so tightly together, he could feel her heart racing. Its quickened pace matching his own.

He tried–and failed–numerous times to start a conversation with her during their dance. But the fact that she never brought her eyes higher than his shoulders stung. All he wanted to do was pull her closer. Tell her he was sorry. Fix this rift that had formed between them.

As the song slowed, and their dance came to an end, he decided to try one more time.

"*My star–*"

She scoffed, fire burning in her eyes as she finally looked at him, but underneath that fire was hurt. He'd hurt her. "Don't you *dare* call me that."

She dropped his hand.

Curtsied.

Then walked to the edge of the floor where Piper and Xander stood.

Frozen to the spot where she left him, Daemon watched as she walked away.

Walked away from the dance floor.

Away from the party.

And away from him.

Seconds. Minutes. Hours. He wasn't sure how long he stood unflinching on the dance floor. It wasn't until his sister looped her arm through his and began to drag him away that time started again.

"You're not seriously thinking of just letting her go, are you?"

Daemon stopped abruptly. "What?"

"Auraelia. You're not just going to let her go, are you? You're not even going to *try* to fix this? I thought you were smarter than that, little brother."

"It's not that simple, Yvaine, and you know it."

"True, but I still think you should at least try."

He sighed, "I can't just leave the solstice celebration. I'm the prince for goddess' sake, how would that look?"

It wasn't Yvaine who answered this time, but his mother. "The celebration will be fine without you. Go on. Go to her."

"But, Mother. What about the treaty?"

"You let me worry about that, alright. Get the girl first, and we will deal with the treaty later." Queen Avyanna winked, and the smile she gave him was full of hope and love.

Daemon's heart raced as hope swelled in his chest.

As his smile broadened, his mother's eyes glimmered with mischief.

"You did say that her favorite color was a deep teal, correct?" Her smile matched his now as she winked. "Good luck."

With that, Daemon turned and hurried across the garden, taking the wide stone steps that led to the castle two at a time.

Once inside, he shadow-walked to the room his mother hinted at.

Here goes nothing.

Chapter Twenty-Eight

Auraelia

She stood in the doorway that led out to her balcony.

After she, Piper, and Xander made it back to the suite, she'd insisted that they return to the party and enjoy themselves. That she was fine, and just needed to be alone.

As soon as they left, she'd thrown the doors open to her balcony. Letting the fresh sea air fill the room, and still her racing mind and heart.

She'd been *fine* until he took her hand.

Finer still, until he placed his warm palm on her bare back.

But she could no longer claim to be *fine* when he called her 'my star.'

That broke something in her. Something she didn't know how to fix.

Auraelia leaned against the door frame, watching as twilight took over the sky. The stars finally allowed to shine after being pushed aside to let the daylight linger.

She felt his presence before he said anything, but still, the sound of his voice made her jolt.

"Auraelia?" He sounded nervous, like he was questioning being there at all.

She sighed and rubbed her hand along her arm. "I can't do this tonight, Daemon. I don't know that I can do this at all, actually."

When she finally turned around to face him, she knew what he would see.

He would see silver rimmed eyes from tears she refused to let fall. Would see a nose that had been reddened by continuous wiping.

He would see a defeated and tired woman.

Something that she never let anyone see. But she was tired of being strong all the time, and she just didn't care to try anymore.

Not tonight.

She barely met his gaze, instead turning her head back toward the darkening sky outside.

Out of her peripheral she saw him take a step towards her.

"Don't. *Please.*" Her voice cracked and turned pleading as she hung her head, and the first tear fell. Leaving a dark stain on her skirt as it rolled to the floor.

"My star, plea–"

"Daemon, don't. *Please* don't call me that. I am *begging* you. Please. Not now, not ever. I just–" She took a breath, eyes searching the ceiling above her for some kind of answer. "I can't take it."

"I'm not trying to hurt you, Auraelia. I–I just want to talk."

"Talk?" She turned towards him, her sorrow blending seamlessly into the cresting anger. "You want to *talk*? What could you possibly want to talk about, Daemon?"

She watched as he opened and closed his mouth like a fish out of water. When he didn't respond, her anger flared.

"Here, I'll start. How about we talk about how you stopped writing to me? How about we discuss how your own *mother* wanted to meet me and you decided that I wasn't good enough. What about instead of telling me that you didn't want this anymore, that you didn't want *me* anymore, you started looking for someone else while I sat and waited for a stupid letter!"

Her voice got increasingly higher as she went on. Thunder boomed in the sky, while lightning crackled between the clouds. It was as if the Sapphire Isle's Goddess–Narissa–was witnessing their argument and agreed with her.

Daemon's eyes got increasingly sadder and more guilty with every blow she landed.

"The worst part is that I *knew* this would happen. I even told you that it would happen, and you said that it wouldn't. You said you wanted to get to know my mind and my heart. But as soon as I let you in, you left."

Daemon took a step closer, but she held out her hand to stop him. "Don't come any closer. I can't bear to be near you right now. I t *hurts* too much. Can't you see that this *hurts me*?! You could come over here, pull me into your arms and I would melt into your touch. Seek comfort in your embrace. But I *can't* do that. I can't let you break me anymore than you already have. I just– can't."

Her tears were flowing freely now. Her vision blurred as they mixed with the dark kohl around her eyes and the paint on her lashes that Yvaine had applied earlier. And she was quite sure that she had rivers of black running down her face.

"Auraelia, please."

"What do you want, Daemon?" Her voice was low and the anguish that filled her heart bled into every word. Exhausted, she turned back toward the balcony–watching the storm roll in from off the coast.

He must have shadow-walked to her, because she didn't hear him move.

"*Please*, Auraelia. Let me explain. And if you never want to see me or hear from me again, I will leave you in peace. Just, please hear me out."

She felt the warmth of his body as he stepped closer to her back, his scent of sandalwood and the ocean permeating all of her senses. She closed her eyes and breathed him in, but she refused to lean into him.

Fought every instinct she had to turn and bury her face into his chest.

"I'm sorry."

His apology surprised her enough that she turned around to face him but kept the space between them. "Sorry? You're *sorry*?"

He nodded, bringing his hand up as if to stroke her cheek, but seemed to think better of it and dropped it back to his side.

"Yes, Auraelia. I'm sorry. I'm sorry that I stopped writing. I hadn't intended to, but I got it in my head that if I stopped, you would forget about me, and it would be easier that way."

When she widened her eyes and tilted her head to the side, he hastily continued.

"Let me explain." He ran his hand through his hair, a nervous habit that she once thought was endearing.

"The treaty between our two kingdoms has always loomed over us. And the closer we got, the more I *wanted* you. The more I *needed* to be near you. And I got *scared*, Auraelia. I didn't know what to do, so I did nothing."

His eyes were full of regret as he searched her face.

"When my mother suggested that I invite you to solstice, it was the day that I returned home. I wanted to, but I wasn't sure how you would receive it since everything was still so new. But as time went on, I kept pushing it off. Until it got to the point where I felt like I couldn't invite you. Auraelia, it had nothing to do with you not being good enough. You're far better than anyone I know, and I wanted you here. Goddess, did I want that. I wanted to show you off to my court. Let you meet my mother, my father, my insufferable sister. I wanted you here with me. I meant it when I said that I am a better man for knowing you."

Auraelia nodded, her lips pursed in thought. "You're sorry?"

"Yes, Auraelia. I am *so* sorry."

Her head continued to bob, then she looked up to meet his gaze. Her eyebrows furrowed slightly. "You got scared?"

Confusion crossed his features. "Yes...?" It was meant as a statement, but it came across as a question.

Her smile was cold as she threw her hands up in the air and slowly backed away from him. She could feel her magic rolling under the surface of her skin, begging to be released. "Oh, well, then that makes this all better, doesn't it? You're *sorry*. You got *scared*. Well guess what, so was I! Goddess! How could you not think that I was going through the same thing?!"

Auraelia let her magic slip past her hold just a fraction. Using the force of the wind to push him away from her. Tears no longer fell, as disgust and anger became front and center.

A mirthless laugh escaped from her lips. "That's pathetic, Daemon. And you know it."

He stood there stunned for a moment, but she watched as frustration crept into his features, and the sadness in his eyes was replaced with anger.

"Don't tell me you wouldn't have done the same, Auraelia."

She laughed. "You're joking right? We were in the same position, Daemon!" She was full on yelling now, but the thunder rolling through the sky drowned her outburst.

"What would you have had me do, Auraelia? Tell me, please. Since you seem to have all the answers." His tone was boarding on condescending, and all it did was stoke her anger.

"Oh, don't be so fucking obtuse. I would have *talked* to you. I would have let you know how I felt. Not just fucking disappeared!"

"But you didn't, did you? You didn't tell me how you felt. You didn't *talk* to me. You just carried on as if nothing was wrong."

"Because I didn't think anything *was* wrong. We *both* knew what being together meant. We *both* knew that there was a treaty hanging over our heads that would make this damned near impossible. *Fuck*! Why didn't you just *talk* to me when you felt overwhelmed? Was I just a good time? Why was it so *easy* for you to just–just *leave* me?"

Her anger pulled back enough to let hurt shine through. "Why, Daemon? Tell me *why*."

"I told you why!" He was yelling now, and angrily running his fingers through his hair as he paced the room. "Fuck, Auraelia. What do you want me to say?!"

"Saying you were scared and that you're sorry is not a reason. I want to know why, Daemon. Why was it so *easy* for you to let this go after you fought so hard to convince me it was a good idea. I want to know *why* you were a coward and didn't invite me here yourself, despite the fact that your mother wanted me here. Why did she have to hold your hand in this? Daemon, I want to fucking know *why*! If you were done, you could have just told me. I would have understood."

Air began to swirl around her as her emotions and temper rose. She closed her eyes and focused on her breathing, reconnecting with her magic the way that Ser Aeron taught her, so that she could calm the storm raging inside of her.

When the anger ebbed enough for her to still the air around her, she opened her eyes and locked her gaze onto his. A mixture of emotions roiled in those moss green eyes. Anger, sadness, confusion.

She took a deep, steadying breath. "Why–why couldn't you just let what happened in Lyndaria stay in Lyndaria? Why did you have to fracture my heart?"

Daemon collapsed in one of the chairs that made up the small sitting area in her chambers. His elbows planted on his knees, as he ran his hands through his hair, leaving his head to rest in his palms.

After a few minutes, he looked up to meet her gaze. "Deciding to let you go was one of the hardest decisions I've had to make, and I've regretted it every day since. As for why–" he sighed as a look of defeat marring his features. "Auraelia, can this even go anywhere? We can't get married, and yes, I know that would be far off if it ever happened, but you know that we couldn't. Not unless one of us abdicates the claim to our throne. And I know you wouldn't–I wouldn't even *ask* you to. And with my father ill, it wasn't something that I wanted to bring up. I couldn't do that to him. He's *relying* on me to take the crown. My *people* are relying on me to take the crown. We have always said that our kingdoms came first, and for the first time in my life I found myself putting them second, and that was unacceptable. But tell me, Auraelia. Can you say the same? Has the thought of leaving everything you know and love behind ever crossed your mind?"

Daemon gave his words time to sink in before he continued. "I didn't invite you, didn't feel as if I could, because I knew the moment that I saw you–that I held you in my arms again, I would throw it all away to keep you. I knew that the minute my mother and my sister met you that they would do whatever they could do to make sure that I could have you, if that was what you wanted, too. Yvaine would take the throne for me if it meant that I could be happy. But I couldn't, in good conscience, do that to her."

Auraelia looked to the ceiling, willing her tears to dissipate before she tried to respond.

"Wh–" she took a steadying breath before she continued and met his eyes. "What happened in the last few weeks that made the treaty such an ominous threat that you thought that I would be better off without you? Better off not knowing that was your decision?"

Daemon stood and took a few steps in her direction. And with every step he took toward her, she took one back until her back met a solid surface. He placed his hands on the wall next to her head, effectively caging her in.

With barely a breath of space between them, her heart quicked its pace. She couldn't think straight with him this close. Even when she was this mad at him, her body reacted to his.

His words were barely more than a whisper. "I *thought* that you would be better off without me, because you deserve to be happy, Auraelia. I *thought* that if I left you alone, you would move on and forget about me. Hate me even. Though knowing that you hated me would have killed me, at least I would have given you the chance to live the life you deserved. But I thought wrong. I was so very wrong."

He let out a breathy exhale that coasted across her cheek. "I was wrong to stop writing. I was wrong to think that I could live without you. Wrong to think that I could stand the idea of you with anyone else. And goddess knows I deserve all your ire, because you do not deserve any of the pain that I caused. And I will tell you that I'm sorry until my dying breath if that's what it would take to lessen the hurt I see in your eyes. But I am, Auraelia. I am so sorry."

She stared at the clasps on his vest, refusing to look into his eyes. "Those are just words, Daemon. How am I supposed to trust you? How am I supposed to believe anything that you say to me when everything has been a lie?" her voice cracked with the swell of emotions.

"I don't know. But I want to fix this, Auraelia. *Please* let me try."

Her heart picked up pace at his words, and new tears rimmed her eyes. He was pleading with her now, and as much as she wanted to, she couldn't let down her guard. The image of him laughing with another woman as she ran her fingers through his hair, played on a loop in her mind.

Auraelia took a breath to steal herself before she asked the question that burned on the end of her tongue. "What about the other woman?"

Daemon pushed away from the wall and ran both hands through his hair this time. "Auraelia, there is only *you*. There has only been you since I saw you shining like a star across that stupid ballroom in Lyndaria. Will only *be* you, until you cast me aside. And then probably for years afterward."

"But–" she swallowed the sob that had worked its way up her throat. "But I saw you with another woman tonight. She was running her hands through your hair and seemed to know you on an *intimate* level."

Daemon's brow furrowed in confusion, then relaxed as realization dawned.

"Fiery red hair?"

Anger once again flared behind her eyes as she nodded.

"That was Sariah. She's Yvaine's ex-girlfriend, but we're childhood friends. She's like a sister to me. I swear it. Auraelia, *please*."

No longer able to hold back her tears, she let them fall freely down her cheeks.

"What do you *want*, Daemon? Because I can't– I *won't* do this again."

He cupped her face in his hands and tilted it up toward his. "*You.* I want you. You are the only woman for me, Auraelia. No one else."

A sob racked her chest.

As she brought her hands up to cup his cheeks, he brought his lips down onto hers. It was soft and simple, but she felt it all the way to her toes all the same.

When he pulled back, he ran his thumbs under her eyes, surely smearing the streaks of makeup that trailed down with her tears.

"Goddess, I'm a mess," she said as she tried to wipe away the tear stains on her face.

Daemon grabbed her hands and wrapped them around his waist before bringing his own back to her face. One gently wrapped around the nape of her neck, while the other cupped her cheek. She leaned into his touch and gazed up at him with misty eyes.

"No, my star. You are a *masterpiece*."

Then he pulled her closer and crashed his lips against hers.

Chapter Twenty-Nine

Daemon

The feeling of having Auraelia in his arms again was like coming up for air. Like suddenly the world had righted itself, and everything was as it should be. They still had things to discuss and figure out, but right now–in this moment– his world was whole once more.

She melted into his touch, her grip on the back of his shirt unrelenting, as if she were afraid he would disappear on her again. He pulled her flush against him, reveling in the way her body molded perfectly to his.

His hand drifted from her neck to her hair, tangling his fingers in the soft waves as he held her to him. When she moaned against his mouth, the sound went straight to his cock and made his heart race.

Their hands became desperate, their kisses more frantic.

It was as if they were both trying to erase the fight they had, while simultaneously making up for their missed time together.

His hand coasted down her back, landing on the patch of bare skin at the base of her spine. Her skin was feather soft and warm beneath his touch, and he wanted to reacquaint himself with every inch.

As his fingers slipped beneath the fabric, dipping slightly to graze the dimples above her ass, his cock twitched behind the laces of his trousers–his need growing by the minute. And if Auraelia's frantic fingers were anything to go by, she was right there with him.

But now was not the time.

He just wanted to–needed to–hold her. Comfort and reassure her that this wasn't going to happen again.

He wasn't sure how much time he had, or how long she was staying in Kalmeera, but he wanted to make every moment count.

Daemon reluctantly broke their kiss. Placing one on her forehead before resting his brow on hers. "Let me help you get cleaned up."

Auraelia pulled back and lifted a brow, rightfully skeptical of his intentions if their history was anything to go by.

He chuckled as his thumb idly traced the ridge of her cheek. "I promise, Auraelia. I just want to help. No ulterior motives. I just–I want to take care of you. I want to start trying to make amends, and if that first step is me helping you get cleaned up, then it would be my pleasure." He paused for a moment, his eyes searching hers. "But if you need space to think, or–"

Auraelia brought a finger up to his lips. "I *think* I've had enough space for the last month and a half, and I'd like some company."

Her eyes were still glassy from the tears she'd shed, but there was a small smile that tugged at the corners of her mouth.

She dropped her hand and turned towards the bathing chamber, and he watched the subtle sway of her hips as she walked away. His heart kicking up a notch as his breath caught in his throat.

Goddess, help me.

He took a deep breath, then followed her in.

He entered to the sight of Auraelia on her tiptoes, leaning across the counter as she tried to get as close to the mirror as possible. The position accentuated the long lean lines of her body, and the muscles of her arm stood out from her balancing her weight on it. Her long golden tresses hung like a curtain to one side.

She was stunning.

He crossed the space in a few strides and placed a hand on her lower back–their eyes locked in the mirror. "Here–" he held out his hand for the cloth she was using to wipe off the kohl, "Let me."

She held his gaze as she nodded, then turned and handed him the damp rag. Placing it to the side, he picked her up by her hips and set her on the counter–her legs falling open naturally to accommodate him between them.

Like this, the slit in her skirt slid open to reveal the entire length of her leg, nearly stopping where her hip and thigh met. The chain garter draped across her tanned skin and jingled softly with every movement of her leg.

Daemon's breath caught in his throat as his eyes roved over her body like a man starved. Swallowing thickly, he stepped further into the space between her legs and picked up the cloth. This close, he could feel the heat between her legs, and he had to suppress a moan that threatened to escape.

When he finally pulled his gaze to hers, the tears had dried, and the hurt had ebbed. And in their place were tiny embers of passion, ones that he was desperate to stoke back to life.

He dipped the cloth into the water that she'd pooled in the basin, and ever so gently wiped the black streaks from her face.

They sat in silence, the air thick with tension and electricity, neither of them brave enough to break the silence.

He worked slowly, wanting to soak in every moment. But every time she leaned into his touch and her eyes fluttered closed, his heart skipped.

When he'd finished, and set the cloth aside, he gently lifted her off the counter, letting her body slide down his until her feet touched the floor.

They stood there a moment– their gazes locked and his hands on her hips while hers gripped tightly on his biceps.

A flush crept across her cheeks, and he watched as it traveled down her throat.

He watched as her lips parted slightly and her tongue made its way across the plump flesh.

Fuck, is it hot in here?

Daemon cleared his throat and took a step away. "I, uh–I'll let you get changed."

He turned and ran a hand roughly through his hair as he headed towards the exit, his mind racing. He was almost to the door when he heard her speak.

"Could you help me with the buttons?"

Daemon stopped and turned. "Buttons?"

A low chuckle brought a tiny spark back to her eyes, "Yes, Daemon. Buttons. I believe there are three on the upper part of the bodice that are holding my dress in place. Would you undo them for me, please?"

He stood dumbfounded for a moment, like she was speaking another language, before he snapped out of his stupor. Nodding hastily, he took hurried steps across the floor. When she turned, giving him her back, flashbacks of their night together after her coronation played through his mind.

Memories of his knuckles brushing up her sides and her skin pebbling under his touch while he unlaced her corset. The way her head would loll to the side, giving him access to the full column of her neck. Flashes of her splayed on his bed, with firelight licking across her skin.

Demon nervously ran his hands up her arms to her shoulders. Gathering her hair before he delicately swept it to one side– exposing the long line of her back.

His hands shook slightly as he undid the tiny buttons, and when he finished, he let out the breath he had unintentionally been holding.

After a muttered, "thank you," from Auraelia, he left the bathing chamber and went back into her room.

Auraelia

She felt the air stir around her, the telltale sign that Daemon had shadow walked, and released a breath.

Closing her eyes, she let her head hang forward, and focused on her breathing.

In. Out.

In. Out.

Her mind was a tangle of thought and feelings. They still had so much that they needed to discuss, but she couldn't deny the fact that she wanted him.

She wanted his mouth on hers, and between her legs.

She wanted his hands on her bare skin, touching every inch of her body.

She'd had that–for a fleeting moment– she had his hands on her. His fingertips coasting up her arms and then skimming the skin of her back as he undid the buttons of her dress. The firm grip he had on her hips as he lifted her onto the counter had her heart fluttering in her chest. And when she slid back down his body, she was so sure that he would claim her then and there.

His eyes had been burning with lust, and the way his fingers flexed against her hips she could tell it was taking everything he had not to act on it.

Well, that just won't do.

Auraelia slipped out of her dress but left the chain and pearl garter around her leg. Then, crossing the chilled marble floor, she grabbed the silk night dress that hung on the back of the door.

It was short– falling to her upper thigh– and clung to every curve of her body before falling to barely cover the swell of her ass. The color was a deep sapphire-blue and the bottom was edged in lace the color of moonlight. The neckline cut low between her breasts–perfectly framing the pendant that Daemon had given her– and had simple embroidery that matched the lace. The back dipped into a *V* at the base of her spine, leaving her entire back exposed.

There were small slits on the bottom at both side seams, and delicate straps that had trouble staying on her shoulders. There was even a matching–barely there–pair of panties that she threw on as well.

Deciding to forgo the robe, she took a fortifying breath and headed out into her bed chamber.

When she opened the door, she fully expected to see him standing on the other side waiting for her. But instead, he sat on the edge of her bed.

He'd taken off his coat and boots, leaving him in just his charcoal-colored leather pants and dove gray tunic. He'd loosened the ties at his neck, letting it hang open to reveal the tattoos across his chest, and his sleeves were rolled up to the elbow revealing the strong muscular lines of his tattooed forearms– which were planted on his knees. He had his hands clasped between them, and his head hung in defeat. He hadn't even heard her open the bathroom door.

Taking full advantage of his distraction, Auraelia drank in the sight of him as she walked quietly across her room until she stood in front of him– her bare feet in his line of vision.

Daemon slowly lifted his head, taking in every inch of her bare skin.

She noticed the way his hands clenched together. The subtle shift of his feet on the floor. Then when his gaze reached the hem of her gown he stopped, the muscles in his jaw tightening as he ground his teeth together.

"*Auraelia–*" He drew out her name through clenched teeth, "What are you wearing?"

A smile that he couldn't see spread across her face, but she kept her tone light and innocent. "It's a nightgown. Don't you like it?"

He squeezed his eyes shut and shook his head. "Fucking, goddess." He took a deep breath through his nose, his head still swinging back and forth like he was trying to shake the images from his mind. "My star, I am trying so hard to behave. And you're making it *very* difficult."

Auraelia pressed a finger below his chin and tilted his face up to hers. When he finally opened his eyes, the golden pools in his irises had taken over the green and his pupils were slowly encroaching as well.

Auraelia let herself drown in his eyes, soaking up every blaze of passion that burned in their depths. "I think I'd rather you be a little naughty."

Chapter Thirty

Daemon

She looked like a goddess.

Standing there in silk and lace, with her honey blonde waves cascading down her back. The moonlight that filtered through the open doors to her balcony casting her in a luminous light. Between the silver glow from the moon, and the stardust that sparkled in her eyes, he could have sworn an actual goddess stood in front of him.

"Auraelia." His voice was barely above a whisper.

Her eyes never left his as she took a step toward him, the movement forcing his hands apart and him to sit up straight.

"Daemon," she purred as she held his gaze, sliding into the space between his knees until his face was level with her breasts.

"We–we should *talk*."

He drowned in the hazy blue of her eyes as she cupped his cheek in her hand and traced his lips with her thumb. She hummed her agreement, but the smirk on her lips said she had other plans.

"*Auraelia–*"

The tenor of his voice deepened as his need for her grew, and when she ran her hand through his hair, he knew he'd lost. His eyes closed, savoring the feeling of her simple touches that he'd craved for so long.

She took a step closer, and as if of their own volition, his hands slowly slid up her bare legs. He let his hands drift further up her body until they found her hips, her skin softer than the silk she wore.

With a gentle pull towards him, Auraelia was sliding her legs on either side of his hips, straddling his lap. The heat of her core nestled above his aching cock.

His hands didn't wander. Instead, they kept a firm hold on her hips–preventing her from rocking against him.

"Auraelia, *my star*–" His voice sounded whiny even to his own ears.

She held his gaze, seriousness banking the lust in her eyes. "We will talk, Daemon. I swear. But right now? Right now, I *need* you. I need to *feel* you."

"You swear?" he asked as his hands drifted from her hips up her side, his thumbs barely brushing the outer swells of her breasts before wrapping around to stroke up her bare back. Her breath hitched, and the minute sound that accompanied it made his cock twitch beneath her.

She licked her bottom lip then pulled it between her teeth, and Daemon zeroed in on the movement as she nodded.

"Fuck it."

Within seconds, his hands were tangled in her hair as he pulled her face to his.

Their lips collided, and it was like stars exploding–bright, beautiful, and *powerful*.

His magic flared as his hands wandered her body, gliding over silk and lace, as he sought out every patch of bare skin, and traced every decadent dip and luscious curve.

She pulled at his shirt, tugging it from where it was still tucked into the waist of his trousers.

Breaking the kiss long enough to help her pull the fabric over his head, he then rotated them to where she was spread out on the bed. Her hair in a messy tangle of waves and pearls around her head.

He stood from where he had placed her on the bed and released the hold he had on his magic. Pulling and shaping the shadows to wrap them in a world all their own. One full of stars. Of constellations and galaxies. Where the sky twinkled, and colors coalesced into vibrant pools of light on an inky black background.

"Daemon." Auraelia's eyes widened, and her breath hitched in her throat as awe swept across her features.

"*No one* is going to hear a sound you make tonight. Not one scream. Not a single moan. Those belong to *me*. And I want to hear them all."

The embers in her eyes were now a blazing inferno of passion and possession.

A stiff wind swirled through their cocoon of stars and slammed into his back. Urging him forward until he almost fell onto the bed.

A smirk pulled at the corners of his mouth. "Patience, Princess. We have all night, and I plan on taking my time with you."

He wanted her writhing under his touch– begging for his cock. He needed to *taste* her. But first, he needed to play out the fantasy that had been playing on a loop in his mind.

Daemon dropped to his knees, and slowly slid his hands up the outside of her legs until he reached her hips. Hooking his fingers in the waistband of her panties, he slid them down and off her legs.

When he stood once more, her brows furrowed, and he smiled a rakish smile.

"Touch yourself."

"Wh–what?"

"You heard me. I want you to touch yourself. Show me what I was missing all those nights you were in Lyndaria. I want to *see* what you did while you thought of me."

A flush crept across her cheeks, but her eyes sparkled from the challenge as they raked down his body–settling on the defined ridge in his pants.

She pulled her bottom lip between her teeth once more, and when she released it, the smile on her lips promised trouble.

She sat up and leisurely slipped the silk gown over her head before tossing it at him. When he glowered in response, she winked and scooted back on the bed until she was propped up on the pillows. Her legs spread wide, and the sight of her glistening pussy made him second guess his decision.

Her eyes stayed locked onto him, while he watched.

Watched as one of her hands glided down her body to the junction of her thighs, while the other palmed her breast and tweaked her nipple.

Watched as she slid her fingers through her slit gathering her arousal before she slowly circled her clit and plunged those same digits inside.

Watched as a thin sheen of sweat formed over her body as she repeated those steps over and over, building her pleasure.

But when her eyes fluttered closed, her head fell back and her breath quickened, Daemon had enough.

Grabbing an ankle in each hand, he yanked her to the edge of the bed until her ass almost hung over the side.

"Daemon!" His name was a squeak of protest, but it was short lived the moment his mouth was on her. This time, when she said his name, it was a husky moan that could make him come in his pants from just the sound.

The taste of her on his tongue had his eyes rolling back in his head in bliss.

"Fuck, you taste good."

It didn't take long for him to work her back to the edge after he'd pulled her across the bed. Alternating between flicks of her clit and spearing her on his tongue, she began teetering on the edge of oblivion.

When he added two fingers, curling them the way that she liked, her fingers dug into his hair. Effectively holding him in place as she rode his face.

As her walls began clenching around his fingers, her hold on his head tightened. The slight pain that accompanied it had him moaning against her, and the resulting vibration against her clit tipped her over the edge, her orgasm crashing through her.

Daemon stayed between her legs, lapping up every drop of her release until her body relaxed under his touch.

With one final lick up her center, he pulled away and slowly kissed his way up her body, pausing every so often to speak. "I've wanted to watch you get yourself off since you wrote me that fucking letter." *Kiss.* "But, fuck, if that wasn't the sexiest shit I've ever seen." *Kiss.*

She giggled and began stroking his hair as he made his way up her body.

"And yet, you couldn't keep your hands–or your tongue–to yourself."

He stopped abruptly and looked up at her through his lashes.

She had a haughty look on her face–her mouth lifted at one corner, brows slightly raised, and a slight tilt to her head.

He lifted his head and matched her expression. "Would you prefer I keep to myself? You seemed to quite enjoy my tongue on your cunt, Princess."

"Perhaps–" challenge flared in her eyes, "But I'm not so sure you could handle it."

His answering growl had need growing in her gaze, and he could feel her heart picking up its pace.

Insatiable creature.

"*Auraelia*, if you don't watch that mouth, I'm going to fuck it."

The wicked smile that pulled across her face had his cock thickening, and the pressure of being confined to his pants was suddenly too much.

Her smile broadened, and mischief sparked in her eyes. "Promises, promises."

Auraelia

Daemon had done exactly as he promised. Fucking her mouth until tears streamed down her face once more, but for an entirely different reason.

She smiled to herself as she leaned back against the tub and soaked in the warm eucalyptus-scented waters. He'd drawn her a bath after he came down her throat, urging her to relax while he went in search of food.

The doors to her balcony were still thrown wide open, letting the ocean breeze drift through her chambers. And the soothing sound of the waves crashing against the cliff side were a balm to her soul.

Though partially sated, her mind was still a tangled web of indecision. There was so much that she and Daemon still needed to discuss. From where they went from here, to how they would handle the treaty, and manage time apart once she went back home.

Her mind was still spinning when she heard the soft padding of footsteps through her room, putting a small smile on her face.

"Well don't you look cozy." Piper's sing-song voice floated across the quiet of her bathing chamber.

Auraelia shot up straight, the cloth across her eyes falling into the water. "What are you doing in here?"

Piper leaned against the frame of the door, her arms crossed over her chest and a look of indignation on her face. "You're joking right?" She narrowed her eyes at Auraelia for a moment, and then her features shifted to one of intrigue.

"*Auraelia.*" Piper drew out her name, a small smirk lifting a singular corner of her mouth. "Did you have a *boy* in your room after you forced Xander and I back to the party?"

Auraelia's lips folded inward, and she pulled her gaze from Piper's unflinching scrutiny.

"You *did*! Oh, my goddess." Her excitement was palpable, but it didn't last– her face falling moments later.

"What is it, Piper?"

"I'm happy for you, Rae, really. But did you at least talk? Please tell me that you talked first."

Auraelia hung her head slightly. They hadn't *talked* exactly, but explanations had been made and they mutually agreed to put off the conversations that needed to be had in favor of enjoying each other's bodies. Was it a smart plan? No, not exactly. But it was one that she was content with at the moment, and one she didn't want Piper adding her concerns to.

She sighed as her eyes migrated back to her friend. "We haven't talked everything out, but we will. Shortly after you left, he showed up in my room. We yelled. I cried. He explained. And we decided to talk tomorrow, once emotions weren't so high. I'm not an idiot, Piper. I know there is a lot that needs to be figured out, I just–I just want to *be* with him right now. No stress. No treaty looming overhead. Just a man and a woman. Please, just let me be a woman who is–"

A small smile crept across Piper's face, and her eyes softened. "A woman who is what, Rae?"

Auraelia matched Piper's smile but didn't answer her question. "So where is he anyway?"

"He went to grab some food. You should *probably* be gone by the time he gets back."

As soon as the last word left her lips, the telltale signs of Daemon's magic permeated the air, and she watched as the shadows in the corner of her bathing chamber darkened.

He was there, but he was waiting for Piper to make her exit first.

Piper's eyes shifted from Auraelia to the darkened corner that kept pulling her attention, and when the connection settled into place her eyes widened in understanding.

She mouthed '*right*' and then slowly began to back out of the room.

"Okay, well, I'm just going to go then. Rae, I will catch up with you in the *morning*." It was a statement and a question all rolled into one. When a flush colored Auraelia's cheeks, she amended it. "*Late* morning, obviously."

She chuckled as her friend winked and then backed the rest of the way out to the door. But before Piper fully exited her chambers, she hollered into the space. "Glad to see you're taking care of my girl, Daemon. Don't screw it up again!"

With the sound of the door latching into place, he dropped his shadows. Placing the covered tray in his hands on the counter, he strolled over to where Auraelia was giggling in the tub.

"How'd she know I was here?" Mirth filled his tone, and she glanced up to see a genuine smile tugging at the corners of his mouth.

"Hmm? Oh, she can read me like an open book. *She* noticed my reaction the moment that *I* noticed that *you* shadow-walked into the room."

"Ahh." His head bobbed in understanding, and he sank down to the floor behind her head. Tapping the edge of the tub to let her know he wanted her to lay back, he gently gathered her hair into his hands and draped it back over the side.

With the gentlest of touches, he kneaded into the muscles of her shoulders as he trailed kisses down the column of her neck.

She moaned as her muscles loosened under his ministrations.

"That feels amazing." Her eyes fluttered closed as she melted under his touch.

She felt him smile against her skin as he continued to trail kisses along her neck and across her shoulders. His hands worked in tandem, massaging her shoulders and then down her arms. He rubbed away the tension that was built up at the base of her skull, then meticulously plucked all the pearls from her hair. Then after unraveling all of the braids, he ran his fingers through her waves, and massaged life back into her scalp.

"You're going to put me to sleep." Fully relaxed, her voice was barely above a whisper.

"We could go to bed, you know."

Auraelia turned her head slightly and cracked one eye. "You're serious?"

He laughed, and the sound made her heart soar. She'd only heard him laugh a few times, and it was quickly becoming one of her favorite sounds.

"Yes, I'm serious. If you're tired, I'll wrap you in my arms and hold you while you sleep."

She sat up, her hair dragging over the side of the tub and sticking to her wet back. She turned fully around in the tub—the water cutting directly across her nipples. A sultry smirk pulled at her lips, while her eyes locked onto his.

"*Daemon–*" his name was a purr rolling off her tongue. She stood slowly, streams of water rolling down her curves. "That sounds wonderful and all. But, if I'm being completely honest, that's not what I want. Not right now."

His smile shifted into one that would make the demons of the underworld second guess themselves. "No?"

She shook her head slowly. Watching as his eyes devoured her naked form–heat licking at her skin from the passion that burned there.

Daemon stood, and rounded the tub until he stood directly in front of her. She turned toward him, her nipples hardening under his intense stare.

"No, Daemon. That's not what I want."

"As you wish, Princess."

Catching her behind her knees, he lifted her from the tub and wrapped her legs around his waist. Auraelia's hands threaded through his hair, pulling his head back so that she could crash her lips to his.

Daemon walked them to the bedroom, where he unceremoniously dropped a dripping Auraelia onto the bed.

She watched him with hungry eyes as he stripped out of his clothes, devouring every inch of skin as it presented itself. From the deep contours of every muscle and the designs inked onto his skin, to the impressive length between his legs. He was a masterpiece.

And he was hers.

When the last piece of clothing was added to the pile on the floor, he grabbed her ankles and flipped her onto her stomach. His fingers were featherlight caresses up her legs and had her wriggling beneath his touch.

He kissed up her spine and nipped at her shoulder, while his hands massaged her backside.

"*Daemon*–" her voice was a breathy plea, but he took his time.

"You want my cock, Auraelia? You want me buried to the hilt inside your pussy?" His words were heated whispers across her skin.

"*Yes*, for the love of every goddess, yes!"

The warmth and weight of his body pulled away, and with a sharp slap to her ass, he gripped her hips with firm fingers and hauled her backside into the air.

A breeze drifted through the open windows and licked across her wet core, sending chills up her spine. But that chill was quickly replaced by the heat of his mouth.

After two licks up her center, his tongue was replaced by the thick head of his cock running through her slit.

"*Daemon-*" she moaned, pushing her hips back into his.

"Say *please*, Princess." She could hear the smirk on his lips, and when she rolled her eyes, another slap landed across her backside.

"I saw that, Auraelia," he said as he rubbed the sore spot on her ass cheek.

She couldn't help the whimper that escaped from her lips as his fingers slipped between her cheeks, adding pressure as they progressed down to her center.

He slid his fingers through her slit before dipping them into her entrance–gathering her arousal on his fingers before trailing them back up between her cheeks. Adding pressure as he circled the tight hole, but never pushing through.

"Say please, Auraelia, and I will fuck you until you don't remember your own name."

He slid his cock through her slit before slapping the head against her clit, sending a jolt of pain-edged pleasure through her body.

"Beg me, and I will fuck this tight, little hole." He added more pressure to the tight ring of her ass as he spoke. "Has anyone claimed you here, Auraelia?"

The pressure he had on her anus increased as he continuously slid his cock against her. Stopping periodically to let his fingers dip into her core, before returning to work her asshole.

She shook her head, then quickly added a verbal response when she felt his hand shift against her throbbing cheeks.

"No, Daemon. No one has fucked me in the ass." Exasperation bled into her tone.

His body pressed down onto hers, as he leaned to whisper in her ear.

"Do you want *me* to fuck you in the ass, my star? Claim your body in every way possible so that no man will ever be able to satisfy you? Because that's what will happen, Auraelia. I'm going to make damn sure of it."

He pulled away, and the loss of his body against hers made her heart ache. But then his hands were on her hips and his cock was thrusting into her pussy.

"*Fuck,* Daemon!" she moaned into the coverlet beneath her as he fully seated himself inside her.

His hand slid down her spine and into her hair. His grip was tight, but not painful, as he twisted it around his fist– pulling gently, but with enough force to lift her head.

"I do believe that's what I'm doing, Princess." As if to emphasize his point, he withdrew slowly before slamming back in. "Now, about that ass."

His movements stilled, giving her a brief reprieve so that she could try to form a coherent sentence.

"I don't know, Daemon, it's hard to think straight with your dick in me."

His chuckle sent a shiver down her spine. It was deep and promised all manners of debauchery.

"I'm not going to jump straight to fucking your ass, Princess." He began moving again, but it was torturously slow, and she whined in protest. "You need a lot of preparation first. We need the right oils and need to slowly stretch that tight little hole before I can even think about getting my cock anywhere near it."

Auraelia grew impatient as he spoke. She needed friction. She needed it rougher, dirtier– and his slow and tender movements weren't cutting it. She clenched the muscles in her core, tightening them around his cock. The move made him groan and tighten his grip on her hair.

"*Behave.*" The way he ground out the word sent a flood of heat to her center, so she did it again. Eliciting another deep growl from within his throat and earning another slap to her ass.

"*Shit.*" The pain from multiple strikes to her cheeks was starting to linger, despite him rubbing the tender flesh after each one.

"As I was *saying*, there's a lot to be done before your ass is ready for me. But since you're unsure, maybe we could try just a finger, see how you like it."

She wasn't overly fond of the idea, but she also didn't hate it. It also helped that she knew if it turned out to be something she was completely opposed to, he would never broach the subject again.

"Fine, Daemon. You can finger-fuck my ass, as long as you *dick*-fuck my pussy."

"Deal."

She could hear his satisfaction dripping in his tone. But true to his word, Daemon drove into her–hard.

His pace was punishing.

The grip on her hair, unrelenting.

And the sound of their slick bodies coming together, mixed with moans of pleasure and strings of curses, was a symphony that she would never tire of.

After circling her clit a few times, Daemon's fingers returned to the tight ring of her ass. Spreading her arousal around before pressing against it until finally the tip of his smallest finger slipped inside.

The pressure was strange, but as her muscles relaxed against the intrusion, it added an unexpected layer of pleasure.

His finger slowly slipped further in, letting her adjust as he went. When she was fully relaxed against that single digit, only then did he begin to work it in and out. The slight friction ricocheted through her body and settled in her core.

She moaned and pushed her hips back against him, meeting his cock thrust for thrust as his finger fucked her ass.

"That's it, Auraelia. *Fuck*, look at you. So, fucking beautiful."

Her orgasm built slowly.

Heat radiated out from her center, filling her body as a blissful buzz settled into her fingers and toes.

Daemon released his grip on her hair and slid his hand down her body– tracing every vertebrae in her spine before slipping it around to circle her clit.

Between the punishing pace in her pussy, the finger in her ass, and his fingers circling her clit, it was too much, and her orgasm came crashing down. Daemon's name was a hoarse cry from her throat as her pleasure ripped through her like waves crashing against the shore in a storm.

Daemon gently removed his finger from her ass and gripped her hip. Pulling her to him as he thrusted into her, building to his own release. With the walls of her pussy spasming around his cock, he wasn't too far behind her.

His fingers moved fervently against her, urging her back over the edge that she had just climbed down from. But with one final thrust, and a pinch to her clit, he sent her flying back into oblivion as she came again right along with him.

He withdrew carefully, then collapsed on the bed next to her and trailed kisses up her arm. They lay there in silence, Daemon tracing circles on her back, as their breathing returned to normal, and their heart rates slowed.

Leaning over, he pressed a kiss to her lips. "I'll be right back."

Before she could protest, or ask where he was going, Daemon disappeared.

Naked.

What the hell?

It wasn't long before she heard the trickling sound of water from her bathing chamber, and she smiled. *Of course.*

Moments later, he returned, only this time he sauntered back into the room instead of magically appearing. Kneeling between her knees, he took the warm, wet cloth and carefully wiped between her legs–cleaning her up like he always had.

Auraelia moaned at the feeling of the warm cloth between her legs, the way it soothed the slight soreness there.

"*Auraelia–*" Daemon removed himself from between her knees and stood from the bed.

Chuckling, she rolled onto her back and stretched her arms above her head. "Don't worry, I'm *currently* sated." She paused, bringing her hand to her mouth as she tried–unsuccessfully–to stifle a yawn. "Actually, I think I'll take you up on that '*wrap you in my arms and hold you while you sleep*' offer now."

A cheeky grin spread across her face as she settled beneath the sheets.

Dameon smiled his beautiful smile as he shook his head. "Your wish is my command, Princess."

He tossed the cloth on the floor by the bathroom, walked to the opposite side of the bed, and slid beneath the covers. Wrapping his arm around her middle, he pulled her to him, her body molding perfectly to his.

A contented sigh slipped through her lips as she relaxed into his warm embrace. His whispered, "*Goodnight, my beautiful star,*" were the last words she heard before sleep claimed her.

Chapter Thirty-One

Auraelia

Early morning sunlight filtered into her room through her still open balcony doors, while the soothing sounds of waves breaking against the mountain side filled the space.

But that wasn't what roused Auraelia from her dreamless sleep.

Instead, it was a large, warm–slightly callused–hand gliding along her thigh and up her body, while a mouth left a trail of heated kisses across her shoulder and neck.

"You're still here," her voice was still ladened with sleep, and the subsequent yawn that escaped made Daemon chuckle against her shoulder.

"There's nowhere else I'd rather be, my star."

Auraelia groaned as she arched her back into a stretch. The movement pushing her ass into Daemon's hardened cock.

"*Auraelia,* you insatiable creature–"

"Excuse me? I just woke up to your hands and lips on *me* and your cock pressed against my ass, and you're calling *me* insatiable?"

His chuckle reverberated through her, waking up every part of her body.

"Touché, Princess. But can you blame me when you're lying *deliciously* naked next to me?"

His hands continued to travel over her body, avoiding every part of her that craved his touch. They skirted around her breasts and the apex of her thighs, sticking strictly to her stomach and thighs.

He no longer trailed kisses up her neck or her shoulder, instead he left whispers of breath across her skin, causing it to pebble in anticipation.

"*Daemon,*" she whined, and pushed her hips back into his.

"Yes?" His hand continued to coast along her body.

"You've woken me up and made me needy."

She reached behind her and gripped his length in her hand, squeezing slightly as she slid her palm up his shaft. His sharp intake of breath was music to her ears.

He pulled out of her grip and rolled her onto her back. Climbing on top, he held his weight on one arm as the other snaked down her body to the apex of her thighs–her legs instinctively spreading for him.

He slid two fingers through her slit, before circling her clit. "Fuck, Auraelia. You're such a good girl. All wet and ready for my cock."

"Yes," she moaned, dragging out the word. Her eyes rolled into the back of her head as he toyed with her.

When she moaned again, his mouth descended onto hers.

Withdrawing his fingers, he wrapped his arms around her middle and rolled–putting her on top.

Auraelia pulled back and sat up. Her slick center settled against the hard length of his cock, and she began to rock against it, spreading her arousal along his length.

Daemon's jaw tightened and his nostrils flared as he tried to let her retain control. She loved this side of him. The one that handed over the reins and let her be in full control.

She felt *powerful*.

"What do you want, Daemon?" she asked as she continued to rock against him.

"I want you to be a good girl and ride my cock."

Auraelia pulled her bottom lip between her teeth before a smirk settled onto her lips.

"Yes, sir."

Those two words sparked something in his eyes. Hunger and possession warred in their moss green depths, while molten pools of gold grew to overtake the green–the telltale sign that his magic was scratching against the surface.

"*Now*, Auraelia." His patience was hanging on by a thread, and he sounded like he wanted to devour her whole.

She slid along his cock twice more before lifting and positioning its head at her entrance.

She sank down his length gradually. Taking him inch by inch until he was fully seated inside her.

The moan that left his lips sent a flood of heat to pool at her center.

"*Goddess*." His eyes rolled into the back of his head, and she could feel his dick pulsing.

"I'll be your goddess."

"Oh, my star, you already are." His eyes locked onto hers, and unspoken words mixed with desire shone back at her.

Her thoughts began to spiral, so she locked them down. Focusing instead on bringing him pleasure and finding her own.

Later. I'll over analyze everything later.

She began to rock her hips against his, her clit grinding against his pelvis as his hands roved her body.

Alternating between spearing herself on his cock and rocking against it, she felt her orgasm grow. When Daemon's grip on her hips tightened, she knew he was close.

She bent down, pressing her lips to his, before whispering into his ear.

"Fuck me, Daemon."

Daemon pulled her lips back to his and rolled her underneath him.

Grabbing a pillow from the head of the bed, he stuck it under her hips before bringing both legs to his shoulders and slamming into her pussy.

Auraelia reached down to circle her clit with one hand while the other pinched her nipple.

"Fuck, Auraelia. My cock was made for this pussy. Come for me, Princess. I want to feel you come all over my cock."

With a few more thrusts and circles on her clit, she did just that. The orgasm barreled through her and pulled him with her.

As they lay there, spent and sated, Auraelia let her mind run rampant.

He hadn't fucked her– he'd *claimed* her.

In that moment, with his cock deep inside of her and filth spilling from his lips, he'd staked his claim on her heart and her soul. And something she wasn't quite ready to acknowledge made itself known.

But as she went to say something to him, the door across her suite opened and closed. The telltale sound of Piper's not-so-inconspicuous footsteps sounded across the suite, heading towards her door.

Shit.

Chapter Thirty-Two

Daemon

Confusion settled onto his face when Auraelia groaned and pulled the silk sheet over her head after one of the best rounds of morning sex he'd ever had.

"Everything alright?"

"Piper." Her voice was muffled beneath the linens, but he understood her nonetheless.

No sooner than the words left her mouth, was there a quick succession of knocks on the door.

"Do you want me to leave?" He didn't want to ask the question, but out of respect for her and her privacy, he did anyway. He didn't want to leave her side at all, for anything. They'd spent too much time apart as it was, and they still had too much to discuss. But he knew that he couldn't smother her either.

It was a delicate balance that they hadn't figured out yet, and he wasn't about to start off on the wrong foot.

She removed the sheet from her face. Propping up on her elbows, she looked at him with warmth in her eyes. "No, Daemon. I don't want you to leave. I want my *nosey best friend to go find food and come back later!*" The latter part of her statement was loudly directed toward the door and met with a cackle from the other side.

"Note taken!" Piper hollered back, before her footsteps retreated back across the space.

"So much for *late* morning," she grumbled as she fell back against the bed.

Daemon couldn't help the laugh that bubbled up his throat, and when Auraelia's brow furrowed in confusion, he laughed harder.

"What's gotten into you?"

"Nothing, just adding another reason to my ever-growing list of reasons for your nickname."

"Care to elaborate?"

Her tone was bordering on annoyance, so he took a moment to calm himself before explaining. "You, my *star*, aren't a morning person, are you?"

"Oh, fuck off," she grumbled, pulling the sheet back over her head as she rolled away from him.

He chuckled, then dove under the sheet as well, pulling her body flush to his–the feeling of her warm skin pressed against his had his dick hardening again. When she pushed back into his hips, a groan rumbled in his throat, and he pulled her closer.

His hands roamed her body as he trailed kisses across her shoulder and playfully nipped the skin where her neck met her shoulder.

"And you called me *insatiable*." Her tone was light with the husky undertones of lust.

His hand slid down her body, slipping between her legs to circle the sensitive bundle of nerves there. As she rocked against his hand, her ass ground against his growing erection.

"Fuck, Auraelia. What have you done to me?" he moaned in her ear, then pulled the sensitive lobe between his teeth. Her low hum in response sent every ounce of blood straight down.

Within seconds he was between her legs, poised at her entrance with her legs wrapped around his hips trying to pull him into her. Her eyes burned with unfettered passion. Green streaks lighting up her gaze as her magic pooled at the surface, and Daemon's magic responded in kind, itching to reach out and mingle with hers.

"Let your magic go, Auraelia."

Confusion and hesitancy marred her features as her eyes searched his face.

"Let *go*, my star. I've got you." Daemon held her gaze as he dropped the hold on his magic.

The shadows swirled and twisted around the space, creating a barrier around the room while tendrils licked across her skin, urging her play.

Auraelia closed her eyes and took a deep breath.

When she opened them once more, Daemon's breath caught in his throat. Gone were the marbled blues and grays of her irises. In their place was a green, so vibrant, he'd only seen it in the heart of an opal.

When she exhaled, a controlled gale force wind tore through the room. The curtains around the windows billowed in the onslaught and the shards of sea glass that hung from her chandelier knocked into each other, creating a delicate chime.

It whipped around them, spinning into tiny spirals that mixed and mingled with his shadows. The air filled with electricity that made the hair on his arms stand on end, as a smirk that rivaled his own crept across her face.

"Oh, this is going to be fun." The grin on his face widened into a full-blown smile before he pressed his lips to hers in a bruising kiss.

Between the amount of magic that was expended and the multiple rounds of sex, they were spent.

They'd each found their release once more, and then collapsed onto the bed–Auraelia by the pillows, with Daemon sprawled across the end of the bed. Their legs entangled between them.

"Daemon–" Her voice was a breathy whisper as she tried to slow her breathing. "As much fun as this morning has been, I need food. And coffee. Lots and lots of coffee. And food. Did I mention food?"

He chuckled and forced himself into a sitting position.

"Your wish," Daemon bent at the waist in a mock bow, "Is my command."

He winked, and with an overexaggerated flourish of his hand, the tray from the night before appeared on the bed beside them, surrounded by ribbons of shadow.

He removed the cloche to reveal a plate of fruits and bread and watched as her eyes zeroed in on the assortment with excitement. As if on cue, her stomach growled and a flush colored her cheeks.

"Eat, Auraelia. I have to actually go get you coffee, but this should tide you over until I return."

He crawled across the bed and kissed her softly on her lips. "I'll even bring back something hot."

Her eyes widened and a smile crept across her face as the prospect of a hot meal.

My girl really loves her food. The thought made him smile, and he pressed another kiss to her lips before standing from the bed.

He dressed in his pants and shirt from the night before, then gathered his boots and jacket before shadow-walking to his chambers.

When he arrived, Aiden was lounging on the couch in his study and his mood was immediately soured. He understood that as emissary for the court, Aiden was responsible for carrying out the orders from the king and queen, but he still would have appreciated a heads up.

"What are you doing here, Aiden? I don't have the time or the patience for your bullshit today."

Aiden sat up but kept his gaze on his lap. "I'm sorry, D. Truly." He looked up to meet Daemon's gaze across the space, and guilt—as well as determination—swam in his eyes. "I was under direct orders from your mother to keep it from you. I'm not sure what game she's playing, and I didn't want to be a part of it, but you know I don't have a choice."

Daemon pinched the bridge of his nose and exhaled. "I know and trust me I will be speaking with my mother about this whole charade. But first I need to talk to Auraelia."

Aiden scrunched his brow in confusion. "What the fuck have you been doing all night if you haven't been talking?"

He didn't need to say a thing. He just tilted his head towards his friend, and with a slight shrug of his shoulders, Aiden knew exactly *what* he had been up to.

Aiden shook his head in dismay. "You really like her, huh?"

Daemon smiled. "You have no idea, my friend. No idea."

After Aiden left, Daemon hurried into his chambers for a quick shower and a change of clothes.

He'd just pulled on his second boot when there was a knock at the door.

You've got to be kidding me.

He hastily walked to the door in his study and pulled it open. "Hello, Mother."

"Hello, my son." Her smile was sweet, but it was the cockiness in her eyes that stoked the embers of his anger.

Daemon stepped aside and let his mother in. "What are you doing here, Mother? And don't give me the whole *'can't a mother come see her son'* bit."

Her chuckle was mirthless. "I wanted to see how things went with Auraelia. *If* they went anywhere." She sighed and turned to face where he still stood by the door. "I wanted to see how *you* were. Are you alright?"

He sighed, and pulled the door closed. Motioning for her to sit on the couch that Aiden had vacated earlier, he walked over to his desk.

"What are y–"

Daemon held up a finger to cut her sentence short. "You're currently impeding my plans, Mother. So, please, give me a moment to handle something that is of utmost importance."

Queen Avyanna acquiesced, closing her mouth with a small smile, she held her hands up in surrender and sat down on the couch where she waited for him to finish.

Once his letters had been penned and sent off to their destinations, Daemon turned his attention back to his mother.

"Now, let's talk about this meddling habit of yours, shall we?"

Auraelia

With Daemon gone, and Piper off goddess knows where, Auraelia wasn't quite sure what to do with herself. She'd lounged in bed and picked at the tray of fruits and bread that he'd left her with, but that would only get her so far. She needed an actual meal. She needed coffee. And he was taking longer than she had anticipated.

Standing from the bed, she padded into her bathing chamber to take a quick shower and try to tame the mess that had become of her hair. Once she was finished, she pulled on her dressing robe and headed back into her chambers.

She was still towel drying her hair when a folded piece of parchment fluttered down and landed on the floor at her feet. Her smile was brief, as disappointment set in at the realization that he wasn't coming back as quickly as he said that he would.

My Star,

I am so sorry that this is taking so long. I returned to my chambers for a quick shower and to change and have since been bombarded by Aiden and now my mother.

I am trying to get back to you as soon as I can. But, since my mother is currently perched on my couch, I can't leave right now.

Don't worry though. I have sent word to the kitchens that you are in need of food and coffee, and it should be arriving shortly.

I promise, I will be back as soon as I can. There are so many things that I would love to show you while you're here, if you'll let me.

Wait for me, Auraelia, please.

-D

The smile returned to her lips as she finished reading the letter again, just in time for the knock at the suite door.

When she reached for the handle on her door, she heard Piper's singsong voice echoing across their shared sitting area. "Rae, there's a tray here with your name on it. Literally. Your name is written on a piece of parchment."

What the hell? Auraelia scrunched her brow in confusion, but she tightened the sash around her waist and pulled the door to her chambers open.

Piper stood in the middle of the room with the covered tray in her hands. "Do you want it in here or in there? Either way, I'm staring at you while you eat until you spill all of your secrets." A sly smile crept across her friend's features, and she shook her head.

"Come on, then." Auraelia stepped aside, sweeping her arm out in front of her in a mock welcome. "I will share my secrets, but I am *not* sharing my food. That man seems to think he can fuck me without feeding me." The latter part of her statement was said more to herself than to Piper, but she heard it anyway and started laughing as she set the tray down on the bed.

"I didn't hear you complaining this morning when I came to *get you* for breakfast."

Auraelia rolled her eyes and walked over to the bed. Plopping down next to her friend, she removed the parchment from in front of the cloche.

> *I hope you're hungry, Princess.*
> *Dress for a ride today.*
> *-D*

It was simple, but it still brought a smile to her face. When Piper snatched it out of her hand, flipping it back and forth like that would make more words appear–her brows scrunched in confusion–Auraelia laughed and removed the cloche from the dish.

The smell of toasted bread, butter, eggs, and bacon wafted through the air with the removal of the shining dome. There was also the sweet smell of blackberry jam, and honey that had been drizzled over strawberries. And coffee. Sweet, glorious, rich coffee.

She added sugar and cream to the bitter liquid before she fisted the mug in both hands and brought it up to her face, her eyes fluttering closed as she inhaled the rich aroma. When she took a sip, her body relaxed as she savored the flavor on her tongue.

When she opened them again, Piper was staring at her like she'd lost her mind.

"Are you okay over there, Rae? Do you need a little time alone with your coffee?"

"Oh, hush, you!" She grabbed a pillow, and smacked Piper over the head sending them into a fit of hysteria.

Once they calmed down, she dug into her food as Piper peppered her with questions about her night with Daemon.

When all the sordid details had been spilled, and there was nothing left to say, a tension filled silence descended into the space.

"So, you still haven't talked? About anything?" Piper asked, her tone full of worry. When Auraelia shook her head and looked away, Piper pinched the bridge of her nose in frustration. "Rae, come on. You're smarter than this." Her tone was harsher than Auraelia was used to, but she also understood why.

Sighing, she nodded in agreement. "I know... I know. We're going to talk, I promise. He said he wants to show me Kalmeera, so I'll try to talk to him then. But trust me, we're going to talk. We have to. I can't leave here without that happening."

Piper nodded, but her shoulders were tense and there was a crease across her forehead that only showed itself when she was trying not to say something.

"What is it?"

Piper looked away and pushed a breath out through pursed lips before she pulled her gaze back to her friend. "I just need you to remember that *you* are worth more than this. *You* are worth more than a sideline seat in his life. You may be '*his star,*' but to our court? Rae, you're the sun, the moon, *and* the stars. You are the future, and you deserve more than what he's been giving you. Don't settle for less. Promise me, you will hold your worth higher than your heart. Promise me, please."

Auraelia reached across the space between them and grasped Piper's hands firmly in hers. Tears welling as she gazed into Piper's silver-lined hazel eyes.

"I promise, Piper. I know my worth. I know it with every fiber of my being because you have reminded me of it my whole life, and I will hold it higher than my heart."

She pulled Piper into a firm embrace, staying there until the tears in both of their eyes had dried.

When they pulled apart, Auraelia released a breath and stood, walking over to the wardrobe where her clothes had been put away.

"You know, Queen Avyanna sent a trunk of Kalmeeran garments for us to wear if we wanted. It's in the sitting area if you want to wear something from there," Piper said from where she was still perched on the bed.

Auraelia turned around slowly, her eyes narrowing as she caught the sly look on Piper's face.

Her curiosity fully piqued, she asked, "What's so special about these clothes, Piper?"

Standing from the bed, Piper backed towards the door with a grin on her face. "Why don't you come with me and find out."

Chapter Thirty-Three

Daemon

An hour.

His mother kept him for a whole hour, and the entire time that she was talking, his mind continuously wandered to Auraelia.

She'd explained her reasoning behind her scheming, but that didn't mean he was any less annoyed by her methods.

Thankful that she brought Auraelia to Kalmeera?

Yes.

Overjoyed at the prospect of things moving in a forward direction with her *because* of his mother's meddling?

Of course.

But annoyed, nonetheless.

Daemon shadow-walked back to Auraelia's suite, but instead of entering unannounced as he had the night before purely out of desperation and the fact that he thought she wouldn't let him in otherwise–he appeared outside the main door that led into the sitting room.

He could faintly hear the conversation between Auraelia and Piper, and though he couldn't make out exactly what they were saying, their words were intermixed with laughter, and it brought a smile to his face.

Taking a breath to center himself and calm his nerves, Daemon knocked–the sound bringing the conversation on the opposite side of the door to an abrupt hault.

As he stood there, he could hear whispered mumbling and a scurrying of footsteps across the space before Piper finally called for him to enter.

He had no idea what to expect when he walked through that door, but it wasn't anything compared to what he saw. Standing in the middle of the room was Auraelia, dressed in traditional Kalmeeran riding clothes. She was a vision of beauty, curves, and all things inherently *Auraelia*. He stood stock still, his breath caught in his throat as he drank her in.

The clothes were simple, but they still accentuated every feature she had. She wore simple, flat, chocolate-brown boots that ended right below her knee. Her leggings were a slightly lighter hue and hugged every curve.

The top was a plain, loose, white linen tunic and she had her sleeves rolled to her elbow. The neckline cut down between her breasts, the ties that crossed the bottom of the deep V doing nothing but drawing attention to the swell of her breasts and the sapphire pendant that dangled between them. Cinching her waist was a Kalmeeran corset in a matching blue with intricately embroidered waves and shells in pearlescent white thread and was secured across the front with brass hook and eye closures.

Her golden waves had been pulled back away from her face and tied into a simple ponytail that cascaded down past her shoulders. There were still a few strands that fell around her face, and he itched to run his knuckles across her cheek and tuck them behind her ear.

She also had her dagger strapped to her thigh. The sheath was attached to a belt around her waist that connected down to a strap around her leg that held it in place.

"You–you look–I, um–" Words evaded him at every turn as he gazed at her.

"Thank you." A sweet smile tilted her lips up at the corners, but with a cocky edge. She knew how good she looked, and the confidence that radiated off her was the sexiest thing about her.

He cleared his throat, and then finally stepped fully into the space as an awkward silence fell around them.

Piper's wide eyes flitted back and forth between him and Auraelia, before rolling to the back of her head as she threw her arms in the air in defeat. "You're both ridiculous. Daemon, where are you taking us today?"

"Us?" he asked, clearly confused.

Just as the word left his lips, Xander stepped through the door and into the suite.

"Yes, *us*. Do you really think we're going to let the future queen of Lyndaria traipse around your kingdom unaccompanied?" His tone was curt, and Daemon could feel his disapproving gaze as he crossed the room.

"Xander–" Piper and Auraelia said his name simultaneously, but Auraelia continued alone. "That's quite enough. If you insist on accompanying me, you're more than welcome, but you will not spoil my day with your sour attitude."

"Auraelia." His tone was chiding, and it rubbed Daemon the wrong way.

"Xander, I mean it. Either slap a smile on your face or find something else to do. Piper will be with me, so if you really don't want to go, you don't have to. I don't *need* you to come with me. I can take care of myself."

His sigh was exasperated, and he shook his head in defeat as he agreed to her terms. With Xander's smile–albeit, fake–firmly in place, Daemon shared his plans for the day.

"I want to take you through the city and show you some of my favorite places. There's the grove of fruit trees right here on the grounds, my favorite bakery in the heart of the city, as well as the market. I also wanted to show you how we handle all the imports here."

Auraelia and Piper's excitement was palpable, and it made him all the more excited to show them his world. He wanted her to be happy here, even if it was only for a short period of time.

Daemon smiled and held out his hand for Auraelia. "Shall we?"

"Wait, wait, wait. Are you going to do that 'shadow-walking' thing?" Piper asked, practically bouncing in place with excitement.

He chuckled then nodded his head. "Yes, I was about to do *'that shadow-walking thing.'* Did you want to tag along?" His eyebrows were raised as he waited for her answer.

He assumed she would say yes, but he hadn't expected her to come bounding across the sitting room and grasp Auraelia's arm in a grip so tight that Piper's knuckles began turning white. Her face was lit with pure joy, and he couldn't help but laugh.

"Alright, alright. I'll bring you first." Daemon turned his attention to Xander, "Did you want to–"

"No, I'll keep my feet firmly planted on the ground, thank you very much." Xander turned and stalked toward the door.

"We'll meet you at the stables," Daemon hollered, his words barely reaching Xander before he turned down the hall.

With Xander gone, Daemon turned his attention back to the two women. "Ready, Piper?" Daemon pried her grip from Auraelia's arm and pulled her into an embrace–her back to his front. "Close your eyes and breathe."

After she nodded, he turned his attention to Auraelia, a smile forming on his lips. "I'll be right back for you. Don't go anywhere, Princess."

Then with a wink, he was gone.

When they landed in the stables, he kept a firm grip on Piper, remembering the way that Auraelia handled her first trip.

"What the *fuck* was that?" she asked, pinching her temples as she sank down to the ground and put her head between her knees.

"Sorry, it's a little disorienting the first time."

Piper blew out through pursed lips and groaned. "First, and *last*. I'm never doing that again."

Daemon was about to leave to get Auraelia, when Xander strolled into the stables.

"What the hell? Piper, are you ok?" his voice and eyes were laced with concern as he made his way over to Piper, and kneeled by her side.

When his attention was directed back to Daemon, his gaze was full of ire, but Piper pulled that gaze back to her when she spoke.

"I'm fine, Xan. Just a little dizzy from the trip."

Xan? Daemon smoothed the furrow that formed in his brow at the informal nickname. Not even Auraelia used one, at least not in the presence of other people.

"Piper, if you're alright, I'm going to go grab Auraelia."

"Yea, I'm fine. Go get your girl." She waved him off and stuck her head further between her knees.

Not wasting anymore time, Daemon funneled his magic into another shadow-walk.

When he materialized in the suite once more, Auraelia was standing at the bookshelf perusing the volumes that lined the shelves.

"See anything you like?" His voice was a low rumble in his throat, and it sent a visible chill down her spine.

When she turned toward him, there was a mischievous gleam in her eye that promised a world of trouble.

"*Auraelia*. We don't have time for whatever idea is spiraling in that beautiful head of yours."

She smirked as she pulled away from the shelves and sauntered over to where he stood.

"Pity." The slight tilt to her head and the way she pulled her lip between her teeth, had a surge of heat pooling in his groin. *It's going to be a long day.*

When she got close enough, he pulled her into his arms and briefly pressed his lips to hers. "Shall we?"

The smile she gave him put all the stars in the sky to shame. "Let's go."

Chapter Thirty-Four

Auraelia

Kalmeera was breathtakingly beautiful.

Birds in a variety of colors flew over their heads as they rode down the main thoroughfare, their calls filling the air as they flitted from tree to tree. The flora around the island was just as colorful as its birds, and their fragrance permeated the air.

There were plumeria trees with delicate white and yellow flowers that were smaller than her palm, and hibiscus bushes with flowers as large as her hand that came in an assortment of colors. Palm trees towered over the streets and houses, their fronds providing shade to the creatures and people of the island, while freestanding plants littered the ground. The yellow, orange and blue flowered plant that looked like the birds in the trees–aptly named bird-of-paradise according to Daemon–had quickly become her favorite, but the amount of greenery that engulfed the isles was absolutely stunning and so very different from what she was used to.

The houses were mostly made of beams and stucco instead of solid stone, with beautiful flower boxes under the windows. Windows of colored glass covered the city, reminding her of the windows in the ballroom back home.

"Are you enjoying yourself?" His question pulled her out of the enchantment the scenery put her in.

"I am. Daemon, it's beautiful here. I wish that Piper and Xander would have been able to come with us."

He raised an eyebrow at her, clearly skeptical, and it made her laugh.

"Obviously, I'm glad to have some alone time with you, *outside of a bedroom*. But she would have loved this."

After her first experience with shadow-walking, Piper didn't feel up to an adventure through the city. Auraelia remembered how she felt after her first trip from the garden to Daemon's chambers back in Lyndaria. She'd been dizzy, but Piper seemed to have taken it harder, claiming a headache and nausea, and the need to lay down.

Xander, goddess love him, had agreed to stay with her to make sure that she was alright. And when he'd offered, Auraelia didn't miss the small squeeze of Piper's hand in his or the faint blush that colored her friend's cheeks. She'd always thought that something might be between them, but every time they were around her, Xander treated Piper like a sister, and Piper picked at him in the same familial way.

She looked around once more, taking in the myriad of colors and the people as they walked to and from the shops. Each one stopping to wave at their prince as he rode down the lane.

She loved discovering this new side of him, completely at ease and smiling freely at anyone who looked his way. She loved the closeness that he had with his people.

Kalmeera was completely open to its citizens. The castle kept their grounds accessible so people could benefit from their gardens, and everyone seemed genuinely happy here.

Though it was probably easier to be accessible with the city right next to the castle, unlike in Lyndaria where it was a good hour ride away. But she wondered if it was the same on the other islands as well.

They rode for a while, Auraelia peppering him with questions about his kingdom that he hadn't told her in the letters. He explained that he and his sister alternated who went to the other islands to check in and make sure that everything was running smoothly. And how they each spent one week a month with their people there.

He told her about the people on Malaena–the middle island–and how they harvested obsidian from the mountainside. Forming it into knives, arrow heads, and other weapons and tools that were needed. As well as using the sand from their beaches to make the colored glass that was found throughout the city.

He explained that Lunaria–the smallest of the islands–was where the temple for Narissa stood. Sitting on top of the highest mountain peak so that they priestesses could see both the sea and the stars without interference. How they lived a simple life without the comforts most people long for in life. He told her of the summer he spent there three years ago, after his magic manifested, learning more about his goddess and how to connect and control the shadows around and within him.

He was giving her a whole new look into his life, and it bandaged the pieces that had been fractured the day before a little bit more.

When they came to the center of the city, she had a feeling that she knew where they were heading. The smell of fresh bread and pastries filled the air, and made her mouth water.

"Please tell me we're going in there."

Daemon's smile broadened, and she matched it with one of her own. "Of course, we are. My woman loves food, so I'm bringing her to get food." Then he winked, and the butterflies in her stomach began to flutter in response.

He dismounted his horse–a menacing, solid black stallion named Poe that looked like Daemon's shadows had been given life–as they approached the small cottage style building.

Every time she looked at his horse, their conversation from the stables brought a smile to her face.

"Poe? You named that behemoth Poe?" Auraelia asked incredulously as the black stallion glared down at her.

Daemon laughed as he stroked the animal's velvety muzzle. "I was only ten, what did you want me to name him? Balthazar? Or maybe Leviathan?"

"I feel like either of those would fit better than Poe at this point."

"Maybe now, but not when he was a lanky-legged colt. Which is what he was when I got him." His voice was full of laughter, and it brought a smile to her face.

She kept her distance until Daemon grabbed her hand and pulled her to him. Handing her a carrot, and keeping his hand on hers, he let Poe sniff her hand. And after he realized she had a treat for him, his ears perked forward, and he'd allowed her to stroke his nose.

The slight pull from Daemon grabbing the bridle of her horse pulled her from the memory. She was borrowing Yvaine's horse, Luna, who was a beautiful moon-white mare with crystal-blue eyes and the temperament of a springtime breeze.

Leading them to a tree covered in fluffy red blooms that stood in front of the bakery, he tied the reins of the mounts around a low branch.

When he helped her dismount, her body slid down his until her feet were firmly on the ground, and it lit a fire low in her stomach.

"It's called a bottle-brush tree." His voice was like velvet, lush and soft.

"What?" She was lost in the closeness of his body, her mind unable to comprehend his words.

He inclined his head to where the horses were secured. "The tree. It's called a bottle-brush tree because of the shape of the blooms."

When he reached up to tuck a strand of hair behind her ear, she leaned into his touch, but the moment was spoiled by the sound of the cottage door opening.

"Prince Daemon!" A stout elderly woman shouted from the small doorway of the bakery. "I'm so glad you've come. I have a surprise for you–who's your pretty friend?"

Her attention was locked onto Auraelia as she continued to cross the yard toward the quaint wooden fence that surrounded the property.

"Auntie, this is Princess Auraelia from the Court of Emerald," he responded as the elderly woman got closer. "Also, how many times have I asked you to stop using my title in informal settings?" His chide was playful, and he pulled her in for a hug when she reached them.

"A princess, huh? Maybe *queen* one day, hmm?" She elbowed Daemon in his side as she jested, and a flush colored his cheeks when his gaze met Auraelia's. The woman then turned her attention onto Auraelia. "It's a pleasure to meet you, Princess. I'm Jodie, but most people around here call me Auntie, and you're more than welcome to do so as well."

"It's a pleasure to meet you as well, but please, call me Auraelia or Rae. Like Daemon, I'm not big on formalities–unless it's absolutely necessary."

Jodie's eyes grew wide, and a smile spread across her face as she grasped Auraelia's hands in her old, wrinkled ones and squeezed.

When she released them, she turned and headed back toward the bakery, hollering over her shoulder, "Come on now, I need to pull them out of the oven."

She and Daemon shared a look, before they both shrugged and followed Jodie into the building.

It was warm inside, but not as warm as his hand on her back as he guided her through the shelves full of baked goods.

Breads of varying kinds filled baskets, while glass cases of pastries lined one side of the room. There were shelves of assorted cheeses, and even some fresh fruit. But the thing that caught her eye was the fresh tray of croissants that Jodie pulled out of the stone oven at the back of her shop.

Auraelia inhaled deeply, her eyes rolling to the back of her head from the delicious aroma. "Jodie, those smell absolutely divine."

"They do, don't they? When Daemon came back from his trip to Lyndaria he wouldn't shut his trap about some chocolate filled pastries that he had, so I decided to give them a try."

Auraelia cut her gaze to Daemon, eyes wide with curiosity. He refused to meet her gaze as a fresh flush, the color of the wax on a cheese wheel, covered his face. She smiled and took a few steps until they were toe to toe, and he was forced to look her way.

"You talked that sweet old lady into making chocolate croissants and then brought me all the way into the city to try them? Daemon Alexander, do you *like* me?" Her voice was only loud enough for his ears.

Out of the corner of her eye, she could see his hands flexing by his side in frustration. His eyes flicked toward the kitchen, presumably to make sure that Jodie was preoccupied, before he lightly gripped her chin between two fingers. The golden pools of his eyes turned molten as his desire flared to life. Keeping his voice low, he growled, and she felt it all the way down to her toes. "Princess, what have I told you about that smart mouth of yours?"

They left the bakery with full stomachs and fuller hearts. Jodie was a delight to be around, and Auraelia loved how comfortable she felt in her presence. It was like being with family instead of with someone she'd just met. Not to mention that the croissants had been even better than she imagined, and she made sure to bring some with her to share with Xander and Piper.

The rest of the afternoon went much like their encounter at the bakery. Daemon took her along the waterways that ran throughout the city. Showing her how they interconnected so that people could travel from one end of the city to the other without having to worry about foot traffic. He took her to the marketplace where people from all over Ixora could come to sell and barter their goods, explaining how their ports and exchanges worked. And everywhere they went, they were met with friendly faces eager to show him their wares. Faces that grew even more excited when they learned he was with the princess from Emerald. He met each of them with a smile and a handshake, taking the time to speak with all who approached him.

He knew his people. And in one day, he'd shown her just how much he *loved* his people and how beloved he was in return.

As they continued their way through the city, he took his time, showing her everything that it had to offer. From pointing out and naming the numerous different plants and birds, to regaling her with stories from his childhood.

The day was perfect. Aside from them being addressed by their titles, she could almost imagine that they were two normal people spending the day together. Getting to know each other without treaties looming overhead, and kingdoms that relied on them.

Almost.

Auraelia was so lost in her thoughts, that she hadn't noticed they were riding out of the city, or that Daemon had been calling her name.

"Auraelia?" Worry tangled in that one word, and it pulled her from her thoughts.

"I'm sorry, what were you saying?" A smile pulled at her lips, and she hoped that it would ease the worry that had etched itself into his features. But the furrow in his brow told her that he hadn't bought it.

"I said I have something to show you."

She laughed, and it brought some light back into her tone. "Daemon, you've been *showing* me things all day."

He smiled in return, causing tiny creases to form by the corners of his eyes. "True, but this is one of my favorite spots on the island. Think of it as my Nefeli Lake."

At his mention of her and Piper's secret lake, she was immediately intrigued, and her smile grew in excitement.

"I think it would be a good place to talk."

And just like that, the illusion of them being just a man and a woman enjoying each other's company, without duty or responsibilities outside of themselves, came crashing down around her.

Despite her knowing they needed to have this conversation, she wanted to be *just* Auraelia and Daemon for a little while longer.

Pasting a smile on her face, she tried to make sure that it reached her eyes as she nodded her head.

"Sounds perfect."

Chapter Thirty-Five

Daemon

The smile on her face wasn't fooling anyone. Despite her efforts, it didn't reach her eyes and he saw the moment his words popped the blissful bubble they had been floating in all day.

It killed him to break the spell they were under.

In a perfect world, they could have continued as they were. Traveling side by side without a care in the world. But they didn't live in a perfect world.

They lived in a world where distance separated them, and treaties could keep them apart.

A world where no matter how much they may wish it were different, they had responsibilities and kingdoms that relied on them.

So, despite every fiber of his being begging to stay in the peaceful moment that this day brought, he knew they couldn't put it off any longer.

The way to Azure Falls was quiet.

Auraelia seemed to be lost in thought. No longer was her head on a swivel, taking in everything around her with wonder in her eyes. Instead, she focused solely on the trail in front of them, her knuckles white as they gripped Luna's reins, and her shoulders tense.

Daemon's thoughts ran rampant. Going through every possible scenario he could come up with, praying that it led to a solution.

None of the options in front of them were easy choices to make. Nor were they what he wanted. He wanted an easy way out. One that gave him Auraelia without forcing one of them to give up their kingdoms.

Unfortunately, that wasn't how the world worked, and it was a fact that they would have to face sooner rather than later.

But at least they could face it together.

"We're here." His voice was barely louder than a whisper, but after traveling in silence, it still made her jump.

After dismounting, he walked over to where she was still seated in the saddle and held his arms out to help her down. Her body slid down his and he inhaled the faint scent of lavender that was inherently *her*.

When her feet were on solid ground, she held his gaze for a moment before turning away to take in the scene around them. "Where is *here*, exactly?"

Daemon smiled. "Come on, let me show you."

He'd stopped them far enough away from the falls that they were barely background noise. Tying the horses off to one of the nearby banyan trees, he grabbed her hand and led her the rest of the way to the falls.

The walk was short, but it required them to climb over a few boulders. And by the time they reached their destination, the sun had begun its descent.

As soon as they crested the final rock, and the sparkling pool of crystal-clear water at the base of falls came into view, Auraelia gasped. Her hands flew to cover her mouth, like the tiniest of sounds would disrupt the calm that radiated through the area. Her shock and awe were palpable, and he wished that he could just hold her and enjoy the moment.

"Daemon. It's—wow. I don't even have words."

When she finally turned to him, her eyes were misted over, but too many emotions swirled in their depths for him to get a good read on how she was feeling. She turned back to where the water was running down the mountain side in delicate vertical rivers before spilling into the pool below–their streams carving deep crevices into the mountainside.

"Thank you for sharing this with me. I will treasure it always."

He reached over to grab her hand and pulled her to him. Her face tilted up to his and he locked her into his embrace. "We need to talk, Auraelia. I don't want to have the conversation either, but we both know that it needs to happen. We can't put it off any longer."

He placed a chaste kiss on her forehead before she dropped it to his chest and sighed.

"I know." When she looked back up into his eyes, resolve and determination shone back at him.

"Come on." Walking to a small, flat rock that jutted out over the pool, Daemon sat and gestured for her to do the same. It was large enough for them to sit side by side without being on top of each other and low enough that they could put their feet in the water.

He helped her out of her boots and rolled the bottoms of her pants up to her knees. While she situated herself at the edge, her feet dangling in the water below, he did the same with his own. Sliding across the stone, he sat close, but left space between them.

They sat in silence for a while. Watching as the sun slowly crossed the sky and sank toward the horizon.

"Rae–"

She chuckled and hung her head back as she closed her eyes. "That's the first time you've ever called me that. I guess that's one surefire way to know that this conversation is going to suck."

Daemon shook his head, a small snicker escaping as he did. "Well, it's definitely not going to be fun, that's for sure."

Silence descended once more, before Auraelia pulled her feet from the water and turned towards him. "Okay, I'm ready. Where do we start?"

He blew out a breath, then turned his head to look her in the eyes. "I guess we start with what we both *want*."

Hope shone in her eyes as she stared back at him. "And what is it you want, Daemon?"

"Simple answer? I want you. But it's not as simple as that." He pulled his gaze from hers and lifted his feet from the water. Placing them flat on the rock face, he rested his forearms on his knees and stared out at the water that darkened with the sky.

Her hand was soft and gentle as she rested it on his shoulder, pulling his attention back to her. "Nothing about this is simple, Daemon. And we're not going to figure everything out sitting here on this rock. But what we *can* do is make sure that we're on the same page. That we both want the same things. I don't want to leave here just as confused as I was when I arrived. I want to *know* where we're going from here."

Daemon's gaze bore into hers. "What is it that *you* want, Auraelia? I've been telling you for days now that I want you, but I haven't heard those words returned."

A flush crept across her cheeks. It was barely perceivable in the dimming light, but he saw it just the same. When she tried to look away, he turned to kneel in front of her. Grasping her chin between two fingers, he slowly turned her face back to his and palmed her cheek as he ran his thumb across her cheekbone. "Tell me, please."

Tears began to well in her eyes, and his heart sank with the idea that she may have changed her mind. But when he went to pull away, her hand held his to her face and she leaned into his touch.

Her tears began to spill over and run down his hand as she spoke. "I want you, too. When you left Lyndaria, you took a piece of me with you, and I don't want it back. I've never felt like this before, Daemon, and I'm terrified."

He wiped away the streams of tears that were flowing freely now and kissed her lips. Pulling away, he smiled and shook his head in disbelief. "Do you know how much I've wanted to hear those words?"

Her laugh was a hiccup through the tears, but she held his gaze. "So, what now?"

"Well, my star, now we figure out what we're going to do about all of this. I know we can't solve the problem with the treaty right now, or even in the immediate future. But like you said, we need to make sure we're on the same page."

Twilight took over the sky and stars began to shine like pinpricks of light through a dark tapestry, as he and Auraelia talked through their options. With their plan falling into place, the weight that blanketed his heart began to lighten.

"So, we'll continue to write? As often as possible?" Auraelia asked, her eyes narrowed slightly with the question. No doubt remembering that it wasn't long ago that he'd stopped.

Daemon nodded and continued to trace the line of her knuckles with his thumb. "I'll also try to come to Lyndaria as often as I can. It's not going to be easy with my father still ill, but I would pull the stars from the sky if it meant that I got to be with you."

Auraelia flushed at his words and tucked a stray piece of hair behind her ear.

As the conversation continued, she decided that she would try to talk her mother into letting her visit Kalmeera as well, but they both knew that with the Fall solstice festivities with Topaz approaching–and all of the preparations that were required to pull it off–it wasn't likely to happen.

As the heaviness of their conversation lifted, so did the corners of her mouth.

"So, it's settled then. Communication and visits whenever possible," she said with an excited gleam in her eyes.

"Yes, and we will both work on trying to find some way out of this damn treaty. One that works for both of us."

Auraelia nodded her head in agreement, and smiled as he brought her hand to his lips, placing a light kiss on her knuckles. He wasn't lying when he said that he would remove the stars from the sky if it meant he got to be by her side. If he had his way, she wouldn't be leaving the Isles at all.

When he released her hand, and met her gaze once more, she seemed genuinely happy. A smile brighter than the moon stretched across her face and stardust sparkled in her eyes.

And he would do anything to keep it that way.

When the moon was in the sky, and the last fragments of sunlight rested on the horizon, Daemon stood and began to pull his shirt over his head.

Auraelia's eyes widened slightly in confusion before she narrowed them. "What are you doing?"

"Going for a swim," he answered as he unlaced the ties on his pants.

Her gaze traveled slowly down his body, stopping briefly at his hands, before bouncing back up to his face–eyebrow raised and a look of skepticism on her face. "A swim?"

Daemon stopped undoing his pants and squatted down in front of where she still sat. "Yes, a swim. Would you like to join me?"

She swallowed thickly, her gaze flicking from his face to the natural pool. "I–um."

Daemon grabbed her hands and stood, pulling her with him. Stepping into her space, he ran his knuckles down the side of her face to her neck, then down her arm–her skin pebbling under his touch. When he turned her toward the water, her intake of breath was barely audible, but it still broadened the smile on his face.

The once crystal-blue waters were now a perfect mirror to the sky above. The moon and stars reflecting in the pool below.

Daemon pulled her back flush to his front and whispered into her ear, "Come swim among the stars with me, Auraelia."

Chapter Thirty-Six

Auraelia

By the time they got back to the castle, the sky was dark, and the moon shone brightly overhead, while the stars glittered like diamonds scattered across the sky, and despite the heaviness of the conversation back at the waterfall, she never felt lighter.

They hadn't solved everything, but the fact that they were now on the same page, working toward the same goals, lifted a heaviness that had been weighing on her heart and made it easier for her to breathe.

They returned Luna and Poe to their stalls in the stables, and Daemon instructed the stable hands to give them extra grains and apples after they were brushed down.

"Walk with me?" he asked as he twined his fingers with hers, his thumb tracing the line of her knuckles.

She smiled, and it was full and uninhibited as she nodded and squeezed his hand tighter in her own. She'd been smiling so much since their conversation that her cheeks were now sore.

Daemon weaved them through the groves of fruit trees that covered the castle grounds. Carefully picking his way so that neither of them ended up with a twisted ankle from stepping on any of the fallen fruit or nuts that littered the ground.

"Did you have fun today?" The tinge of worry in his voice had her pulling him to a stop.

She reached up to run her fingers through his hair, the silky strands gliding through her fingers like silk, then ran the pads of her fingers across the stubble on his cheek. When he leaned into her touch, her heart soared.

She kept her voice soft, her eyes scouring the moss green depths of his. "Of course, I did."

Relief washed over his features as a small smile tilted up the corners of his mouth. Lacing his fingers tighter through hers, he started back in the direction of the castle. As they neared the edge of the grove, he pulled her toward a bench beneath a large plumeria tree that faced the courtyard where the celebration the night before had been held.

An easy silence fell over them, and she leaned against him as he draped his arm around her shoulders and pulled her close.

She tilted her head up, taking in the sharp lines of his jaw and the delicate fan of dark lashes that framed his moss green eyes. "Thank you for today. It meant a lot to me that you would share that part of your life."

Daemon turned his head toward hers and pressed a soft kiss to her lips. Then he smiled, and her heart lodged in her throat.

"My star, I would show you the world if you asked me to."

Tears sprang to her eyes at the sincerity of his words, and he wiped them away before pressing another kiss to her lips.

The rest of her time in Kalmeera went by too quickly. One day bled into the next until there were no more left, and she was standing on the gangplank that led onto the Nevermore. Taking one final look at the multitude of colors that filled this part of Ixora, she wished she could bring a piece of it home with her.

Daemon wasn't able to make the trip back with them, so they had said their goodbyes back in the privacy of her rooms.

She was sitting on her bed, hands clasped between her knees and her head hung low, when Daemon appeared swathed in shadows. Her trunk was still lying open, and half packed while Piper scurried between her own chambers and the sitting room. Leaving Auraelia the privacy she needed.

"What is it, Auraelia?" His voice sounded as defeated as she felt, and he crossed the room in two long strides, kneeling at her feet as he pulled her hands into his.

"I don't want to leave. Being here has been a dream." She looked up to meet his gaze, and the anguish that coursed through his eyes broke her heart. "I was able to just be. *Be a normal woman, spending time with a normal man."*

Daemon stroked her cheek, and she leaned into the caress–savoring the warm, calloused touch of his hand on her skin. He smiled, small wrinkles forming at the corners of his eyes, but the pain of her leaving still lingered there. "Auraelia Rose, do you like *me?"*

Her laugh came out as a hiccup as tears began to stream down her face. The memory of her asking him that question in the middle of the small bakery in the city seemed like so long ago. Daemon wiped away her tears, pulled her to her feet and into his arms.

"We were never normal, my star." His words were muffled against her hair.

"I know." She took a ragged breath, and then pried herself from his arms. Wiping the remaining tears from her face.

The rest of their time together was spent in a tense silence. Looks that said more than words would ever be able to crossed between them as he helped her pack the rest of her things. And when he signaled to his staff that her and Piper's trunks were ready to go, tears began anew.

There were so many words that she wanted to say, but there was no time to give them a voice. So instead, she pulled him to her and pressed her lips firmly against his. Praying that everything she wanted to say was portrayed in that one kiss.

When they pulled apart, Daemon pulled the sapphire pendant from beneath her tunic, admiring the way his shadows played with the light that streamed through the stone.

"You don't know how happy I was to see that you wear this every day." When his eyes met hers once more, they were glassy from unshed tears, but he cleared his throat and let the pendant fall back between her breasts.

He then reached into his vest pocket, and Auraelia's brow furrowed in confusion.

In his hand was a delicate silver chain that was shorter than the one that held her sapphire pendant. But instead of another blue stone, this necklace held an oval cut raw emerald.

"Where did you–?"

"The market. I saw you eyeing the stone while we walked around, and while you were preoccupied with the fabric vendor from Pearl, I slipped away and purchased it." A flush colored his cheeks the most beautiful shade of pink.

Pushing up onto her toes, she grabbed his face and pulled it to hers, planting her lips firmly on his. It was meant to be short and sweet, *but it quickly turned into something more. Her fingers gripped his neck, while his roamed her back and pulled her flush against him.*

The kiss was devastating and beautiful.

It said everything they needed, and wanted, to say without them uttering a word.

But when Piper cleared her throat at the door, they pulled apart. Both of them breathing heavily, their eyes never straying away from each other's face.

"Rae, I'm sorry, but it's time to go. Everything is loaded onto the ship, and we need to leave soon if we want to make it back before it gets too late."

"I'm coming, just give me a minute."

Out of her peripheral, she saw Piper nod before turning back toward the sitting room.

Daemon tucked a strand of hair that had come loose from her braid behind her ear, then leaned down to press a kiss to her brow and fastened the necklace around her neck.

She reached up and ran her fingers across the stone.

It sat right below the hollow of her throat, and warmed against her skin as her magic swam to the surface, recognizing the familiarity of the element.

"Thank you, Daemon. It's beautiful."

Daemon gave her a shallow nod, as he ran his hand across her cheek once more. His eyes tracing every line of her face, committing it to memory. He kissed her once more on the lips, then pressed another to her brow before linking their hands together. "Come on, you have a ship to catch."

Tears welled in her eyes, and despite her efforts, a single drop trailed down her cheek. She gripped the emerald pendant in her hand, drawing comfort in the way her magic pulsed through the stone, and let it calm her racing heart. She took a deep breath–a feeble attempt to steel herself against the sadness that was trying to consume her–and turned to board the ship.

As she stepped aboard, the flurry of people around her—all bustling about as they prepared the Nevermore to depart—were nothing but a blur of shapes as she made her way across the deck. Sounds were muffled, and everyone seemed to be moving at high speed while she had slowed to a crawl. Muted sounds turned to nothing, and it was as if the world fell silent.

It wasn't until Piper stood before her, her hands grasping her shoulders, that the world slowly drew back into focus.

"Rae. *Rae*! Are you ok?"

Auraelia shook the fog from her mind and met the worried gaze of her friend. "Yeah, I'm fine. Is everything set to go?"

Piper nodded, then linked her arm through Auraelia's, pulling her toward the bow of the ship.

They stood linked together in silence.

Her head rested gently against Piper's shoulder as they watched the city drift out of view, until it was nothing but a pinprick of light outside the tunnels that led out of Kalmeera.

"Oh, sweet goddess, that's nice." Piper threw herself onto Auraelia's bed, her face sinking into one of the feather pillows at its head.

"Do you mind?" She stood at the end of her bed with her arms laced across her chest.

Piper rolled onto her back, leaning against the pillows with her arms crossed behind her head. "Not at all, actually. That trip was entirely too long, and riding back in a coach just made it longer. And your bed is much closer than mine at the moment."

She smirked, but Auraelia rolled her eyes. "You know the horses wouldn't have been able to carry all of our luggage. Especially since

Queen Avyanna sent us back with those trunks full of Kalmeeran garments."

Piper shrugged, and then readjusted herself on the pillows.

Exhausted, and not in the mood for Piper's antics, Auraelia went into her bathing chamber.

After her shower, she walked back into her room, only to be met by Piper sprawled across her bed sleeping, a small snore echoing through the quiet.

She dressed quickly and slipped between the sheets.

Pulling them up below her chin, she closed her eyes as she curled in on herself and let her mind wander. Images of strong arms that had held her while she slept the last three nights mixed with the sound of his laughter played an endless loop through her memories. They were so vivid, that she could have sworn that she could still smell him. His signature scent of sandalwood and salty ocean air tickled her nose.

She cracked her eyes, and there laying on her pillow was a note with a midnight blue wax seal.

Careful not to disturb Piper, she sat up and quickly broke the seal. It was short and sweet, but it brought a smile to her face and filled a small portion of the hole that had formed in her heart.

> Missing you already, my star.
> Yours,
> - D

Tucking the letter under her pillow, Auraelia laid back down. A smile on her face as she drifted off to sleep.

Chapter Thirty-Seven

Daemon

The first night without Auraelia had been rough, and as the weeks went on it only got harder. It'd been a month since she left, and Daemon spent every waking moment trying to fill his days so that he wouldn't drown in the growing chasm in his heart.

The day was hotter than usual, the midday sun beaming down on him as he stood out on his balcony looking over toward the docks–his heart growing heavy with the memory of her leaving.

He'd escorted her to the front doors of the castle, not daring to go any further for fear of not being able to let her go. They'd said their goodbyes, but physically letting go of her hand as she climbed into the carriage that would bring her to the docks took more strength than he had.

Returning to his rooms, he stood on his balcony and watched the Nevermore pull away from the dock, until it disappeared into the tunnels that led out of his city. He then spent the rest of the day in his rooms with the curtains drawn, getting blindingly drunk.

It wasn't until Yvaine came to bring him to dinner, that he had even realized what time it was.

Too drunk to stand on his own, she shouldered him into his shower and turned it to the coldest setting. The freezing water was sobering as it seeped into his clothes and shocked him back to his senses.

"Daemon, I know this shit sucks. But we still need you to–at the very least–act like you're not falling apart at the seams." She stood outside his shower with a scowl on her face and arms crossed as the frigid water pelted against his body.

"Sis, I don't know what stick you sat on, but kindly pull it out your ass. I'm allowed to wallow for a day, after the love of my li–" he stopped mid-sentence, sobering immediately at what had just slipped through his lips.

"Did you–did you just say what I think you did?" Yvaine stood up straighter now, her eyes widened, and her mouth hung slightly agape.

He didn't answer. Just stared at the wall as streams of thoughts filtered through his head faster than he could process them.

"D!" her shout startled him out of his stupor. "Did you, or did you not, just admit to being in love with the princess of the Court of Emerald?"

"I-um–" His mouth was suddenly dry, and he had to peel his tongue from the roof of it. "Yeah, I think I did." His brows furrowed, his eyes searching the tiles of his shower for answers he wouldn't find as the realization barreled into him.

He loved her.

Somewhere in the recesses of his mind, he'd known what it was all along. He'd known for sure as soon as he saw her standing at the top of the stairs at solstice. He was just too scared to put it into words.

And saying it out loud, was something else entirely.

But the fact that Yvaine had been the one to hear his confession, instead of Auraelia, made his chest hurt and his head throb.

Yvaine sank down on the floor next to the shower. The water was still streaming down on top of him, but he was numb to the cold as his heart beat harder in his chest.

Yvaine sighed, "Damn, little brother."

Daemon glanced over at his sister and nodded. "Yep."

They sat in silence for a while, both just staring at the wall as the sound of water filled the space.

Turning from the docks, Daemon headed back inside his study. Auraelia's most recent letter sitting unread in his vest pocket.

In the time since she'd left, not much had changed within the kingdom. But by the grace of the goddess, his father had been improving slowly over the last few weeks.

Color had returned to his face and the rashes on his body began to heal. The swelling in his arms and legs receded slowly with each passing day, and he was able to keep food down as long as it was light and not heavily seasoned.

It wasn't much, but it was progress, and the relief on his mother's face was evident. There were times where his healing would regress, and he would sleep the days away, but overall, he seemed to be improving. But, even with the fluctuation in his health, the sudden respite of the king's symptoms made Daemon wary. His doctors still weren't sure what had caused the illness, and now they were unsure what was causing the symptoms to subside.

It was unnerving.

But through it all, his letters to and from Auraelia were what kept him calm and focused.

They let go of trying to keep their correspondence light and free from strife, instead opting for a more honest form of communication.

Daemon kept her up to date on all his findings regarding the treaty—which unfortunately, wasn't anything they didn't know already.

It didn't matter how many times he'd gone through it, it always read the same and gave him the same outcome. When he'd started digging into the document after Auraelia left, his mother had been there to help. Looking over it with him and throwing out her own theories and potential solutions. But as his father's health improved, and then subsequently declined once more, she'd been too preoccupied to help him. Instead choosing to stay by her husband's side through the ordeal and lending him her strength.

It made his heart ache to see his mother so torn, but it also made him yearn to have that kind of love in his life.

Love he knew he could have with Auraelia, if only he could only find a way around the centuries-old treaty keeping them apart.

When it felt like he could look no further, he turned to Yvaine. Praying that a pair of fresh eyes would be beneficial, but it didn't yield any new information then either.

"Just start a minor war, that would break it," Yvaine said one afternoon as she flipped through the pages of a history book on Ixora.

Daemon rolled his eyes and pinched the bridge of his nose in frustration. "Yvaine, please *try* to be helpful."

"I'm not *wrong*. But I can see how that may cause more issues than it solves."

"Yvaine—"

"Just trying to lighten the mood, little brother." She shrugged, and then turned back to the book in her lap.

While he dealt with his dead end, Auraelia was dealing with problems of her own in Lyndaria.

Sinking down into the chair behind his desk, Daemon pulled out her letter. His thumb brushed across her seal, sending tiny pieces of dried lavender fluttering down onto his desk.

Daemon,

I'm so sorry to hear that your father's symptoms continue to fluctuate. I wish that I could be there with you, and for you, but please let me know if there is anything that I can do for you or your family.

And I know you're busy with everything there and trying to find some way out of this treaty for us, but I need to ask you a favor.

What do you know about the Court of Garnet? I'm not sure if you recall the conversation—or lack thereof—in the council meeting you attended here, but mother has been quite tight-lipped about everything in regard to that court in particular and it's piqued my interest.

She's constantly changing the subject when it's brought up with the council, saying they can discuss it later.

She tries to hide it, but I see the worry in her eyes when Garnet is mentioned. And since I don't have access to the queen's records, because I'm not yet queen, I need an alternative to getting information.

I'm so sorry to put this on you with everything you're dealing with, and if you don't have the time, I completely understand.

I'm probably overreacting anyway.

I miss you, Daemon. Fall solstice can't get here soon enough.

Yours,

-A

Daemon blew out a breath, the lavender petals flying off his desk and scattering across the floor. Standing, he crossed the space to the wall of bookcases where all of his volumes on Ixora and the various courts were housed.

There was a little bit of everything. From the types of fabrics one would find in Pearl, to the warrior histories of Opal. There were countless tomes about the treaties and contracts between each court, and even more on the various goddesses that were worshiped throughout their realm. But the one thing he couldn't find was any volume pertaining to the Court of Garnet.

Not even a scroll.

Well, that's strange.

Chapter Thirty-Eight

Auraelia

The voices in the council chambers came to an abrupt halt as she walked into the room. Everyone turned in her direction as she stood in the doorway, Xander and Piper flanking her on either side.

Her jaw tightened and her hands clenched into fists with the realization that, once again, they had been arguing over the Court of Garnet and left her and Xander out of the discussion.

It didn't make any sense.

As the future queen, that alone should have ensured her inclusion. But Xander was the queen's advisor, and even *he* was being excluded from the conversation.

All eyes shifted back to where Queen Adelina sat at the head of the table. She sat straight, with a smile on her face and her hands clasped in front of her. To anyone else, she would be the picture of unphased.

But Auraelia saw through her facade.

Worry lines creased the queen's brow and her knuckles turned white from the grip she held on her own hands.

"Mother." Auraelia stared her down from where she stood, before turning her attention to the rest of the room. "My Lords. My Ladies. Please, don't stop on my account."

Auraelia stalked around to the chair designated for her next to her mother and sank into the plush cushion as Xander took his seat on the opposite side.

The tension in the room was palpable.

Tense looks marred every council member's face, as they avoided her gaze and suddenly found the parchment on the table much more interesting.

"So." She leaned back in her chair, her hands steepled together in front of her chest. "What were we talking about?"

Her mother nodded towards the members surrounding the table, and they immediately stood to take their leave. "We were just finishing up." She never once looked at Auraelia. Not as she spoke, and not as the nobility filtered out of the chambers.

"Mother!" Auraelia stood in a rush. Her chair flew backwards in her fit of rage, her magic skittered to the surface and prickled at her skin, begging to be released.

"Auraelia, you will calm yourself and conduct yourself as the future queen of this court, or you will be dismissed."

The coldness of her mother's words sent a wave of shock through her system, her magic no longer swirling beneath the surface in an angry current.

Auraelia turned and picked up her chair from where it landed, returning it to the table and sitting down once more.

"Mother, what's going on? You're excluding Xander and me from meetings altogether now?"

Her mother sighed, and it was in that moment that Auraelia really saw her.

The dark circles under her eyes and the wrinkles in the corners had deepened. Her shoulders were tense and she seemed to be carrying the weight of the world on them. Yet, in the two months since she'd returned from Kalmeera, Auraelia had been progressively pushed away from anything regarding the welfare of the kingdom, which included council meetings.

The fact that her mother refused to share the burden of whatever weighed on her heart, frustrated her to no end. Instead, she avoided her at every turn, except when she would insist on a training session to see how her magic had progressed.

"Auraelia, I'm tired. I don't have the time, or the energy, to have this conversation right now."

"Make time." Xander's tone was harsh, and it made the hairs on her arm stand on end.

Xander never spoke out of turn. He kept to himself and observed, calculating every possibility before opening his mouth. But when she looked at him now, anger rolled off him in waves, and his usually calm eyes were swirling storms of gray.

Queen Adelina stood abruptly and slammed her hands onto the table, the sound echoing through the chamber.

"I will *not* explain myself, or my decisions to my *children*. If I say now is not the time or place, then that is final. Am I clear?"

"Goddess damn it, Mother. As the future queen of this court, I deserve to know what's going on with my people! I'm tired of you avoiding me and keeping me in the dark with whatever is happening with Garnet." Her magic sparked beneath her skin the way lighting crackled across the sky.

Her mother righted herself and slowly turned her gaze toward her daughter, her eyes hard as she spoke through clenched teeth. "You may be the *future* queen of this court, but I am *the* queen, and you will do as you're told and drop this. *Now*."

Auraelia and Xander locked eyes across the table, her jaw was clenched so tightly that she wondered if she would crack a tooth.

She stood from the table and turned toward her mother. "Yes, *Your Majesty.*"

Auraelia dropped into a deep curtsy, then turned on her heel and stormed from the room with Xander and Piper close at her heels.

She charged through the castle, heading to the east wing where she could slip out the back and head to the stables.

Xander had gone his own way after they left the council chambers, mumbling something under his breath about needing a drink. She could have joined him, but she needed to get out.

Out of the castle and away from all of the secrets.

She couldn't breathe.

"Rae!" Piper cried from where she was trying to keep up behind her. "Rae!"

Auraelia finally stopped when she came to the bottom of the stairs that ran along the outer wall of the castle that would lead to either the stables or the training pitch.

"Fuck, Rae. You could have at least let me catch up." Piper's breathing was slightly labored, and it brought a smile to her face. "What the hell are you grinning at?"

"Oh, nothing. Ser Aeron would have your ass if he saw you right now, though."

"Oh, fuck off." Piper pushed her shoulder, causing her to stagger back a step.

Auraelia inclined her head, a Cheshire grin creeping across her features. "Want to blow off some steam?"

Piper's eyes narrowed, as suspicion twisted her features, and she crossed her arms across her chest. "Depends on what you have in mind."

Auraelia glanced over toward the training pitch, and Piper's eyes widened.

"No. No, not no. *Hell no.*" Piper slowly began backing away from her friend, her arms stretched out in front of her like she was trying to calm a vicious animal. "We already trained once today, and I'm still sore from that. Don't make me do it again, *please*. I'm begging."

Auraelia chuckled and looped her arm through Piper's. "Come on, it will be fun. "

They had taken all but two steps when ribbons of shadow wrapped around her fingers and parchment appeared.

"Oh, thank the goddess. Saved by the letter." Piper pulled on Auraelia's arm and led them back toward the stairs that led into the castle.

Back in her room, Auraelia stared at the letter.

In the last two months, their letters had been more about seeking answers than building their relationship. Both of them drowning in their own problems, while still trying to maintain transparency and open lines of communication.

She'd asked him if he had any information about Garnet, but he too, had come up empty handed. It was as if the court existed in name only.

Auraelia carefully peeled the wax seal from the paper and unfolded the letter.

> *My Star,*
> *How are you? Have you found anything out about Garnet, or has your mother decided to clue you in? Unfortunately, we both seem to be in the dark about something.*
> *My father is better, he's able to walk around now which is wonderful. But he and mother both seem to be hiding something. They won't meet my gaze, and when I ask them what's going on, my concerns are brushed aside.*
> *There have been emissaries from other courts here recently, all taking meetings with my father, but like you, I haven't been included in them.*
> *I'm not sure what's going on, in either of our situations, but I don't like it.*
> *The one thing keeping me going, is knowing that I will see you soon.*
> *Until then, my star.*
> *Yours,*
> *-D*

    Auraelia refolded the parchment and added it to the stack tucked away in her side-table drawer.
    They weren't getting anywhere.
    Not with the treaty.
    Not with Garnet.

And now with Daemon's parents acting strangely, it was another facet to their ever-growing list of problems.

Exhaustion washed over her, and she sat down on the plush covers of her bed and removed her boots.

Laying back, she stared at the constellations that covered the canopy over her bed, her mind a tangled web of thoughts that she couldn't unravel, no matter how hard she tried.

Her eyes grew heavy, and it wasn't long before sleep claimed her.

Chapter Thirty-Nine

Daemon

Daemon sat on one of the benches in the garden, rereading the most recent letter from Auraelia. He didn't need to be near her to see how stressed she had become; he could see it through her writing.

Since her departure from Kalmeera, two and half months ago, things within both of their kingdoms had been strange.

Mainly with their parents.

She was still battling her mother over council meetings and still had no information on Garnet. And with him fighting his own battles, he hadn't been much help.

And after months of holding their breaths over whether this time his father's health would continue to improve, he was finally back to normal. They still had no answers as to what caused his illness in the first place, or how it was cured, merely vague reassurances from his father that he was *'fine'* and *'better than ever.'*

His mother was ecstatic at the news, but Daemon was skeptical. And when he pressed for more information, his father would give him a stern look and tell him to be thankful.

It made no sense.

He had just put Auraelia's letter back in his pocket when his mother's silhouette came into his peripheral vision.

"Mother?" It was barely a whisper, and his brow furrowed in confusion. He hadn't seen her without his father plastered to her side in over a month. But there she was, standing atop the steps that led out into the garden.

He stood from the bench and began walking toward the stairs. But as soon as she saw him heading in her direction, she turned and headed inside.

"Mother?" Daemon hollered after her, praying that she had somehow overlooked him, and wasn't actually running from her own son.

But she didn't stop.

"Mother." He tried again, only louder this time. Quickening his pace to try and catch up to where she was disappearing down one of the castle corridors, but she wasn't slowing.

In fact, she began walking faster.

"Mother!" He was practically jogging at this point and was over this chase. He needed to talk to her, and she was going to listen. "Fuck this." The words were a low mumble that only he could hear.

He let the hold he kept on his magic slip. Feeling the swirls of shadows pull to the surface, and shadow-walked to the hall she was about to turn down. Leaning against the wall with his arms crossed, he dropped his shadows as soon as she turned the corner.

Her surprise was audible, her gasp resonating through the hall. "Goddess, Daemon. You startled me."

"I'm not sure how I could have *startled* you, Mother, when I've been calling after you—"

Queen Avyanna opened her mouth to protest, but he pushed away from the wall and stalked toward her. "I *know* you heard me. Your spine visibly stiffened the first time, and you quickened your steps every time after."

"Daemon–"

"What's going on? What aren't you telling me?"

She sighed, her head drooping in defeat. "I wish I could–"

Just as she began to speak, one of his father's stewards stepped into the hall. "Your Majesty, King Evander requests your presence."

You've got to be fucking kidding me.

Daemon looked past his mother and toward the interloper. "Is my father okay?" He tried to keep his irritation from his tone but failed.

"He's fine, Your Highness." Even from where he stood, he could see the thin sheen of sweat that was forming on the man's brow.

"Then, surely, he can wait a moment while I speak with my mother." Annoyance dripped from every word, but he didn't care. He was tired of being kept in the dark about whatever it was that his parents were keeping from him, and his mother finally seemed to want to share the information.

Queen Avyanna placed her hand on his chest, drawing his attention back to her. "I need to go to your father."

"But, Mother–"

"I'm sorry, my son." Immense sadness filled her eyes as her gaze met his, her eyes turning a bright cornflower blue as silver lined their rims.

She cupped his cheek and gave him a gentle smile, then turned on her heel and slipped down the hall.

Daemon stared after her, but when he noticed the steward trying to discreetly slip her a piece of parchment with a blood red seal, Daemon's annoyance grew into a fiery rage.

Her words echoed in his mind and twisted something deep within his stomach.

Something was wrong.

A loud boom echoed throughout the quiet of the castle library, the doors ricocheting off the walls as he pushed them open and stormed into the room.

The library was one of his favorite places in the castle.

Spiraling staircases of iron and windows made of multicolored glass covered the area, casting the room in a kaleidoscope of colors. Large wooden desks covered the majority of the first floor, while the upper level held floor-to-ceiling shelves that housed innumerable volumes of books and scrolls.

At his entrance, the priestess in charge looked up from where she was sitting behind a large mahogany desk–her eyes narrowing at him as he stalked across the room.

The library was a quiet and peaceful space, and Daemon had thoroughly disrupted that peace.

"Is there something that I can help you with, Your Highness?" She tried to keep her voice light and cheery, but there was an undercurrent of annoyance.

"I need anything, and everything, you have on the Court of Garnet."

At the mention of Garnet, the priestess's eyes widened slightly. Shock briefly crossed her features before she composed herself once more. She cleared her throat and cast her eyes downward, then continued to work on whatever she was doing before his disruption.

"I'm not sure we have anything on that particular court, Your Highness."

Rage burned beneath his skin, his shadows scratching beneath the surface, begging to be released as his temper grew.

The muscles in his jaw tightened as he clenched his teeth to keep his anger in check. His hands flexed at his sides as shadows began to pool at his fingertips.

"Priestess," his voice came out as a warning growl. "I know we have something on that damned court, and you will tell me where it is. And you will tell me *now*."

She looked up from her work, fire burning in her gaze as her lips set into a hard line. "I'm sorry, Your Highness. But anything we may have on that court is locked away in the archives. And the only person with access to it–"

"Is my father." Daemon's nostrils flared as realization set in.

"Correct. Only the king's magic will open the archives. So, until you are king, there is nothing I can do for you."

He huffed out a breath, gave the priestess a curt nod, and then left the way he came.

There was no way to get any information on Garnet without talking to his father. The same father who had been avoiding him for the last month and a half.

He knew he wouldn't get anything from him, and it looked like his mother wasn't going to be much help either.

Taking a deep, steadying breath, he shadow-walked back to his rooms.

He needed to let Auraelia know what he learned, even if it was only that he had no way of learning anything without his father's help.

With his letter sent off, he settled onto one of the couches in his study–a glass of whiskey dangling between his fingers and his head propped on one of the cushioned arms.

It wasn't long before he felt his magic coiling through the air, and a letter appeared on his chest swathed in ribbons of shadow.

He grabbed the parchment and sat up, placing the glass of amber liquid on the table.

Quickly opening the note, he read her words and a smile pulled at his lips as one line resonated above the rest.

"I can't wait to see you in a few weeks."

Chapter Forty

Auraelia

The last three months were simultaneously the longest and the shortest she'd ever experienced.

Long, because she missed Daemon, and knowing that she would see him for fall solstice made the time creep by. And short, due to her days being filled with trying–to no avail–to find any and all information that she could on Garnet.

But it was finally two days before the solstice celebration, which meant preparations were in full swing and the lords and ladies from other courts would begin arriving later that evening and through the following day.

Auraelia and Piper had been busy in the kitchens since the early morning. Helping chop, dice, and sauté the multiple different fruits that were being turned into sauces and purées for various dishes.

The smells that filled the large kitchen were decadent and delicious.

Freshly baked breads and cakes, assorted pies and pastries, and of course–at Auraelia's special request–trays and trays of buttery, chocolate croissants.

The game keepers were outside preparing the various meats that would be served. They stripped the birds of their feathers, and relieved the boars of their hides, then cleaned the flesh before submerging them in different brines so that the flavors would permeate the meat.

The kitchens became more crowded as midday approached and the two women took that as their opportunity to escape.

They were halfway to the stables, when a deep rumbling voice called from behind, causing them to stop in their tracks and cringe.

They would recognize that voice anywhere. It could be soothing one moment and haunting your nightmares the next.

"Princess Auraelia, Lady Piper. Training pitch, *now.*"

Their shoulders dropped as their heads fell back in exasperation, both muttering an annoyed, "*Yes, Ser Aeron,*" before they quickly headed in the direction of the pitch.

Auraelia and Piper were curled over, their hands resting on their knees as they tried to catch their breath.

They had been training for hours.

The sun had already started its descent in the sky, but still continued to pelt them with waves of heat. And even though her muscles cried for a break, she still managed to pull a breeze through the yard in an attempt to cool them.

"That form is going to get you killed, you know." A voice as sweet and smooth as honey traveled across the yard, jolting Auraelia upright.

She turned in the direction that it had come from and a large smile pulled across her face.

"Lady Aesira!" Auraelia jogged across the field and launched herself at the women, pulling her into a tight embrace.

Lady Aesira–along with Lord Arlo–was head of the Court of Opal, and she was as beautiful as she was deadly.

She had gorgeous, deep mahogany skin that was enviably perfect and full lips that were kissed with pink. She kept her hair shaved close to her scalp, and when Auraelia asked her why when she was little, she explained that it kept her cool, but she also liked the ease of it. She didn't have to worry about it getting pulled during training or battle or keeping it in protective styles like Ser Aeron and his locs.

Her eyes were a deeper shade of amber than Ser Aeron's, and pulled more tones of red than gold, but they held the same warmth.

Lady Aesira made frequent trips to Lyndaria throughout Auraelia's youth. Checking in on Ser Aeron and making sure that everything was coming along as it should be with her training. She even stepped in on many occasions to train Auraelia herself. Teaching her different ways that a woman could move, that would be difficult for a man to react to–let alone teach.

She taught her how to handle a staff, and about different pressure points and their purposes–both for combat and in healing.

She was like a second mother to Auraelia.

"You're early," she said when she finally released Lady Aesira and stepped back, giving Piper room to embrace her as well.

"Yes, well, it seems I was not early enough, since both of your stances were abysmal." Her tone was reprimanding, but her eyes were lit with joy and laughter.

The three women chuckled as Ser Aeron approached and bowed. "Lady Aesira. It's good to see you again."

"Oh, brother. Why so formal?" Lady Aesira winked, before pulling him in for a hug.

Auraelia and Piper exchanged a confused look before turning back to the two warriors.

"Brother?" They asked in unison. As long as they had known Aeron and Aesira, their relationship had never been a topic.

"Am I not allowed to have family?" Ser Aeron asked, one quizzical brow raised in their direction.

Both Piper and Auraelia's mouths opened and closed like a fish out of water as they tried to come up with something to respond with. Thankfully, Lady Aesira broke the tension with her laugh.

"Ser Aeron is my older brother. But, like Emerald, Opal follows the matriarchal line, so I took over once our parents passed. He was my right hand until he came here, and he is definitely missed." Her eyes softened as she looked at her brother, and Ser Aeron's softened in return.

"Now." Lady Aesira clasped her hands together and directed her attention back to Auraelia and Piper. "Shall we get back to your training?"

The moon was high in the sky by the time she made it back to her rooms. Her muscles screamed in protest as she slowly shuffled across her sitting room and into her bed chamber.

The hours of training with Ser Aeron alone were enough to make her not want to move for a few days. But with Lady Aesira's additional training regimen, she didn't think she would be able to function at all. Piper had gone off to her own rooms, leaving Auraelia to fend for herself.

Once in her bathing chamber, she turned on the shower as cold as it would go, and slowly peeled off her clothes leaving them in a pile on the floor to deal with later.

Before stepping into the frigid stream of the shower, she turned on the faucet of her tub so that it could fill with hot water while she showered.

The cold was a shock to her system, but it slowly seeped into her sore muscles and eased some of the ache.

She hurried through her shower. Washing quickly, then finger combing through her hair to make sure it wasn't a tangled mess when she got out.

Stepping out of the shower, she padded lightly over to her tub where steam curled above the water and the scent of lavender and chamomile filled the air.

Dipping her toes into the water, she hissed through her teeth at the intense heat before her body acclimated. She progressed slowly until she was submerged up to her shoulders, her head tilted back against the lip of the tub as a contented sigh slipped past her lips.

She wasn't sure how long she had been soaking, but the water had begun to cool, a sign that she's long since passed the healing effects of the heat. Slipping beneath the surface, fully submerging herself in the last bits of warmth that remained, she stayed there until her lungs began to ache.

When she emerged, something was different.

Her eyes were closed, but she felt her magic rise to the surface, and it seemed to dance beneath her skin.

She wiped the water away from her eyes and breathed deeply.

The smell of sandalwood and ocean air filled her nostrils the same moment she felt his presence.

When her eyes snapped open, her head jerked toward the door of her bathing chamber.

"Daemon." His name was barely louder than a whisper as it crossed her lips.

He was such a beautiful sight.

From his tightly fitted leather trousers and bare feet, to the loose black tunic that laced at the neck and hung open. The open V of his shirt made the perfect window for the ink that was scrawled across his chest, and his sleeves were rolled to the elbows displaying the muscles and tattoos on his forearms.

His hair was perfectly tousled, and the scruff of his beard was slightly longer than the last time she'd seen him.

He leaned against the frame of her door with his arms folded across his chest, as a smirk of pure sex tilted up one side of his mouth.

"Hello, my star."

Chapter Forty-One

Daemon

Her eyes widened, and his heart hammered in his chest as they stared at each other.

How was it that she was even more stunning now than she was three months ago?

He hadn't meant to shadow-walk in on her bathing, but it was a happy accident.

"Daemon." His name was barely a whisper, but he heard it all the same. Just as he heard the tiny catch in her throat as it slipped past her lips.

Saw her slate blue irises brighten as tears welled in her eyes, and the pink flush that covered her cheeks and cascaded down to color her chest.

"Hello, my star." He sent a silent prayer to the Goddess Narissa that his voice sounded steadier than he felt. His entire being was vibrating with need for her.

He tightened the hold on his magic as it lashed beneath the surface, trying to scratch and claw to the other half of his soul.

Within seconds, she was on her feet. Water sloshed onto the floor with her quick movements, but before she could step out of the tub, he closed the distance to her.

As he lifted her from the tub, she immediately wrapped her legs around his torso, her fingers tangling into his hair as she pressed her pillowy soft lips to his.

Lavender enveloped his senses, and every care he had ebbed away. Everything in that moment was *right*.

Auraelia was in his arms once more, and that was all that mattered.

He carried her into her room, their lips never parting even as water dripped along the floor. His hands slid along her slick body, as he reacquainted himself with every dip, curve, and dimple. When he gripped her ass, a moan slipped past her lips and onto his, but he felt her body tense beneath his hold.

Gingerly, he laid her out on her bed, her wet body darkening the already deep blue coverlet. "Is everything ok?" His face tightened with concern as he scanned every inch of her body for an entirely different reason.

Her flush deepened, but when she winced in pain as she pushed up onto her elbows, worry and anger melted into one. "Auraelia–" Her name sounded like a growl even to his own ears.

"I'm fine, Daemon." She sat up quickly and grabbed his hand in reassurance, but her face contorted with pain as she moved.

"You're in pain."

"I am. But it's because Ser Aeron and Lady Aesira decided that Piper and I needed to train until we could barely walk today. Nothing else." A small chuckle left her lips, and his body relaxed.

"Now, come here." She tugged on his hand in an attempt to pull him onto her, but he slipped his hand from hers, a sly smile tugging at his lips.

Her brows furrowed, but he cut her off before she could protest.

"My star." He drew out his name for her, then tugged his—now wet—shirt over his head.

He watched as she drank in the sight of his bare chest, before traveling down to the prominent ridge in his pants and back up again. He'd never get tired of watching her eyes dilate with desire whenever she saw him, or how she mindlessly pulled her lower lip between her teeth.

He noticed the subtle shift of her legs as they pressed together in a feeble attempt to relieve the pressure building there, and it only made his smirk widen. "As much as I love adding pain to your pleasure, this is not the way to do it."

Her eyes snapped to his, "I told you—"

"Yes, I know you said that you're fine. But let me *take care* of you."

It took less than a heartbeat for his words to hit their mark, and he delighted in the way her face shifted from confusion to excitement and desire.

"Lie back, Auraelia."

She did as she was told, and as he kneeled at the edge of her bed, he slid his hands up her legs to her knees and pushed them apart. Her skin pebbled beneath his touch, and her nipples hardened into stiff peaks.

Wrapping his hands behind her knees, he gently pulled her to the edge.

Her sex glistened with evidence of her arousal, and the sight made his cock throb.

He draped her legs over his shoulders and moved in.

When his breath ghosted across her wet center, her hands tightened into fists as she gripped the coverlet in anticipation, and a whimper escaped through her barely parted lips.

One lick up her slit had him moaning against her. She tasted like sunshine and chocolate, and everything good in the world. He could drown in her essence and die a happy man.

Dropping all pretense of teasing her until she begged for release, he doubled his efforts, alternating between long languid strokes up her center, with nibbles on her clit.

He switched fucking her with his tongue, for slipping his fingers deep within her core. Curling them to stroke the spot inside of her that made her writhe.

He loved watching her come apart for him, and this time was no different.

Even as his dick grew painfully erect, he kept his focus on her pleasure. He glanced above the soft mound of curls, and watched her body for every sign that her orgasm was near.

He knew the obvious signs, the walls of her pussy fluttering around him until they clamped down in a vice-like grip would have been a dead giveaway, if he didn't know it could be faked. But he knew Auraelia's body almost as well as he knew his own.

He watched for the thin sheen of sweat that would cover her skin.

Listened for the sound of her breath quickening as it intermingled with moans of pleasure.

But the moment her body locked, and her breath caught in her throat... that was the moment that he lived for.

The moment her eyes would roll to the back of her head, her legs would shake, and her back would bow off of the bed with the force of her release.

And that was what he was after now.

Summoning his shadows, he let the velvety tendrils trail featherlight caresses across her sensitive skin as he slid one hand up her stomach to cup her breast. Pulling the delicate tip of her nipple between two fingers, he pinched and tugged on the peak.

Her breath began to quicken, and a sheen of sweat began to form, making her skin glisten in the low light of the room.

Daemon concentrated his efforts, plunging his fingers in and out of her core as his mouth devoured her pussy. And as he pinched her nipple in sync with a sharp suck on her clit, she fractured around him.

He drank every drop of her release as he coaxed her down from her high.

Only when her body finally relaxed, did he finally stand.

She curled her legs up and rolled onto her side. Taking him in with her half-lidded eyes. When she reached for the waistband of his pants, Daemon stepped away, and her lips pulled down into a frown.

"Rest, Princess."

"But what about you?" Her voice was low and sultry as her eyes trailed down his chest to the thick bulge in his pants, and the sound made him ache.

"Auraelia, you're sore and tired. I'm fine. Tonight was about you, my star. Though I'm quite content with how my night played out." He waggled his brows, and she laughed.

"I mean it, Auraelia. You need your rest."

She nodded, but then scrunched up her face when she went to pull the covers over her naked body.

Daemon's brows furrowed in confusion when she pushed the sheets away and moved to stand. "What are you doing?"

"They're wet. I'm not sleeping in a wet bed."

Realization dawned, and he began rifling through her wardrobes and trunks for alternate bedding.

Her chuckle pulled him from his task, and he turned toward her. "What's so funny?"

She shook her head, and despite her apparent exhaustion, a warm breeze circulated through the room. Daemon watched in awe as the coverlet was lifted from the bed and began to tumble in a large ball of hot air. His mouth hung slightly agape as his gaze flicked from her to the sheets suspended in midair.

Slowly, the linen floated back down onto the bed as if it hadn't been disturbed, and she winked.

Daemon walked over to the bed and felt for any residual wetness—there was none.

"How in the—what did you—" His mind was reeling. He'd seen all kinds of magic, seen her use her magic on many occasions, but this was new.

Auraelia laughed, "You're not the only one with a neat party trick now."

Daemon shook his head and swept her into his arms and kissed her hard. Her body immediately melted against his, and the moan that sounded deep in her throat was a straight shot to his cock.

Reluctantly, he broke the kiss and walked her over to the bed. It was still warm when he pulled the sheets back and tucked her beneath them.

When he went to stand, she grabbed his hand in a vice-like grip.

"Will you stay?" The gaze that stared back as his was one of longing and hope, but also sadness.

He smiled, and gently squeezed her hand. "There's nowhere else that I'd rather be." He bent down and placed a chaste kiss to her temple before standing once more. "I just need to take a cold shower before I climb into this bed with you still gloriously naked, or I won't be able to keep my hands—or my dick—to myself."

Auraelia's laugh was the most beautiful sound he'd ever heard. And evidently, when she was exhausted, she was more prone to hysterics which resulted in tiny snorts intermixed with her laughter.

When the first one slipped, she stopped immediately and pulled the covers over her face.

That won't do.

Daemon chuckled and pulled them back down, and though her hands covered her face, he could tell that it was the color of a ruby.

"Princess, did you just *snort*?" Gently, he pried her digits away from her face and looked at her with adoration.

Her flush grew even deeper, and she groaned.

"There is nothing for you to be embarrassed over, my star. Your laugh is one of my favorite sounds. Snorts and all."

She scoffed and slapped at him playfully and when she snorted once more, he kissed the tip of her nose before kissing her lips.

When they finally calmed, he stood and headed into the bathroom to shower.

His cock was painfully hard, but instead of taking care of it himself, he took the coldest shower possible.

By the time he was finished, Auraelia was curled onto her side and sleeping soundly.

Slipping into the bed behind her, he gently pulled her to him.

He'd missed this.

Missed the way her body molded perfectly against his. He even missed the way her hair tickled his nose.

With a contented sigh, he pulled her more firmly into his hold and peacefully fell asleep for the first time in months.

When he woke the next morning, Auraelia was securely tucked into his arms, and he was sure he was still dreaming.

It wasn't until she rolled over and nuzzled into his chest as her arms snaked around him and mumbled, "Good morning," that his mind truly let him believe it.

"Good morning, Princess," he replied, before pressing a kiss to the crown of her head.

She slowly drifted back to sleep, so he held her and basked in her closeness. Letting her scent further embed itself on his soul as he watched particles in the air dance in the early morning sun that filtered in around the edges of her curtains.

They stayed that way for a while.

But as the morning crept on, he knew he would have to leave soon.

"Auraelia." He gently pulled away from her and placed delicate kisses to her temple and cheek. "Auraelia, my star, I need you to wake up."

Memories of their first morning together in Kalmeera fluttered to the forefront of his mind, and he chuckled.

And at the sound, Auraelia's eyes opened a crack. "What's so funny?"

He smiled at her and kissed the crease that formed between her brows. "Nothing, my star. You just remind me of one of Narissa's sea monsters in the morning."

Her eyes grew wide, and her mouth hung open in shock.

The laugh that tumbled out of him was short-lived when Auraelia managed to pull the pillow out from under his head and began to hit him with it. He let her get a few hits in before he wrenched it from her grasp.

She was on her knees now, and he let his gaze devour every inch of her naked form.

When she finally realized that she was bare, she grabbed her pillow and hit him once more before he grabbed her by the waist and pulled her beneath him.

"As much as I love the foreplay, Princess. I'm afraid I don't have time for all of the things that I want to do to you." Daemon pressed his hard length against her center, and she gasped at the contact. Auraelia wrapped her legs around his hips as he slowly slid cock along her slit. "Fuck, you're soaked already."

"Fuck me, Daemon. I need you inside me. *Now*." Her pleas were music to his ears, but she should have known the demand wasn't going to get her what she wanted.

Daemon let a smirk pull at his lips, "What do you say?"

When she began to roll her eyes, he raised his brows, and she stopped herself. Blowing out a breath, she said the one word he wanted to hear. "*Please.*"

It was sarcastic, but he didn't care as he began to inch his way into her.

"*Fuck.*" His head fell to her shoulder as he slowly sank into her. "After the last three months, and last night, I don't know how long I'm going to last." He could hear the defeat in his voice and hated it.

Auraelia lifted his face to hers, and fierce determination filled her gaze. "Daemon, I need you to move. I've been wound tight like a top for the last three months, and I need you to fuck me. *Hard.*"

His smile turned devilish as he looked into those pools of blue and gray. "Your wish is my command, Princess." Then he drove into her.

Draping one of her legs over his shoulder, he furiously worked her clit as he pounded into her.

He could feel his climax building.

The heaviness in his balls.

The tingling at the base of his spine.

He refused to leave her wanting, so with renewed effort, he doubled down on her pleasure. Swirling and pinching her clit as he watched for the signs he needed before he could let go.

"Play with your breasts, Auraelia."

Her compliance to his demands was instant. She palmed her delicate globes and twisted her nipples between her thumb and forefinger.

Then like bricks in a line, everything fell into place.

Her breath, the sheen, and then her body locked in around him as her climax ripped her apart and pulled him with her.

Daemon collapsed next to her. The only sounds in the room coming from the birds that chirped outside the window, and their erratic breathing.

"Auraelia–" he whispered when their breaths returned to a semi-normal cadence.

She sighed, then sat up and looked over her shoulder at him. "You have to leave, don't you?"

It was his turn to sigh now. "Unfortunately, yes. I have to go meet my parents and Yvaine at the dock in the city and arrive *with* them."

A bewildered look crossed her features, but it didn't take long for her to realize his meaning. "No one knows you're here."

It wasn't a question, but he nodded anyway.

When a tense silence fell over them, Daemon pulled her back down into his embrace. "I will be back here later today to be formally introduced to your court with my parents. I *will* be back, Auraelia."

She didn't need to say that him leaving right now would hurt. His own heart rebelled against the very idea–but he had to.

They both had to keep up appearances, and they were still no closer to finding a solution to their problems involving the treaty, which meant they couldn't be seen together in more than a friendly capacity.

Daemon kissed the crown of her head then let her go.

He dressed quickly, and with a kiss on her lips, he let his shadows carry him away.

It was midday by the time his parents arrived in Lyndaria.

The sun was shining, there was nary a cloud in sight, and the light that reflected off the water looked like fallen stars floated on its surface. It was a beautiful day, but Daemon's mood was immediately soured at the sight of his parents' ship.

It was larger than the Nevermore. And where his ship was dark and sleek, the Sea Serpent was all light colors and–in his opinion–gaudy.

The hull was stained a medium brown, and its sails were a mixture of sky blue and white, making them blend into the sky on bright days. Accenting the sides of the ship was the unnecessary gold filigree that added to the ostentatious display.

He stood on the docks, arms folded across his chest, as he watched the royal vessel pull into port. The sight of the ship, along with the knowledge of who was aboard, twisted his lips into a scowl.

Only when lines were secure, and the gangplank had been dropped into place, did he peel himself away from the mooring pole and stride over to greet his parents.

"Mother. Father. I hope that your journey was pleasant." His tone was cold and detached. Though he could feel his mother's saddened eyes boring into the side of his face, he kept his expression flat and emotionless.

His father's annoyance came off him in waves, but Daemon did his best not to react, while also refusing to meet their gaze. Instead, he looked around as the crew of the ship scurried about, finishing up their duties and carrying all of their belongings down the gangplank.

They'd spent the last three months either tiptoeing around him, or avoiding him completely.

He'd had enough, and he wasn't going to stand there and smile and pretend that everything was okay between them when it was quite clear that the opposite was true.

Out of the corner of his eye, he saw his father scowl and open his mouth to say something.

Turning, Daemon squared his shoulders in anticipation of the impending argument, but as his father began to speak, his mother gripped her husband's elbow and sent him a warning glance.

Instantly, King Evander's rage was doused, and he hung his head.

Pulling his arm from his wife's grasp, he stormed down the gangplank.

When his father was halfway down the dock his mother stepped up to his side and looped her arm through his.

"You're not going to tell me anything about whatever it is that's going on with you two, are you?" Daemon's tone dripped with frustration, but also acceptance.

Queen Avyanna squeezed his bicep gently, and out of the corner of his eye, he saw her face drop. But when he turned to her, meeting her gaze head on for the first time since they arrived, she plastered a fake smile on her face that didn't quite reach her eyes. "There's nothing to tell, my son." Her tone grated against his nerves. It was the same tone one would use to placate a child.

He sighed in exasperation and shook his head in defeat. He was tired of fighting with them over this. Tired of trying to force answers that they weren't willing to give.

"Whatever you say, Mother."

And with that, he guided her down the gangplank and to the waiting carriage at the end of the dock.

Chapter Forty-Two

Auraelia

The rest of her day was spent either in last minute fittings for her gown or running around to lend a helping hand with final touches for the celebration the next day. So, by the time evening rolled around, standing in the throne room welcoming every lord and lady throughout Ixora was *not* what Auraelia considered a good time.

She was tired and hungry, and if she drank anymore of the wine being passed around, her night would not end well.

The throne room was large and airy and had multiple sets of double doors that led into the main hall of the castle. On the far side of the room was a wall of windows that perfectly framed the dais and the two rarely used thrones that sat upon it.

They were carved from the original emerald mines on which the court had been founded, and mostly consisted of the dark gray stone that surrounded the brilliant green gems. But when the sun set, and the last rays of light shone through the windows behind the dais, it illuminated the shards of emerald that poked through to the surface.

Hours went by, and Daemon and his parents still hadn't arrived at court. The anticipation had her nerves prickling beneath her skin and made her stomach churn–especially since every other representative had arrived already.

Lady Aesira and Lord Arlo arrived the previous day, so they were the first to be announced. They were followed by Lady Orna and Lady Blyana from the Court of Topaz, Lord Kaemon and Lady Levena from the Court of Pearl, and many other nobles and their families from throughout Ixora.

She stood off to the side of the dais with Piper, deep in conversation with the Ladies from Topaz about the upcoming festivities, when there was the sharp rap against the floor that signaled the arrival of another dignitary to court.

Auraelia held her breath and counted each strike of the staff as it crashed against the floor with a resounding *boom*.

One.

A single pound of the staff meant nobility, but no one of extreme importance.

Two.

Two, was for the leaders of each court who were not royalty.

With each strike of the staff, the sound rang out and seemed to hang heavily in the air. As the pause after the second strike lingered, Auraelia felt her heart sink.

Then finally, *three.*

Three taps were reserved for reigning monarchs and their families, and since Queen Adelina only used it for their family in formal settings, and everyone in their household was currently present, it could only mean one thing.

Daemon.

With her heart lodged in her throat, Auraelia turned and climbed two steps up the dais to stand a step below her mother. And as the royals from the Court of Sapphire entered, the steward announced them to the room.

"Announcing, King Evander and Queen Avyanna of the Court of Sapphire Isles, followed by Crown Prince Daemon, Princess Royal Yvaine, and Lord Aiden of the Court of Sapphire Isles."

There was another crack of the staff against the floor, which signified the end of their party, and Auraelia looked on as they made their way across the floor.

Queen Avyanna looked magnificent.

Her raven locks that reminded Auraelia so much of Daemon's, were twisted away from her face and cascaded down her back. She looked like a walking sapphire with her deep cobalt gown accented in gold. The bodice was form-fitting to her waist, then flared out into a skirt that flowed like the waves on the sea. It was beautifully simple, and seamlessly blended Lyndarian fashion with the structure and whimsy that was common in Kalmeera.

Even her crown was beautifully understated with golden branches of what looked like coral sprouting upward from a band of sapphires.

Even if he hadn't been announced, one look into his moss-green eyes and Auraelia would have known exactly who the man to Queen Avyanna's left was–Daemon's father, King Evander.

They had the same strong jaw. Same slightly bushy brows, straight nose, and vibrant green eyes.

He and his father looked so alike, yet so very different.

Where Daemon's hair was dark and unruly, his father's was a light, chestnut brown and combed into perfection. His skin, a cooler tone in comparison to Daemon's rich olive complexion. And where Daemon seemed more relaxed and carefree, his father looked straight-laced and stoic.

But their similarities were not lost on her.

Like the way King Evander looked longingly toward his wife. She knew that look. She'd been on the receiving end of it many times from Daemon. There was so much love that translated between their gazes, that it made her heart skip.

He was wearing something similar to the formal garb she'd seen Daemon and Aiden wear on their last trip to Lyndaria, though much more garish.

The fabric was a deeper shade of blue than his wife's gown but decorated with the same luxurious gold accents. He wore a snow-white cravat at his neck, which was pinned with a large sapphire brooch, and the crown that encircled his head was a perfect match to the queen's.

Then, like an invisible string that pulled on her heart or a siren's call, her gaze drifted away from the king and queen. As if he felt it too, Daemon's eyes found hers in the same moment.

He stood a few paces behind his parents, flanked by Yvaine and Aiden.

Yvaine was gorgeous as usual, in a sky-blue version of her mother's gown without the gold accents, and she had a slit up to her mid-thigh. Her short blue-black hair had been styled into small waves with one side pinned back, and she wore a simple circlet of silver and sapphires around her brow.

Aiden, who stayed a step behind the royal siblings, wore a tunic of dove gray with charcoal-colored pants and a royal blue brocade vest.

His eyes seemed to roam around the room in search of something—or someone. When they finally landed on Piper beside the dais, he quickly averted them as a flush of color spread across his cheeks.

Everyone in their party seemed to be dressed in shades of blue.

Everyone, except Daemon.

Auraelia's gaze raked down his form. Taking in every inch of him as he strolled across the room. From the way his trousers hugged every muscle in his legs to the tight fit of his coat across his shoulders and torso.

Dressed from head to toe in black, just like the first time they met. The only color in his ensemble coming from the sapphires that were embedded in his circlet.

He looked like night incarnate, a living shadow.

The thought brought a smile to her face, and as if he knew what she was thinking, he smiled in return.

When they reached the end of the dais, Queen Adelina descended the steps and exchanged greetings with the visiting king and queen, while Daemon and Aiden bowed, and Yvaine dropped into an elegant curtsy.

Once the formal introductions and greetings were out of the way, Queen Adelina's voice rang out over the crowd. "Now that all of our guests have arrived, let the festivities begin!"

As the last word left her lips, servers flooded into the room by the dozen. Some carried trays of bite sized foods, while others continued to circulate trays of wine and bourbon.

There were musicians set up in the main hallway, and as they played, their music filtered in through the doors and filled the room with lively melodies.

Auraelia descended the steps, and after curtsying to King Evander and Queen Avyanna, she excused herself to mingle with the crowd. Her gaze drifted back to Daemon, still by his parents as they introduced Yvaine to her mother and decided that she would find him later. Piper met her a few steps from the dais, her face screwed up with anger.

"Are you alright?" she asked, looping her arm through her friend's as they both grabbed a glass of wine from a passing tray.

"Fine. I just–why did he have to come?" Piper's aggravation dripped from every word.

"Who? Aiden?" As a friend, Auraelia understood Piper's frustration to a degree. But since they hadn't really discussed Aiden since Kalmeera–though it wasn't from her lack of trying–she wasn't quite sure what Piper's residual hostility toward him was for. But as a royal, she understood that Aiden didn't have much say in the matter. He was the emissary for their court, and if anyone in the royal family said he needed to be somewhere, that's where he would be.

"Yes, Aiden. Who else would I be talking about? Goddess, he's just so...so...*Aiden*." Her hand was balled into a fist at her side as her frustration bled into anger.

"Piper, I have no idea what that means. Especially since you haven't told me what happened between the two of you in Kalmeera. I've been asking you for months and you keep pushing it off, saying you're fine, when it's clear you're not."

Piper closed her eyes and took a deep breath to try and stay her anger. "I'll tell you; I promise. Just not here and not now. Okay?"

"Fine. Oh, and Piper? I know you're upset with him, but being here is not his doing. He's just doing his job. So, try and cut him a little slack, okay?"

Piper rolled her eyes, but nodded and tapped her glass against Auraelia's before taking a large sip and downing half of its contents. When she lowered her glass, Xander stood in front of her, and she almost choked on her drink. One corner of his lips pulled upward and there was a gleam in his eyes that Auraelia had begun to notice only showed itself around Piper.

"Thirsty?" The teasing tone that laced Xander's words made her snicker and earned her an elbow to her ribs.

"*Ouch!*" she exclaimed, narrowing her eyes at Piper as she rubbed her side.

Piper gave her a snide look in return, then drained the rest of her glass and turned her attention to Xander.

"As a matter of fact, yes, I am. Care to grab me another?" Piper dangled the empty glass in his face, drawing her lips up at the corners in a challenge.

Xander's eyes never left Piper's as he grabbed the glass and placed it on a passing tray. "How about a dance instead?" His brows lifted in a challenge of his own, and a flush painted Piper's cheeks as she accepted.

Auraelia watched as Piper linked her arm with Xander's, and they strolled away toward the makeshift dance floor in the throne room.

Seeing her brother with her best friend was odd, but there was no denying the chemistry between them. Even if they were both adamant that they were merely friends, it was quite clear to those who knew Xander that he wished it was more.

What was stranger still, was that she couldn't picture them with anyone else. Piper brought out a softer side to her brother that not many people got to see. Though Xander would have protected Piper without question before, there was a new kind of tenderness and affection that filled his gaze every time that he looked her way.

She wasn't sure when the shift happened, but she was glad that it had. They both deserved happiness, and she wasn't going to be the one standing in their way–they were doing a fine job of that all on their own.

Now that she was alone, she took a lap around the room, stopping on occasion to make small talk with the guests or to grab a canapé from one of the servers. All the while, keeping her eyes peeled for Daemon.

She was about to look for Piper when Lord Syrus approached and asked her to dance.

She remembered him from their dance in Kalmeera. Remembered his greasy, blond locks that fell in front of his muddy brown eyes, and the sinister smile that was firmly planted across his face. He radiated false confidence and superiority, and his mere presence made her uncomfortable. But as one of the hosts, it would be impolite to decline. So, she summoned a false smile, and let him lead her out to the dance floor.

His hand, that was supposed to be on her upper back for this particular dance, continuously slid down her spine. Despite the numerous times she politely put it back into position, it still drifted lower.

Auraelia sent a silent prayer of thanks to the Goddess Rhayne when the song mercifully ended. With a terse smile, she nodded her thanks and scurried away from the floor–leaving Lord Syrus with a dumbfounded look on his face.

Crossing the room, she found Lady Aesira and Yvaine discussing various fighting stances and techniques and decided to join in on the conversation.

She felt him before she saw him.

Felt the caress of his magic across the back of her neck, and it sent shivers down her spine. Phantom touches twined around her fingers like they were holding her hand, while some snaked beneath her dress and up her legs.

They were touches that let her know that he was watching.

Touches of longing and of possession.

It was intoxicating.

She was about to excuse herself when she felt a strong presence at her back.

"Good evening, ladies." The smokey tenor of his voice made her skin pebble, and she had to focus on keeping her breaths even and her knees from giving out. "You wouldn't mind if I borrowed Princess Auraelia for a dance, would you?" By the sound of his voice, he was trying to hold onto the final threads of decorum before they slipped from his grasp.

He hadn't laid a single finger on her, but his mere presence made her skin buzz and the fine hairs on her body to stand on end. His body practically vibrated with rage and *need*, and it sent a wave of heat to her core. She knew he'd seen her dancing with Syrus. She'd seen him leaning against one of the walls as Syrus led her across the floor. Saw the way his eyes lit with anger and his magic swirled in their depths. He'd clenched his jaw so tightly that veins began to protrude at his temples, especially when Syrus' hand continuously dipped too low.

She hadn't meant to make him mad, or jealous. But if that's what it took to get him to be near her, then so be it.

Yvaine smirked, "Not at all, dear brother. But does the princess *want* to dance with you? I seem to recall that you step on the ladies' feet."

Lady Aesira's eyes widened and a smile tugged at the corners of her mouth. She took a sip of her bourbon to try and hide her chuckle.

"Dearest sister, I do believe that was *you*. The princess and I have partnered before, and if I remember correctly, I have always left her toes unscathed."

Auraelia covered her mouth to stifle a snicker, and Yvaine shrugged then turned her attention back to Lady Aesira, their conversation picking up right where it left off.

"Your Highness." His voice was a silky caress and low enough for only her ears.

She turned, and he bowed as he extended his hand for her to take. She dropped into a curtsy, then placed her hand in his and let him lead her out onto the dance floor.

All eyes were on them as Daemon led her in their dance.

His hold was strong and sure, never faltering as he spun her around the floor. But his shoulders were tense, and there was a small wrinkle between his brows.

"What's wrong?" She kept her voice barely above a whisper, but it was loud enough that it brought his gaze down to hers.

"I didn't like seeing you dance with that snake." Auraelia's brows lifted. For a man calling someone else a snake, Daemon's tone dripped venom.

"Lord Syrus?" she asked.

He didn't answer, but his nostrils flared with annoyance and the grip on her hand tightened slightly.

"Ahh. Well, Daemon. I'm not overly fond of him either, but he asked me to dance and as I didn't have a legitimate reason to say no, I had to agree."

He took a deep breath, and roughly exhaled through his nose before speaking. "I don't like seeing you smiling and laughing with other men. I selfishly want to be the only one who gets to bask in the warmth of your gaze. But seeing you touched by another man? Fuck, Auraelia. It fills me with inexplicable rage, and I want nothing more than to rip the offending limbs from their bodies–" his gaze was intense as it locked on to hers, "You're *mine*, Auraelia. Mine."

His possessive words vibrated through her body and resonated with something in her soul. Something about the way he claimed her set a spark in her chest.

Her eyes softened under his strong gaze, and she smiled. "I know, Daemon. I'm yours, just as much as you're mine."

The song came to an end, and they begrudgingly went their separate ways. Keeping up the pretense that they were merely holding up political alliances.

The rest of the night was much of the same.

She made the rounds through the room, making sure to welcome people to court and to Lyndaria. Giving them suggestions of places in town that may be of interest and encouraging people to explore the area.

She danced with Xander and Ser Aeron, but Daemon didn't seek her out again. Though she understood why, it didn't keep her from wishing that he would. But it didn't stop him from touching her from a distance.

He continuously sent his shadows to trail velvety caresses up her arms or across her back, forever letting her know he was watching. The few times that their paths crossed, they did so close enough that their fingers would brush, and each time was like a lightning bolt shooting through her.

By the time the festivities came to a close, and she and Piper made it back to her suite, Auraelia was an exhausted bundle of need.

Every look, every touch–phantom or otherwise–throughout the night sent a wave of heat through her body.

"Piper, would you please undo this goddess-forsaken gown? I feel like I'm melting."

Piper chucked as she stepped up behind her and began undoing the laces on the back of the gown.

It was a simple dress made of gorgeous deep teal satin that shifted between being more blue or green depending on the lighting. The bodice was a sweetheart design, with a vee cut down between her breasts that was backed with shimmering mesh.

It was beautiful, but with the voluminous skirts, it was heavy–and hot.

"Is lover boy coming up tonight?" Piper asked as she undid the final lace.

"No, I don't believe so. His entire family is in the emerald suite in the east wing, so it may be hard for him to sneak away." A tinge of annoyance seeped into her words.

Piper snickered, then covered her mouth to try and stifle a yawn. "Well, I don't know about you, but I'm going to bed. I'm exhausted, and we have a *long* day tomorrow."

With a sigh, she nodded, then thanked her friend and walked across the sitting area to the door that led into her chambers.

Pushing it closed behind her, Auraelia let her dress fall to the floor and kicked off her heels. Propping her foot up on the edge of her bed, she gently rolled down her stocking, careful not to let it snag on anything.

When all that was left was her panties, she slipped beneath the covers on her bed, and let her eyes drift closed. But despite her exhaustion, she was wound too tight to sleep.

In the quiet of her room, her thoughts filled with images of Daemon.

Memories of their time together in Kalmeera. Their trip through the city and nights together in her room. Their bodies sliding against each other as he fucked her beneath the waterfall. She envisioned the way he looked whenever their eyes met across the throne room. The way it felt to feel his shadows secretly swirling along her skin.

Her arousal built with every image that filtered into her mind, and she needed relief.

Sliding her hand down her body, she stopped to palm her breasts before traveling further to the apex of her thighs.

She was soaked, and her fingers slipped between the lips of her sex with ease.

She swirled the pads of her fingers around her clit before plunging them into her entrance.

Rolling onto her stomach, she rocked against her hand. Pushing her fingers deeper into her core while her thumb teased her clit.

It wasn't long before release found her, and some of the tension faded away.

She rolled back onto her back and was about to pull back the covers when she heard a sharp intake of breath and every hair on her arm stood on end.

"That was the hottest fucking thing I've ever witnessed."

"Fuck, Daemon!" She reached behind her and tossed a pillow in the direction of his voice.

He caught it with ease and chuckled.

She'd been so caught up in finding her release, that she hadn't noticed when his magic filled the space.

"I would love to, Princess. But unfortunately, I can't stay. I'm just here to kiss you goodnight, and I was barely able to sneak away to do that. Thankfully, Yvaine covered for me." He tried to keep his tone light, but there was sadness there too.

Auraelia slipped from her bed and turned the dial on the sconce that hung on the wall over her side table so that it cast the room in a soft glow.

At the sight of her naked body, his eyes widened, and his throat bobbed as he swallowed. "Fuck, Princess. You're really making it hard on me here."

Her gaze trailed over his body.

He'd lost the coat and vest, but the tunic was barely tucked into his pants and the laces at his throat were loose. As her eyes traveled further, a smirk pulled at one corner of her mouth when it landed on the hard ridge in his pants. "I can see that."

Daemon groaned, then crossed the room and swept her into his arms.

His kiss was all consuming, and his hold on her didn't yield or wander.

He devoured her, and she melted into him.

When he broke the kiss he rested his brow against hers, their breath mingling in the space between them as they tried to slow their breathing.

"I'm going to go now before I get caught doing something I shouldn't."

Auraelia tried to respond, but his lips sealed against hers once more, and then he was gone.

She fell backwards onto her bed and groaned.

Chapter Forty-Three

Auraelia

It was late morning by the time she rolled out of bed the following day–roused by the smell of fresh coffee.

"Morning, sunshine." Piper sing-songed while holding the steaming mug beneath Auraelia's nose.

"How are you always so chipper in the morning?" She groaned, but once she was in a sitting position, Piper handed her the cup of coffee then perched on the edge of her bed with one of her own.

She took a sip, letting the bitter liquid warm her from the inside out. Then, after another, she finally broke the silence that had descended.

"So, are you going to tell me about Aiden now?"

"I was kind of hoping that I would get a pass for today since it's solstice." A cheeky, yet hopeful, grin spread across Piper's face.

"Not a chance. Especially after the way that you reacted to seeing him again after three months. What happened?"

Piper stood, set her mug on the table next to Auraelia's bed, and began pacing the room.

Auraelia sat quietly and listened.

"When Aiden left Lyndaria after your coronation, I thought that was it. He never wrote, so I wrote him off. And when your mother sent us to Kalmeera, and he was an asshole on the way there. When he wasn't acting like I didn't exist, he talked down to me, and it just reaffirmed my decision. But–" Piper stopped pacing and began twisting her fingers–her nervous habit when she was about to say something that she thought Auraelia wouldn't like.

"*But?*" Auraelia prompted, in what she hoped was a reassuring tone.

"But, when I started ignoring *him*, he came crawling back like a lost little puppy, and you know how much I love puppies. Rae–he apologized. Said he didn't know that I wanted anything else from him, and that he missed me and wanted another chance. So, I gave him one.

"We spent some time together the night of solstice, and then it happened again. I didn't hear from him until the night before we left. He apologized–*again*–and said that he wanted to try writing letters like you and Daemon, and I stupidly agreed. I wrote to him when we got back, but I never heard from him.

"So, when I saw him last night, everything that happened–or didn't happen–was shoved in my face and it made me angry. I hate him. *Hate* him, Rae. But at the same time, I *want* him. Which makes me hate him even more."

Auraelia sat in silence for a moment, then looked at her friend. "What about Xander?"

"What about Xander?" Shock briefly crossed Piper's features before morphing into confusion, but Auraelia caught the panic that crossed her friend's eyes before it disappeared.

"Do you like him?"

"Xander? He's–he's like a brother to me, you know that." Piper began to fiddle with the ends of her hair avoiding Auraelia's gaze.

"Piper, if you're worried about what I would think–"

Piper's gaze snapped to hers and there was a fierce determination in her eyes. "Rae, I do *not* like Xander like that. He's–he's *Xander!*"

Auraelia shook her head, "Whatever you say, Piper. *I'm* just saying *if* you want to go there, I'm not going to stop you. And I'm pretty sure he wouldn't either."

"Rae–"

Just as Piper started to speak, the door to Auraelia's suite opened and a flood of lady's maids entered the room. Some held trays of food and drinks, while others came holding dress boxes and sewing kits.

It was time to get ready for the solstice celebration, and every year there was a theme– this year was no different.

Last year, it had been metamorphosis, and both Auraelia and Piper had painted butterfly wings next to their eyes.

This year's theme was living gems, and she couldn't wait to wear the gown that she'd designed.

It was a deep shade of emerald, and the skirt was made of layers upon layers of tulle in varying cuts and lengths that were all edged in gold to mimic the veins that coursed through the natural gems.

Like her dress from Kalmeera, the bodice was made from strips of pleated fabric that crisscrossed over her torso. There were cutouts on her sternum and the side of her waist that wrapped around to the back of the dress, which were left open save for the thin straps that went across her shoulder blades.

Her ladies moved in a synchronized dance around her. They curled and pinned her hair into a magical looking updo and used emerald pins to secure the gold version of her circlet that her mother commissioned for the occasion.

The gold cuff that they slid onto her arm was cold against her skin, and the scalloped chains that hung down her bicep swayed delicately with her movements.

Her makeup was minimal, with only a little bit of rouge on her cheeks and a barely-there color on her lips, but her ladies brought an immense amount of focus to her eyes. Her lids had been dusted in champagne gold powder and then a deep brown in the outer corners, and they had even painted her lashes as Yvaine had.

When she was fully dressed, and her ladies gave her a moment of peace, she slipped on the final piece of her ensemble and smiled to herself. There was only one person who would see the addition, and she couldn't wait to see his face.

Auraelia walked into her sitting room where Piper had been getting ready and stopped in her tracks–her friend looked stunning.

Piper had chosen peridot as her gem and wore the color beautifully.

Her gown was a sweetheart cut that tapered in at her waist before flowing out into a beautiful chiffon skirt of varying shades of muted yellow and bright greens, and the uppermost layer was a shimmering gold.

Her eyes had been dusted in the same champagne gold powder, a dark line of kohl had been flicked upwards past the outer corner to make her eyes appear larger, and her lips were painted deep, berry red.

Piper's naturally straight hair had been left loose, but she'd slicked down the front sections then pinned them behind her ears and added tiny crystals.

The final touch to their looks was to dust any visible skin with a sheer, shimmering, powder that would make them sparkle beneath the light like gemstones.

Once both women were ready, the swarm of help filtered out, leaving them a moment's peace before they had to join the rest of the party downstairs.

"Piper, you look beautiful," Auraelia said as she grasped her friend's hands firmly in hers, giving her a reassuring squeeze.

Piper returned the gesture and smiled. "So do you. Are you ready?"

"As ready as I'll ever be. Let's have some fun tonight."

They both nodded as a knock sounded on the door.

Auraelia called for them to enter, and Xander stepped into the suite.

She watched as his eyes consumed every inch of Piper, and she had to fold her lips inward to keep the grin from her face.

"You look beautiful." There was awe in his voice, and as if he realized he hadn't yet looked toward his sister, he cleared his throat and snapped his focus to Auraelia. "You *both* look beautiful."

She didn't say anything about his misstep, she didn't need to. Her Cheshire smile said everything. "Thank you, Xander. Is it time to go down?"

His gaze had traveled back to Piper, and she didn't miss the deep flush that radiated down Piper's neck as she attempted to keep her gaze from Xander's.

When he didn't answer her, clearly lost in his own thoughts, she called his name in an attempt to pull his attention back to the task at hand.

"Hm? Oh, sorry. Yes, it's time to go. Are you both ready?"

"Yes, we're ready." Auraelia took a few steps toward the door and halted. Turning back to where Piper was still standing still as a statue. "Piper? Are you coming?"

Piper finally turned from the window that had evidently become intoxicatingly interesting when Xander entered the suite and met his gaze head on. "Yes, sorry. I'm coming."

Auraelia's gaze leapt from Piper to Xander, and back again. The tension between them was palpable, and she had a feeling it wouldn't take much of a spark for them to ignite.

Rolling her eyes, she stalked toward the door muttering, "You're both idiots," as she walked past Xander.

The celebration was in full swing by the time they made it downstairs.

The entire main area of the castle had been turned into a staging area. The throne room was open to the main hall, as were the doors that led into the ballroom and the ones that led out into the gardens.

Music played and laughter filled every corner as people danced and talked with free abandon. It was wonderful, and Auraelia couldn't help the smile that formed as she made her way through the crowd.

She loved their Fall solstice celebration. Loved how it brought all of the courts together to celebrate the beauty and unity of their realm.

It wasn't long after they arrived that Xander asked her to dance, and her surprise must have been evident because his brows furrowed in confusion. When they were fully ensconced in the flow and rhythm of the dance, he probed as to why she'd looked so shocked.

"I just thought that you would ask Piper."

"Why would you assume that?"

She looked at him incredulously. "You're joking right? I could cut the tension between the two of you with a rusty butter knife."

"Rae–"

"Don't try and deny it, Xander. I don't have a problem with it if that's what you're worried about. But for the love of the goddess, *please* figure it out. I have my own longing glances to deal with that I don't need to be a third-party spectator to yours." The latter was said with laughter and love, and Xander sighed.

"You really think there's something there?"

"I do–" Auraelia hesitated a moment, debating whether or not she should say something, then decided that it was better than not saying anything. "I also think that she's in denial. She's torn between acknowledging her feelings for you, and the confusing ones she has about Aiden."

Xander tensed at the mention of the Sapphire Isles emissary. "He's not good for her, Rae."

Auraelia let out a short, exasperated breath. "That may be, but it's not our place to tell her not to be with someone. Especially since you and I both know it would just drive her to them. And *maybe* she doesn't know that there is a better option right under–well over–her nose." She smiled and winked at her brother.

She loved both of them so much and just wanted them to find happiness.

Xander chuckled and shook his head. "Yeah, well, we'll see what happens."

They finished out the dance in comfortable silence, then parted ways. Him, presumably in search of Piper, and her in search of Daemon.

She could feel him. Feel the pull of his soul to hers, taught like a tether holding a ship to the dock during a storm. But she couldn't seem to find him.

Auraelia walked out of the ballroom and into the gardens.

It was early, the sun had barely begun its descent and blue still blanketed the sky. The torches that had been set out to line the pathways remained unlit, as were the candles floating in the fountain, but the garden still felt magical.

The mixture of voices and music filtered out through the doors, but as she walked further into the organized chaos that made up the garden, the noise floated away on a breeze, leaving her in a relaxed silence as she wandered the gravel paths.

She hadn't gone far when the hair on the back of her neck stood on end, and her magic began swirling beneath her skin.

She smiled but continued her walk. Running the tips of her fingers along the rose bush that lined this particular path, careful not to prick her finger on their thorns. "You know, it's not nice to sneak up on people," she said into the void of silence that surrounded her.

Daemon's deep chuckle rumbled from behind and sent a shiver of anticipation down her spine. "I suppose you're right–" his arms snaked around her waist, pulling her flush against his body as he ran his nose up the column of her neck before stopping at her ear. "But it's not really sneaking if you can *feel* me behind you." His words were barely a whisper, and they sent a wave of awareness through her body.

Her nipples stiffened into peaks behind the fabric of her dress, her skin prickled, and a heavy heat settled in her core.

Daemon's hands skimmed along her stomach, his fingers brushing across her bare skin through the cutouts.

She leaned into the touch and rested her head on his shoulder.

"I *need* you, my star. I could think of nothing else after I saw you last night." He pulled her hips back into his and pressed the hard ridge of his cock into the soft curve of her ass.

She moaned and reached behind her to palm him over his pants. He hissed between his teeth then spun her around and gripped her chin between two fingers.

Auraelia locked her eyes on his and ran her tongue along her bottom lip.

"*Fuck*, Princess," he groaned, his eyes rolling into the back of his head, before he devoured her mouth with his own.

Dropping the hold he had on her chin, he slid his hand in her hair at the nape of her neck, pulling gently to angle her the way he wanted her.

She *loved* the way he kissed her.

Loved the way that he could hold her tenderly one moment, then have his hand around her throat the next.

The way she felt at ease around him, like she was just a woman, and he was just a man.

She loved...*him*.

The revelation hit her like a strike of lightning.

She knew that she cared for him and had tossed around the idea that maybe it was love. But standing here with him, in the middle of the garden where it all started, it became crystal clear.

Auraelia pulled back, breaking the kiss, and looked–really looked–at Daemon.

He was beautiful. All sharp lines and bold features, with a softness in his eyes and a pureness in his heart.

And he was hers.

"What is it? Is everything ok?" Worry lined his face, and a little wrinkle formed between his brows.

She reached up to smooth the line, then cupped his cheek in her palm and smiled up at him. "Everything is fine, wonderful even."

Auraelia's gaze traveled south, taking in the man who held her heart and was a piece of her soul.

He was once again dressed from head to toe in obsidian, and she couldn't help the laugh that bubbled up her throat.

"What's so funny?" he asked, perplexed by her outburst.

"Black? Again? Did you lose a trunk of clothes on the way here?" She shook her head, her tone full of mirth.

"Onyx is black. I think I fit the theme quite well."

"Sure, you did." She patted his arm in mock placation, and he pulled her into his arms as she crumbled into a fit of laughter.

When she finally calmed, she pulled his lips to hers once more, and the chaste kiss dissolved into something more.

Her hands flew to the laces on his trousers, while his skimmed across the bare part of her back.

Completely lost in the moment and the heat of his touch, she hadn't realized that he'd shadow-walked them to the sanctuary gate until the cold iron bars were pressing into her back.

Daemon slowly lifted her hands above her head, then secured them to the gate with his shadows, leaving her completely at his mercy. He broke the kiss and took a step away, letting his eyes roam down her body and she pulled against the bindings.

"You're not going anywhere this time, Princess. We're finishing what we started here all those months ago."

Her breath caught in her throat as silky ribbons of shadow licked across her body, while Daemon undid his pants.

She wanted to touch him, but more than that, she wanted him to touch *her*.

Once his pants were hung precariously on his hips, he stalked over to her and dropped to his knees.

As he bunched up her skirt, he chuckled as looked at her over the volume of fabric that had accumulated in front of his face. "I seem to recall telling you that the skirts were a bit much the last time we were here, too."

"*Daemon. Please,*" she groaned his name in anticipation, but it was also laced with aggravation, and it made him smirk.

"I do love when you beg."

He began to hike her skirts higher, but stopped when he reached the garter she'd worn to his solstice celebration. A look of awe and wonder crossed his face as he fingered the chains that dangled against her skin then pressed a kiss to the inside of her thigh where it rested.

He continued to push her skirts higher once more, and she knew the exact moment he realized that she was bare beneath all of that fabric. And if his muttered, "Fuck," wasn't a clear indication, the fact that his mouth was on her mere seconds after, definitely was.

He consumed her.

Flattening his tongue as he took long languid strokes up her center. And when he added two fingers into her entrance, and swirled his tongue around her clit, she thought she would combust right then.

But Daemon stopped his assault with his tongue and stood, his fingers still plunging deep within her as his thumb worked the sensitive bundle of nerves. Using his free hand, he pushed his pants down off of his hips and freed his considerable length from its confines.

"I want to spend the rest of the night with my head between your thighs. But right now, I need your sweet pussy wrapped around me."

She nodded emphatically, and in the next moment, he removed his digits from her core and replaced them with his cock, his mouth fusing to hers to stifle her moans.

Her legs were wrapped firmly around his waist as he drove into her. The cool bite of the gate as it dug into her back added to the mix of sensations, and it wasn't long before she was spiraling into bliss with Daemon right behind her.

Once their hearts stopped racing and their breathing returned to normal, he returned her feet to the ground and recalled his shadows from her wrists.

They hadn't even had time to fully right themselves, when Piper came barreling into the sanctuary garden with a crazed look in her eyes.

Auraelia pushed her skirts back into place and scurried around Daemon to reach her panicked friend. "What is it, Piper? What's wrong?"

Piper's eyes were wide and there was fear swirling in their hazel depths.

"Something's wrong. I don't know what exactly, the vision is fuzzy. But, Rae, I think–I think I saw your mother...die."

Chapter Forty-Four

Daemon

"Die? What do you mean, you think you saw my mother die? What are you talking about?" Auraelia's voice was edged in panic as she grasped her friend's shoulders, shaking her as if that would force the information in Piper's brain to dislodge and transfer into her own.

Daemon hurried across the space and pulled her from Piper. "Auraelia, give her a moment."

She roughly pulled out of his grasp, his arms falling limp at his sides, as she extended her hand toward Piper. "Show me."

"Rae, I don't–" Nervousness and worry contorted Piper's features at Auraelia's request.

"Piper, it's my *mother*. We don't have time; I need to see it. Please."

Piper acquiesced and grasped Auraelia's hand in hers.

Daemon watched Auraelia squeeze her eyes shut. Saw them flick back and forth behind her lids as she watched the vision unfold.

Piper on the other hand, had her eyes wide open—her gaze growing distant as the vision took over her sight.

He knew the instant the vision concluded, as Piper blinked away the fog and Auraelia's eyes shot open—her face whiter than fresh snow.

"Auraelia?" Her name did nothing to jar her out of the state of shock she had fallen into after seeing Piper's vision. But the moment his hand landed on her lower back, she spun away from him and sprinted toward the castle.

He and Piper were quick on her heels, and despite their cries begging her to slow down, her pace never faltered. It wasn't until she reached the courtyard right outside the ballroom, that she finally slowed to a brisk walk.

With her pace slower, Daemon shadow-walked and grabbed her elbow from behind, pulling her to an abrupt stop. "Auraelia, slow down, please."

She whirled on him, anger and fear warring for dominance in her eyes. "Slow down? My mother could be lying dead on the floor of the ballroom right now, and you want me to *slow down*?"

Piper grasped Auraelia's face between her hands, forcing her to focus on her face and everything that she said. "Rae, breathe. You can't barge into the ballroom; you'll throw everyone into a panic. Just—take a moment to calm yourself before you go storming through the room like a hurricane."

"I don't have time for this." Auraelia wrenched her face from Piper's hands and continued toward the ballroom.

Daemon was close on her heels, and as they wove through the throng of guests just outside the doors, the chime of glasses clinking together filtered out into the garden as everyone took a sip from their glasses.

"No. Goddess, please, no," she muttered under her breath as she shoved her way toward her mother once more.

As the clamor of the toast began to die down, it was as if the world tilted on its axis, causing it to spin in slow motion.

Queen Adelina looked down into her glass, her eyes widening as it slipped from her fingers and fell to the floor, shattering against the veined marble of the ballroom.

"No, no this can't be happening." Tears began to well in Auraelia's eyes, and her head shook slightly in disbelief of the events that were unfolding in front of her eyes.

The queen's face flushed and twisted into one of pain. She clawed at the bodice of her gown as if it were burning her skin, and her eyes frantically searched the crowd around her.

When her gaze landed on Auraelia, a look full of more love than Daemon thought he would ever be able to comprehend latched onto the princess, but there was regret in her eyes as well.

Auraelia began chanting, "No," over and over again, and she watched the queen crumple to the ground.

A collective gasp filled the air as Auraelia hurled herself across the floor and fell to her knees next to her mother. As she pulled her mother's head into her lap tears began to stream down her cheeks.

He couldn't hear the words that fell from the queen's lips, but when he heard Auraelia sob, "Please, don't leave me," his heart shattered.

When the queen's arm went limp at her side, and her eyes fluttered closed, Auraelia's head fell back as she released a blood curdling scream that sent wave upon wave of raw, unfiltered magic pulsing throughout the room.

He'd never felt a blast of pure power like that.

It caused the ground to shake and knocked people off their feet.

It chilled the air and blew out the windows that lined the walls of the ballroom.

Hurricane force winds swirled through the space, ripping the carefully curated decorations from their places and throwing them like projectiles around the room.

An unnatural lightning storm raged outside as rain poured from the sky in sheets.

Auraelia's hair and skirts began to lift around her as if she were suspended in water, and the emeralds she wore were incandescent with the sheer force of her magic that funneled through them.

Even the sapphire pendant that he'd given her seemed to be fueling the magic as it ripped through her.

As her scream died down and turned into a hoarse cry that sounded like it was being painfully ripped from her throat, the wind began to subside. Though the unnatural rain and lightning still persisted, it seemed as if the world had tilted back into alignment once more.

Daemon attempted to rush to her side, but a tight grip on his elbow stopped him in his tracks.

When he turned to see who it was, shock and rage filled his entire being, as the deep moss-green eyes of his father stared back at him.

"It's not our business, son."

"The fuck it isn't! Someone just murdered a monarch, what makes you think they won't come for you next?" Daemon forcefully ripped his arm from his father's grasp and stalked towards Auraelia.

Chapter Forty-Five

Auraelia

Numbness.

Confusion.

Despair.

Emotions warred against each other as she stared down at her mother's lifeless body. She'd thought they could make it in time. Thought they could warn her so that she would be able to avoid the poison that had unjustly taken her life.

But they'd failed.

She'd failed.

Tears streamed down Auraelia's face and splashed against her mother's once rosy cheeks.

She could barely make out the sounds of frantic screams around her. Could hardly understand the commands that Xander was undoubtedly issuing to lock down the ballroom in hopes of finding the person responsible.

Her entire body buzzed from the magic that had been released through her grief.

She vaguely recalled the weightless feeling as wave after wave of power ripped through her. Could hardly comprehend the strength it took to blast through the countless windows that once filled the walls around the ballroom.

The sound of the torrential rain outside mixed with claps of thunder and lightning, and the howl of the wind, mimicked the storm that raged inside her, further muffling the sounds that surrounded her as she sank further into the nothingness that the black void of grief provided.

She was drowning. She felt like her head was being held underwater and she couldn't fight her way back to find air. The longer she stayed there, the more she didn't *want* to fight. The more she wanted to succumb to the numbness.

It was Daemon who broke through to her.

Daemon, who sat on the floor next to her and laced his fingers with hers–fingers that now looked like they had been dipped to her first knuckle in a shimmering emerald green–and whispered, "I'm right here, my star. I've got you."

With those few words, the pressure that held her beneath the surface and pulled her into the endless void, released enough that she was able to suck air down into her lungs.

And with that breath, the storm that raged around them slowed.

The wind died down, the rain slowed to a shower, and the thunder and lightning calmed into a distant rumble.

"Well, well, well. That sure was entertaining." A honeyed voice pierced through the noise of the ballroom, rendering it into an eerie silence, and filled her with a fiery rage.

"Who said that?" Xander asked. His voice was authoritative, but this close, she could hear the undercurrent of pain. Could feel the anguish that radiated out of him, because it was one and the same with hers.

Movement from across the room caught her eye, and she turned to the wall of broken glass that looked out over the garden.

There, standing in one of the shattered doorways, was a woman she'd never seen before.

She was incredibly underdressed to have been a guest at the celebration. Dressed in black leather pants and thigh high boots, a ruby-red corset over a white tunic, and a hooded blood-red cape that obscured her features and fell to her knees.

Even with the hood, Auraelia could see the feline grin that spread across the woman's face.

"I did." Her tone was matter-of-fact and it was like a red-hot poker had been shoved into Auraelia's stomach.

The mystery woman pushed off of the wall and removed her hood.

She had long moonlight white hair that was pulled into a braided ponytail at the top of her head and fell to her shoulders. Her cheekbones were razor sharp, and she had full, blood-red lips.

But it was her eyes that caught Aurelia's attention, as they were eerily similar to her own.

Auraelia narrowed her gaze at the woman, and finally found her voice. "Who are you?"

"I'm Lady Davina of the Court of Garnet, and I'm here to take your throne, Princess."

Shock rolled through the room, as people began muttering to themselves and to their neighbors.

"I'm sorry, *what*?" Auraelia gently laid her mother's body on the ground and stood. She was exhausted and her stomach roiled as a wave of nausea slammed into her, but she wasn't about to let this stranger see that. Wasn't about to *give* her anything. Taking a step forward to block her mother's prone body, Auraelia straightened her spine; her magic once again rising to the surface.

Davina laughed, then cocked her head to the side. "Was I not clear, *cousin*? I'm here to take your throne." Every word in her latter statement was harshly enunciated to drive the point across.

"Cousin? We're not—"

"I see your mother kept some secrets from you, Princess. Here, allow me to fill you in." Cockiness bled into her tone, and she spoke with an air of superiority.

When Auraelia failed to respond, Davina continued, her feline grin spreading further across her face.

"Years ago, before you or I were even a blip in this world, our grandfather decided that his wife was not enough for him and took a mistress. When both women fell pregnant, it became a race to see who would provide the female heir to the line.

"Your mother—" Davina lackadaisically waved her hand in the direction of the fallen queen, "Was born mere seconds before mine, so she was given the title of heir. And since that self-righteous male had secured his precious lineage, he cast my grandmother aside and sent her, and his newborn babe, to live in Garnet. Where my grandmother then married the lord of the court."

A hush fell over the room as Davina spun her tale.

"My family has stayed tucked away in that remote, frozen, no-man's-land for decades, and we've had enough. So, here I am, to take back what could have been rightfully mine to begin with. I have just as much a claim to that throne as you do, and I intend to have it."

The nonchalant tone in her voice grated Auraelia's last nerve, and her magic swirled throughout the room as her temper rose.

"You killed her, didn't you?"

"Who? Your mother? Yes...but also, no." Her smile was sickly sweet. "I merely provided the necessary supplies." Reaching into the pocket of her cape, Davina pulled out a delicate white flower and gazed at the tiny bud with all the tenderness a mother would give her newborn babe.

"Did you know that Lily of the Valley was poisonous? Or that consuming five or more of its berries could kill a person?" she asked no one in particular.

Auraelia watched as Davina continued to swirl the stem between two fingers.

"You'll never get the backing from the other courts," Auraelia said, filling her voice with as much confidence as she could muster.

Davina stopped twirling the flower, and turned her pity filled gaze to Auraelia. "Oh, my dear, sweet cousin. I have the entire Court of Sapphire Isles backing my claim."

"Like hell you do!" With the mention of his court, Daemon shot to his feet and moved to stand next to her.

"Ah, you must be Prince Daemon. It's so nice to put a face to the man I'm intended to marry."

"I'm not marrying you," he scoffed.

"Oh, but you are. Just ask daddy dearest."

"I would never agree to a marriage with you."

Davina giggled, her eyes growing wide with mock innocence. "I didn't need you to agree. Your father leapt at the proposal when I explained that I knew how to cure his illness."

"You–you cured my father?" Daemon's brow's furrowed, and confusion filled his words.

Davina tilted her head from side to side, like she was trying to find the best way to answer his question. "Again, yes...but also, no. I simply *stopped* supplying the poison that was wreaking havoc on his system once he agreed to my proposal."

Auraelia whipped around to face Daemon, but his eyes were searching the crowd for his father.

"You won't find him here. He and your mother fled back to Kalmeera shortly after the queen dropped dead."

Rage surged through Auraelia, and her fingertips began to spark with electricity. "How *dare* you!"

Davina's eyes lit with glee. "You want to play, cousin? Because I am *dying* to play with you."

The instant the words left Davina's mouth, Xander placed a shield around their group.

Auraelia rarely saw her brother use his gifts.

He was one of very few shields in Lyndaria, and he was the most powerful one at that. Able to cast over entire armies, but also able to form individual shields around multiple people at once.

His abilities were extremely impressive, but they weren't needed in times of peace. Peace that was slowly fading away with every second that passed in Davina's presence.

Davina's eyes widened in surprise as she took in the shimmering dome that covered Auraelia, Xander, their mother, and even Daemon. Her gaze, which was now aimed back to Auraelia, was full of malice as it trailed down her arms.

The electricity had formed into ribbons of lightning and began to wrap around her arms like pieces of armor, but Davina's gaze continued until it stopped at the tips of her fingers.

She tilted her head to the side like a cat contemplating a mouse, then she smiled once more. "Though, with a little practice, we may yet be evenly matched."

"What do you mean?" Her words were spoken through gritted teeth.

Davina sighed and shook her head. "Your mother did you a disservice, cousin. Keeping secrets from you all these years. Your fingers–" she gestured to Auraelia's hands, "That happens when you've fully tapped into your magic."

Davina held up her own hand, and just like Auraelia, the tips of her fingers were stained. Only Davina's, were a red so dark it could have passed for black.

Auraelia watched as Davina twisted her fingers in front of her face, admiring the way the tips shimmered in the light. "Well, cousin, if you don't want to play, perhaps I should play with someone else, hmm?"

With a flick of her wrist, there was a piercing scream that came from the edge of the crowd, and Auraelia would know that sound anywhere.

Piper.

Xander's shield faltered when he realized who was screaming, and it was just long enough for Auraelia to send a bolt of her lightning at Davina.

She barely grazed her shoulder, but it was enough to pull her focus, and stop her from doing whatever torture she was inflicting upon Piper.

Xander reinforced his shield and pushed it out to cover everyone else in the area.

"Daemon, go find Piper. *Now.*" Auraelia's gaze stayed locked on Davina as she spoke and felt the air shift as Daemon shadow-walked to her friend.

Davina gripped her shoulder where Auraelia's lighting struck, and when she pulled her hand away, it was tinged with blood–her once carefree demeanor twisting into one of rage and retribution. When she laughed, it was full of hatred, her nostrils flaring in anger as she stared at Auraelia. "This isn't over, Princess. As a matter of fact, it's only the beginning."

Davina looked over Auraelia's shoulder to where Daemon was standing once more, with Piper sagging against him. "Oh, and Daemon. Better hurry home to mommy and daddy. We have a wedding to plan."

As she turned away, her cape fluttered behind her in the wind that drifted in through the shattered windows. When she crossed the threshold, a man appeared in a flurry of snow, and then they were both gone.

Xander dropped his shield, and it was as if every person in the room exhaled at once, but they were all still frozen in place. Their gazes turned to Queen Adelina, where she still laid against the cold marble floor.

Auraelia kneeled next to her mother and grasped her hand, before she turned her gaze to Piper. "Are you okay? What did she do to you?"

Piper sipped from a glass of water and shook her head. "I'm not sure. It felt like there was a cold hand wrapped around my heart and squeezing it." A shiver coursed through Piper at the memory.

Auraelia turned back to her mother's prone body. "I need to know who gave her the poison." It was said more to herself than anything, but Xander reached over and grabbed Auraelia's hand in his.

"We'll find the person responsible, Rae."

She nodded and sat there in silence as her thumb idly stroked her mother's hand, the events of the day playing out in her head.

But as Piper's vision filtered back through her memories, an idea formed.

"Piper–" her head whipped toward her friend, "I need you to try and trigger a vision."

"What?" Wrinkles formed on Piper's forehead as her brows shot up toward her hairline.

"I need you to trigger the vision you had of my mother. Maybe if you hold her hand, or–or touch her in some way, you can get a clearer vision."

"Rae, I don't know about this."

"Piper, *please*. I'm begging you. Please. Just...try?" Tears began to well in her eyes once more. She needed this, needed some kind of hope to cling to.

Piper's gaze flicked over Auraelia's face, sorrow filling her eyes as she agreed.

Sliding over until she sat behind the queen's head, Piper placed a hand on each of Queen Adelina's temples.

As soon as Piper made contact, she inhaled sharply as the vision took hold and her gaze became distant. Only a few minutes passed before Piper pulled her hands away, severing the vision caused by the contact. "Rae–"

Auraelia grasped Piper's hands in her own, and for the second time that day, she asked her friend to share her gift.

The feeling of being underwater wasn't nearly as suffocating this time around as the vision played out in her mind's-eye.

The milky white clouds that prefaced every vision Piper shared faded away, leaving crystal clear images. Images that flew through her mind at such a rapid pace that it made her head spin.

Auraelia watched as her mother spoke with guests.

Watched as she danced with Xander.

And finally, watched as one of Auraelia's very own lady's maids laced her mother's glass of champagne before her toast.

Bile rose in her throat as she watched her mother die for the second time that day.

As the vision ended, her vision clouded once more, like curtains falling across a stage at the end of a performance.

She'd done it.

Piper had been able to manipulate and steer the vision to show her the information she needed.

Opening her eyes, Auraelia smiled at her friend. "Thank you."

As she turned to Xander, her smile dropped into cold disdain, and the warmth she'd just given Piper switched to one of seething fury. "Bring me, Kyra."

It wasn't long before Kyra had been dragged kicking and screaming into the ballroom, and more of the queen's guards lined the walls.

Auraelia stood next to her mother's lifeless body, her eyes seeing no color other than red as the woman responsible for the lethal dose of poison stood in front of her.

"Kyra, you have murdered the Queen of Lyndaria and the Court of Emerald." It wasn't a question. She didn't want–or need–her to confess to the crime. She had all the proof she needed in Piper's vision.

Kyra didn't respond, but her eyes were fixed to the lifeless body that lay on the floor by Auraelia's feet.

"Do you have *anything* to say?"

Kyra pulled her gaze up to Auraelia's face, but when she opened her mouth, the only sound that escaped was her gasping for air.

The guards that had been holding her upright, released her as she crumpled to the floor.

Auraelia's head cocked slightly to the side and her lips pressed into a firm line, as she watched with fire in her eyes and ice in her heart.

Watched as Kyra clawed at her throat, her face beginning to turn shades of pink and purple from the lack of oxygen.

"You stole my mother from me. Murdered her, in cold blood." Auraelia took a step forward, her lip pulling up into a snarl. "Now, you will pay the same price."

Letting her pain and anger drive her, Auraelia held out her hand and slowly began to close it into a fist–the closer her fingers got to her palm, the more Kyra struggled.

Blood vessels began to burst in her eyes, turning their whites, crimson.

But just before she closed her fist completely, Daemon stepped in front of her and pulled her hand open.

"Auraelia, you don't want to do this."

Her hardened gaze burned into his, "And why is that? She murdered my mother, Daemon!"

"I know, my star, I know. But you don't want your first act as queen to be murdering someone. Especially, in front of every delegate in our realm. Please, Auraelia. Don't do this." His voice was only loud enough for her ears as he pleaded with her to stop.

His softened gaze locked onto hers, and she felt a crack form in her need for vengeance.

"My mother is dead," her voice cracked, and tears lined her eyes.

"I know. I'm so sorry, Auraelia."

Not caring who was watching, she buried her face in his chest and sobbed.

Daemon wrapped her in his arms, told Xander to throw Kyra in a cell, then shadow-walked them away from the prying eyes of court, and into her rooms.

Chapter Forty-Six

Auraelia

The days following her mother's death were some of the hardest that she'd ever lived.

She'd spent the first night curled up against Daemon, as sobs wracked her body until she fell asleep. Only to be woken by recurring night terrors of watching her mother die over and over again.

Her throat was raw from the force of her screams, and her eyes were swollen shut from the number of tears that she'd shed.

She refused to eat.

Refused to see anyone aside from Daemon–even Piper and Xander.

By day two, her tears had run dry, and she spent the day curled on her side staring at the wall, until sleep and the nightmares claimed her once more.

She could hear Daemon outside her chamber door updating people on her status.

Could hear the frantic and demanding tone of Xander's voice, and the crushing sadness in Piper's, but she couldn't gather the strength to care.

Sleep.

She just wanted to sleep.

When day three came, Daemon was no longer taking no–or silence–for an answer when it came to hygiene and food.

He ladled warm broth into her mouth, while she stared blankly ahead. But as soon as she was finished, she curled onto her side once more and fell into another round of fitful sleep.

After waking drenched in a cold sweat from yet another night terror, he stripped her out of her nightgown, and carried her into her bathing chamber.

When he placed her into her tub, she didn't care that the water was scalding. She welcomed the burn. Welcomed anything that made her feel something other than immense grief and the pain in her heart.

She let him care for her. Let him wash her body with slow, gentle strokes. Let his hands massage the soap into her hair and work out the knots that had formed at the base of her skull.

She responded to his commands, but only barely. Lifting a limb when instructed or tilting her head back when he needed to rinse the suds from her strands. But not even his touch could soothe the endless ache.

She was numb to everything and everyone around her.

Brick by brick, she slowly began to build a wall around her crumbling heart.

When he finished, he let the tub drain before wrapping her in a towel, then lifted her into his arms once more and carried her back into her room.

He spoke to her while he dried her off, but his words sounded like they were coming from far away. When he tried to get her to look at him, it was like she was looking through a pane of glass that had been fogged over on an early fall morning.

She could see, but there was a haze in front of her eyes, and nothing was clear.

Dressed once more, she crawled back into bed.

Keeping her back to him as she pulled the covers up to her chin, she silently begged for one night of dreamless sleep.

When she awoke, it was the following morning, and she thanked Rhayne for answering her prayer.

Daemon sat in the bed next to her–fully clothed–with his back against the headboard, and his eyes closed. But the moment she stirred, they popped open and for the first time in four days, she saw him a little more clearly.

His hair was disheveled, he had dark circles under his eyes, and his normally neat stubble was overgrown and unkempt. When she met his gaze, she saw all the worry and sorrow that permeated their depths.

"Auraelia? Can I get you something?" He raised his hand and moved it toward her face, but thought better of it at the last moment, and pulled away.

She pushed up into a sitting position and nodded. "Water." After screaming for days on end, and not talking at all when she was awake, her voice was hoarse and grated against her sore throat.

Shock flashed across his face at the sound, but he smiled and sprang into action–crossing the room to where a tray with a pitcher and glasses sat next to a plate of simple foods.

He returned to the bed with the glass, and after a few sips, she attempted to speak once more.

"Where's–" she stopped and cleared her throat in hopes that it would loosen her vocal cords. "Where are Xander and Piper?"

Daemon sat next to her on the edge of her bed. "They're probably still in your sitting room. They've barely left your suite since–"

He stopped himself before he said anything that could potentially make her spiral back into overwhelming grief.

They sat in silence for a moment before she cleared her throat once more. "Your parents–" Daemon's spine stiffened slightly, but she continued. "What happened?"

His face fell as a sigh slipped through his lips. "My father...shadow-walking is a familial trait. I'm assuming that after he tried to stop me from going to you after—" He stopped himself once more. The unspoken words hanging between them like a heavy weight. "He took my mother and ran."

Auraelia nodded, her gaze falling to the glass she held in her lap. "Can I see them? Xander and Piper, I mean."

"Of course, I'll go get them. Are you hungry at all?" he asked before standing to leave.

Auraelia thought for a moment, then as if her stomach had a mind of its own, it grumbled in response to his question.

Daemon chuckled then stood. "Is there anything in particular you would like? There's a plate of fruit and cheese on the tray if you'd like that for now."

"I think some tea and maybe some soup could be good for my throat. Do you mind?"

He smiled, then cupped her face in his hands and shook his head before resting his brow on hers. "Whatever you need, my star. Whatever you need."

He placed a chaste kiss to her brow, and then turned to leave.

Auraelia watched him walk through her door, and the crevice that was trying to cleave her heart in two, widened a little more.

"Auraelia!" Piper bounded into the room and threw herself onto Auraelia. "Don't you *ever* do that to me again, do you hear me?" Piper scolded her, but there were tears in her eyes, and Auraelia pulled her into a tight embrace.

"I'm sorry." Tears flowed freely between them, and they stayed locked together for a long moment, each using the other to help bandage the wounds that had been cut so deep they would probably never fully heal.

When they finally broke apart, Xander fully entered the space. "Are you ok, sis?" His eyes were puffy, and his nose was red, and seeing him so worried and upset sent Auraelia back into tears.

"I'm so sorry, Xander. I–I shouldn't have left you to deal with that on your own. She was your mother too. I'm so, so sorry." Her words came out in strangled sobs as guilt slammed into her. Crossing the room in two long strides, Xander folded her into his arms and let his tears stream down his cheeks.

"It's ok, Rae. I'm okay. I was just so worried about you." He pulled back and palmed her cheeks in his hands, looking her over as if the wounds on her soul were visible to his eyes. "Are *you* okay?"

Auraelia let out a choked laugh and shrugged. "I don't really have much choice in the matter, do I? For the sake of our people, I have to be."

As silence descended over their group, Auraelia pulled herself from bed and wrapped her robe around her shoulders.

When she turned back to Xander and Piper, there was a fierceness in her eyes. "Xander, there's something that I need you to do for me."

His brow furrowed, but he nodded. "Anything. What is it?"

She took a deep breath, then straightened her shoulders. "I need to move into the Queen's Suite, and then I need you to shield it."

"Shield it? Shield it from what?"

Piper's eyes filled with sadness and understanding as she grasped what Auraelia was asking. "Not what, Xan. *Who.*"

Xander's head swiveled from Piper to Auraelia, and then he sighed when he realized what she meant. "You want me to shield your chambers from Daemon? But why?"

Auraelia's gaze fell to her hands, where she absentmindedly rubbed the shimmering green stains on their tips. "Because I need to shield my heart from him. He's betrothed to another."

"But, Rae. You love him." Piper stood from the bed and walked over to her, pulling her hands apart and clasping them in her own, "Don't you?"

"I do, but I *can't*. It hurts too much."

Piper nodded, then turned her head toward Xander. "We need to move her now, while he's down in the kitchens."

The queen's chambers–her *mother's* chambers–were exactly as they had always been.

Her robe still hung on the door to the bathing chamber.

There was a stack of unfinished books on the bedside table, none of which she would ever know the endings.

It was as if her mother had just walked out the door and would be back any minute demanding to know what Auraelia was doing in her rooms.

And the smell of peonies still permeated the air.

Auraelia ran her hand across the large wooden footboard of the bed and collapsed onto the bench that sat in front of it as a sob ripped through her chest.

Her head fell heavy into her hands as her grief tore through her again.

There was a heavy-handed knock on the door that led into the attached sitting area, and she immediately knew who it was.

Knew he was here in response to the letter she'd written him before running to the safety of her mother's suite, and the security of Xander's shield over them.

"Where is she?" Daemon demanded, his voice carrying through the closed door of the bedchambers.

"Daemon, how nice to see you again." Xander's response was cold, and it sent a shiver down her spine.

She stood from the bench, and quietly walked to the door, pressing her ear to the wood.

"Don't give me that bullshit, Xander. Let me talk to her." He was angry–rightfully so–but there was also pain behind his words, and it wrapped a strangling hand around her heart.

"She told you everything she wanted to say in the note. Now please, don't make a scene." Xander kept his voice calm and level, but there was a firm edge to it.

"Daemon, don't make this harder than it needs to be, please," Piper said. She sounded like she was just on the other side of the door, adding another barrier that he would have to cross if he wanted to get to her.

She could hear the break in his voice when he turned his attention to her friend. "Piper, please. Talk to her. Don't let her do this. *Please.*"

She could feel the sobs that she had been holding begin to force their way out, so she hurried away from the door, and headed to the bathing chamber. After closing it behind her, she turned on every faucet and let the sound of the water wash away the sound of the pain in Daemon's voice.

Let it drown out the thoughts that made her doubt every decision she'd made.

Minutes passed before there was a gentle knock on the bathing chamber door. "Rae? He's gone, can I come in?"

Auraelia took a deep breath, suffocating the remaining sobs that were threatening to escape, then called for Piper to enter.

The room was full of steam, the mirrors were fogged, and she was a sweaty, sobbing heap on the floor.

Piper sank down next to Auraelia and pulled her head onto her shoulder. "What was in that letter you left him, Rae?"

She sighed, and pinched her eyes closed. "I told him to go home."

"Rae—"

"I know, Piper. Trust me, I know. But it's so much more complicated now. It's a fight between Emerald and Garnet that I had no idea existed. It's him being betrothed to *her*. It's—it's just too much."

Piper grabbed her hand and squeezed. "I know, but we don't even know if what Davina said was true."

Auraelia bolted upright and planted a kiss on Piper's cheek. "You're a genius."

"Thank you...but what did I say?" Confusion and worry filled her tone.

Auraelia stood and ran the back of her hand across her damp brow. "I need to get into the archives. There has to be something in there about all of this, right? And now that I'm...queen...I have access to the records."

"I guess? But, Rae, it's late and you haven't really eaten in almost four days. Please, for Xander's and my own peace of mind, will you *please* put this off until tomorrow. We can talk about what we need to look for over dinner."

Auraelia released a breath, but acquiesced and stuck her hand out for Piper to take.

After pulling her friend from the floor, the two women set about turning off the faucets, then headed into the sitting room where Xander stood looking out over the garden of peonies.

As she came to his side, she looped her arm through his and rested her head on his shoulder.

"I think they started dying the same moment she did." His words, though barely above a whisper, cut through the silence like a hot knife.

And as she looked out over the garden, she realized what he meant. The once full and bright blooms seemed to have dulled and wilted. Like they, too, were mourning the loss of the queen.

Piper walked across the room and wrapped her arms around Auraelia's waist.

The three of them stayed that way, watching the sun make its trek downward in the sky, until there was a knock on the door that announced the arrival of their dinner.

Chapter Forty-Seven

Auraelia

Auraelia woke bright and early to sunlight streaming through the banquette window in the sitting room.

She, Piper, and Xander had been up most of the night trying to figure out the best way to handle things with Garnet, and it seemed as if they'd talked themselves to sleep.

Rising from her spot on the deep cushioned couch, she carefully stepped over where Piper had fallen asleep on the floor surrounded by pillows. But as she passed where Xander was sleeping in one of the armchairs, his arm shot out and gripped her wrist.

"Sneaking off by yourself, Your Majesty?" he asked, cracking one eye in her direction.

"Don't call me that."

He released his grip and peeled himself from the chair, raising his arms over his head in a full body stretch, then sighed.

His eyes were full of empathy as he looked at her. "I know you're not ready to hear it, but the title is yours. And anyone you come into contact with outside of this room, is going to use it."

She closed her eyes and exhaled. "I know."

Xander put his arm around her shoulders and pulled her into an embrace. "Come on, let's go see what's in these archives."

"What about Piper?" Right as she asked, as a small snore sounded from the pile of pillows on the floor.

Both Xander and Auraelia covered their mouths to stifle a laugh. "Let her sleep. She can join us later."

The Court of Emerald's archives were located through a hidden passage in the council chambers, behind a door that could only be accessed by the queen.

There was a pin next to the lock, and to open it, Auraelia would have to prick her finger and let the blood drip into it. The lock was said to have been imbued with magic by the Goddess Rhayne herself, and only the blood and magic of the reigning queen could access what was behind the door. How it knew who was on the throne was a mystery in and of itself, but Auraelia didn't question it as the door swung open.

They'd been searching for hours, and still hadn't found anything of significance by the time Piper joined them–bringing a carafe of coffee and a tray piled high with pastries with her.

Auraelia and Xander–after much insisting from Piper–stopped long enough to eat and have a cup of coffee before they dove back into their work.

By lunch, they still had nothing, so Auraelia told them to take a break and she'd let them know if she found anything.

Begrudgingly, they agreed and left.

Hours passed as she sifted through piles of books and roll after roll of parchment, and still, she found nothing.

Lifting the stack she'd just finished going through, she headed back into the archives to put them away, but when she walked through the door, it was like she'd walked into a different chamber entirely.

Red leatherbound books that hadn't been there before stood out like beacons, and she almost dropped the stack she held in her hands.

She hurriedly put the other books away, then pulled every red spine she could find and headed back into the main chamber.

Tome after tome proved everything that Davina had said to be true.

From her–*their*–grandfather's mistress, to Davina's grandmother being sent away to Garnet with her newborn.

Her mother had a half-sister, and she'd never mentioned her.

Auraelia and Xander had, at the very least, one cousin that they never knew about.

And as she scanned through pages and pages of truth, after a lifetime of lies, rage boiled in her veins.

Her mother *lied* to her.

The entire council *lied* to her.

Kept her and Xander in the dark for so long, and now their mother had been murdered because of it, leaving her to deal with the fall out.

Auraelia slid her arms across the table in a fit of rage, sending all the books and parchments skittering across the floor.

Thunder and lightning crackled through the sky, and she could feel her magic buzzing beneath her skin.

She needed to get out.

Needed to scream and release her anger where she couldn't hurt anyone.

Throwing open the doors that led out into the garden, she ran.

Rain fell in sheets as thunder rolled across the sky, and lightning danced between her fingers.

She ran to the furthest edge of the castle grounds and screamed until her lungs gave out.

The waves of magic that rolled off of her made splinters of the trees that had stood on the grounds for decades, and there was a perfect circle where her lightning had scorched the earth.

"Auraelia!" A voice that would be forever ingrained on her soul called through the torrential downpour, and she had to steel her spine before she turned to face him.

"Daemon, go *home*." She was exhausted, both from the amount of magic that she'd just expended, and from the endless stream of thoughts that swirled through her head.

She loved him, but he was marrying someone else.

Marrying the same person who murdered her mother.

Davina hadn't lied.

She's going to have to fight for the crown she believes is her birthright.

Did she want this?

Her whole life had been a lie.

Her mother was dead, and she was alone.

It was too much, and she couldn't handle this–*him*– right now.

"I'm not leaving until we talk, Auraelia. You owe me that much."

"Owe you? My mother was murdered, and you think that I *owe* you something? I have to go to *war* because of the secrets my mother kept, and you think that I owe you?"

He was standing in front of her now, the rain pelting both of them as they stared at each other. "Don't do this. You don't have to go to war."

She scoffed and threw her hands in the air. "I don't? Please, *Daemon*, tell me how I can avoid a war. Should I just give up my crown and end up with nothing? Let her have you, my kingdom, and my people? Is that your solution?"

"I'm not marrying her, Auraelia. I'll abdicate the throne before I let that happen." He sounded so sure, but she knew it wasn't that easy.

He was a prince, and his father was still the king, which meant he had to do as his king bid.

"Daemon, you and I both know that your father won't let that happen." She hung her head and sighed in defeat.

He pressed a finger beneath her chin and lifted her gaze to his. "Auraelia, let me help you. I can't let you—"

She recoiled from his touch and took a step back. "Let me? I'm sorry, *let me?*" She took a deep breath in an attempt to calm the storm that raged inside of her before it flowed out and worsened the one that surrounded them. "Let's get one thing straight. You do not *let me* do anything. Everything I do, every choice that I make, is *my* decision and mine alone. I may ask for advice, or for an opinion, but it stops there."

Her body was shaking with anger, and she could feel the static that came before lightning pooled at her fingertips.

"My star, please." His gaze softened, and he tried to reach out to her, but she stepped away. Her head shook back and forth as sorrow filled his eyes.

"I'm not 'your star,' Daemon—" She gestured to the storm that surrounded them both. "I am the storm that blocks out the sky and brings ships to their breaking point. I am the wind that tears their sails, and the sea that pulls them under…"

She paused as a moment of clarity shone through the turmoil in her mind. Her emeralds hadn't been the only stone to funnel her magic that fateful day. The sapphire he'd given her shone just as brightly. And while she ripped through book after book in the council chambers, she'd stumbled upon her own family tree. Her father had been from the Sapphire Isles, and her lips tilted up into a small smirk at the realization.

"I am blessed by *both* Rhayne and Narissa, and I will bring this realm to its knees if that's what it takes to keep my family and my people safe. And if you're not with me, then you're against me."

Daemon shook his head, and let his arms drop to his sides. "I'm not against you, Auraelia..."

She took a few steps to close the gap between them and stared at him square in the eyes. "Then you're in my way. You can't help me, so move, or drown in the chaos. I no longer care."

Auraelia brushed past him and headed back toward the castle. She'd only gotten a few steps away when Daemon grabbed her elbow and turned her to him.

"Don't do this, please. Don't sink to her level, don't let vengeance drive you to be something you're not."

Auraelia pulled her arm out of his grasp, her eyes softening a fraction as she saw the tears that mingled with the rain that rolled down his cheeks.

"Everyone is the villain in someone else's story. I will do what I must do to keep my people safe. If that makes me the villain, then so be it. Goodbye, Daemon." She gave him a small, sad smile, then turned and continued on her way to the castle.

"Auraelia," he called after her once more, and she stopped, but didn't turn. "I love you."

His words were a dagger to her chest, and it took everything she had not to run back into his arms.

To tell him she felt the same and that they could figure this out together.

But she couldn't.

She knew that if she didn't make him leave, he would stay, regardless of the repercussions. Knew that if their roles were reversed, she would do the same. But she refused to let Davina use him or his people as collateral damage when they had nothing to do with this war. Davina was already using them as pawns, and Auraelia wouldn't play into her hands.

Instead, she turned her head to look over her shoulder and said the opposite of what she felt. The one thing that would crush them both.

"Don't."

She returned to the queen's suite in the castle–since it was still under Xander's shield–and was met with the mystified faces of Xander and Piper.

"Do you want to talk about it?" Xander asked, though he looked uncomfortable as he braced for the response.

Auraelia took a deep breath in and held it.

She let the bricks stack around her heart until they were so high that nothing, and no one, could get through. Then she reinforced it with her magic.

She let herself go numb.

Numb to the pain of her mother's death.

Numb to the agony of cleaving her soul into pieces when she walked away from Daemon.

And finally, numb to the anger that still roiled inside at the knowledge that she would go to war over secrets that she was only discovering.

Then she looked to her brother and her best friend.

And when she could no longer feel anything, she exhaled.

"Let's prepare for war."

Epilogue

Auraelia

Madame Sylvie's hadn't changed at all in the months since she'd last been there.

The space was still swathed in shades of crimson and black, with hints of gold. There were still multitudes of women, of all shapes and sizes, roaming throughout the room in varying stages of undress. The smell of cinnamon and clove still clung to the air. And there was still the small corner bar, with the petite redhead behind it.

Only this time, instead of shooting daggers, Vee's eyes widened to the size of saucers as Auraelia strolled up to the bar and took a seat on one of the few stools.

Even with her hood on, it was clear that Vee remembered who she was, and knew who she had become.

"Hello, Vee," Auraelia said, her voice friendly as she propped her elbows on the bar top.

"Yo–Your–" Vee stuttered as she struggled to piece together any semblance of a sentence.

Auraelia reached across the bar and grasped her hand. "Rae is fine, Vee. You can even call me 'girl' for old times' sake, if it makes you more comfortable. I'm just here for a drink and a chat."

Vee nodded and dropped her shoulders, the tension peeling away as she relaxed. She then turned and pulled Auraelia's favorite bottle of honey bourbon from the shelf behind the bar and poured her two fingers. "So, what can I do for you, *girl*?" Vee asked as she picked up another glass that needed to be dried.

She took a swig from her glass, and let the burn settle on her tongue before the sweet undercurrent of honey took over. "I need information."

"Information on what, exactly?" Vee asked, a crease forming between her auburn brows.

"On Garnet." She took another sip of her drink and eyed the woman from beneath the edge of her hood.

Vee's face blanched, and the glass she'd been drying fell to the floor and shattered. "Shit," she exclaimed, then dropped to the floor to clean up the shards.

Auraelia stood and walked to the other side of the bar. When she squatted down to help pick up the glass, Vee froze.

"You don't have to do that, Your Majesty," Vee said under her breath. It was said so quietly that Auraelia almost missed it, but hearing her new title still sent a wave of unease through her.

It'd been a month since her mother's death, but the wound was still fresh.

"That may be, but I'm choosing to. Vee..." Auraelia placed the last remaining pieces of glass in the cloth, and grabbed both of Vee's shaking hands in hers. "I know you're from the Court of Garnet. I found a log of registered businesses in our archives, and on the form you completed, you put your court of origin as Garnet."

"I always hoped this wouldn't catch up to me," Sylvie sighed, then looked up to meet Auraelia's gaze. "What do you want to know?"

A smile tugged at Auraelia's lips. "Everything."

TO BE CONTINUED...

Bonus Chapter

Chapter Three: The Masquerade

Daemon

"Fuck, this is boring," Aiden complained under his breath as he sidled up next to Daemon. "And this mask is itchy. Why did they have to have a fucking masquerade?"

Daemon sighed, his eyes rolling to the back of his head. "Is there anything else that you'd like to bitch about tonight?"

Neither of the men were overly thrilled with the fact that they had been sent to Lyndaria to oversee the crowning of the next heir apparent for the Court of Emerald, but since their king had commanded it, they went.

Aiden huffed out a breath and took a sip from his glass, the amber liquid sloshing against the wall of the crystal tumbler before he stalked away mumbling under his breath.

The ball was for the princess of the Court of Emerald, and though there was fanfare when the queen entered the room, neither the princess nor the prince had been announced, and he found that rather...odd.

Daemon took a sip of his own drink, enjoying the satisfying burn of the whiskey as it eased down his throat. It was smokey, and there was a sweet flavor of honey that lingered on his palette long after the burn subsided.

He stood on the far side of the ballroom by the large wall of windows, where wide double doors in the center led out into the gardens. From this vantage point, he had clear lines of sight to every area of the room.

He looked around, taking in the multi-colored glass that made up many of the windows and filled the panes on the ceiling. It was beautiful, and he was sure that most–if not all–of the colored glass had come from the Sapphire Isles. But despite its beauty, he felt like he was standing in a birdcage. And the colors, frills, and feathers that the ladies of this court donned for the ball only added to that effect.

Draining the last of his drink, Daemon turned to where the refreshments had been set out for the evening when the hair on the back of his neck suddenly stood on end.

It was as if the air had become charged with static.

He ran his hand across his neck and tried to shake the feeling. But when his shadow magic vibrated beneath his skin and began pushing against the surface like it was being pulled from his very being, he turned toward the entrance of the ballroom.

His breath caught in his throat, and the world around him slowed to a crawl as he took in the living star that strolled into the room.

She looked like the midnight sky in the midst of a storm, full of twinkling stars and streaks of lightning, and her blonde hair shimmered beneath the warm glow of the lights–giving her a halo effect.

But the moment Daemon caught sight of her eyes as they peered through the holes in her mask, he was done for. Even from across the room, they shone brighter than the moon on a cloudless night.

She was radiant.

He was about to take a step in her direction, when another man approached her and her companion.

Red-hot rage filled his vision while his shadows coiled beneath his skin, poised to strike against the man who had the audacity to approach what was his.

The wayward trail of his thoughts jarred him.

He didn't know this woman.

Didn't know if she was even available.

Daemon shook his head, attempting to dislodge the possessive thoughts and watched as the interaction between the small group played out. When her companion took the arm of the masked man instead, relief washed over him.

He watched with fascination as she made her way around the room to observe the gathered crowd and stopped occasionally to eavesdrop on group conversations.

He'd planned on approaching her. Planned on asking her to dance. But as she meandered closer, he decided to stay put and let her come to him.

It took two full songs for her to make her way to where he stood, and when she smiled his heart skipped. He would have thrown the world at her feet just to see it once more, and it wasn't even directed at him.

She turned her back to him, her hips swaying slightly to the musician's melody as she watched the dancers glide their way across the floor.

Emboldened by her proximity, Daemon closed the distance between them, and slid his arm around her waist. The scent of lavender and chamomile filled his senses, and he had to hold back the groan that threatened to escape.

Leaning down so that his lips brushed the outer shell of her ear, he smiled. "Hello, my star."

She involuntarily jumped into his embrace, but when he attempted to tighten his hold on her, she twisted out of his grip.

"Excuse me, who do you thi–" Eyes the color blue calcite, and full of ire, glared back at him. But that roaring fire cooled to embers the moment they clashed with his, and the whole world shifted.

There was something about her. Something significant that he couldn't quite put his finger on. It was as if the stars had all aligned the moment her eyes locked onto his, and he wondered if she'd felt it too.

Putting on an air of cocky confidence, he raised a brow as one corner of his mouth tilted upwards. "Who do I think I am? Oh, my star, that would negate the purpose of wearing a mask, now wouldn't it?"

Despite the mask covering the top half of her face, he could still see the flush that spread across the apples of her cheeks.

"I'm sorry, you must have mistaken me for someone else."

When she turned to leave, his heart sank, and his magic lashed against the hold he kept on it. But when he reached out, and his fingers curled around her wrist, his shadows settled–turning from raging serpents to ribbons of velvet.

Her pulse fluttered through the point on her wrist, and he began to idly trace delicate circles around it with his thumb.

Tugging on her arm just enough to get her to turn back in his direction, he smiled when she finally met his gaze. "Not a chance, my star. Now, would you care to dance? You're much too beautiful to be a wallflower."

The moment her chin dipped in a nod, he pulled her to the floor. Not daring to give her the chance to change her mind.

His arm wrapped around her waist–pulling her close enough to him that if she took a deep breath, her breasts would brush against his chest–while his other hand clasped hers gently, and he led her around the floor.

They danced in contented silence, but he didn't miss the way that her gaze traveled over his face and chest when she thought he wasn't looking. When he met her gaze head on with a smirk on his lips, she flushed a deep crimson, and turned her face away to mask her embarrassment.

He wouldn't have that.

Though he didn't understand it, he *craved* her gaze. Savored the way she looked at him, and how the heat of desire replaced her earlier anger when she thought he wasn't looking.

Releasing her hand, he gently gripped her chin between his thumb and forefinger, bringing her face back to his.

Her eyes flicked back and forth across his face, and her mouth fell open as she struggled to find her words.

An easy smile lifted the corners of his mouth, and he did the one thing he could think of other than fusing his lips to hers. "My name is Daemon."

Returning his hand to hers, he continued to lead her through the dance. As the song came to an end, he pulled her from the floor and dropped her hand to grab two glasses from a passing tray.

His body felt like it was on fire.

He needed to cool down, to calm his mind before he pushed her against one of the windows and took her right then and there in front of everyone.

They'd barely spoken, but there was a fire in her eyes that knocked him down to his basest of needs.

Daemon handed her one of the glasses, then took a swig from his own and headed out the doors that led into the garden.

Outside, the noise of the party dwindled down to background noise, and he sent a prayer to the goddesses of Arcelia that the goddess he found tonight would follow him out–then thanked them emphatically when he felt her presence at his side.

They walked in companionable silence for a while, and he stole glances at her when she wasn't paying attention.

The moonlight danced across her skin, and sparkled against the shimmering threads that were woven throughout her hair. They both still wore their masks, and though he liked the air of mystery that they provided, he wanted to see her face. Wanted to know who she was.

As they wandered down the garden's paths, the lights from the ballroom faded away, leaving only the glow of the torches to light their way. Grabbing her hand, he pulled her to a stop. "Will you tell me your name?"

Her eyes lit with mischief, lips pulling into a sultry smile. "That would negate the point of wearing a mask, now wouldn't it?"

There was a challenge in her eyes now, and that–coupled with the way she threw his words from earlier back at him–sent all his blood rushing south.

She entwined her fingers with his and pulled on his hand, leading him further into the garden. He'd held hands with countless ladies, but none had felt as intimate as having his fingers woven through hers.

Turn after turn, they traveled deeper into the maze of flowers.

"Where are you taking me?" he chuckled, as they rounded yet another corner.

He had no idea where they were, or where they were going, but he would gladly get lost with her.

She finally came to a stop at a slightly overgrown path that was lined with trees and tugged on his hand. "Come on."

Mindlessly, like a man lured by a siren's song, he followed her.

The branches were tangled so tightly that only trickles of moonlight filtered through to illuminate the ground. At the end of the path was a small clearing where an old iron gate was nestled into an ivy covered stone wall.

Daemon furrowed his brow as he took in the space around him. "What is this place?"

"I believe it's a sanctuary." Her breathy response made his cock throb in his pants, and it took everything he had not to reach down and adjust himself.

"A sanctuary?"

"Mm-hmm...Problem?" Her smile was pure sin as she pulled her hand from his and sauntered over to the gate.

Daemon watched the subtle sway of her hips with every step she took, until she turned towards him once more and leaned against the bars.

He stayed rooted where she left him.

No matter how badly he wanted to–and, goddess, did he want to–he wouldn't touch her again without consent.

His nails dug crescent shaped dents into the palms of his hands and his jaw began to ache from being clenched so tight.

"You got me all the way out here, my star, now what are you going to do with me?" The words came out as a low growl as his need grew.

Her eyes widened slightly, and even from a distance he heard the hitch in her breath. "I'm not sure. It's not like I really planned this." She looked away mid-thought, but when she met his gaze once more, desire burned in the blue-gray pools of her eyes. "What would *you* do?"

That one sentence snapped all resolve he had, and his shadows swirled beneath his skin–begging to be released. Craving her touch as much as he did.

Daemon strengthened the hold on his magic and began to stalk toward her with a sinful smirk of his own plastered across his face.

"Oh, my star, wouldn't you like to know."

Want more?

Want more of Auraelia and Daemon?
More Piper, Aiden, and Xander?
Want to know what happens with Davina and the whole of Ixora?
Don't miss book two of the Gems of Ixora Duet, coming 2024.

Acknowledgements

Oh, lord. Where do I start?

To my READERS, thank you so much for taking a chance on a newbie author. Thank you for diving into the world of Ixora and for taking a chance on Auraelia and Daemon. By reading their story, you helped breathe life into their characters, and I will forever be grateful for the time you gave to them and to me.

To my ARC team, thank you so much for everything! Thank you for taking a chance on a newbie like me and for diving into the unknown world of Ixora. Thank you for breathing life into my characters. I would not have been able to do this without you.

To my BETA crew, you ladies were amazing and I couldn't have made it to the finish line without you. Your insight into the story and its characters brought a new perspective that made my story better, and for that, I will always be thankful.

To my ALPHA and favorite trash panda, DELYNDA. Girl. I would not have finished this book without you. Thank you for pushing me to write. For holding me accountable and being the biggest hype woman. Thank you for being the president of the Daemon fan club, and for loving him as much as I do–if not more. Thank you for staying up until all hours of the night talking out plot points and holes. For laughing at nonsense ideas and being all around awesome as I made my way through this book and the process of getting it out into the world. You've become one of my best friends, and I am so thankful that you "forced" me to be your friend.

CHRISTINE, my sister from another mister and bestest friend. Thank you for being there for me from day one. Thank you for encouraging me to keep writing and hyping up my book when I felt like I would fail. Thank you for being my first Alpha, and falling in love with my characters. For letting me bug you at all hours when I was stuck or felt like I couldn't go any further. For constantly reminding me that I COULD do this, and that even if no one else likes this book, I did the damn thing. You've been a constant in my life for years, and I will never be able to thank you enough for everything that you do for me. Love you girlie!

SARA, girl, where do I start for you? I am so glad that our daughter's became friends, and that a random conversation in a hallway at ballet turned into a friendship I will cherish forever. Thank you for pushing me to write this story. For listening to me drone on about the dream I had for months on end, and convincing me to turn it into a book. Thank you for reading through it (even if it took you forever haha) and being a sounding board. For sitting on my couch drinking coffee with me while the kids were at school and letting me spoil the ending so that I could make sure it made sense. Thank you for helping me look up names and their meanings for characters, and for spending hours looking up and laughing at synonyms for...*things*. Thank you for loving my characters, and for being an amazing friend. I wouldn't be here without you.

To my G.R.I.T.S. girls. The ones who are every piece of Piper and are an intricate part of who I am as a person. Kirsten, Christine, and Alexis, I would not be where I am today without you wonderful women. Each of you are the Piper to my Auraelia, and I will never be able to thank you enough. Thank you for listening to me ramble about this book and the struggles that came with writing it. But most of all, thank you for being there for me every step of the way, regardless of time or distance. I love you ladies.

SYDNE, thank you for taking a chance on me to be on your ARC team, only to turn around and be a part of my BETA team. Thank you for every note you left on my manuscript, my book would not be what it is without you. Your prompts brought a new depth to the story that I didn't know it lacked until it was there. Thank you for suggesting that I change part of the ending. I may not have liked it, but in the end you were right. Thank you for commiserating with me over Indie Author life, and helping me through the steps that it takes to get your baby out into the world. I hope you're ready for book two!

MOM, where would I be without you? I don't even know where to start. You're my hero and inspiration. You're constantly showing me that I can do anything that I put my mind to, and that it doesn't matter how late you start, just as long as you start. Thank you for reading my book. For making it through the "chocolate habanero spicy" scenes without batting an eye. For encouraging me to continue writing and for supporting me throughout the process. I love you, and if I'm half the mom to my kids that you are to me, then I think I'll be okay.

MAKENZIE and LORELAI. My two beautiful girls. Thank you for being patient while mommy followed her long time dream. You won't know it, but you two are all throughout this book. In name, in sass, and stubborn attitudes. It's because of you that I finally had the courage to pursue this dream, and I hope that I will make you proud...just never read it. I don't think I'd survive that. I love you both more than anything, and remember that you can do anything that you set your mind to.

KEGAN. Love of my life and piece of my soul. I would not, COULD not, have done this without you. Thank you for your unwavering support in everything that I do, and for making sure that I follow every dream and crazy idea that I have. Thank you for letting me fangirl at you over my own characters. For letting me become a hermit when I needed to work out chapters or edit my manuscript. Thank you for hyping up my book to guys who would probably never read it, but you have somehow convinced them that they need to. Thank you for letting me read you chapters completely out of context, and for nodding along like you knew exactly what I was talking about.

Thank you for bringing me chocolate croissants and coffee.

Thank you for everything. I love you so very much.

To my editor, SAMATHA. Thank you for everything. Thank you for being patient with me as I worked my way through publishing this first book. Thank you for pointing out a plot hole that everyone missed, and for being my grammar police. My book wouldn't be what it is without your help and influence, so, thank you.

To my amazing character artist, STEFANY (@suusliks on Instagram), thank you for being so patient with me while we worked through bringing my characters to life. Thank you for your amazing attention to detail. I can't wait to work with you again.

To the brilliant BIANCA, with Moonpress Designs, who designed my gorgeous cover. Thank you for taking my jumble of thoughts and ideas and turning them into a cover fit for bookshelves. Thank you for being patient with me as I worked through what I did and did not want. You were a dream to work with, and I can't wait to work on book two with you (I actually have an idea for this one haha.)

About the Author

As a lover of life and art, Jessica is constantly looking for the beauty in the world around her.

She's married to a United States Navy Sailor and together, they have two beautiful daughters and a dog. With their military life, they move often, but currently call Hawai'i home.

When she's not reading or writing, you can find her crafting in one way or another. Whether it's painting, sewing, messing with clay, or working on things for her small shop (Girlie Flamingo Design), she's always got the creative juices flowing.

She's always been an avid reader, using the written word to escape to lands of mythical creatures and happily ever afters. The beach and the bookstore are her happy places, tattoos are her therapy, and though she loves coffee, she could live off of Dr. Pepper. As a Louisiana native, she's a lover of spice...both in food and in her books.

For more information about the author and the books she writes, make sure you follow her on social media.

WWW.FACEBOOK.COM/GROUPS/JESSICAHOFFASREADERGROUP/

@JESSICAHOFFA.AUTHOR

@JESSICAHOFFA.AUTHOR

Printed in the USA
CPSIA information can be obtained
at www.ICGtesting.com
LVHW092350101024
793498LV00002B/6

9 798988 414216